TYPHOON – the story of a woman as wild and
destructive as a storm;
of a man pulled irresistibly into her path;
of a passion so strong it could survive everything . . . except the Typhoon.

JOHN GORDON DAVIS – author of HOLD
MY HAND I'M DYING and THE YEARS OF
THE HUNGRY TIGER – has once again
produced a novel of breath-taking action and
extraordinary drama, a novel that grips the
attention from the first surprising page to the
last. A novel which culminates in terror, and in
tragedy . . .

John Gordon Davis

Typhoon

CORGI BOOKS
A DIVISION OF TRANSWORLD PUBLISHERS LTD

TYPHOON
A CORGI BOOK 0 552 11185 6

First published in Great Britain
by Michael Joseph Ltd

PRINTING HISTORY
Michael Joseph edition published 1978
Corgi edition published 1979

Corgi Books are published by Transworld Publishers Ltd,
Century House, 61–63 Uxbridge Road,
Ealing, London, W.5.
Made and printed in Great Britain by
William Collins Sons & Co Ltd Glasgow

To Max Lucas

PART I

One evening at the end of winter, a young woman with blonde hair and blue eyes was sitting at a corner table in Pacino's Restaurant, New York. It was an expensive Italian restaurant, elegantly informal and old-world, and it was crowded as usual. Opposite her sat an elderly man who was her lawyer. It was the day after her twenty-fifth birthday. They had just left his offices, where he had astonished her by announcing that she had inherited two hundred and fifty thousand dollars under the will of her mother, who had died seventeen years ago.

Vanessa Storm Williams had been quiet a long moment, thinking. Now she said:

'I don't believe my mother had that much money. It was my father, wasn't it?'

The lawyer looked surprised. 'Your mother, Miss Williams. Why should you doubt it? The will's been properly probated. For that matter your father isn't particularly wealthy. You should be happy,' he added.

She looked him in the eye. 'Why have you brought me here tonight?'

The lawyer looked more surprised. 'Your mother was a client of mine way back. Just a sentimental gesture, to celebrate your birthday and inheritance. I was an admirer of hers, I used to be very fond of the theatre in the old days. She was very good . . .'

'Not that good – not a quarter of a million bucks'

worth.' She added: 'I don't mean to seem ungracious but I meant: Why did you bring me to *this* restaurant ?

He spread his hands. 'But I'm Italian. And I think this is the best in town.'

'You know who owns this restaurant, don't you ?'

He looked taken aback. 'Yes, of course.'

She said quietly: 'Carlo Pacino. Of Mafia fame.'

'Indeed. That is common knowledge. It is also common knowledge that it's one of the best restaurants in the state.'

'There is also a Pacino's in Chicago and a Pacino's in San Francisco. And they're all fronts for Mafia business.'

He waved a hand around at the crowded tables. 'It is a highly successful restaurant . . .'

'Carlo Pacino is a client of yours, isn't he ?'

'I have many clients. I don't discuss them, of course. But yes, I can safely say Mr Pacino is a client of mine.'

She knew she would get no information out of him. Then she gave him a smile. When she smiled she was dazzling; her big blue eyes shone. The lawyer smiled back.

'Something else I should discuss with you: What are you going to do with the money ?'

She looked at her glass.

'Nothing. Until I know where it came from. I've got my own money.' The lawyer looked at her with a touch of exasperation. Then she leaned forward and flicked her eyes sideways. 'Carlo Pacino – is he here ?'

'I don't know.' His eyes went around the room. 'He often is.'

She said: 'That's why you've brought me here, isn't it ?'

Just then a tall ageing man came beaming between the tables towards them. He had silver hair and big Italian eyes. The lawyer stood up.

'Carlo!' They shook hands warmly. 'Allow me to introduce Vanessa Williams.'

Carlo Pacino looked down at her, his kind old Italian face expectant.

'Miss Williams.' He held out both his hands to take hers. 'Enchanted.'

She did not raise her hand. 'How do you do.'

The old Italian straightened, embarrassed. 'I always read your newspaper columns . . .'

The lawyer said hastily: 'Will you sit down, Carlo?'

'May I?' The old Italian looked at her hesitantly.

She gave her dazzling smile. 'It's your table, Mister Pacino.'

The restaurant door flew open, crashed against the wall, then there were bloodcurdling shrieks, and a gang of Chinese burst in, flashing meat cleavers on high. They charged through the restaurant, yelling and shrieking and slashing with their cleavers, and women screamed and everybody scattered. Carlo Pacino was reeling backwards across the restaurant, one arm upflung over his face, the other grabbing inside his coat for a gun. Two bodyguards were scrambling up from a corner table wrenching out their guns – two shots rang out and they crashed back against the wall. And the first Chinese got Carlo Pacino.

The cleaver came flashing down on his raised forearm and split his skull open and he sprawled over a table; four more shots rang out above the screaming and shrieking, and now the Chinese were slashing at the furniture with their cleavers, the big knives crashing through the tables and chairs and the bar and the crockery and the bottles. For one terrible minute the Chinese smashed up the restaurant, then suddenly they raced out of the door into the night, and they were gone.

ONE

This hot summer's day a big junk was tied up to the public pier in Central District of Hong Kong. She looked like any other of the thousands of junks in the harbour, but a large crowd of people was gathered round her, and a television crew was there. A reporter was standing in front of the camera, and saying:

'But this junk is something special. For she is not built of wood, or any other conventional boat-building material. She is built of . . . *concrete*.' He raised his eyebrows. 'Ordinary builders' cement. And here is the *un*-ordinary man who built her.'

The camera rolled back to take in a tall, tanned man in short trousers and several days' growth of beard.

'Mr McAdam,' the reporter said, 'this may sound a silly question, but how does a boat made of concrete *float*?'

Jake McAdam replied: 'It's the question most people ask. Particularly the Chinese fishermen, for whom I designed the junk: "a boat of stone", they say. And the answer is: It floats the same way as a boat made of steel floats.'

'And you built her yourself?'

'Myself and my boatman, Mr Wong.' He indicated a short stocky Chinese with one squint eye: the camera swung on to him and Wong blushed furiously and turned away.

'And how on earth does one build a boat with concrete, Mr McAdam?'

'That's exactly what my bank manager wants to know.' The reporter grinned. 'First you build a frame out of ordinary plumbers' piping. Over this frame you stretch several layers of chicken wire. Then you mix up a big mess of cement and sand. And then, in one day, you plaster the netting wire tightly with cement. And there's your hull. The deck is made the same way. And the fishing holds, and the engine room. All the bulkheads. Even the water and fuel tanks are made out of concrete. And there you are.'

'You've just come back to harbour from your sea trials. Are you pleased?'

'Delighted. I took her deep sea about three hundred miles. We met some big seas. She handled beautifully. And she's much faster than an ordinary junk.'

'Why?'

'Because she's much lighter than a wooden junk, which has heavy ribs and beams. And lighter than steel. That's a most important feature. Fishermen with concrete junks will travel faster and use less fuel. I've also made the hull a little slimmer than an ordinary junk, giving her a much better hull-speed. And she's stronger than a wooden boat. And she's much cheaper to maintain because there is no caulking to worry about, no wood to rot, no nails to rust. And, of course, she's much cheaper to build. Cement and chicken wire don't cost much. Timber costs a fortune these days. This same junk,' he pointed at his vessel, 'built of timber, would cost the Chinese fisherman three times as much. And she performs better.'

'Mr McAdam, what is your purpose in publicizing this boat? For the last few days, I believe, you've been touring the fishing harbours showing her off?'

'Yes,' McAdam said emphatically. 'And I'm going to continue making a noise about her. Because every year a

11

thousand new junks are built in Hong Kong. How many thousands of tons of timber is that? How many trees have to be cut down? – How many *forests*?' He waved his hand earnestly, launching into his theme. 'And that's just for tiny Hong Kong. Think of China – the most populated nation in the world – how many forests must they cut down for the *hundreds* of thousands of new junks they build every year? Then think of the rest of teeming Asia. In twenty-odd years' time the world population is going to be almost double. How many fishing boats must there be to feed the billions? – and how many forests must be cut down to build them? We've been spendthrift, gobbling up the world's resources as if the well would never run dry.' He paused for emphasis. 'The forests are vital to our environment. They make the oxygen we breathe. And they're the home of a host of creatures. And they're beautiful. Ways *must* be found to protect the balance of nature, upon which our very lives depend. And building concrete boats is one of those ways.'

The reporter said: 'You also manufacture solar heating units and wind-chargers. Do you do that to help save the environment?'

He was delighted to get a plug in about his solar heaters and wind-chargers: 'Yes. Solar heating and wind-chargers give clean energy. Natural, God-given energy. And free. No electricity bills. No fuel bills. And no pollution.'

'And are you now going to start manufacturing concrete boats on a large scale?'

'Yes, but I'm not so interested in the business side of it – I'm interested in selling people the *idea*. I built this boat on a remote piece of beach. Without electricity and without much fresh water. That's how easy it is. I'm now going to build a proper boatyard, yes. But what

I really want to do is get the *idea* taking root.' He pointed to China. 'I want to persuade the Communist Chinese to start. The Thais. The Vietnamese. The Koreans.'

He could have gone on, but the reporter had enough footage. Soon the crowd began to disperse.

Jake McAdam lived in an apartment that looked down the steep mountain over the rooftops and across the harbour to Kowloon. At night the harbour lights were fairyland, shining on the water in deep stripes and sparkles of all the colours, and the window lights were sparkling, hazy glows. It was a magnificent, expensive view; the apartment block was called Dragon Court.

At four o'clock that afternoon McAdam left Wong in charge of the junk at the public pier and took a taxi back to his apartment. It was the first time he had been home in ten days.

On the front door a small brass plaque read: *The Oriental Israelite, Registered Office*. In the corner of the living room was an iron spiral staircase. At the top of it was a door, leading into the apartment above. It was a womanless place. The windows were all closed; it was hot and stuffy. His footsteps sounded loud as he went opening windows. There were no ornaments. But on the wall was one large portrait of a very beautiful Chinese girl. He had painted it himself. And it was very good. But he did not paint any more these days. He had many other paintings, but they were locked away upstairs, in the apartment at the top of the spiral staircase.

He went into the kitchen, got a beer out of the refrigerator, snapped the cap off. He walked down the passage to his study to look for mail. The floor seemed to be heaving gently under his feet, because of his long time on the junk. The study floor was shining but the

13

desk was a mess of papers and books, for the makee-cleanee amah knew she should not touch papers. But there was a big neat pile of mail. He switched on the air-conditioner and took a swig out of the beer bottle, then stood at the desk flicking through the letters.

There were several from his banks, which he did not care to open. Tomorrow. Then there was an invitation to a cocktail party for that very night. From 'The Ladies of the American Mess', To meet Ms Vanessa Storm Williams.

Jake McAdam smiled. The parties of the American Mess girls were always good. They lived in an adjacent apartment block, below and to the side, and from his windows he could see theirs. They usually did not bother to draw their curtains and from his desk in his office, without trying, he often saw them walking around in the nude, or in their underwear, which was always a pretty sight. They were good-looking girls. McAdam glanced down at their windows now, and he saw something he had never had the good fortune to see before; a girl on the living-room carpet, making love.

He could not see who the man was. She was on top of him, long legs astride him, and her blonde hair swinging around. McAdam stared at them an astonished moment, then for another moment he wrestled with his conscience; then he sat down on the corner of his desk philosophically and watched them.

But it was almost over. After a moment she slowed her movements, and then she stopped; she crouched limply on top of him then she slowly toppled off. She rolled on to her back on the carpet with her arms and legs and hair outflung. McAdam got up regretfully from his desk.

Then, with a smile, he picked up his telephone. He consulted a list. Then he dialled a number, and looked back at the window. A moment later he saw the girl get up off the carpet and disappear.

'Hullo?' she said.

'Hullo, is that Olga?'

'No, Olga's at work, can I give her a message?'

He could imagine her standing naked at the telephone, sweating.

'This is Jake McAdam – I've just found an invitation to a cocktail party tonight at the Mess, and I've phoned up to accept with thanks.'

'Oh, good. I've heard about you, Mr McAdam, I look forward to seeing you.'

Not as much as I look forward to seeing you properly, madam.

'Is the party in honour of anybody's birthday?'

'No. It's my party, actually. To meet the important people of Hong Kong.'

'And I qualify?'

'Oh yes, you qualify.'

'Well,' he grinned, 'welcome to Hong Kong, Miss Williams.'

TWO

Usually, the American Mess parties were elegant humdingers. Theirs was a large old-fashioned five-bedroomed apartment built in the Victorian days when apartments were like houses, with a long wide veranda and a big sunroof; often the girls sunbathed topless up there, and there was always a pretty array of scant female underwear drying on the lines. There were about ten semi-permanent members of the Mess, but at any given time half of them were away living with boy-friends and there were always new faces. Hong Kong is a crossroads. Usually the American Mess parties flushed out the beautiful people of Hong Kong.

But this one was different. The front door was open and as he approached he heard only the muted sound of polite conversation. He walked in. There were only about thirty people, and most of them seemed to be men. He stood in the living-room door, looking for somebody to pay his respects to. He saw Derek Morrison, his bank manager, and thought: What the hell's Derek doing here? Then he saw old Whacker Ball, who wrote the monthly *Oriental Israelite*, and thought: *Whacker?* A Chinese waiter was passing with a tray of drinks and he took a glass of beer. He saw Mervin Katz, of the Royal Hong Kong Observatory, and Kurt Marlowe, the American pilot who was going around with Olga at the present. Then a hand fell on his shoulder and he turned around. 'Hullo, Champion!'

'The Seldom-Seen-Man,' Bernard Champion beamed. 'I saw you on television.'

'What qualifies you for this party? It's only for the important people.'

'I'm a very important representative of the police. But tell me – how were the sea trials, really?'

'Beautiful. She handles like a yacht.'

'Thank God.'

'What kind of party is this? – Who is this Vanessa Williams anyway?'

'Vanessa *Storm* Williams, please. Some kind of high-powered Yankee journalist come to sort out Hong Kong in four weeks.'

There was Olga coming towards him. 'I saw you on six o'clock television. Handsome brute, aren't you?'

'Hullo, Olga.'

'Come and meet your hostess.' She took his elbow.

'I'll be back in a minute, Champ,' he said.

'No, you won't,' said Olga.

He saw her on the veranda, talking. She was tall and her blonde hair was perfectly groomed up on top of her head and she wore a white low-cut dress that hung off her shoulders; she was laughing at something and her mouth was wide and sensual and her eyes were sparkling, and he thought she was beautiful.

'How do you do, Mr McAdam! I've heard so much about you I know you already.'

Which, he felt sure, was true. Ms Vanessa Storm Williams was the sort of journalist who would do her homework on her guests' background. And have them eating out of her hand.

'Who actually do you write for?'

'I'm freelance. Until recently I wrote for the *New York Times*. I used to work for a group that owned a bunch of glossy women's magazines. I was one of those frightfully snotty ladies who wrote about Every Woman's Right to Have Multiple Orgasms. And worried damsels sick about how they should be vaginal and not clitoral – which is nonsense by the way, in case it worried you.'

'Orgasms are clitoral? – that's definite now?'

'Oh yes, the clitoris is back *in*.' She added: 'I believed it for a while because *I* have vaginal orgasms.'

'You do?'

'But then I'm an unreliable case because I can have one in a dentist's chair if I put my mind to it.'

He burst out laughing. He was going to ask her about the multiple orgasms, then he changed it in his mouth. 'What aspects of Hong Kong do you want to write about?'

Her mood changed immediately.

'How about having lunch with me Friday next week?'

He was taken by surprise. 'I was going to ask you to dinner.'

'I can't until next week. Lunch, Friday? So we can talk quietly.'

'Fine.'

'About everything. What makes this place tick. But the thing I'm interested in most,' she said, 'are the Triad Societies.'

He drew on his cigarette, nodded.

'They'll be the hard ones to investigate. They're secret societies, you know.'

'I know.'

'And deadly. But so secret we don't know much about them. Except they're into every type of organized crime. And their tentacles have spread around the world.'

She said: 'Are they more powerful than the Mafia?'

'In my opinion, yes. Much more. We know who the Mafia are. What they're into. The only trouble is proving it in a court of law. But with the Triads? We don't know who they are. They're in every walk of life. And the Mafia are confined to America. Whereas the Triads are all over the world. Wherever there're Chinese communities. And that's everywhere.'

She nodded. 'The American police tell me their power is on the increase.'

'Dramatically. They've moved into Europe in a big way. London and Amsterdam – Heroin traffic. Narcotics – '

'And in America.'

'Indeed. They're muscling in on Mafia territory. And anybody who challenges the Mafia has to be extremely powerful. They've taken the London underworld by storm – and the police. The European police forces don't know what's hit them. They don't understand the Chinese. The Chinese mentality. The clannishness and

18

secretiveness. And,' he shook his head, 'their cleverness. You've got to be a Chinese to understand. Or an experienced Hong Kong policeman.' He shrugged. 'But I'm afraid you'll find our Anti-Triad Bureau not very helpful. They'll only speak in generalities. They know a lot, but they also know there's a helluva lot more they don't know. And most of what they do know they can't prove in a court of law under the Laws of Evidence.'

She said: 'You used to be a senior policeman, didn't you?'

He smiled. 'However did you guess?'

'I'm well informed.'

'But I quit nearly nine years ago. At the grand old age of thirty-one.'

'Why?'

'Personal reasons.' He felt for his cigarettes and held the pack out to her. She took one. He held his ligher out to her and she bent forward. He could see down the top of her dress when she did that. She was not wearing a brassiere and her breasts were big and firm and her nipples were brown against the white. Then she straightened up. She looked at him with a twinkle in her eyes.

'Enjoy that, Mr McAdam?'

'I'm sorry.'

'Like hell you are.' She pulled the top of her dress up a little. 'And now you're a successful businessman.'

'Better say that quietly: my bank manager's here, and he'll burst into nervous hysterical laughter.'

She grinned. 'And the publisher of an intellectual magazine.'

'Thank you for the intellectual. "Publisher" is too strong a word, however. I simply pay the printing costs. Old Whacker Ball does all the work. Staff of one. We don't make any money.'

19

'He's here, by the way.'

'Good man for you to talk to. Knows everything. And what he doesn't know he thinks he knows. He's a good critic of the big wide world. And he doesn't like anybody. Not even me, and I'm his partner.'

She smiled. 'It's a very good paper.'

'You aren't on our mailing list, are you?'

'No, but the *New York Times* is. I've read up most of your back numbers. Very anti-communist, I notice.'

'Yes. Every time Whacker gets a cold he thinks it's the Russians waging bacteriological warfare.'

She smiled. 'But you do the editorials?'

'Only sometimes, when I'm steamed up about something. Which drives Whacker mad. But he can't stop me, can he? Seeing I own the thing. And I don't write them, I dictate them, then give the tape to Whacker to put into English. Which drives him madder.'

They were both laughing.

'Why do you call it the *Israelite*? You aren't Israeli, are you?'

'No. I'm Anglo-American. Dual nationality.'

Bernard Champion took a swallow of his whisky and breathed into his glass, and it made a weary sound.

'I'm the *only* person you should pay any attention to on the subject of corruption. Don't –' he jerked his head – 'listen to McAdam.' He shook his head anxiously at her, in difficulties where to begin for the uninitiated. 'Listen . . . Hong Kong had a branch of the police force called the Anti-Corruption Bureau. And McAdam once wrote in his *Oriental Israelite*: "Putting the police in charge of Anti-Corruption is like putting a rabbit in charge of a lettuce." *That* shows how prejudiced he is.'

She said, 'Is Jake anti-police?'

'On the contrary. He's just an idealist. In a less than perfect world.' He groped for words. 'Hong Kong is imperfect. But it's a perfect success story! It's unique. It's a capitalist bastion on the Red China coast, for heaven's sake. Such a contradiction is bound to have imperfections – but it *works*. Listen: here's an example. Print this story.' He paused for effect, then went on: 'There's a Chinese gentleman in Hong Kong called Herman Choi. He's a multi-millionaire in any currency. He donates huge sums of money every year to charities. Many good works. Have you heard of him?'

Indeed she had. But she shook her head. She did not want to spoil his story. 'Go on.'

'It is not surprising, therefore,' Champion went on, 'that this philanthropic gentleman should be rewarded for his good works by getting a knighthood. And I have it on the grapevine that in the Queen's Birthday Honours, which are to be published next month, that is what he is going to get. Ho-man Choi is about to become *Sir* Herman Choi.'

She nodded encouragingly. She had been in Hong Kong five days and she had heard this too.

'However,' Champion said, 'apart from his philanthropy, which he can well afford, Sir Herman Choi is also a big wheel in the 14K Triad Society. And he is one of the world's biggest traffickers in narcotics. Heroin.'

She feigned surprise. 'Christ!'

'Exactly,' Champion said. 'We can't prove it. And you can't quote me. But the police know it. The question is: why do we knight this blackguard?'

He looked at her with brown earnest eyes. She said: 'Go on. Why?'

'Part of the answer is that under the law a man is presumed innocent until proved guilty, and even more so if we can't even get him *into* court, let alone try him.

21

We must all presume blindly in his innocence. And the rest of the answer is – ' He paused. 'This Crown Colony exists for one reason only: Money! And the fact is that without the donations from the Mister Bigs of our Triad Societies most of our charities would go bang. And the Mister Bigs of the Triad Societies relieve our Finance Secretary of a lot of bother with his Budget every year. Every little million dollars donated helps because dear Government hasn't got to contribute. Which helps our Finance Secretary get *his* knighthood in due course. And Ho-man Choi has let it be known that if he doesn't get his knighthood this year his donations will cease. So. Sir Herman it is to be. Print that. And,' he looked hard at her, 'consider what a poor flatfoot Chinese constable on the beat thinks about that. *Print* that,' he said again, 'because it's the only weapon we have against the bastard. There's no more drug traffickers in China, d'you know that? And opium was the downfall of China. But no more drugs in China. Because Mao Tse-tung shot them all. That's the only way to stop the bastards. You can't traffic in drugs if you're dead. But we British? We give them knight-hoods.'

'That's a good quote.'

'I'm telling you this so that when you investigate cor-ruption in this colony you get things in perspective . . . So that when you talk to the likes of Jake McAdam you realize the nature of the place. You're going to be talk-ing to a lot of people and getting a lot of information. Particularly about the police. If I can help you I'll be pleased to do so. Because you're writing about my home-country, for practical purposes. And I'm bloody proud of it.' He glared at her. 'It's a roaring success story. For all its warts. It's got the highest standard of living in the whole of Asia. The factory worker, the

22

coolie, the fisherman, they all work like hell and they're paid well. Trade increases twenty-five per cent per year! Everybody prospers, from the lowest to the highest . . .'

She managed to interrupt. 'And the Triads? How does official corruption tie up with them?'

'It doesn't,' he said. 'The Triads are a phenomenon all of their own. There is no connection.' His tone got hard. 'Except this: Triad power has increased enormously in Hong Kong in recent years. And spread world-wide from Hong Kong. And why? Because the Hong Kong police have been *emasculated* in recent years. The Hong Kong police have been made the scapegoat of so-called corruption purges! Experienced policemen have been hounded out of office, driven to retirement left, right and centre. Their morale is low, their efficiency as a police force in this dog-eat-dog place diminished! And crime has increased as a consequence – and the Triads . . .'

There was a babble of voices, laughter, cigarette smoke. The invitations had read 7–9 p.m., but it was ten o'clock already and nobody seemed to have left.

'Do you,' a voice said suddenly beside McAdam, 'think I'm *eee*-vil?'

He looked down at Monica. She had piercing green mauve-painted eyes, slanted upwards, and big freckled breasts with a deep tight cleavage. '*That* little prick – ' she pointed a long mauve fingernail across the room at Jack-the-Fire – 'thinks I'm *eeee*-vil.'

'Did he say why?'

She looked at him with her mauve and green eyes. 'Say, McAdam, why haven't I ever screwed you?'

'Because you never told me you cared.'

'I don't care a damn. But *that* little prick – ' she pointed her long fingernail again – 'complains I've screwed *every*body. That I'm *eeee*-vil.' She turned and looked up at him. 'Why don't we put the record straight? And have a *mad* affair. And really give him something to complain about.' She leered up at him aggressively.

'I don't think so,' McAdam said regretfully. 'Jack-the-Fire –' he indicated with his head – 'is a friend of mine.'

She digested this. 'You got to be the only bastard in the whole world who'd let that stop him. You know that, McAdam? You're a bastard.'

'Who, me?'

'You love 'em and leave 'em. But at least you don't bullshit them.'

'Thanks, honey.'

'Don't mention it. I don't know how you get away with it and still be a gentleman. To be a gentleman bastard you got to be a bullshitter. But maybe that's your line. Honest-Jake. Gennelman-Jake . . . You set yourself up as a challenge. And they go for it, hook, line and sinker. And drop their pants. Is that your line, McAdam?'

'I haven't got a line.'

She looked at him unsteadily. 'Say, Mac, when are we all going to go swimming bare-assed off your new boat I saw on television?'

'Any time you like.'

She looked at him unsteadily. 'To-*night*!' she announced. 'I feel like being *eeee*-vil! I feel like swinging bare-assed from the chandeliers.' She shot a finger at him. 'Don't go away, McAdam – I'm going to organize a party.'

Harry Howard was only fifty years old, but he looked about sixty, his face lined with the worries of thirty years of making a fortune in the cut-throat textile business and stock exchange, and coarsened with drinking too much to relieve the worry that he might lose it. Because Harry Howard drank too much worrying about his fortune he had to work harder to save it and stop worrying. The harder he had to work the more he drank too much worrying about all the work he had to do. 'What's good on the Exchange, Harry?' McAdam said above the noise.

Harry Howard looked up at him, his sad eyes bloodshot.

'What,' he asked, 'am I doing at this party? Never heard of the woman.'

'Isn't she worth looking at, though?'

'Wants to know all about the problems of industry in this god-forsaken place. Management. Import-export. Shipping problems. Personnel. Income tax. Employment of women. You name it, she wants to know about it. Got me taking her to lunch next week,' he ended, mystified.

McAdam raised his eyebrows.

Harry Howard said: 'Smart as a whip. What profit-sharing schemes do I have? Worker-participation in management? Industrial conciliation? Export quotas? Overseas protective tariffs? Competition with China? The Common Market?' He waved his drink. 'Had me nailed down in two minutes, promising her a breakdown on the whole fucking Far East economy.' He shook his head. 'And me so fucking busy. What will Isabel say if she finds out?' He shook his head again. 'What a power-house . . . Wouldn't like to be on the wrong side of her.' He added, bemused: 'What tits.'

McAdam smiled widely. 'What's good on the Stock Exchange, Harry?'

Harry turned and focused on him unsteadily. He took a gulp of his drink. He said thickly:

'Isabel doesn't love me. I'm going to divorce her.'

McAdam forced the smile off his face.

'The bitch doesn't love me . . .' He looked at McAdam, then quavered, 'Do you know what that's like?'

'Come on, now, Harry.'

Harry looked at him, and for a moment he was going to burst into tears, then his eyes bulged and he announced aggressively: 'I'm going to get laid.'

'I think you should go home.'

'I'm going to go to King Winky's an' get laid,' Harry said aggressively. 'Then I'm going to go home and divorce her.'

'Where's your car-keys, Harry?' He held out his hand.

Harry blinked at him. 'Where'd I leave the car?'

McAdam patted Harry's jacket pocket. He slipped his hand inside and got the keys. 'I'll get them back to you tomorrow.'

Harry blinked at him. 'She'll give me hell if I come home without the car.'

'What does it matter if you're going to divorce her?'

'I always lose the car,' Harry Howard mused. 'Every fucking morning I wake up absolutely exhausted and there she is standing over me going *Nag-nag, nag-nag and furthermore where's the bloody car?*' He took a gulp of his drink, then glared around: 'All right, I'm going to King Winky's now.'

'Okay, Harry.'

Harry Howard looked at him. His bloodshot eyes looked almost sober again.

'The Lucky Man,' he said.

'What?' McAdam said.

Harry Howard took a big breath.

'The Lucky Man Development Company. You asked

me what's good on the Exchange.'

'Thanks, Harry.'

He glowered. 'Still a secret. Chinese outfit. Friends of mine. Into everything. Particularly real estate. Now they're turning themselves into a public company to raise capital.' He looked at McAdam, bloodshot eyes steady for a moment. 'The news won't break for a month . . . When it does there'll be a queue a mile long all screaming to buy. Boss-man worked for me for years. Made a fucking fortune out of me. He owes me plenty of favours.' He swayed. 'I can get you a block of shares at par.' He added: 'Double your money in a year.'

McAdam's mind was working fast, juggling overdrafts. 'Thanks, Harry.'

Harry swayed, looking at him; he started to add something, then he muttered: 'Phone me when I'm sober.' He added: 'Shouldn't have told you at all. Trouble is I like you.'

He knew Harry Howard wouldn't tell him anything when he was sober. 'Tell me now, Harry.'

Harry looked at him, swaying. 'The boss-man knows a lot of people in the right places . . . And he's acquired a lot of valuable building sites . . . And he's about to start building some very big apartment blocks. And that's all I'm going to tell you. Now I'm going to King Winky's.'

THREE

It was a glorious night. The junk lay at anchor in the middle of Repulse Bay. There was a moon shining big and bright, the sea was silver and black and it was sultry hot. Two hundred yards away the long curved beach was silver in the moonlight, and the lights of the apartments twinkled through the dark palms and trees.

McAdam climbed up the swimming ladder on to the deck of his junk, dripping, naked. The cassette tape recorder was playing. There were clothes and glasses everywhere. There were the faraway noises of splashing and laughing from near the beach. He stood on the deck in the moonlight looking at the sparkling wedge of sea, the sky full of stars, the mountains brooding low and black and beautiful. And out there, the South China Sea. And his beautiful boat lying in the middle of it, perfect, strong, and she was ready to take him anywhere. Anywhere at all, to the Philippines, San Francisco, the Mediterranean, around the world. And he had built her, with his own two hands, out of plumbers' piping and netting wire and ordinary builders' concrete. And by God he would do that one day. Just victual her up and set sail. Away into the sunrise, alone with the great, blue, swelling sea and the vast blue sky, the sails full and the bows surging. Oh yes, soon he would do it. While the world was still beautiful. Before all the oceans were covered in oil from goddam tankers breaking up and the ocean beds killed by sewage and industrial waste, before all the skies were clouded with gasoline fumes and industrial smoke.

He looked at his boat, with pleasure, in the moonlight; then he picked up a towel and draped it round his waist, turned and went down the hatch into the cabin. He got a cold can of beer out of the refrigerator. Then he lit a cigarette and went back up the hatch on to the wheeldeck. A woman was coming up the swimming ladder, blonde hair plastered wet.

'Hello.'

Vanessa Williams smiled. 'Hi.' She climbed up on to the deck. She stood there in the moonlight, twisting the water out of her hair, the water running down her big breasts and over her belly, glistening in her pubic hair.

'Can I get you a drink?' There was splashing as some people dived off the swimming raft two hundred yards away.

'I've got one somewhere.' She picked up a glass. Her legs were long and strong and perfectly shaped. He wondered if her knees were a little red from the carpet that afternoon.

He took a big swallow of his beer. He looked at her eyes, studiously avoiding her naked body. She lifted the glass to her mouth. He almost nerved himself into making a move at her. Then didn't. He cleared his throat.

'About these multiple orgasms you used to write about?'

She looked at him over the rim of her glass, taking a long slow sip, her eyes twinkling in the moonlight.

'That's a corny approach if ever I heard one, McAdam. Tell you what. Let's skip the preliminaries. And I'll show you.'

He was taken aback for a moment. Then he smiled with nervous relief. He took her hand quickly. There were people swimming back towards the boat now. He hurried her down the hatch steps, into the saloon, towards his aft cabin, and opened the door. He led her in. He closed the door behind them, then locked it. He was shaking a little. They could hear splashing towards the boat. He turned around and looked at her.

He took her in his arms, shaking, her breasts pressed against him, and he kissed her hard, his hands urgently feeling her body, fumbling, and her flesh was cool and wet and smooth and soft; she was still grinning as he kissed her hard, then her hand went to his loins and she took his hard penis and rubbed it against her wet pubic triangle, and all he wanted was to get her on the bunk and throw himself on top of her and push her firm thighs apart and thrust up into her warm wet body and he was trembling. He broke the kiss shakily and began to push her urgently towards the bunk, and she was grinning as she said 'Easy, boy . . . Lie down. On the deck.'

He smiled shakily and got himself back under control. He lowered himself to the deck. On to his back. She stood there over him, looking down at him, amused.

'At sea a long time, were you?'

Her long golden legs were astride, her hands on her hips, her belly and breasts towering over him, glistening with water in the moonlight shining in through the port-hole. She stood there a long moment looking down at his body, then suddenly she got down on to her knees. She knelt beside him, then leant slowly forward, and slowly lifted his penis in her cool hand. Then she leant slowly, slowly towards it. He lay there watching her, breathing hard, trying to keep control; she leant forward until her mouth was six inches from his loins, and he could feel her warm breath, then she stopped, her mouth poised, partly open, her eyes heavy, staring, her breathing hard; for a long moment more she knelt there in the moonlight, and he lay, watching her, desperately waiting: then she gave a moan and sank her mouth deep 'over his penis.

And later, on top of her, his arms straight, resting on the heels of his palms so he could look down at her body, thrusting hard in and out of her, her white breasts lolling heavy on her golden chest, her long legs wide open and straight and half up in the air, her eyes closed and her mouth half open, her arms flung wide on the deck, palms up, abandon all over her beautiful face, he thought it was the most exciting experience of his life. She was not making love to him, she was revelling, oblivious to everything but her lust.

A lot of other things happened that bright moonlit night. Twenty miles away five young Chinese males were swimming the fifteen miles across Mirs Bay from the shores of China towards the islands of Hong Kong, mouths gasping, eyes fixed on the distant black silhouette of Kat O Chau Island. A snake-junk belonging to Vacations-in-Happiness-and-Tranquillity set sail from the muddy harbour of the Portuguese colony of Macao at the mouth of the River Pearl, bound for the archipelago of Hong Kong forty miles away, with forty-eight Chinese men and women packed down in her black fishing holds. A total of seventeen million dollars was lost and won at illegal gambling places playing fantan, roulette and mahjong. An average of three point one people committed suicide, as usual. The parents of Mui Sai-sai, who was aged seven, sold her into concubinage to Mr Chan Kit-ling for one thousand dollars. A freighter from Singapore put into Hong Kong harbour carrying a substantial cargo of toothpaste and pickles and coffee, and contained invisibly in each sealed tube and jar were plastic capsules of pure heroin. A hundred and twenty-seven Hakka men and women stood sifting thousands of pounds of human excreta out of nineteen sewerage points to put on their paddy fields as fertiliser. The midnight goods train from China came steaming across the Shamchun River into Hong Kong carrying People's pigs and vegetables for the capitalists. A fishing junk from Thailand chugged through Hong Kong's black islands towing five tons of raw opium in big plastic bales behind her under the water. Minnie Chan of the Seven Oceans Bar got the clap from an American sailor, although she did not know it yet and would not know it until she had a number of angry friends. Lam Fat-li, who was doing very well as a clerk in the Hong Kong & Shanghai Bank, was robbed by three Chinese youths at knife point of his wristwatch and five dollars while he was sitting on a bench cuddling with Miss Nancy Ho. Eleven other courting couples were robbed at knife point of a total of eleven other wristwatches and twenty-seven dollars. Mr Choi Ho-man, otherwise known as Herman Choi, OBE, held a dinner party for the leaders of the Scouts and Girl Guides and the Society for the Blind and Physically Handicapped to discuss fund raising measures. Man Lo-ling, a Communist fat cat who ran the Middle Kingdom Import-Export Agency, held a stag party for some of his business associates, serving stewed dog and monkey brains followed by a sex act by two American girls sent over by King Winky, who ran a very successful brothel. The Fire Brigade was called out to five house fires, one big factory fire and to rescue people from three jammed elevators in two different apartment blocks. A Royal Hong Kong Marine Police launch sighted the Thai trawler and decided to check it out, and the junk crew cut the ropes dragging the bales of opium, noting exactly where they sank. In a tenement apartment Mr Kwan was busy bleaching the print off one thousand American one-dollar bills while his friend Mr Chan was happily working the little Itaglia printing press printing one hundred dollars on to each of them. Herman Choi received a coded telephone call at his bedside from a Chinese lady friend of his wife's cancelling a dinner invitation for the next night, which meant that the Thai trawler had had to cut the ropes dragging the opium because the Marine Police had hove to, and Herman Choi replied that the dinner should be postponed until the night after tomorrow if that suited, which meant: send the divers down the night after tomorrow if the coast is clear. Harry Howard went to King Winky's whorehouse and got laid and felt terrible remorse afterwards and rushed home to his wife whom he did not want to divorce any more now. Jake McAdam and Vanessa Williams ravished each other.

PART II

Two thousand miles away, over the warm Pacific, a vast mass of warm, moist air was moving from all directions across the sea in a long, slow, clockwise curve with the rotation of the earth; and as the air moved it slowly sucked moisture up out of the warm sea. Where the masses of air came together they were rising upwards, because of their warmth, sucking up moisture all the way, and as the air rose it expanded in the lower atmospheric pressure, and as it did so it was cooled down a little; and as it cooled the moisture in the rising air began to condense and clouds began to form.

At first these clouds were only misty white and grey. Then, as they rose higher and expanded and cooled more, the moisture began to condense more and more, and now the clouds were turning darker, and now the moisture was condensing into tiny drops of water, and it began to fall. At first, for a long time, it fell only very finely, drifting down out of the darkening, rising clouds; then it began to fall more heavily, and more heavily still, down on the warm Pacific.

FOUR

At six o'clock every morning, before first light, her alarm clock rang and she was instantly awake, no matter how late she had gone to sleep. All the apartment blocks were still in darkness, the harbour still; just the lights of the freighters at anchor and the neon lights of Kowloon silently shining in rainbows on the sea. But it was oily humid already. She got up immediately.

First, naked, she did the Ten Basic Exercises for Women in the middle of the living room. Then she went to the bathroom and sponged herself off with her bucket of cold water, for there was a drought in Hong Kong and the water mains were only turned on every fourth day. Then she drank a pint of fresh Californian orange juice, ate a carton of yoghurt and one boiled egg, and swallowed a vitamin pill. Then she left the American Mess in the sunrise and set off briskly down the steep winding roads of Midlevels towards Central, to the Government Information Services Library, which was open twenty-four hours a day to members of the Press. There she read up old newspaper files.

Whacker Ball of the *Oriental Israelite* was almost always there. Whacker was an old China hand who had given up the unequal struggle with the demon drink. Once upon a time he had been a widely respected reporter, until the struggle had become too unequal. Whacker knew a great deal about China and Hong Kong, but he didn't like writing news about it any more. He just liked criticizing. So he and McAdam had started the *Oriental Israelite*, wherein Whacker could criticize everybody. Another reason why Whacker liked night work was that he enjoyed drinking in daylight. 'That's when most other people in this town do their drinking, isn't it?' he said to Vanessa. 'In this first-class town for second-class people.'

'Present company excluded, of course,' she said. 'Why do you call it the *Israelite*?'

'Good name. The wandering Jew. Everybody against him. Works like hell. Tough as nails. Resilient. Wise. And the *Oriental*. Inscrutable. Smart. Hard-working. Et cetera. Bloody good name,' he ended aggressively. He added tangentially: 'Somebody's got to tell the people the truth.'

'I think it's a very good magazine. And particularly valuable in a place where there's no democracy.'

'Democracy?' Whacker Ball rasped on principle. 'Who needs democracy? That's the trouble with you Americans. You think what's good for Boysie Idaho is good for Timbuktu. Even if the poor noble savages haven't got roads even, let alone hamburgers with a college education and chock-full-o'-nuts and angina pectoris. When are you goddam Americans going to leave the rest of us alone? Where has your precious democracy got the Third World? Political war-lords and poverty: ripe for the Russians to take over. The democrat begat the liberal and the liberal begat the anarchist. And the anarchist begat the United Nations. What the world needs is a bit more truth and no-nonsense authority.' He ended provocatively: 'This is a very conscientious government. Of a very difficult place.'

'Conscientious for whom? For the ordinary people of Hong Kong? Or for the big tai-pans? Big business, the banks and the industrialists?'

· Whacker snapped, 'The banks and tai-pans are the only reason for Hong Kong's existence. It's them who provide all the employment for the people.'

'What about Social Welfare?'

'What about the refugees? Why do they keep flooding into Hong Kong, why do they call it The Golden Mountain Where Men Eat Fat Pork? You may bullshit yourself,' he barked, washing his hands of her for at least half an hour – 'just don't bullshit your poor readers! Go back to the Library,' he snapped, forgetting that they were in the Library, 'and *think* before you write, woman.' He stumped out, looking like the back of a small elephant. 'And *read*, girl, *read* before you presume to think!'

She sat in the Library in the red China dawn and read. She wrote in her Gregg shorthand:

'True that Hong Kong is governed by the Hong Kong & Shanghai Bank, Jardine-Matheson, the Jockey Club and His Excellency the Governor, in that order. But also true that Peking does not want Hong Kong governed any other way. Because Hong Kong is China's window on the world: China earns most of her foreign exchange through Hong Kong. Because China does much of her espionage through Hong Kong: it enables her to put the screws on Britain. Because Hong Kong *suits* China. And the Hong Kong Chinese know a bargain when they see it. Making money while the sun shines. Hong Kong, Borrowed Place, Borrowed Time. Tomorrow China may change her mind, tomorrow there may be another power struggle in Peking. Tomorrow Peking could capture Hong Kong with a telephone call.

'But I do not think so. There has been a volte-face in China since the great Mao Tse-tung died. The King is dead – Long Live the King! The Cultural Revolution is

38

with him, in the mausoleum.

'It has been long, glorious, astonishing, bloody, exhausting, destructive. Mao Tse-tung, old Mao who had led the Long March, the Great Rectification Campaigns, the Great Thought Reform Campaigns, and the Three-Antis and the Five-Antis Campaign, the Hundred Flowers Campaign and the Anti-Rightist Campaign and the Great Leap Forward, had finally launched the Great Proletarian Cultural Revolution to remake Man in his Communist image, to ensure there were worthy successors to his Communist Revolution. Put more crudely, he waged a power-struggle to get rid of his political enemies in the Chinese Communist Party.

'The Cultural Revolution spread to Hong Kong too, and for six months the Communists rioted against the British and made running battle in the streets. The Cultural Revolution exhausted China, nearly wrecked her. But Mao had shaken up and purified the Party and the People. Then, exhausted, he had let the Great Proletarian Cultural Revolution grind down, and let the pragmatists get back to the business of making China money.

'The world gave a sigh of relief. And of excitement, because maybe eight hundred million customers were going to do business with the world.

'Hong Kong got back to Business as Usual.

'Then began the Ping-Pong Diplomacy, remember?

'Then came President Nixon's historic visit to China, remember?

'Then China was admitted to the United Nations, right? And we got out of the Vietnam War.

'And then Chairman Mao Tse-tung died. And the Peking pragmatists really took over.

'And Hong Kong booms as it has never boomed before. The stock markets are wild. The investment money is flooding in from Europe and America, cashing in on the great Chinese gambling fever. Because coolies, amahs, stevedores, rickshaw boys, fishermen, sampan women and the great legions of the Chinese white collars are hocking their life savings and their gold teeth to buy; every Tom, Dick and Harry is raising millions of dollars by issuing paper share certificates to the clamouring queues of Chinese.

'Why?

'The answer is "Hong Kong Mentality". The feverish, last bastion of capitalism on the Red China Coast. The old China Coast mentality, of Shanghai before the battles not so long ago. The Golden Mountain, where it's all still happening, the wheeling-dealing inter-national money-melting-pot where anything goes, any-thing at all: the great Chinese money-mad mentality, work like hell and get rich quick. And the money comes pouring in from around the world to cash in.

'While Hong Kong lasts. Borrowed place living on borrowed time. Because China could take the place back tomorrow, with a telephone call.

'But what's all this got to do with us in America, the Land of the Free? The answer, ladies and gentlemen, is that this is a thumb-nail sketch of the cross-roads of East and West: the "Hong Kong Connection" in the vicious heroin traffic that is poisoning America and Europe and the world; it is an introduction to the fertile fields in which the conductors of this traffic operate, the Triad Societies, who are now out-gunning the Mafia and the cops combined.'

FIVE

At the stock exchanges there was clamour and gesticulating, and the clerks chalking up the prices and the jobbers shouting and the people crowding on the public floors; and in the scores of stockbrokers' offices across the town there was pandemonium, the clattering of the teleprinters and the clamouring of the telephones, the buying and the selling, people jostling to fill out buy-and-sell orders.

Every day the soaring stock exchange was front-page news. Every week in the newspapers there were editorials shaking their heads about it. Prices were totally disproportionate to the shares' values, they said. But the average Chinese investor could not read the editorials, all he understood was that you buy and sell at a profit; it was like betting money on a winner at the races at Happy Valley, except that at the stock exchanges all the shares were winners. The people who could understand the editorials understood the Chinese gambling fever and they gambled on the gambling fever continuing to push the share prices up. The foreign money came pouring in and the share prices soared higher and the Chinese gambling fever got hotter. It was a dangerous spiralling circle, the editorials said, it was bound to crash. The smart investors would decide to take their huge profits and quit and it would be the mass of unsophisticated who would be left holding the baby. But they had been saying that for two years now. Every week there were announcements in the newspapers of new companies offering their shares, every week there were long lines of people queueing to buy, every new issue was oversubscribed many times. A lot of small-time businessmen made a lot of money overnight by the simple expedient of printing paper share certificates in their small-time businesses and offering them to the public. Which is nice work if you can get it. And anybody could get it.

But Jacob Hogan McAdam would not take it.

It was a beautiful, bright Friday. It was a beautiful day to be taking a beautiful woman to lunch. But McAdam was in serious spirits. He was sitting in the sub-manager's office of the Hong Kong & Shanghai Bank, staring grimly out of the window. He had just heard his favourite money-lender, his good drinking friend and financial adviser, that very same Derek Morrison who had always lent him money for his other businesses, for his apartment purchases and his factory and his *Oriental Israelite,* for the stock exchange and for air-tickets and to pay his grocer – this very same bank manager had just refused to lend him half a million Hong Kong dollars to build his boatyard.

'I've never let you down.'

Derek Morrison was grimly apologetic. 'Not yet. But you still owe us a lot of money.'

'But my assets are worth well over a million Hong Kong dollars.'

'And you owe us over a million dollars, Jake.'

'All those debts are safely secured.'

'You're mortgaged to the hilt to us. You've got no more security to offer us for this new loan, have you?'

'Yes. *Me.*'

Derek Morrison shook his head briefly.

'Jake. The only way for you to raise the money you need is to go public. Turn your proposed boat-yard into a public company and sell forty-nine per cent of the shares on the stock market.'

McAdam stared out of the window.

'No. It's dishonest.'

'It's *not* dishonest,' Derek Morrison said wearily. 'It's the corner-stone of the capitalist theory, the stock exchange and the public's participation in industry.'

'The money-mad Chinese public will buy anything at the moment. They don't know the risks involved.'

'So you agree it's a risky project. So why do you expect us to lend you the money?'

'Because you know me! And you're the professional money-lenders, for Chrissake!'

The banker sighed and sat forward. He said carefully: 'Right, Jake. We're professionals. And we know you. And . . . in all honesty and sincerity, we admire and respect you. Hard-working and as honest as they come. But, Jake? You're not a businessman.'

McAdam turned and stared at him. 'I beg your pardon?'

Derek Morrison smiled apologetically.

'You're not, Jake. Oh, sure – you've made money. You're imaginative and you work like hell. And you're as lucky as hell. But the fact is . . . you don't *care* enough about money. You don't *worry* enough about money. And it's *our* money, remember. You don't seem to go into these business ventures of yours because you want to make money. You go into them for some ulterior motive. Take your *Oriental Israelite* magazine.' He held up his hand. 'Let me finish, please. Look at your balance sheet. By the time you've paid costs you're making about one per cent on your annual investment. You could make six times that simply by putting the money in the bank, without doing any work.'

'I *don't* do any of the work.'

'It's an excellent magazine but it's a bum investment. Why do you do it? Because you *want* to. Because you

43

want to tell the world what you think. Fine. Admirable. But it's not business. You've got no asset there you can pledge.'

'My apartments are a sound investment.'

'Sure. But they're mortgaged to us to the hilt. Take your solar-heating factory. Look at your balance sheet.' He pointed at his desk. 'After paying costs, and interest on your mortgage to us, there's hardly any profit.'

'Any business of that size takes years to make a decent profit, you know that.'

'Indeed. But yours is going to take twice as long. Why? Because you over-pay your workers. And then give them a bonus on top of that. You can't do that in business.'

'As a result they work hard and they're happy. I never have any labour-trouble.'

'I should think not. But look at your sales. It's a small factory, Jake.'

'It's growing well.'

'And now you want to go in for manufacturing boats,' Derek Morrison said. 'Concrete boats. Oh sure they'll float, I was only kidding you about that. But the hard fact is that this colony has hundreds of efficient boat-builders and there's a public prejudice among the fishermen about boats built of concrete – '

'There was public prejudice a hundred years ago against boats made of steel.'

'Indeed. But it's risky. And then I only have to probe a little into your motives and what do I find? Not a business motive. You don't want to compete with the ordinary boat-builders, you're quite happy to teach them how to build concrete boats too. Your purpose is not to make money like a businessman, its conservation. You don't want to corner the market, you want all the boat-builders of Asia to mass-produce boats in com-

44

petition with you so they won't cut trees down. Jake . . .' he shook his head at him. 'We're not a philanthropic organization.'

'Look –' McAdam shifted around in his chair earnestly. 'I've given you the wrong impression, I've put the cart before the horse. Of course I intend making money! I've got my first enquiry already – ' He tapped the file on the desk. 'For a fifty-foot yacht – '

'Jake, you haven't even got a boatyard yet – and that'll cost a lot of money.'

'It won't. I'll build it with my own bloody hands!' He shook them in front of his face. 'If I could build a completed thing like a junk on a bit of naked beach, I can build a big shed and slipway! And then it *would* be worth a lot of money – a permanent asset. Christ, after all the money you've lent me to buy shares on this crazy stock exchange, why won't you lend me money for a sensible asset like that?'

Derek Morrison said: 'Jake, I'm not saying we'll never help you. But you must come to us with a better scheme than this. More than just a rented deserted beach and a good idea. You'll have to raise some capital to show us. And after all the times you've gambled on the stock exchange, why do you adamantly refuse to turn your project into a public company and raise the money you need on the stock exchange? That's the answer to your capital problem.'

McAdam sat back.

'That's entirely different. And I don't *gamble* on the stock exchange. I make my ten per cent and get out. Ten per cent profit is enough for any man. But when I turn myself into a public company, I'm saying to the public: "Invest in *me*." I'm saying to the unsophisticated coolies and amahs: "Trust me, put your hard-earned savings into my skills." It's like asking a stranger

45

for a loan – like borrowing ten bucks off a coolie. What does the public know about me? But they'll invest in me because they'll invest in anything on the stock market. Well, I won't take money from coolie gamblers. And then they turn around and sell their ten dollar share to some other sucker for twelve. When it's still only worth ten, really.' He shook his head. 'No.'

'But your fifty-one per cent of the shares would be worth twelve dollars each too,' the banker pointed out.

McAdam shook his head. 'I'm not having that. I'm not having some poor coolie pay twelve dollars for Jake McAdam when I'm only worth ten. And then I've got the hassle of stockholders' meetings and dividends, and all that. And if the stock market crashes, my shares crash too. No.'

Derek Morrison shook his head. 'Your subtleties escape me.'

'I'd feel a goddam fraud,' McAdam said.

The hot humid air hit him as he went through the doors of the air-conditioned bank, out into busy Queen's Road Central. All right, he thought. The Hong Kong & bloody Shanghai Bank had not shut the door on him entirely. He would raise some money somewhere. And get things started. And then go back to them. And they weren't the only bloody bank in this town. It wasn't so bad.

And, by God, it was a beautiful day! The sun shone dazzling on the harbour, the junks, the ships, and the Mountains of Nine Dragons beyond were misty mauve in the heat haze. He slung his jacket over his shoulder. As he passed the bronze lions guarding the bank's doorway he gave them a stroke. The Chinese said that was supposed to bring luck.

He walked towards the foreshore and the Foreign

Correspondents' Club – the best club in Hong Kong, for atmosphere, company, news and the beautiful people. The China-watchers of the world hang out there, and it has a big elliptical bar so newspapermen can shout and argue with each other more easily. It has a fine view over Central, the most expensive real estate in the world; the mighty Communist Bank of China with its big stone lions at revolutionary attention, the mighty Hong Kong & Shanghai Bank next door with its big bronze lions imperialistically recumbent, the Hong Kong Hilton, the Hong Kong Club, the Supreme Court.

He pulled out a tie from his jacket pocket and slung it round his neck as he entered the club. He went straight through to the dining-room to check out his table with the head-waiter. Then he glanced around the bar for Whacker Ball. He wasn't there. Whacker was usually there by noon, arguing the problems of the world and complaining bitterly about his lot and dictating his black opinions into his pocket tape recorder. He went to the coin telephone.

'Yes!' Whacker Ball barked.

'Are you sick? It's way after twelve.'

'How's a man got time to have lunch in this job?'

'Have you found anything out? About the Lucky Man Development Company?'

'Yes. And I want you to know this is the last time I do this kind of research for you. That's no part of our contract. The company is one of Herman Choi's deals. Get it? *Choi* – Luck. *Ho* – Good. *Man* – Man. The guy's a peasant, what else do you expect?'

He saw the elevator doors open, and Vanessa Williams enter the foyer. She walked confidently into the bar, her blue skirt swirling, bringing the sunshine with her.

SIX

He wanted to take her hand across the table as he said it, but instead he just stroked his finger once over the back of her wrist. 'That was wonderful love-making the other night.'

'That wasn't love-making, Hogan. That was just good fucking, and you know it.'

He wondered if he had heard right. Then for an instant he was embarrassed. Then amused.

'Why do you call me Hogan? Jake's the name.'

'It's your middle name, isn't it? I've done my homework. Besides, you *look* like a Hogan. Even if your surname was Hogan I'd call you Hogan.'

'How does a Hogan look?'

'Like you. Nice. Rugged. Not *too* handsome.'

He smiled. 'Well. At least you agree the other night was good.'

She smiled. 'It was excellent, Hogan. You've been around long enough to know when you've done it well. And I'm paying for lunch.'

'You are not.'

'Yes I am, I'm a Visiting Member.' She snapped open her handbag and pulled out a notebook, flicked it open. Then she put a small pocket tape recorder on the table and switched it on. 'I'm going to be picking your brains – and it all comes off expenses.'

He sat back. He was amused, and impressed.

'Pick,' he said. 'We'll fight about the bill later.'

She folded her knuckles under her chin and looked at him and said:

'I'm missing out somewhere. I've got a lot of facts.

But I don't understand the *heart* of this place. I don't understand the *Chinese*. What makes them tick. Why're they so different . . .'

He was also impressed by the amount she could drink. And she obviously loved it. The same way she smoked cigarettes: sensually, savouring beneath her concentration.

And he tried to explain it to her; she had to go back in time to understand why it is so today, back to the days when China was called Chung-kuo, which means the Hub of the Universe, the Celestial Kingdom, and all other peoples were Outer Barbarians, Foreign Devils. And he told her about the Hoppo, the high mandarin who was appointed by the Emperor to be the only person who could trade with the Barbarians on behalf of the whole of the Celestial Kingdom, a land the size of all of Europe; and how the Barbarians were confined to their Hongs, to their wharves on the banks of the River Pearl in Canton, with a big brick wall around them so they could not offend the rest of the Celestial citizenry.

And he tried to explain to her that that is what Hong Kong still is today: a *Hong*, where the barbarians are contained without contaminating the rest of China, and the Chinese are still the Celestial citizens. And Hong Kong is still that kind of Old China of before the battles not so long ago. For before Mao Tse-tung finally marched his Red Army triumphantly into Shanghai the British Colony was only a tiny tavern of the China Seas, a mere bazaar between her bars and brothels, without even enough water to drink: but when the Red Armies marched into Shanghai the people who did not want to be liberated fled in their hordes to the tiny enclave down the China Coast called Hong Kong, and

49

the little harlot-harbour staggered, no houses, no schools, no work, no food, not even enough water to drink: but it was these refugees from China with their Shanghai know-how who put her to work in back-yard Chinese sweatshops, making anything from shoes to ships and sealing-wax, with nothing but sweat and muscle and sang-froid: and her stagger became a swagger.

And for all the Chinese gunboats they still keep coming, swimming Mirs Bay in dead of night and in the snake-junks from Macao and creeping through the jungles past the People's Liberation Army guards to the tiny colony of Hong Kong.

'These are the people that make Hong Kong,' he said. 'And the government officials are still the mandarins of yesteryear.'

The afternoon sun beat down on the harbour and the heat haze hung thicker, mistier, all the way to the horizon, oily hot and still. The dining-room was empty now, and the bar almost empty; he knew he should go. He had drunk far too much wine and then Irish coffee, and he had the taste for it now and he wanted to carry on drinking and then take this woman home to bed – but he had to get out there and raise half a million dollars. She said quietly:

'I'm gunning for Herman Choi.'

He sat back.

'I see . . . That will be very dangerous. Because he will gun for you. Literally.'

'I'll take my chances on that. Because somebody has to start somewhere. On cracking the narcotics rings. And the Triads. And I'm going to do it. Starting at the top. The normal powers of government aren't having much success, are they? Neither in the States nor

50

Europe. Nor right here in Hong Kong, where the Triads start. And the Hong Kong police are supposed to be the experts on Triads.'

'Then how are you going to be able to do it?'

'As a journalist. By exposing them. The pen is mightier than the pistol.'

'Like Woodward and Bernstein exposed Watergate?'

'Right. Woodward and Bernstein did it, didn't they? What a legal investigation couldn't do. Like the cops can't do it now, because they can't get evidence that would be admissible in court. And,' she said, 'you yourself do it, in a way. With your *Oriental Israelite*.'

'In an entirely different way.'

'You mean you don't pick on people who may shoot you?'

McAdam just smiled at her.

She looked at her watch. 'Can we talk again soon?'

'Of course.'

'I really should go now.'

'So must I.'

She looked at her watch again.

'Tell you what. I can postpone my appointment for an hour. Let's go back to your place and fuck.'

He stared at her a moment, astonished. 'No,' he said.

She drew elegantly on her cigarette.

'Do I shock you, Hogan?'

It was his instinct to say No, but he looked her in the eye, and he enjoyed telling the truth.

'Yes.'

'I believe in speaking the truth, Hogan . . . Not only is honesty the best policy, it's such fun.'

He sat back, smiling. 'Go on.'

'Because most people are so unaccustomed to it that they're shocked. And why should the truth shock a

51

civilized man?'

'Indeed.'

'It gives one such a feeling of freedom. So tell me why you're shocked. Men often tell me they want to bed me.'

'I believe it.'

'Then why,' she smiled pleasantly, 'should not women be permitted the same liberty in this day and age? When we fulfil equal roles. And fuck just as much.'

He couldn't help feeling the shock every time she said the word.

She added: 'When you have issued the same invitation, were the ladies shocked? Or do you only speak the truth when you feel on strong ground?'

'When inviting women to bed with me, yes. Otherwise I use more conventional approaches.'

'Whispering sweet nothings in her ear? Little kisses on her pretty neck? Pressing your cock against her pudendum. And finally a courageous pass at her tits? Ah yes, all good wholesome stuff. Don't get me wrong, I enjoy the fumbling and bumbling of convention too from time to time. But when I'm horny I like to get straight to the point.' She leaned her face in her hands and looked at him. 'So. I am not on strong ground with you?'

'On the contrary.'

'Now that's what puzzles me, Hogan. It seems you're being illogical. You see: I read you as a man of the world who's seen and done most things and who's unshockable. And who's fucked me once and presumably is looking forward to it again.'

He lifted his glass and sipped. 'It's not illogical. But I must tell you how I read you.'

She kept her eyes on his and inclined her head once.

'You are a thoroughly self-assured, thoroughly liberated young lady who knows exactly what she wants

52

and who makes no bones about getting it, be it your professional needs or your sexual.' She inclined her head in elegant agreement. 'And to those ends you will use people.'

She cocked her eyebrow. 'Don't we all?'

'And I have no objection to your using me, whether for my knowledge of Hong Kong or as a stud. I'll enjoy it. But if I'm to be used it will be on my terms.'

She was listening attentively, enjoying it. 'And your terms are that *you'll* do the soliciting – when *you* feel like it, not when I choose to grab your cock under the table.'

He had to try hard to keep a straight face. 'Right.'

She rolled her tongue inside her mouth to smother her smile. 'Do I detect a male chauvinist pig?'

'Not on the evidence. My male ego is flattered. Do I detect a Woman's Libber?'

'Not at all. I'm liberated, always have been; what do I need them for?' She sat back and drew on her cigarette deeply. 'Well. Where do we go from here?'

'You're beautiful.'

'Thank you. You're a bit of a smasher yourself.'

He said conversationally: 'Tell you what. You've got an appointment and I've got to raise half a million dollars. Let's say to hell with both problems and go back to my place and fuck.'

'God, you're a smooth-talking bastard!'

SEVEN

Afterwards she lay spreadeagled on his double bed, one long beautifully shaped leg bent, golden hair outflung, her breasts lolling white against her tan. And her pubic hairs were fair. She watched him studying her.

'Yes, I'm a natural. Though I've been most other things. Just to test whether gennelmen really do prefer blondes.'

He stretched out his hand and stroked slowly up her smooth thigh, up over her hip: it was the first time he had studied her naked, quietly; even her feet were sleek golden things, her toe-nails painted red; the texture of her, every line and curve and cleft of her was a sexual thing, to touch and look at and smell and taste, and where her thighs touched there was a secret olive line, and then the beautiful triangle of curly hair. She was the most naked woman in the world.

'What other colours has your hair been?'

'Flaming red.'

'And before that?'

'I liked being red. That was a real turn-on. It made me feel wanton. Before that I was pitch black. And originally blonde.'

'How do you feel now?'

'*Really* wanton. They say blondes have the best time, don't they? Would you like to try me red?'

He looked at her, surprised. Her eyes were twinkling.

'I've got a wow of a red wig. How'd you like red hair flamed out all over the pillow? . . . And then black? Like having a brand new woman every time.'

He smiled. 'You *are* a brand new woman.'

'But one needs variety, doesn't one?'

He looked at her, taken aback.

'You're unaccustomed to the truth, Hogan. You're shocked again.' She reached out and stroked his nipple. 'Isn't variety the spice of life?'

'Possibly.'

'Oh yes, it is.' She played with his nipple. 'I can't understand sexual jealousy.'

'But you must have been in love sometime.'

'Oh yes.'

'And weren't you jealous of your lover then?'

She smiled her outrageous smile. 'If he had any sexual energy left after I'd finished with him for the day, good luck to him!'

'Seriously.'

'If he'd started falling for somebody else I'd have got uptight. Because I'd have thought I would lose him forever. But if he just went and had a screw when I wasn't around and came back to me, no way would I be jealous.'

'Then I don't think you've been in love.'

'Bullshit, Hogan!' she said pleasantly. She rolled on to her side and propped herself up on her elbow. 'D'you think I've been around twenty-five years and don't know what love is? I've been very much in love. But even then, say walking down the street, walking on air –' she twiddled her hands and fingers – 'absolutely singing inside, tra-la-la, and I happen to see a sexy man . . . I've thought: *Hmm, wouldn't mind screwing you!* And don't tell me men in love don't do the same when they see a sexy wench. And *why* –' she gave his penis a playfully aggressive tug – 'should us wenches be any different?'

He grinned.

She went on: 'Screwing around on the side has got

nothing to do with being in love, Hogan. It's just satisfying a sexual appetite. Which in *my* case – ' she blinked her eyes tizzily – 'happens to be robust. It's got no more significance than masturbation. Except – ' she made her eyes sparkle again – 'it's much more fun.'

He didn't believe she knew what she was talking about.

'You must've been in love, Hogan. Didn't you ever have a girl on the side from time to time?'

'As a matter of fact I was the faithful kind.'

She looked surprised.

'It's just satisfying an urge,' she said. 'Like having a meal. What love is . . . real, mature love between two mature people . . . is you love the total person. Their minds as well as their bodies. You want them to be happy in mind and body. Being in love . . . is an entirely voluntary association of two people. In fact,' she said, 'in the same way as one can come home and tell the other what a fantastic sexual experience they had. And the other should be able to say, if they truly love each other: "That's fantastic darling – lucky old you!" '

He smiled at her. 'Yeah?'

'Certainly.' He wasn't sure if she was teasing him. Her smile widened. 'In fact, it should be a turn-on.'

'A turn-on, huh?'

'Oh yes. Imagine your beautiful lover with a beautiful woman . . . Particularly the description of the details.' She smiled at him. 'Sex is such a . . . wildly exciting business. The more one gets the better, not so? And variety is the spice. So? . . . share your experiences.' Her finger went out and stroked his nipple again. 'Better still, to be there and actually share it with them.'

He had been expecting it, but it was still a small shock. 'Three in a bed?'

She half closed her eyes. 'Super . . .' He smiled at her

imitating the English. 'Assuming, of course, that everybody turns everybody else on, all sexually attracted.' She added: 'I'm a little bisexual, you see.'

He made himself shrug.

'Who isn't?' she said evenly. She added: 'Almost every girl I know who's honest is, a little anyway. They all admit they are interested. Even if they're scared of trying it. In case they find out they like it and turn lesbian.' She added: 'Don't misunderstand, I'm not lesbian.'

'No, I didn't think you were.'

She fingered his nipple absently. 'I'm just a bit kinky. I don't screw women alone. Oh, I've done it, sure, to try it out. But that's not my scene.'

'What is your scene?'

'Bisexually? Three in a bed. Then it's all mixed up.' She smiled, enjoying shocking him. Then she added: 'I'm not hooked. It's just . . . fun. Kinky. I'm only bisexual up to a nice wholesome point.'

He believed her. And it was very erotic. She trailed her fingertip slowly down his chest and stomach towards his groin.

'I still shock you, Hogan. Underneath that worldly exterior there lurks a very straight guy. You may deserve your reputation for loving 'em and leaving 'em, but you're a pretty straight guy all the same.'

'Yes?'

'Ah yes . . . I'd like to truly liberate you, Hogan. Introduce you to the truth about yourself. About all of us. Because underneath that straight guy that's lurking underneath that worldly guy – ' she clasped her hand round his penis and shook it aggressively – *there lurks a lovely animal!*'

He was laughing quietly.

'But we're luckier than animals, aren't we? Because

57

we're the *naked* animal. We're the only animal – ' she half closed her eyes – 'who's got the joy of nakedness. Of touching nakedness. Of looking at nakedness. Of being a voyeur! Of *sex for sex's sake* . . .'

She let the words linger a moment. Then she said brightly: 'I'm right, you know, Hogan. Nature evolved us to be as horny as hell. That's why we're over-populating the goddam earth.'

He laughed.

'And so I've got to build concrete boats.'

'Right. Shall I see if I can arrange it, Hogan? Three in a bed.'

He shrugged. 'Who do you have in mind?'

'Somebody beautiful. With lovely long legs.'

She walked cheerfully out of the bedroom door ahead of him, down the corridor, dressed again. In her high wedge heels she was almost as tall as him. She glanced in the next bedroom doorway. 'Is this where you work?'

'Yes.'

She walked into his big sparse office. She pointed at a big colourful poster on the wall. 'Ah, the Nitrogen Cycle.'

'Yes.' He was impressed. Not many people would identify the chart immediately, if at all.

'Yes, that's your thing too, isn't it?' She was crossing the room looking at the posters on the wall. 'Do you belong to Friends of the Earth?'

'Yes. Do you?'

'Friends of the Earth, the Appalachian Trail Conference and World Wildlife.'

He was astounded. She just didn't look the type. 'Great! I also belong to the Greenpeace Foundation. And the World Wildlife and the Sierra Club. Have you done any walking in the Appalachians?'

'From Maine to Georgia.' She added: 'I'm tougher than your average blonde broad with big tits.'

'Christ.' He was really impressed. 'All two thousand miles?'

'All two thousand one hundred and fourteen of the bastards. Have you?'

'I've only done about five hundred miles of it.' It was hard to imagine her, reeking of sweat, slogging over those mountains in hiking boots with a fifty-pound knapsack on her back. 'How long did it take you?'

'Six months. Five hundred miles is quite enough. Six months is a long time to go without being laid.'

He threw back his head and laughed. Hell, he liked her. He sat down on the corner of his desk. 'Were you alone?'

'You meet other idiots along the way doing the same trail. I teamed up from time to time. But – ' she held up a finger and cocked her head at him – 'Vanessa Storm Williams doesn't screw absolutely everybody, you know, don't misunderstand her.'

'Why did you do it?'

'After that sonofabitch I was in love with gave me the old cold shoulder. Never again! I wouldn't let any man get to me that much again!' Then she added: 'But I always wanted to do it. Those mountains.' She shrugged. 'Plenty of people have done it, it's no big deal. It was either that or a trip to Africa which I couldn't afford.' Then she said: 'I really must go. Thank you.'

He took a step towards her, and kissed her lightly. 'We've still got a dinner date sometime.'

'Yes.' She let him go and turned towards the door.

'I'll phone you next week and we'll make a date.'

She was preceding him towards the front door. A flicker crossed her face but he did not see it. 'Fine,' she said.

Suddenly everything seemed very formal. He opened

59

the front door for her and pressed the elevator button. The doors slid open immediately.

'Adios, Hogan.'

'Adios.' She gave him a short bright kiss, then the elevator doors closed on her smile. He stood there a moment, leaning against the wall.

PART III

It was humid, oily hot, even at sunrise. She was walking up Nathan Road, sweating already. Bernard Champion had offered to send a car for her any time she liked, but she had declined. It was good to walk and sweat.

Total immersion. That's what she believed was necessary for good journalism. To write about something conscientiously you had to get out there and experience it and truly feel it.

She strode lightly, carrying only a light sackcloth shoulder bag. She was heading for the Man Ping resettlement estate and squatter area for the third time. She was meeting Superintendent Bernard Champion there at noon. Her hair was piled up on top of her head to try to keep her neck cool, a jeans skirt swirled just above her knees. Half her blouse buttons were undone to keep cool. She was not wearing panties. She seldom did; it gave her a feeling of freedom. And if ever a gust of wind let anybody see anything, good luck to them. She was in a happy mood. The more she saw of this place, the more she loved it.

Just half a mile up the golden mile of Nathan Road, cutting right across the middle of Kowloon, she came to Boundary Street. She pulled her little tape recorder out of her bag and said softly into it as she walked:

'Boundary Street . . . In a way this street sort of epitomizes Hong Kong. Although it looks just like another road, it is a very remarkable street indeed. For Boundary Street is the official border between the British Crown Colony of Hong Kong, which was ceded to Britain for ever by the old Emperor of China, and the New Territories, which was only leased to Britain. In less than twenty years' time all the land on the other side of Boundary, all the factories, houses, apartments, tenements, and all the three hundred square miles of mountains and valleys and farms beyond, will all revert to China.

'About half of Hong Kong's teeming population lives and works on the wrong side of Boundary Street, and half of them are under twenty years of age. In twenty years' time Boundary Street is going to be a most heart-breaking street indeed . . .'

An hour later she came to the resettlement estate. It was her third visit, but this time she did not have her interpreter with her. Now she almost knew the place. A whole mountain had been bulldozed flat, and on top the Government had built the vast new resettlement estate: twelve massive concrete blocks each twelve storeys high, concrete canyons reaching up, every apartment the same; masses of identical-looking laundry hanging out of the windows on bamboo poles, thousands of people all with the same black hair and brown slanted eyes, and all the time the noise: the sing-song blare of Chinese radio, the screams of the thousands of children playing, the hammering and the jammering, the clattering of mahjong, the minibuses, bicycles, carts, wheelbarrows, hawkers.

She went to a cooked-food stall, sat down on a little stool and ordered green tea. She lit a cigarette and settled down to watch the world go by. She knew a lot of the people by sight already.

EIGHT

Chan Fat-ho was an illegal hawker. The Government refused to license him because there were too many hawkers already in Hong Kong's narrow, teeming streets. If the Government issued a licence to every hawker who applied for one there would not be room to move.

Chan Fat-ho lived in the squatter area immediately below the Man Ping resettlement estate. The rows between the shacks were narrow dirt paths that turned to mud in the rains. At every third row there was a water pump, and in every fifth row a latrine. And that was it. At the bottom of the squatter area were factories built like apartment blocks, factories on top of factories, all the way down to the teeming harbour.

But this was a good squatter area. It had water and latrines. Many other areas were simply tolerated by Government, vast patches of shacks cut into the steep jungled mountainsides, and the shack-dwellers carried their own water up and latrines were another matter. Chan Fat-ho was well-off. In due course, when his number came up, the Government would resettle him.

Every morning at sunrise Chan Fat-ho left his shack with his bamboo pole slung over his shoulder. From each end were suspended two tin cages, which contained his paraphernalia. He went shuffling up the zig-zag path worn in the high man-made cliffs. Next to the estate began the massive blocks of factories, and there was a minibus terminus. It was a good area for hawking food, but it was illegal because of the congestion.

Chan Fat-ho set his pole down on the sidewalk. Then he hurried into the estate and filled his four-gallon tin with water. He put a big pot of rice on the stove to boil: on the other burners he put noodles and congee. He set the frying basins sizzling with gizzards. Immediately his first customers began to turn up. Chan Fat-ho hopped around on his bony haunches cooking, dishing out, chucking on more, taking money. All the time the people were hurrying along the narrow sidewalks into the minibuses and factories, and the cargo lorries were arriving and discharging and loading. All down the crowded street other hawkers were also doing good trade. There was a lot of competition, the food was good, and for one dollar Hong Kong, twenty-five US cents, you got a gutful.

Vanessa finished her breakfast of fried noodles and gizzards and watched the street. She felt she knew Chan Fat-ho quite well now. They gave each other a smile each time and she had learnt a few Chinese words. She knew his routine.

It went on like this all day. Half a dozen times he had to run to the markets to buy more rice, vegetables, noodles, fish, meat. When it began to get dark, Chan Fat-ho lit his paraffin lamp and kept going. Now it was the night shifters at the factories who were his best customers. The night was as busy as the day. After the night shifts had had their midnight break, Chan Fat-ho packed up for the day. He shouldered his bamboo pole and started shuffling off through the resettlement blocks, down the man-made cliff back to his squatter shack. That is what he did seven days a week every week of the year.

But twice a week Chan Fat-ho received a visitor who did not want rice or congee. Vanessa had seen this, too,

64

and her interpreter had explained to her what was happening. On Mondays the visitor was the Rent Collector from the local branch of the 14K Triad Society. In fact this branch of the 14K was only small fry, into protection and extortion, controlling the use of the communal lavatories and garbage bins, protection money and drug peddling within the Man Ping estate. All the same, it was a multi-million dollar business. Every week their Rent Collector came to all the hawkers and collected ten dollars for use of their piece of sidewalk.

'Jo-san Chan-san,' the 14K Rent Collector said.

'Jo-san, Elder Brother,' Chan Fat-ho said. He counted ten dollars out of his lucky red plastic bowl and handed it over cheerfully.

The Rent Collector made a mark in his notebook. 'How is business?'

'Very good, Elder Brother.'

'See you next week, Chan-san,' the 14K Rent Collector said.

The interpreter had explained it to her: Chan Fat-ho paid the protection money cheerfully because he had no option and anyway it was money well spent. He could not complain to the police because he was an un-licensed hawker. If he had complained, the police would have arrested the Rent Collector, and then the 14K Triad Society members would have beaten up Chan Fat-ho, destroyed his equipment and driven him from every street in Hong Kong, if they hadn't actually murdered him as an example to others. On the other hand for a mere ten dollars a week Chan Fat-ho was allowed to make a living, and allowed to use the lavatory and water.

Chan Fat-ho's other visitor was an officer from the Hawker Control Force. Once a week the officer came and sat on one of the little tables outside a licensed stall. One by one the hawkers went up to the stall, ordered a cup of green tea and left a ten-dollar note folded under the cup. Finally the owner slipped the officer the wad of ten-dollar notes. If anybody had failed to pay, the owner related any explanations, apologies and promises to make it up next week. This did not happen often, because everybody was doing good business.

Then the Hawker Control Force officer made his way to a tea house in the next street and paid the Rent Collector of the 14K Triad Society twenty per cent of what he had collected. He paid him philosophically, because if he did not the 14K Triad Society would denounce him to the police as a corrupt officer. The 14K Triad Society was content with only twenty per cent because the Hawker Control Force was a large body of men who, after all, had the strength of the Royal Hong Kong police behind them. It was much better for everybody to be satisfied with a reasonable share.

The Hawker Control officer took the rest of the money back to his office and distributed it according to the rules. Once a week, he met the bag-man from the local police station. He paid over to the police bag-man the agreed share of all the hawker, gambling, and general protection money collected. At the end of the month, when the chief bag-man had collected all the monies from all his bag-men within his jurisdiction, he distributed the money amongst those fellow policemen who wished to participate, at the agreed scale, depending on rank.

It was nine o'clock. She was about to get up and explore the alleys and the factory blocks. Suddenly a big green Urban Services Truck came around the corner and stopped. Immediately, half a dozen Hawker

66

Control Force officers de-bussed in uniform. A murmur went up in the crowded street, and suddenly everybody was watching. The uniformed officers went busily down the street, inspecting licences.

She looked across the street at Chan Fat-ho. He had already started packing up his gear resignedly. Crowds were gathering.

'Show me your licence, please!' the beetle-browed Hawker Control officer said.

'I do not have a licence, First Born,' said Chan Fat-ho.

'You are under arrest for hawking without a licence contrary to Hawker Control Ordinance. Anything you say may be taken down in writing and used as evidence. Get into the vehicle,' the officer said unnecessarily, for Chan Fat-ho was already getting into a vehicle, along with all the other unlicensed hawkers. People were hanging out of the factory windows. In five minutes the Hawker Control had cleaned up the whole street.

Vanessa followed in a taxi. The vehicle drove ponderously to the local Magistracy. Into the big courtyard. De-bussed, the hawkers were hustled into the charging office. Dockets were filled out:

Elizabeth the Second, by the Grace of God, Queen of Great Britain, Northern Ireland and the Colonies and Dominions beyond the Seas, Defender of the Faith

versus

Chan Fat-ho

An hour later they were shepherded into the courtroom and stood in a long line outside the dock. Vanessa was sitting in the public gallery. The clerk stood, reading out twenty charges, all the same, in English, and at the same time the interpreter was walking down the line of hawkers interpreting the charge, which everybody knew by heart.

'How do you plead?' the clerk repeated. 'Guilty or not guilty?'

'Guilty . . . Guilty . . . Guilty . . . Guilty . . .' the interpreter intoned.

The magistrate said:

'Ten dollars . . .'

And the interpreter walked down the line again, saying:

'Ten dollars . . . Ten dollars . . . Ten dollars . . .'

They shuffled out of the courtroom and down to the Sheriff's office and paid. And that was that. It all only took a couple of hours. And it was only once a fortnight or so.

Chan Fat-ho picked up his bamboo pole and went loping back through the teeming streets, back to the resettlement estate, set down his gear and started cooking again. Chan Fat-ho was satisfied. His customers were satisfied. The Hawker Control Force officer was satisfied. The 14K Triad Society was satisfied. Everybody was satisfied.

'Except us, of course,' Bernard Champion said a little nervously. They walked between the towering canyons of the estate. Chinese children gathered around them, adults stared at them: the big policeman in his starched khaki uniform with the blue-shaved, sweating face and the black curly hair covering his arms and legs, the epitome of barbarity in Chinese eyes, and the tall woman with the golden hair, another curiosity.

She was a little ill at ease. Champion was so eager to

help her, to please her. She knew that underneath that policeman's exterior he was in love with her. And that was her fault. She should have kept business and pleasure separate. Champion was a senior and knowledgeable policeman who could help her a great deal, but he was not the kind you could love and leave. She wanted to cross-examine him. And that was going to be hard.

'For many reasons,' Champion said, 'the illegal hawkers flourish. Because there is a *need* for them. Because they supply good cheap food on the street. But *because* Hong Kong is so congested we *must* try to keep the streets clear for traffic. But,' he said, 'how do we stop the Triads' protection rackets? The Chinese *expect* to have Triads about, it's a fact of life. There are forty-odd thousand Triad Society members in this colony. And there are only fifteen thousand cops. And these Triads are *secret* societies. Their discipline is iron. They'll kill anybody who stands in their way. They kill each other without hesitation if one of the oaths is broken. They'll never inform on each other. To catch a Triad man you've got to catch him red-handed. And he won't lead you to the rest of his society. You don't smash his gang. On the contrary: while he's in prison his society will support his family. And the Triad boys operating around the resettlement blocks may be small fry but they still have the might of their whole society behind them. If anybody gives these local boys a hard time, he tells his head office and *they* come along and sort it out. And just twenty miles up there is China, remember. Looming like a typhoon. And China can take this place back with a telephone call. And it's going to happen in twenty years anyway, when the New Territories lease expires. What's going to happen to these people then?' He looked at her, his eyes big:

'Who wants them? So they don't care about a bit of extortion from the Triads and a bit of corruption. And it's nothing compared to Thought Reform Labour Camp.'

'And what happens at their jobs?' he went on. 'Charlie Wong works in a factory. At the factory there're a dozen things going on against the law. Dangerous unfenced machinery. Insufficient windows. Insufficient lavatories. No first aid kits. Dangerous goods. Once a month or so the inspector from the Labour Department calls. He could charge the boss with half a dozen infringements. But usually he doesn't. So the boss slips the inspector his "tea-money". Everybody knows it and everybody's satisfied. Particularly the Finance Secretary, with Hong Kong's fantastic balance of trade because of all the hardworking factories.'

He looked at her. 'And multiply that a thousandfold! Look down there at those factories! That's all we've got. And *outside* those thousands of factories – what's happening? The illegal hawkers. The illegal taxis. The illegal gambling. The illegal restaurants flourishing.' He pointed round the playground. 'That's the mentality these kids grow up with. And,' he looked around, 'what kind of life is this anyway, for a kid?' He waved his hand. 'You can hardly be surprised if he joins a Triad Society himself. It is the one way to be guaranteed protection. And have a bit of fun and power. And then anything can happen to him.'

They were passing an ice-cream cart. He stopped and said to the hawker in Cantonese: 'Give these children ice-creams.'

There were squeals. The hawker was grinning, gold-toothed, as he handed out ice-creams. Another dozen children came running up gleefully. He gave the hawker twenty dollars and bought two more for Vanessa and himself. The hawker was having a field day.

They walked on, eating their ice-creams. He said:

'You cannot apply your American standards. You cannot even really apply British law successfully. The only way to clean up the Triads and so forth is with *China*'s law. Massive rectification campaigns. Thought Struggle. Everybody marching in the streets and denouncing each other. And everybody guilty unless proved innocent. That's the way Mao Tse-tung cleaned up China!'

She said: 'Would you advocate that?'

He looked at her, surprised. 'Good heavens, no.'

She said, walking along, head down: 'To rid the world of the Triads and Mafia? And the scourge of narcotics? Once and for all?'

'Would you?'

'It bears thinking about,' she said. 'You're making a very convincing case about the impotence of English law to deal with the problem of the Triads, Bernard. And it's getting just as bad in America. And in Europe. So, what are we going to do? Are we just going to let them go from strength to strength? With us impotently stumbling after them, hog-tied by our law? What's it going to be like in fifty years' time when the world population's doubled? All the cities are going to be like it is right here in this resettlement estate. Should we not consider applying China-type law?'

He looked at her, genuinely shocked.

'But, good God, Vanessa! The whole basis of our society . . . What sets us above the Russias and Chinas, is the Rule of Law! Enshrined in our constitutions . . . Human Rights. The freedom of speech. Freedom of the press. God, if you don't have the Rule of Law you have a dictatorship. Look –' he laughed apologetically – 'What I'm saying is that this is a unique place.'

She said: 'And this is where the Triads come from. The likes of Herman Choi. Isn't he a classic example of your impotence? Perhaps we have to apply a unique solution.'

NINE

He had reserved a table for lunch at the Sheraton. She would much rather have had a bowl of noodles at a cooked-food stall but she did not have the heart to suggest it. He was so anxious to do everything well. And on the table was a vase of red roses. If ever a man wore his heart on his sleeve it was Bernard Champion. But he was still being earnestly businesslike, helping her. She hoped she could keep the rest of the lunch that way. Thank God he had relaxed a little with a drink.

He said: 'There's several others like Herman Choi, of course. But he is the biggest one. Yes, we know all about him. In a sense. In another sense we know nothing about him.'

Her tape recorder was between them on the table.

'But he's only been into narcotics the last fifteen years or so. That's probably why he joined, to get the benefit of Triad secrecy. He's been a businessman all his life – a good one too.' He added: 'Harry Howard's the man to talk to about Choi's earlier life. Choi used to work for Harry.'

She nodded. He went on:

'Choi doesn't physically handle any of the narcotics he deals in. He doesn't even see it. He provides the finance. The management. By remote control. Through his flunkeys. And even the flunkeys probably don't see the stuff. *Their* flunkeys do. And no layer of flunkeys knows more than one man in the layer above him. He buys his raw opium from the Golden Triangle, that's the northern states of Burma, Thailand and Cambodia. From there the stuff is shipped to Hong Kong waters by a variety of methods, mostly by Thai fishing trawler. It is taken to his factory here and processed by his chemists into heroin.'

'But this factory isn't a permanent thing?'

'Oh no. It could be anywhere. All it needs is a few gas stoves and a selection of pots and chemistry equipment. You could get the whole lot on to the back of a mule. Of course, he varies the site of the factory from shipment to shipment. Also, none of these people know Herman Choi. Never see him.'

'And from the factory?'

'The refined heroin is packed. Some of it goes to retailers who put it into small one-shot packets for sale on Hong Kong streets through peddlers. This market of course he shares with other dealers. But the bulk is shipped overseas. To Europe. Via England and Holland, mostly. And also to America, more and more, lately.' He smiled. 'The Mafia are very worried about it.'

'So is the American Government. And how is it shipped to these places?'

He spread his hands. 'Every way you can think of. Hidden in pickle jars and toothpaste tubes, very often. And by couriers. They agree to take a bag of it in their luggage for, say, two thousand dollars. Plus their air ticket. They're met at the airport of destination by the pick-up man. Of course, if Customs find it, the pick-up man melts away. Or the stuff is planted on jet-liners. An accomplice in America gets it out.'

'How does he arrange for the stuff to get put in the pickle jars and toothpaste tubes? If you found out who shipped those things you could get back to Choi.'

He shook his head gravely, apologetically.

'No, you catch the man in San Francisco to whom the goods were shipped. But when you try to trace back here to the person who *shipped* the cases, all you'll find is a fictitious name.' He explained: 'You yourself could buy a big consignment of pickles right now. Take them home, empty them out, stick plastic containers of heroin inside, put some pickles back on top. And ship the lot to Freddie Wong's restaurant in San Francisco. This town's full of import-export agents who'll ship anything for you. All you do is sign a fictitious name on the invoice. And then disappear.'

She thought. 'And I could also get a job as a courier . . .'

Champion looked alarmed. 'What do you mean?'

She said, 'How do these people get propositioned by Choi's boys to carry stuff in their luggage? If you could set that up, you'd get somewhere. How does Choi find these couriers?'

Champion stared at her. 'You're not thinking of setting yourself up as an *agent provocateur*, are you?'

She looked at him, then shook her head. 'No.'

'There are over half a million tourists a year to this tiny place. Thousands of hotels, bars, rooming houses. Over eighty thousand drug addicts, hundreds of peddlers. It's not hard to find a courier. But once the courier has agreed to the job, he won't see the man who propositioned him again. The stuff will be delivered to him by an addict. Or even by an innocent hotel bellboy. If we catch the man delivering, that's all we've caught. And he'll probably be a drug addict. One of Choi's army of dedicated messengers, doing it in exchange for a free fix. He won't tell us who he got it from: he doesn't even know who it was – because it was another stranger.' He looked at her soulfully. 'We try, of course, but we never get back to the Herman Chois.'

74

He smiled at her, trying to make a joke: 'Don't try that, Vanessa.'

She had not wanted a second bottle of wine but he had ordered it (the best) before she could demur. She knew what was coming and she had figured out how to head the subject off. God knew, she did not want to hurt him. But still he took her by surprise. Suddenly, as if he had taken a deep breath to nerve himself, he leant across the table and took her hand. She looked up at him, almost startled.

Apparently speech had failed him. He was hunched forward, his big hairy hand heavily on top of hers, his eyes wide in ardour, his mouth half open to speak, his big, blue-shaved cheeks blushing. She blinked and collected her wits. She opened her mouth to say something, anything, and then Champion's throat croaked and she stopped. Then he stopped. They stared at each other for an agonized moment, then she recovered. She put her other hand on top of his and squeezed it. 'Jake,' she said brightly, 'Jake McAdam – why did he quit the police force?' She removed her hands from his and took a cigarette. 'Was he . . . in some kind of trouble?'

Champion sat back, blushing, and fumbling for a cigarette. He lit hers hastily, shakily. His heart was still hammering.

'Have you asked him?'

She was fully recovered now. And relieved that was over. 'No. But the girls I share with say one minute he was headed for the top of the police, the youngest superintendent ever, and then one day he just quit.'

Champion inhaled deep. He smiled apologetically: 'I think you better ask him. I'm as close to him as anybody, and he's never really told me much. But there're rumours.'

She said: 'Was it something to do with a woman?'

'That's one of the rumours.'

'The girls think it was a Chinese girl. And in his apartment, you must have seen it, there's a big portrait of a very beautiful Chinese girl. Which he painted himself.'

He nodded. 'That's the rumour.' He wanted to ask when she had been to his apartment, but he didn't. 'He had lots more of that same girl. That's no secret, they were hanging all over that huge apartment of his. Then one day he just took them all down. And just left that big one. I asked him why . . .' Then he stopped.

'What did he say?'

Champion was uncomfortable. He guessed he wasn't being disloyal. 'He just said that it was time to forget the past.'

'But he was out of the police force by then? When he took the paintings down?'

'Oh yes. He'd been out about four years. This was about five years ago.' He added: 'And since that day, to my knowledge anyway, he hasn't painted again.'

She thought. 'Was she a spy?'

She saw professionalism flicker across his face. 'I've no idea, Vanessa. And I really wouldn't know, because anything like that would be an Official Secret.' He shook his head. 'There's absolutely no reason to think that. But one thing is absolutely certain . . . and that is that Jake was not a spy.'

She said: 'Have you any idea what happened to the girl?'

He shook his head. 'I didn't even know he had a big relationship with a Chinese girl. Until after he'd left the force. Then I saw the paintings one day.'

She said persistently: 'He was in Special Branch, wasn't he? The department in the police that deals with espionage.'

'Amongst other things. Did he tell you that?'

'Olga. She's known him since forever. And she didn't

know he had a Chinese lover, either. And she thought she knew all about him. She knew his wife, how she ran off. How uptight he was about that. She knew all the girls he took out. Then, she says, he suddenly disappears from the social scene. Or he's always alone when she saw him, never with a girl. And meanwhile, he's a big wheel cop. In Special Branch. Then suddenly he quits. *Then* the pictures of the Chinese girl appear.' She raised her eyebrows at him. 'A lot of coincidences, don't you think?'

Champion breathed nervously, wanting to ask why the interest in McAdam. He said: 'But Jake was always a lone wolf. Even when he was married he refused to have anything to do with the Colonial social bullshit, as he called it. Excuse me . . .' She smiled and nodded encouragingly. 'Then his wife left, and he eventually started taking out women again. But he was always a dark horse. Olga wouldn't know as much as she says. Nobody would.'

'And then?'

'Yes. Jake was a brilliant policeman, no doubt about it. And an intellectual – got a BA in political philosophy at Oxford, and all that. And a good service record, fighting the Communists in Malaya years ago. And,' he added, 'lucky as hell. In his investigations, I mean.'

' "Somebody-Up-There-Likes-Me-McAdam". His nickname, I believe.' She added: 'Olga again.'

'Right. And he was headed for the top, yes. They promoted him to superintendent at thirty. In those days that was genius. In Special Branch. That was when we were having our big Communist riots here during Mao's Cultural Revolution in China – you know about those riots?'

'Yes.'

'Terrible. Lasted six months. Civil war. Running battles every day in the streets. And every day we expected Mao's Red Guards to swarm over the border.' He shook his head. 'Anyway, it eventually died down; then, about a year after the riots ended he suddenly resigned.'

'And . . . ?'

'He just dropped out of sight. I saw him occasionally. Wouldn't talk about it. He looked like hell. But he didn't go away on a holiday, or anything. He had quite a bit of money, but nothing spectacular. He borrowed money and bought two apartments, one on top of the other. As you know. Prices were rock-bottom after the riots. Then he did something strange. I thought it was crazy. Instead of renting out the upper apartment, he joined the two with a spiral staircase. And then he knocked out most of the walls in the upper apartment and turned it into a massive artist's studio. And this is a very pricey apartment. And his reason is, he's going to devote his life to painting.' He raised his bushy eyebrows. 'And he does. Just painted, morning, noon and night. And he did quite well. The upper apartment was his gallery as well as his studio. He held lots of exhibitions. Sold a lot. Then . . .' he raised his eyebrows again: 'One day he just quit painting.'

She waited.

'Then he began to get back to normal. For him. He started taking out women again. And then going into business. Buying apartments. All on mortgage. And starts a factory. He's got a thing about conservation and the energy crisis. So he starts a factory for solar heating and wind-chargers. Like a bull at a gate, he was. Borrowed all kinds of money. In debt up to his ears. Flies to the States, studies solar heating factories, comes back bursting with solar energy. Then, he just about got that factory on its feet, and he throws his money into that *Oriental Israelite* of his. With that nutter, Whacker

78

Ball. And now, as you probably know, it's concrete junks.'

'Whacker's not a nutter, he's damn good.'

'Yes,' Champion grinned. 'But he's not exactly your ideal partner, is he? Lives at the YMCA, with a few of his old China hand cronies. All they do is drink and solve all the problems of the world. But Jake liked the way Whacker could criticize everything. And his wit. So the next thing we know is, they've started this intellectual magazine. With Jake's money. Also borrowed. And of course,' Champion said, 'any profit goes to pay Whacker. I doubt Jake makes a cent out of it. But oh no, he won't give it up.'

She nodded thoughtfully. He started to say something, then stopped. Then he said:

'Jake knows a lot about this town. Is he . . . helping you much?'

She looked at him, then smiled her warm, dazzling smile. She said: 'I think she was a spy . . . You're being a great help, Bernard. Thank you.'

Bernard Champion's heart turned over like a porpoise.

TEN

Bernard Champion sat bulkily on a sack of cement with a bottle of beer, watching McAdam and Wong laying bricks at the deserted piece of beach that McAdam had rented. Champion had brought two Chinese children from the orphanage, whom he supported, and they were swimming now. In the little bay the concrete junk was tied up to a new floating jetty which McAdam had built of oil-drums and old timber.

'Why can't you use ordinary sea-sand in the cement?'

'Because of the salt.'

Champion said pensively: 'I really am impressed. All this in two weeks.'

The walls of the big boat-shed were two feet high already. 'It won't fall down on you or anything? How do you know you're doing it right?'

'I bought a book.'

Champion shook his head, then said tentatively:

'Are you sure it's worth it? I mean, if the banks are all down on the idea, are you sure it's . . . right?'

'Oh, yes.'

Champion looked unconvinced. But he didn't want to say anything discouraging. It was very hot. McAdam and Wong were both glistening with sweat. Champion watched Wong.

'He's good, too.'

'He's a first-class chap. He'd work under water if I told him to. But painfully shy.'

'You've done so much . . .'

'The spectre of bankruptcy. A great incentive.'

'But you're not that broke.'

'Damn near it. According to my bank manager.' He slapped on mortar with his trowel and fitted a brick on top of it. 'No, I'm not broke yet. But I haven't got any liquid assets.' He smacked the brick hard with the handle of his trowel and added: 'Just spent a fortune telephoning my banks in Switzerland and New York.'

'No joy?'

'You try convincing a Swiss banker on a long distance telephone about concrete boats. Guy's probably never seen the sea.' He scooped up mortar and slapped it on to the wall. 'And the Americans think the world's flat. If the boat floated at all it would sail off the edge.'

Champion smiled. 'Why didn't you write?'

'I'm in a hurry. I've got an order for one boat already. If I'm quick.'

'So how did you pay for all these building materials?'

'Credit. Thirty days. Oh, I've got enough money for this lot, he'll get paid. But that's about the end of it.'

'Then what'll you do?'

'Starve.'

'I'll grub-stake you. I mean for groceries and that.'

McAdam smiled as he emplaced a brick. 'Thanks, Champ. Don't worry, the bank will grub-stake me. They've got too much money invested in me, they need me alive. Living money's no problem, I don't get around enough to spend much, anyway. It's big money they're nervous about.'

'But you haven't got enough materials here to finish, have you?'

'No. But if I can just get the roof on. That's a big step.'

'And then?'

'Then go back to the bank. With something impressive to show them.'

'And if they still won't lend you the money?'

McAdam snorted. Slapping mortar and a brick. 'Then I'll just have to sell my apartment.'

Champion shifted his bulk irritably. 'And live where?'

'Right here. On the junk.'

'Jesus. Why not sell the junk?'

'The junk won't fetch nearly enough. That's my whole argument, isn't it? – it's a very cheap boat. I'm looking for something like a million Hong Kong dollars in all. Of course I'll sell it if I have to. But it's the only bit of advertising I have. Living proof for the fisherman.'

'How can you live on a junk, for heaven's sake?'

'Just watch me.'

'But you don't want to live like that for long. At your stage of life. It's a pretty Spartan thing.'

'Tart her up a bit. No,' he admitted, 'I don't want to live like that. But when I get sick of it I can live right here.' He pointed with his trowel at the old Chinese cottage.

'For Heaven's sake, it's a ruin, almost. What a way to *live*, Jake. A bloody hermit.'

'I like the simple country life.'

'But this isn't the countryside, this is Robinson Crusoe stuff. God, you're a successful man, really.'

McAdam smiled as he worked.

'Thanks for the "really".'

'Look, you've walked out of one successful career already. Now you've got your life together again. Now you're going to risk it all for . . .' He waved his hand. 'To stop people cutting down trees. Is it worth it?'

McAdam straightened, trowel in hand, sweating. He looked as if he was about to deliver an exasperated lecture. Then he abruptly scooped up more mortar.

'Yes. There's more to life than making money. Who needs the stuff, anyway?'

'You do.'

McAdam tapped the brick down firmly. 'I'll get enough, Champ.'

Champion sat hunched, watching him work.

'And your apartment. That's not going to bring you much. Isn't it mortgaged? Or should I say "they"?'

'Yes.'

'And it's not going to be an easy apartment to sell, I'm here to tell you. It's a double-storeyed house in the sky. You won't sell that lot easily. Not until you put back all those walls you knocked down. And that's going to cost a lot of money. You could easily end up with a half-finished boatyard – unable to function – and you're forced to sell your apartment cheap. So cheap you *still* can't finish here.'

'Yes,' McAdam said. He scooped up mortar.

'Well?'

'I said yes.'

Champion watched him work. He thought for several moments then he said:

'A million dollars, huh? A quarter of a million US.'

'To do it properly. But I can get by with much less. When I get the roof on this shed, I can start building boats. But it's uneconomic, I could only do one at a time. Unprofessional.'

Champion smiled to hear McAdam talking about economics.

'Why not play the stock market a bit? It's easy money.'

'What do I use for money?'

Champion made up his mind.

'I'll lend you some. Provided I do the investing for you. You can pay me interest.'

'Thanks, Champ. But I only borrow from the professionals. The banks – that's what they're there for. Not my friends.'

Champion said: 'I'll lend you a couple of hundred thousand.' McAdam straightened again and stared at him. Champion added: 'American dollars. But only to invest in the stock market. Not into this boat-yard. Because even if the stock market goes down, you'll still have the shares, and they'll go up again. But I'm afraid . . .' He waved his hand at the wall. 'This business is too dicy for my money. But what you do with your profit on the stock market is your affair.'

McAdam stared at him. 'How the hell have you got two hundred thousand US dollars loose?'

'What the hell!' Champion said indignantly. 'I'm a bachelor, I've got a good salary. And I've played the market all my life, you know that – and the horses. I've got nothing to spend my money on. Except gluttony.'

'But –' McAdam shook his head. 'Thanks very much for your kind offer. But how can you afford that, even if you've got two hundred thousand; why isn't it sensibly invested?'

Champion said gruffly: 'It *is* invested. But I can borrow a couple of hundred thousand against it, easily. And you pay the interest, that's all. It's a hell of a lot better than trying to sell your apartment, and living like a hermit.'

McAdam shook his head.

'There's good stuff on the market,' Champion said. 'And a few real good ones coming.'

'Like Lucky Man?'

'I believe that's one of them.'

McAdam shook his head again. 'Many thanks, Champ. But no, I just couldn't do it. It's either the bank's money, or my own.'

Relief flickered across Champion's face. 'Well, think about it,' he said. 'And think about *this* place.'

They sat on the end of the jetty in the dusk, wet from a swim, feet hanging in the water, drinking beer from the bottles. The children were splashing. McAdam was completely taken aback: it was hard to believe what Champion was saying. Champion stared at the sea, half embarrassed.

'I've heard of it happening like this,' he said. 'A guy's about forty, bachelor, set in his ways. Thinks he'll never get married. Then one day he meets a girl, and – boom! He really falls in love. And gets married. And I mean in love . . . Not some infatuation. And it's a great success.

84

Never looks back.'

McAdam looked at Champion's profile. Then Champion smiled sheepishly. McAdam wanted to put his arm around the guy and squeeze him. He started to say something sensible, then changed it. 'And how does it feel?' he said carefully.

'Oh . . . It feels wonderful,' he said lamely. '*She's* wonderful.'

'That's great, Champ. But listen – '

'You listen to me.' Champion held up his hand. 'I've come all the way out here to tell you I'm in love, now don't go spoiling it!' Then he gave his nervous panting laugh to cover his embarrassment. 'A man's entitled to a little starry-eyed nonsense, isn't he?'

'Absolutely.'

Champion hunched over the end of the jetty and stared at his feet. 'What were you going to say?'

McAdam regretted it. 'Nothing.'

'Go on!' He added gruffly: 'I need to talk about it.'

McAdam took a big wary breath.

'What I was going to say is . . . it may be . . . it's not uncommon, I believe – with people who've got profound scruples about – ' he was going to say 'screwing' and changed it – 'going to bed with a girl before marriage – that when they do, they wake up with a disproportionate, unrealistic amount of feeling. Which is partly guilt and partly . . . sexual infatuation.'

'Well, that's not the case. I'm not entirely inexperienced, you know.'

'I'm sorry.'

Champion glared at the sea a long minute. McAdam took a swig of his beer, waiting. Then Champion waved his big hand self-consciously and said to his beer: 'I don't just mean her body.' He shook his big head. 'That's fantastic enough. It's *her*. She's highly intel-

85

ligent. And so vivacious. And charm. And guts. And soul . . .' He looked at McAdam and gave up.

McAdam decided he had to say it. 'And hard as nails,' he said quietly.

Champion looked at him as if he had slapped him.

'She is *not*!' he said indignantly. 'God, Jake! That's your trouble – you expect women to be nice docile creatures who'll look at you with big adoring eyes and let you run the world! So when you meet a woman who's as smart and get-ahead as you – a modern woman who's capable of doing a man's job – somebody who's liberated, you say she's tough as nails!'

'I'm sorry – I shouldn't have said that. Look. She's a fascinating woman. She's a great girl. But Jesus, Champ, does she ever know what she wants – '

'And what's wrong with that?'

'Nothing – but she'll break your heart in the process! She'll love you and leave you. Because she's one of those modern women who doesn't *want* to be tied down – she doesn't *want* a permanent relationship. Especially in Hong Kong! She's a ship that passes in the night, for Chrissake. She wants to get her information, enjoy herself, and piss off back home to the Land of the Free.'

Champion was glaring at him. 'That can be changed. She won't be the first Women's Libber to fall in love.'

All right, McAdam thought. He'd said quite enough to make himself unpopular. He hoped Champion would drop the subject. If that was what Champion wanted he would never see the woman again. Champion cleared his throat and said awkwardly:

'You're seeing her soon, I believe?'

Here we go, McAdam thought. He said casually:

'Yes, I'm taking her to dinner on Saturday night.' He added: 'She's got her knife out for Herman Choi.'

Champion nodded, staring at the water. He took a deep breath, then said:

'Have you been to bed with her?'

'Oh Jesus!' McAdam glared at Champion. 'It would be none of your damn business if I had.' Champion shot him an agonized look, then dropped his eyes and hunched forward, embarrassed. McAdam's heart went out to him. 'Look, Champ, I'm just helping her in her job, that's what she invited us all to her party for. But if you feel uptight about it I'll beg off – I'm busy enough here!'

'Don't be silly.'

McAdam felt bad for having spoken so sharply. He put his hand on the man's shoulder and shook it.

'Come on, end of bullshit. You're not in love with anybody except San Miguel Breweries, and the French wine industry.'

Champion smiled sheepishly. 'Sure.'

ELEVEN

Jake spent the next two nights at the boat-yard, laying bricks until midnight by lamplight. Then on Friday night he stayed up very late dictating his editorial for the next issue of the *Oriental Israelite*. The Vanishing Wilderness, Part Six. Which had absolutely nothing to do with the high-powered, bad-tempered essays that Whacker Ball had stuffed the pages with.

Before dawn he was suddenly wide awake, worrying. About money. He got straight up and started laying bricks again. At eleven o'clock he had to drive back to Kowloon to his factory that made solar-heating units and go over the accounts. At noon he had a meeting with his accountant. By twelve-thirty he had finally faced a few facts.

For the next twelve months he would be technically,

legally, in a state of bankruptcy, his liabilities exceeding his assets. Which meant that if one single thing went wrong, if he failed to pay any debt on due date and a court writ was taken out against him, he would lose everything. Lunch-time he spent pacing in the Botanical Gardens, the sun beating down, the sweat making his shirt stick to his back. At two o'clock he got back into his car and drove back to his apartment. He telephoned four estate agents and put his apartment on the market.

Then he drove grimly fast back through Hong Kong and through the Mountains of Nine Dragons, back to his boat-yard on the remote beach of Tolo Sound. And stripped off his city clothes and started laying bricks again. Within two hours he had to throw down his trowel, shower, get back into his city clothes and then drive back to Hong Kong to take Vanessa Storm Williams to dinner. Which he dearly wished he did not have to do. He did not care that he was late.

She answered the door, and she was radiant.

'Forgive me for being late.'

She leant back against the door.

'You're tired. Should we just go to your place and have ham and eggs?'

'Oh no!' And he really wanted to take her out somewhere, now. He wasn't so tired anymore.

He had decided to take her to Aberdeen, because that's what tourists usually like to see, then to the floating restaurant. They took a walla-walla across the tiny harbour. The sun was getting low, the China Sea was flat, blue, golden, glassy smooth. The fishing junks were jam-packed, row after row of them, forests of masts, their great wood hulls gleaming browny-yellow, fishing nets and ropes everywhere. Sampans and walla-wallas were criss-crossing, and in the middle of the teeming

Chinese harbour were the two big gaudy barges, all lit up; the floating restaurants.

Any anxieties about the financial deep water he was heading for with his boat-yard dissipated. He loved this place: the hurly-burly of the Chinese boat-yards, the hammering and the roaring of machinery and the timber everywhere, and the smell of wood and oil and steel and sweat, the slipways jammed up against each other, junks being built everywhere, even a hundred yards up an alley. He was entirely at home here, in the hustle and bustle, the creation of boats that can sail the high seas and brave typhoons, that can sail round the world – he loved it. And he was glad that he was part of it. They picked their way through the boat-yards, carrying a bottle of cold beer each. She could feel how he felt, the confidence of a man in his element.

He pointed at three Chinese chiselling at a single teak log, forty feet long, and he had to speak loudly. 'That's the keel of a new boat. Those guys are about to build a forty-foot deep-sea fishing junk without a single plan or even a drawing.'

She looked at the log and shook her head. 'No plans?'

'Just build her by eye. Even the curved ribs, they'll just saw them into shaped sections by eye. Perfectly balanced. Deep-sea vessel. The builder won't even know the exact length the junk will be.'

He took her elbow. He pointed at the boat-yard next door. Nothing separated the two places except piles of timber. The skeleton of a fifty-foot junk stood there against the darkening sky: a long plank of teak bent over a fire with a heavy weight on one end.

'Bending the plank for the hull?'

'Right. No change in two thousand years. Except this.' He stepped over some timber and picked up a nail.

'The old junks were held together with wooden pegs. Then they started using iron nails. Which rust.' He tossed the nail down. 'In ten or fifteen years' time timbers will start rotting and have to be replaced. Damn shame. No problems like that with concrete.'

They sat at a wooden table in a teahouse and drank another cold beer. She looked about her. 'If I could paint, this is the sort of place I'd do. But your concrete junks will change all the romance of it, Hogan.'

'Partly, yes. But – look at all this timber. And the enormous cost of it nowadays. Something must be done.'

She looked at him, then said casually: 'Why did you stop painting, Hogan?'

He was surprised she even knew he used to. 'I burnt myself out.'

She studied her cigarette. She was about to say something, but he leant back in his chair and said: 'You've really done the trick with Bernard Champion.'

She was taken aback at the change of subject. 'What do you mean?' She knew what he meant.

'He's in love. Try not to hurt him.'

'I'm sorry. He's such a hell of a nice guy. I didn't mean him to take anything seriously.' She added: 'He was completely normal and confident when I first met him.'

'He's a very serious man, under that bulky, jolly exterior. And, actually, a very strong Catholic.'

'Yes, I've had an inkling of that. But there've been other women in his life, surely.'

'Precious few.' He leant his elbows on the table and took a mouthful of beer. 'You see, Bernie's really the marrying kind. For all he protests he's not a confirmed bachelor. He's just naturally shy, with women. He just has great difficulty getting it together – socially,

90

I mean. Oh, he can be the life and soul of the party. But he won't compete. He takes a back seat, as soon as anybody else shows any interest in the girl.'

'But he's a lovely guy. He must have had plenty of opportunities.'

'He's had a few girl-friends, sure. But they've always been the girls he thought he wanted to marry. And raise lots of kids. But it's come to nothing every time.' He added: 'And they've all been the most beautiful girl in the room. Always falls for the beautiful ones, old Champ.'

'And in between these girl-friends?'

'Bites the bullet. Sex is only for marriage. Confession and so forth.'

She drew on her cigarette.

'Oh, God. You trying to tell me something, Hogan?'

'None of my business. But I presume you're going to be seeing a lot of him?'

She frowned. 'Yes! He's a mine of information. And I'm going to Macao with him, to the bullfight.'

'What I'm saying is: Don't break that guy's heart.'

'I don't want to break anybody's heart. Live and let live. I've only just come to town.'

'Right. And you're off as soon as you're through.'

He did not take her to the floating restaurant. She had been there and she thought it beautiful, expensive, and a tourist trap. She wanted to go to McAdam's boat-yard.

It was a beautiful night. The moon shone big and bright on Tolo Sound, a long, wide wedge of silver on the dark sea. The mountains were silver-mauve in the moonlight, and the village lights of Shatin and Tai-po were twinkling.

There was no road out to the boat-yard, just two

tracks worn by his car. His old station wagon bumped along on the ridge of the mountain. Then he turned down towards the silvery sea. The car went grinding down the hill in low gear. She saw an old Chinese house in the headlights, then he stopped the car and switched them off, and she saw the bay properly in the moonlight. It was a small horse-shoe of a bay. Around the edge of the beach he had planted a crescent of banana trees and palms. The sea was sparkling silver-black and the rocks silvery grey. To the side were the rising walls of the big shed. But it was the cottage that she was looking at.

'It's absolutely charming.'

It was made of stone and the roof was of old Chinese tiles. It had two rooms, and round the doorway was an old peeling picture of Tin Hau, goddess of the seas. There was a big hole in the roof which McAdam had covered with a plastic bag.

He unlocked the door and lit a candle. There was a wooden bed, which he had knocked together himself, a table and two chairs. A bamboo cane stretched across one corner with clothes slung over it. In another corner was a small gas refrigerator and a stove. Piled everywhere were books and papers.

She smiled as she looked around her. 'And the other room?'

'My work-room.' It was dominated by a table covered with plans and geometry equipment. Round the walls hung a large assortment of tools. Against one wall was a stout carpenter's bench. This room was tidy.

'It's great, Hogan. You haven't got electricity, of course?'

'I'm going to mount one of my wind-chargers up on top of the hill. Eventually, when the business is in full swing, I'll have to get the electricity company to blow a power line through. Then that village a few miles back will have the benefit of it too: poor bastards haven't even got a fridge.'

'You're in business, remember. Not the Peace Corps.'

'Beer?'

'I thought you'd never ask. But let's take them with us while you show me the rest of your spread.'

He opened the refrigerator happily.

He got a flashlight and led her out into the moonlight. They walked between the trees towards the far side of the bay. There was a low stone wall. He shone his flashlight over; there was a startled grunt and a big pig clambered up, ears forward. And scrambling up groggily were a dozen pink piglets.

'Ahhhh . . . Why didn't you tell me you had pigs?'

'I wanted you to love me for myself. A guy with a good pig can't be too careful.'

He led her on to the next sty and shone his flashlight. Two ducks were sitting huddled in straw, staring into the light, their beautiful round eyes startled.

'That's the drake. And one duck who won't sit on her eggs.' He shifted his torch to one corner and there sat another duck. She was all fluffed up, her head up. Out of her feathers poked ducklings' heads, staring round-eyed at them.

'Aren't they beautiful?'

He opened the sty door and led the way in. The mother duck fluffed up dangerously. McAdam crouched down, making whistling noises. He lifted her up an inch, and there were all the ducklings' legs. He carefully closed his hand round one and pulled it out. He held his palm open to Vanessa.

'Oh.'

The little yellow duckling stared at them, round eyes wide. She took it and lifted it to her cheek and held it there.

'Why won't the other one sit on her eggs?'

'She's not as bright as your average duck.'

She laughed, clutching the duckling to her bosom. The ducks quacked, the mother pig huffed, the chickens in the sty next door squawked, and then he was laughing at her laughing.

She put the duckling back under its mother, gave her an admiring word, and followed him out of the sty to the next. She saw half a dozen chickens perched on a cane. He shone his flashlight to the corner. There was a hen, fluffing up her feathers indignantly. Little heads appeared and disappeared in her feathers.

'Ducklings!'

'I gave her the other duck's eggs to sit on.'

'Oh fantastic!'

'You have to wet the eggs with water once a day, like a duck does when she comes back from her swim. She didn't think that was right at all. And when they hatched out she didn't know what to make of them. And when they legged it straight into the duck pond she nearly had a heart attack.'

'Where's the pond?'

'There's a tiny stream that trickles down the gully behind the house. I've made a few little dams up there. I pipe water off by gravity to the rest of the place. Come and see my new shed.'

He took her hand. They tramped back along the beach in the moonlight. There was a pair of railway tracks running down the beach into the sea. 'Is this your slipway?'

'Right.' They walked up the tracks to the shed.

It was the size of a tennis court, concreted; the walls about three feet high already. And piled everywhere were sacks of cement and bricks and sand and piping and timber.

'You're not just a pretty face, are you? How many

94

junks can you build in here at a time?'

'Three. All in different stages. Two curing while the third is being put together. Then while the last one is being cured, the carpentry is being done on the first one.'

'Cured?'

'Letting the cement harden – settle down. We have to spray the cemented hull with water for three weeks, night and day. There'll be pipes everywhere.' He added: 'We use sea-water, of course.'

'How did you cure your junk, then?'

'I sank her.'

'You *what-ed* her?'

'I just ran the hull down the slipway into the bay here. Opened all the cocks and she sank like a stone. Left her there for three weeks. Then hauled her up and put the engine and carpentry in.'

She said: 'How the hell did you refloat her?'

'Dozens of car inner tubes. Tied them to her hull, then pumped them up with an air-compressor. Once you get her breaking surface, close all the cocks. Then pump her out.'

'You and whose army?'

He smiled. 'Wong and I. You should meet Wong,' he added, 'he'll interest you. He's a refugee. He swam fifteen miles to get to Hong Kong. And he knows China.'

'Anybody who builds concrete boats for you has got to be a pretty interesting guy, Hogan.'

TWELVE

They had a lovely time, that night.

Sometimes a small breeze wafted in off the sea, and the moon shone down on them big and bright. They lay on a blanket on the silvery beach, made love, and drank cold beer, talking, and then made love some more. And they swam, the glorious, erotic feeling of swimming naked, and they came splashing up to each other, grinning all over their wet faces at each other, for the pleasure of what they were doing, and they kissed, sucking, salty kisses, and he ran his hands over her satin body under water, down over her hips and up between her thighs; and she opened her lovely legs to him under the moonlit South China Sea.

They lay on the blanket under the moon, water glistening on them, talking, about anything but mostly about themselves; she lay on her side, propped on her elbow, her rounded hip jutting in the moonlight.

She said suddenly: 'What happened to the Chinese girl, Hogan?'

He turned his head slowly and looked at her.

'How do you know about a Chinese girl?'

'The painting. And the rumour.'

He looked back at sea. 'Don't pay attention to rumours, Vanessa.'

'But the girl you painted . . . she was for real, wasn't she? You knew her well?'

He scooped up sand and let it run through his fingers.

'Yes. She was for real.'

'What was her name? Or can't you tell me?'

'Her name was Ying,' he said.

'Was she an artist, too?'

'She was a school-teacher. And an artist, yes,' he said unwillingly.

'Was she a good artist?'

He could answer that. 'Yes.'

'Have you got any of her paintings?'

'Yes.'

She said: 'You used to exhibit them, I believe. In your gallery.'

'Sure.'

She traced her finger in the sand. 'Whatever happened to her?'

He breathed deep and looked at the sea. 'I don't know,' he said.

'Did she go away?'

'Yes.'

'Where to? . . . To China?'

It was really the last question he was going to answer.

'Yes.'

'And she's still there?'

'Yes.'

She said: 'Do you ever hear from her?'

He could answer that too. 'No.'

'Or of her?'

'No again.'

She hesitated. Then asked: 'Was she a Communist?'

He turned his head and looked at her. He smiled thinly. 'Why the questions?'

She smiled. 'You fascinate me, Hogan. I promise I won't write a story about it. Was she?' She added: 'Most people who go to China are Communists.'

'True.'

'Or can't you tell me, because it's something to do with the Official Secrets Act?'

McAdam turned on his side and propped himself up on his elbow. He looked her in the eye as he took a sip of his beer.

'Let's talk about you,' he said.

She smiled. 'Can I ask just one more question?'

'You can ask.'

She said: 'Do you still love her very much?'

He looked at her. Then he said:

'Let's talk about you, Vanessa.'

She lay on her stomach on the blanket, the moonlight shining silver on her supple nakedness. 'My mother was an actress. In the theatre. And Dad's a politician.'

'What kind of politician?'

'Senator. He was a Congressman for years. He was the youngest Congressman for a long time. Since the Boston Tea Party, to hear my mother tell it.' She added: 'She died rather young. Dad was only thirty then, his first term in Congress.'

'How did she die?'

'Car crash. I was only small. But I remember how proud she was of Dad. They made a very dashing couple, I believe. The beautiful young actress on her way to stardom, and the handsome young Congressman.' She smiled: 'I think they both thought they were on the way to the White House. And maybe they were.' She added: 'She *was* extraordinarily beautiful.'

'I can believe it. And what happened then?'

She sighed cheerfully.

'I went to stay with my aunt, my mother's sister. Because Dad was always in Washington, sorting out the world. I was shunted off to a boarding school for rich little bitches whose mummies didn't want them underfoot. And then Dad went and married one of the mummies – a rich big bitch.'

'And you didn't get on with her?'

'Did I, hell. But I suppose I wasn't too easy to get along with, myself. I wanted my own mummy. And my Daddy to myself.' She shook her head. 'He was almost always in Washington, anyway. My wicked step-mother was *very* Boston Brahmin, that's where her family spread was. No, occasionally I went up to Washington to visit big Daddy and get spoilt rotten for a few days, the rest of the time I went home to my aunt in Long Island.' She added: 'She married an Italian businessman. Restaurant-owner. I almost grew up on spaghetti.'

'How do you get on with your stepmother now?'

'I still hardly ever see her. But she's an old rich bitch, now, isn't she? And I'm a young rich bitch.'

'And your father?'

'He's still up in Washington, of course. Still too busy. I hardly see him. But we get along great. Still tries to spoil me when we see each other, to make up for having been such a rotten father. Seems to think I still like lollipops.' McAdam smiled. 'He's given up his designs on the White House. But he's very much the elder states-man. Frightfully proper. And very Boston Brahmin too, now, unfortunately.'

She turned her head and gave him her brilliant smile.

'Okay?'

The moon began to get lower in the starry sky and it was the coolest time of the China night. He made a fire on the beach, and fetched a frying pan and eggs and bread and sausages and some ice and another bottle of wine. She took the pan from him.

'This is something I know more about than you, Hogan.'

She crouched in front of the fire with one of his shirts on and fried the eggs and sausages, the flames flickering yellow on her; he brought the small wooden table and set it up between the fire and the sea. They sat at the table on the beach, and ate fried eggs and sausages and drank crisp cold wine and she put a flower in her hair, and her hair flickered golden in the firelight. The night began to turn grey in the east and now the moon was sitting on top of the mountains, and a light early morning mist was beginning to drift in from the sea.

'I must go soon, Hogan. But first I want to see the sun rise over China.'

The grey began to turn to pink in the east, and then to a red and orange glow; they climbed the long grassy hill, hand in hand, and stood on the top silhouetted against the dawn, and the morning breeze blew cool on them. All the islands were turning to mauve, and the early morning mist was drifting in below them, slowly billowing round the islands, creeping along the rocky shorelines; and now the east was turning red, fanning up into the sky, and then the sun came up. First just a crescent of flaming gold, then up it came before their eyes, slowly, slowly, then faster and faster, swelling above the horizon, and now the glow was spreading riotously right across the eastern sky, red and orange and gold, and now the whole horizon was on fire and the sea sparkled blinding gold and silver and the early morning mist was turning to shifting pink, and the grass on which they stood was golden sparkling green.

The following Wednesday Vanessa went out to McAdam's boat-yard to get Wong's story. She came in the very early morning by bus with an interpreter arranged for her by Bernard Champion, crowded up with fishermen and Hakka peasants and ducks and geese; then from the main road she walked the four miles to McAdam's bay, swinging along, enjoying it. But there was nothing sociable about the visit.

She did the interview with Wong sitting in the shade under the banana trees, while McAdam carried on working. She had been fascinated by the tubby round-faced Chinese man and how he had swum fifteen miles from China during the year of the Hungry Tiger. But getting the story out of him had been like drawing teeth; and all the time she had been very aware that McAdam was working. She was welcome to take his labour away for a couple of hours but he wasn't going to stop for her or anybody. Fine. But she did think he might take time out for a cup of coffee with her. After all, they weren't exactly business acquaintances. And by God, how he worked! In shorts, the sweat running off him, with studied, concentrated swiftness. Like a Trojan, and the walls seemed to grow up in front of her eyes.

When the interview was over she firmly refused his polite offer to drive her back to the main road: working hours were clearly for working around here. She stood in front of him, very aware of the sweat glistening on him and the strong smell of man, and gave him her dazzling smile and said almost formally:

'Many thanks again. Let me know when you're coming to town, I'd like to cook you dinner.'

And she turned on her heel brightly and started walking up the hill in the blazing China sun, her skirt swirling.

Which impressed him. Of course a journalist should go out and get her story but it was a long, hot way back. It impressed him that she refused to disrupt him and considered a four-mile hike all in a day's work. He thought about her a good deal that day as he worked, sweating, laying bricks in the broiling sun. The image stayed with him, her walking over the hills, her long golden legs. And she wouldn't be wearing panties.

PART IV

Wong Ting-tak, which means Wong Man-of-Great-Virtues, had fled to Hong Kong three times in the Year of the Hungry Tiger, before the borders were closed again. Altogether Wong Ting-tak was arrested, fed and deported three times by the Hong Kong Police, and each time he crept back across the river and across the flattened fence and into the steep jungled foothills, running, scrambling, dodging, and each time he was arrested again and deported.

The third time the People's Liberation Army guard did not just let him go, he ordered him to return back to his native village. There were the border guards all along the river again, and there were the long lines of exhausted hungry people trudging back across the valley, heading back into the great, mauve, misty mountains of China.

When darkness came Wong saw some young people leave the road and go creeping into the paddies towards Deep Bay, and he followed them. Creeping, sloshing, crouching, exhausted, hungry. That night they heard the gunfire of the People's Liberation Army shooting the people again. The searchlights of the Hong Kong Police were sweeping the river and the paddies beyond. It took them all night to creep down the valley, to the coast of Deep Bay. When the dawn came they threw themselves down between some big rocks, flat out on the sand, and slept.

When Wong woke up it was already sunset again, and the others had gone. He sat up, staring, then he scrambled up. He saw their footprints leading down into the sea. Wong stared. His heart was thudding; then he wanted to throw back his head and howl: *'Come back! Wait for me!'*

He threw himself back down on the sand. For five minutes he lay there, feeling the fear. The lights of the Hong Kong fishing village of Laufaushan were coming on across the bay now; it was fifteen miles away. He lay there a long time, then he got up on to his knees, and prayed. Wong was not a religious man, and he had never prayed before to Tien Hau, goddess of the seas, but he prayed to her now, to keep him afloat. Then he prayed to Lu Pan, the god of carpenters. He prayed to the god of the West Wind, although he did not know what good it would do, for he knew by the sunset that he was going to head east. Then he prayed to the god of the East Wind also. He prayed to Kwan Tai, the god of Martial Honour; Kwan Tai had nothing to do with him, but Wong was running out of gods. He also prayed to Mister Rabbit, who lives on the moon, for the moon had something to do with the sea. Then he could remember no more gods, and he just lay crouched there on the sand, sweating, and sand stuck to his mouth and hair and eyelids.

Wong was full of fear, such as he had never known. It was the fear of death. Wong knew he was a strong man, and he could swim, but he did not know how far. Then at last he took a long quivering breath and got to his feet. He flinched as his foot first touched the water. The sweat was running down his chest. He waded as far as he could, until the sea lapped up over his chest. Then he gave a whimper and he screwed up his sweating face and kicked off the bottom.

Wong swam, his arms slapping the water, kicking his legs, gasping and blowing, out into the flat black sea and the night; he swam like that for maybe a thousand yards, and it seemed he must have swum a very long way; he was exhausted by the great hunger in his belly, from the many days of walking, the running. He stopped swimming to rest, and his heart was hammering in his ears and the sea was smacking into his face; he trod water, desperately trying to gasp his breath back and get the great ache out of his arms and shoulders and his legs. He looked about him and he could not make out the beach he had swum from, and he could not see the lights of Laufaushan above the black smacking sea. All he could see was the big black shape of a mountain looming up into the sky with the glow of the lights of the Golden Mountain Where Men Eat Fat Pork behind it. He rolled on to his back to try to float, but the water smacked over his face, and he had to roll over on to his chest again; wallowing and gasping, face screwed up, and the black bitter water smacking into his mouth, and all the time the terror of the vast black sea all around him. For maybe a minute Wong wallowed, then he started swimming again.

Thus Wong swam, thrashing and breast-stroking until he could swim no more, then rolling over on to his back, gasping and spitting, then rolling over and breast-stroking and dog-paddling again, spluttering, blind. The sea smacked up and he gasped it into his mouth, the terror-choke of sea, and he retched it out and gasped again, and sea smacked into his throat again and his face sank under and he clawed wildly up again, spluttering, gasping, blinded, and all the time the agonizing ache in his arms and in his legs. The black faraway land rose and sank away, and he felt terror and exhaustion such as he had never known. For three hours Wong swam like that, and he only knew that he could not make it back across the terrible sea to China, to turn back was as terrible as to thrash onwards.

The black current suddenly surged Wong sideways, and with the renewed strength of terror he thrashed and kicked, but he was finished, and the current took him. Wong could not fight it; he pawed the sea with his head thrown back, gasping and spitting, and the black sea took him down Deep Bay.

For two hours the sea took him in the China night. The black silhouette of the faraway land slid past him, but Wong did not see it going. All he knew was that he must keep his reeling head up. For two hours the current swept him along, gasping, spluttering, terrified, then he hit the oyster raft.

The raft was made of bamboo and the oyster cages hung down into the sea. Wong was dragged a long way down the big old piece of bamboo, ripping his flesh, before he flung his arms over it and clung. And he was crying, with exhausted, gasping, desperate, clinging joy; he did not know what he was clinging to but he knew it was solid and that his head was above water. He clung and clung, and it was the best feeling in the world. He saw the first grey in the sky, then the land, the grey mountains not a mile away, and the oyster rafts all round. Wong clung there whimpering, gasping, for a long time; then he pulled himself slowly along the raft in the first light, and started to swim slowly through the rafts, and as he clung to each one and pulled himself along it, the joy and knowledge of them was the sweetest thing he had ever known.

THIRTEEN

She was strong and she could take the heat. And she
believed in doing her homework properly. But she
could not take bullshit.

She had been there, to the Golden Triangle of northern Thailand and Burma, where the terrible stuff came
from, she had hiked for days with her knapsack on her
back, her leg muscles expanding with the hard work. She
had seen the opium poppies growing in the high mountains, stayed with the simple mountain tribes who grew
them (delightful people all), listened to their problems.
She had even got right into the fortified stronghold of
the Chinese bandits who bought the opium from the
tribesmen, she had seen the stuff stacked up in ware-
houses, seen the jungle refineries that turned it into 999
heroin, she had seen the mule trains taking the stuff
away, heavily guarded by soldiers armed with American
M16 automatic rifles, M79 recoil-less rifles, grenade
launchers and mortars, headed for the docks of Bangkok by secret routes and rivers; she had even chatted up
the smooth Italian gentleman with his Bronx accent and
natty white suit and his Beechcraft aeroplane at the
airstrip cut into the jungle, who was buying on behalf of
a Mafia family; she had even nearly slept with the bastard in the naïve hopes of getting some more information – dumb, girl, dumb.

She had been the guest of the bandit General and
tape-recorded him saying: 'It is the law of necessity. We
have to continue the war against the evil of Commu-

nism, even harder now that you Americans have abandoned the struggle in Vietnam and Cambodia. We must liberate China! An army must have weapons. To buy weapons you must have money. In these mountains the only money is opium.'

Bullshit. The generals had not fired a shot at China for over twenty-five years.

Like so much of the rest of it. Like the earnest United Nations officer who had told her: 'It's not just a question of making the hill tribesman grow another kind of cash crop instead of opium poppies. We would also have to supply hospitals, because opium is the only pain-killer these people have. And we would have to teach them to terrace. And lay on water and irrigation. And build roads so the tribesmen can bring their produce to the market towns. It is a problem of finance.'

More bullshit. Because the staggering fact was that it cost the Thai Government alone (not counting what it was costing Uncle Sam and the others) well over one thousand million dollars a year to try to combat the problem: and with a fraction of that kind of money they could build a Mayo Clinic on every hilltop of the Golden Triangle and give them a Tennessee Valley Water Authority irrigation set-up and pay every tribesman a pension for growing nothing at all, for Chrissake – provided they did one little thing first: send in paratroopers and shoot the living shit out of those opium warlords once and for all.

And why not? They knew where the bastards were. If she could get into their stronghold with just her press-card, why the hell couldn't the military?

Because of the Rule of Law. Because every man is presumed innocent until proven guilty in a court of law. Well, Byline Storm Williams, pouring her sweet sweat out on a Hong Kong rooftop, is here to tell you that you have to fight fire with fire. Not with the Laws of Evidence. A problem of finance, my poor achin' ass.

Except – oh *yes*! – the problem of financial *profit*. Now *there's* the rub. If a village's whole annual crop of opium sells for two thousand dollars it sells as heroin for over one million dollars on the streets of London or New York – a profit of fifty thousand per cent. As long as there're profits like that there will be traffickers. But: no profit, no traffickers. So the trick is for Government to supply the addicts with their heroin, at cost price, which is peanuts: every addict is medically certified, registered, and he comes along to a clinic every day for his dose. Why not? But no. More bullshit. Instead of kicking the chair out from under the traffickers' asses by slashing their profit, we repose our pathetic confidence in the pathetic Laws of Evidence.

And the evidence was right there in front of her binoculared eyes, on that chunk of jungled mountainside that she had been watching for almost three days with the police. It was in hundreds of other places in this colony, in the ever-shifting heroin dens, in the traffickers' cars that cruised the streets picking up the addicts free of charge, in the peddlers on the streets, the hundreds of look-out boys watching for the police, the addict-children acting as couriers, in the Triad bully-boys peddling pep-pills laced with heroin at schools to breed more addicts. *That* was the evidence. In the last week she had watched the police raid the drug dens on that piece of mountainside over there three times, and the following day they had been back in business.

And at the other end of the spectrum of evidence were the forts of the opium warlords of the Golden Triangle, the smooth Italian-Bronx gentleman with the zippy Beechcraft aeroplane and the luxurious mansion of Herman Choi just two miles away from this rooftop.

But the Laws of Evidence could not connect the two.

Well, *she* could. And would.

It was a big area. There were two roads, and lots of footpaths and ladder paths between the huts made of plank and tin, and the whole area was flanked by apartment blocks. Above was just mountainside and bush. Through her binoculars (her sweat on the eyepieces stung her eyes) she could see the addicts, skinny wretches, making their way to the dens. She could spot eleven of the look-out boys dotted about, each in sight of the next, just sitting on the road-sides and on tops of the shacks.

Sometimes it was one of the skinny, wretched addicts who delivered the big bag containing the little packets of heroin to the dens, sometimes it was a little girl or boy. A car delivered the big bag to the addict or the child on the busy main road below. But now, as she watched, a car drove brazenly up the mountain road. She saw a look-out boy wave. The car sped along the road between the huts, then it braked opposite the den and a bag was held out of the window, and the addict grabbed it. The car sped away and the addict walked towards the den. The radio of the inspector beside her rasped:

'Scramble. Black Hillman sedan number – '

She scrambled up with them and ran across the rooftop and clattered down the stairs. They burst out of the apartment building and ran flat out along the access road. There were plainclothed policemen running flat out ahead of them, more coming up from the main road below. There were look-out boys and addicts running down the paths and up into the bushes. A car screeched to a halt outside the den and the policemen flung themselves out. They bounded up the path towards the den. Addicts were throwing themselves out of the door and windows and crashing off into the bushes. The den door slammed in the first policeman's face. He kicked it open with a crash and burst in.

Ten minutes later it was all over. She stood inside the hut with the panting policemen and surveyed the haul. The inspector was complaining to his men about their lack of synchronization. On the floor the exhibits were being arranged for police photographers: a plastic bag half full of little packets of white 999 heroin or Number 4, another bag of packets of reddish grey powder, Red Chicken, or Number 3; candles for heating the heroin in the little strips of tin foil, cardboard tubes for sucking the fumes up off it into the mouth – 'chasing the dragon'. The other common system was putting the heroin in the tip of a cigarette and smoking it, held upwards so the stuff didn't fall out – 'firing the Ack-ack gun'. She had seen it all before in other raids in other places, from plush dens like casinos down to hovels like this.

The den operator was handcuffed, sitting against the wall nursing a big bruise on his head, scowling. The addicts were sitting around the walls, looking vacant. They were emaciated, their faces hollow, eyes sunken, their bones pushing against their dirty skins, hair wiry and sticking up. They were all high on their euphoric plateaux from the heroin they had smoked, but they all looked wretched: in a few hours, when they were in the police cells, the narcotic would wear off and the depression would set in, then the physical agonies of withdrawal.

The addict who had taken the bag of heroin from the car driver was there but he had not yet had his fix and he was shaking. But the bag was gone – somebody had made off with it into the bush. Two of the eleven look-out boys had been arrested: they were about twelve years old. They had even found the little girl who sometimes acted as courier. The inspector's radio rasped, then he said to her excitedly:

'Bloody marvellous! They've caught the Hillman! Had a shootout in Chai-wan. The driver was just an ordinary illegal taxi, he didn't know anything about it, but we've got the guy who was seen handling the bag –'

'Great,' she said.

She thought, *Big Deal*. What'll he tell you? He's a Triad man. If you can convince the jury that you saw him hand over the bag you still can't prove that it contained heroin because you haven't found the bag. And even if you had found the bag in the den how could you prove it was the same bag? She shook her head and turned away. If the den operator was a Triad man he would be paid whilst he was in prison, and in any case there were plenty more where he came from. And as for the addicts, all eleven of the poor wretches, what did they matter? There were plenty more where *they* came from. And getting more and more every day. And even for the short time they would be in prison they would be supplied with heroin by the Triads.

She thanked the inspector and left the hut, followed by the faithful detective corporal whom Bernard Champion had assigned to her. When she reached the road she saw the fire engine had arrived. Jack-the-Fire was in charge, but he did not see her. They had come to burn the den and surrounding bush as soon as the police had finished collecting their evidence.

Big deal. A scorched earth policy. Of a few huts. And two miles away the mansion of Sir Herman Choi stood resplendent, impervious. End of story.

But not end of bullshit.

FOURTEEN

The next week-end there were bullfights in Macao, the tiny Portuguese colony forty miles away across the River Pearl. Bernard Champion had invited her to go with him.

Friday was the hottest day so far of that hot summer. The sun blazed down on the glaring South China Sea and on the teeming concrete and the narrow sweating streets, and the sky was mercilessly blue. It was still sweltering hot at midnight when they boarded the S.S. *Fat Shan* for Macao. There were a lot of people crowding through Immigration and up the gangways; the Macao bullfights were a big annual event.

Bernard Champion had used all his considerable influence to get the best of everything. Flowers and champagne in her first-class cabin, the best room in the Estoril Hotel in Macao, the best seats at the bullfight. And everything very proper: separate, though adjoining, cabins and hotel rooms. In case she thought him presumptuous. Now, as the ferry steamed down the fairway, they stood at the stern rail watching the beautiful harbour lights go by under the China stars.

Big Bernie Champion was nervous. He was in a new white tropical suit and tie, holding his champagne, feeling very formal. He wished he could relax. He desperately hoped he could keep her to himself this week-end, that they wouldn't have to join crowds of friends. He was dreading having to take her down to the bar soon; they would be all over her, making jokes. And he would stand there tongue-tied like an idiot.

'Isn't it beautiful?' she said.

113

'Oh yes. It is.'

She wished to God he would relax. And she was embarrassed by all the expense he had gone to for her. She had expected to spend the night against the bar like everybody else. But first-class cabins. Separate. She had expected to sleep with him some time, because after all she had accepted his invitation to a week-end in Macao, even if quite long ago, and that was fine, he was a great guy. But now that McAdam had warned her about what she was doing to him, she hoped like hell that they could keep to their expensive separate accommodations and that he wouldn't be hurt.

She watched the rainbow of neon lights gleaming into the water, and the fairyland glow of the vast apartment blocks and the twinkling lights of freighters with the cargo junks clustered round them. Out of the corner of his eye Champion covertly looked at her golden neck and shoulders and the lovely cleft of her breasts and the full curve of her body. He found courage and awkwardly put an arm around her waist.

She stood close to him for just long enough, then gave him a warm smile. 'How about the *New York Times* buys *you* a drink, officer?'

As he had feared, it was jumping down in the big cocktail bar, jampacked with people, most of whom he knew. The first person he saw was McAdam. With old Captain Neil O'Bryan and Harry Howard and Mervin Katz.

She was surprised. She had not seen McAdam for ten days, since she had had the interview with Wong, and he had not contacted her. She had presumed (she damn well *hoped* it was the case) that he was simply too busy to come to town for that dinner she had kindly offered to cook him. And now here he was squandering a whole week-end.

'Hullo there!' She gave her dazzling smile as she made to pass him.

But Champion gave an inward sigh of relief and steered her towards him through the people. 'Hullo Champ! Hullo Vanessa!'

'You're looking fit, Hogan!'

He was. His face was deeply tanned and he must have lost ten pounds in weight. 'You're looking robust yourself,' he said to Vanessa. He turned to Champion and nodded at his new white suit. 'Are you in the ice-cream business?' he grinned.

McAdam was feeling fit, but dog-tired. He had intended working through the week-end, but at sunset he had suddenly thrown down his trowel and declared a holiday. He had given Wong fifty dollars and climbed wearily into his car, driven home, packed a bag and gone down to the docks and bought a ferry ticket from a scalper. He did not intend to see any bullfights. What he needed was people to drink and talk English with, about anything at all except concrete boats. He did not have a hotel room reserved in Macao. He didn't care where he slept, he didn't care about anything except getting a rest from that boat-yard. And he was very regretfully aware of Ms Vanessa Storm Williams. But no way was he going to tread on Champion's territory. Champion was introducing her to old Captain Neil O'Bryan.

'He's the captain of the *Fat Hong* – famous old ferry boat that used to do the China Coast run and River Pearl in the good old days. Ghost ship now. Eh, Cap'n?' Champion beamed at him and gave a nervous laugh.

'Not given up the ghost yet,' Captain O'Bryan said sharply. 'She'll go plenty yet.'

McAdam thought, poor old Champ. The change in the guy since he fell for this one. Where was the big, burly, gut-laughing, quick-witted Champ of last month?

'Why a ghost ship?' Vanessa said.

Captain O'Bryan shifted on his bar-stool moodily. 'Sank four times in forty years. Can't get crew any more.'

'When was the last time?' she said, fascinated.

'Bloody pirates planted a bomb on her in the Pearl in 'fifty-two. Sank like a bloody stone, lady.'

'Were you on her when the pirates planted the bomb?' said Vanessa.

'Sitting on the bloody toilet, madam,' he said. 'Thought it was something I'd eaten.'

They all burst out laughing. O'Bryan grinned, his aristocratic old face weather-beaten: he loved an audience.

'How did she sink the other times?'

'Armed as a gunboat during the Communist Revolution: one. Typhoon Mary in 'forty-eight: two. Hong Kong harbour. Blown all over the bloody place. Bloody great tidal waves. Like a stone again. Then those bloody pirates.'

Vanessa was rapt. 'Were many people drowned?'

O'Bryan looked at her, his old eyes blue. He didn't want to talk about it any more.

'A lot.' He looked back at his gin. 'The screams . . .' he said to his glass. And you saw and heard it all in the hot China night.

Harry Howard was drinking too much again because he was trying to relax too fast because he worked too hard. Harry had a whole week-end's pass from his wife. Mrs Isabel Howard did not like bullfights, but if she loved him she would come with him once a year, wouldn't she? No, she would not. And that was okay with Harry

Howard because he did not like bullfights either and he had not come to see the bullfights, he had come to get drunk and to get laid and then he was going to divorce his wife. Harry Howard was going to lay Cheri Fontaine, alias Vicky Forbes, the big girl who was going to do the strip show soon on the dance floor.

McAdam wanted to talk to Harry Howard sometime about the tip he had given him about the Lucky Man Development Company, but right now Vanessa had moved in on Harry, aside. God, McAdam thought, doesn't she ever stop working? He knew who she was questioning him about: Herman Choi. He looked at the line of her body and had to make himself look away. Champion moved up to him and said with a bright forced smile: 'How are you getting on – about selling the apartment?'

McAdam didn't even want to think about it. 'No joy yet. Too big, the agents say. I'll probably have to rebuild the upper one first.'

'Yes . . .' Champion glanced covertly at Vanessa.

'For Christ's sake!' McAdam put his hand on his friend's shoulder. 'How can you be uptight about old Harry?'

'I'm not uptight,' Champion whispered. He added: 'I just hope this doesn't keep up all week-end. She's a glutton for work.'

'Well,' McAdam said significantly, 'she hasn't got that long here.'

Champion took a big gulp of his drink. 'Maybe.'

Oh God, McAdam thought. 'Show her around Macao, keep her away from the popular bars.'

'Yes,' Champion said. 'She wants to find out about the refugees and all that.'

'Good. Work on that.'

*

117

The ship churned evenly across the South China Sea under the stars. In the bar there was hubbub, music, the air cloudy with smoke.

Mervin Katz of the Royal Observatory was with his girlfriend, Veronica, the Pan Am air-hostess from the American Mess. Jack-the-Fire was there with his girlfriend, Monica. McAdam saw the beautiful Kurt Marlowe, the pilot for the United States Navy Meteorological Department, making his way towards them through the people. He did not want Kurt Marlowe joining them, he could not stand the conceited ass. Trouble was he wasn't an ass. Kurt Marlowe came up behind Vanessa, slipped both arms around her waist and snuggled up against her bottom, grinning his perfect smile. 'Hullo, darlin'!'

'Oh hullo, Kurt, you're back again.'

Her smile was less than warm, but Champion flinched inside. 'Hullo everybody,' Marlowe said.

McAdam leant back against the bar. 'What's the weather going to do next week, Dogs?' he said to Mervin Katz, ignoring Marlowe. 'When are we going to be able to bath again?'

'Speak for yourself,' Marlowe smiled perfectly.

'There's not a typhoon within a thousand miles,' said Katz.

Kurt Marlowe said, 'Typhoon Rose is within fifteen hundred miles. I flew into her this morning. From the Philippines. Bad bitch.'

'I'd love to see over your Royal Observatory some time, Dogs,' said Vanessa.

'I thought you were investigating corruption?' Katz said. 'Show me how I can make a buck on the side out of the weather and you'll be my pal for life.'

They all laughed, except Kurt Marlowe, who said to Vanessa: 'I'll fly you into a typhoon any time you like.'

'Gee, thanks a million,' Vanessa said dazzlingly, and McAdam smiled. Then there was a roll of drums and a cymbal clash. And Cheri Fontaine, alias Vicky Forbes, burst through a door on to the central dance floor.

She had a big creamy smile and long plump legs that always had a bruise; her magnificently enormous breasts bounced before her and her enormous little girl's eyes fluttered nervously, and the band burst into 'Buttons and Bows'. Big Cheri started miming the words with her big eyes rolling, and went into her bump and grind routine.

Kurt Marlowe was dancing with Vanessa. The music was 'Slow Boat to China'. Vanessa had tried to lean well back in Marlowe's arms and talk brightly, but he was having none of that: he was holding her close, nuzzling her brow and cheek, and short of walking off the floor she had little option but to endure it. She could feel his erection pressing against her. That was par for the course, but it annoyed her. The guy presumed that it would turn her on. Almost all the girls in the American Mess had been ga-ga about Kurt Marlowe at one time or another, and he was one of the best-looking men she had ever set eyes on, but he did nothing for her. In fact he irritated her. Because underneath that perfect smile and profile and prematurely grey hair there was massive conceit and calculating shrewdness.

Champion kept his back studiously to the floor, as if nothing was happening. He had hardly contributed anything all night, except his ready panting smile. McAdam's heart went out to him: the poor guy was in for a miserable week-end. He longed for Champion to stop suffering, but most of all he desperately wanted to get some sleep somewhere. 'I must find a bench,' he said.

119

Champion said: 'You can have my cabin. We've got one each.' He was about to refuse then Champion said unhappily: 'In fact you'll be doing me a favour.'

He pretended not to understand. The music ended. He glared at Marlowe: he was trying to keep her on the floor for the next dance; but she succeeded in leading him off it.

'That's very kind of you, Champ,' he said.

Marlowe whispered in Vanessa's ear as they approached; then he turned and walked away towards the toilet.

'Excuse me,' McAdam said.

He found Kurt Marlowe in the toilet off the promenade deck, combing his hair at the mirror. McAdam leant against the door and said quietly:

'Please, Marlowe, do us all a favour: Lay off that woman.'

Marlowe paused, comb poised, then turned to face him.

'Do *me* a favour, Jake. Mind your own business. Stop trying to spoil my fun. You've had your share, now it's my turn.'

Afterwards he did not know why he did it, and he was by no means proud of himself. But he lunged forward and in one movement grabbed Marlowe by the scruff of his neck and wrenched him off balance, flung open the toilet door and slung him out. Marlowe reeled across the deck, arms and legs flailing. He rolled over and over, then crashed to a stop against the rails.

Nobody saw it. McAdam straightened his collar with satisfaction. He had to resist dusting his hands. Then he turned and walked back into the bar.

He said good night and asked Champion to show him his cabin.

*

120

McAdam sprawled on the bunk in his clothes, eyes closed, while Champion moved his suitcase next door into her cabin. He came back. 'Good night, mate,' he said.

McAdam kept his eyes closed, fighting sleep.

'Thank you, Champ. I'll fix up with you . . .'

'Nonsense.'

McAdam smiled, eyes closed. 'Champ?'

'Yes?'

'I think I may be needing to borrow that two hundred thousand off you.'

Champion flinched. 'Sure,' he said. 'I told you, any time.'

'Lucky Man Development. Harry Howard can get me a big block of shares at par, says they're a winner. Know anything about them?'

Champion said: 'They're the one to go for, I hear. You're very lucky. But they're not coming on the market for another few weeks.'

McAdam said, eyes closed: 'Thanks, Champ. I can last that long. I'll let you know. Maybe somebody'll buy the apartment.'

'Sure,' Champion said.

The next thing he knew, Champion was shaking him, smelling of toothpaste and aftershave lotion, and telling him they were docked in Macao, did he want to share their taxi?

McAdam shook his head, eyes closed tight.

'I've got a spare room at the hotel for you, if you need it.'

McAdam shook his head. The next thing he knew the Chinese purser was shaking him, telling him the ship was about to sail back to Hong Kong. McAdam kept his eyes closed and said:

'How much for this cabin back to Hong Kong?'

'Forty dollars extra,' the purser said.

He burrowed his hand into his pocket without opening his eyes and pulled out a note and held it out.

He didn't want to see any bullfights, all he wanted to do was sleep. Most of all he didn't want to take Champion's hotel room and share their week-end.

PART V

It was the 10th of June, the official birthday of Queen Elizabeth the Second.

The room in San Francisco's China-town had a door at each point of the compass, representing the gates of the City of Willows, where the virtuous monks of the Shao Lin monastery founded the Triad Society hundreds of years ago to rid China of the foreign Manchu emperors and restore the Ming to the Dragon Throne. The room was hung about with the flags of heroes, and there was the altar with a large red wooden tub filled with rice to represent the countless thousands of Triad Society members. Next to the tub were the Red Club, symbolizing punishment, and the Sword of Loyalty and Righteousness. On the left sat the 489, the Master of the Society, and on the right sat the 438, the Incense Master. The other officials sat facing each other. The most powerful of these was the 426, the Red Rod, for he was the executioner.

At the eastern door stood two guards, armed with big swords. The group of recruits, who were called New Horses, came and gave the Triad handclasp, and the Guard intoned:

'Why do you come here?'

The New Horses replied: 'We come to enlist and obtain rations.'

The Guard said: 'The red rice of our army contains

sand and stones. Can you eat stones?'

The New Horses replied: 'We can eat stones.'

Then the New Horses were allowed to pass the Mountain of Knives, crawling beneath the crossed swords of the guards, and the Incense Master lit five joss-sticks and cried:

'Tonight we pledge brotherhood in the Red Flower Pavilion. The brethren of Hung will live for myriads of years.'

Three paper figures, bearing the names of traitors who had betrayed the society, were placed in a kneeling position, and the official known as the Vanguard smote off their heads. Then he intoned:

'I bring you numberless fresh soldiers, iron-hearted and valiant, who wish to be admitted to the Heaven and Earth Society.'

The New Horses approached the altar, passing under three arches, each arch guarded by high officials, and bearing a banner proclaiming the principles of the Society. They knelt before the altar, each holding lighted joss-sticks. Then the Red Rod tapped the back of each with his sword and cried:

'Which is harder, the sword or your neck?'

And the New Horses replied: 'My neck.'

Then the Red Rod official read the thirty-six oaths. And the New Horses repeated them, and after each they struck the floor with the joss-sticks, for thus would their lives be snuffed out if they broke the oath.

Then the Incense Master set fire to a piece of yellow paper, for this was the supernatural pall that appeared to protect the founding monks of Shao Lin when the Manchus put their monastery to the torch. The New Horses passed through a fire of joss paper, for this was the Fiery Pit the five monks passed through to escape the Manchus. Next they stepped on to three round marks on the floor, one by one, for these were the stepping stones that appeared in the river to save the monks when the Manchus destroyed the two-planked bridge. Then the Fruit Seller gave to each New Horse a red date, for he had fed the fleeing monks, and the Water Seller handed each a cup, for he had quenched their thirsts.

The Vanguard intoned:

'Loyally and faithfully we perpetuate the Hung family. The wicked and the treacherous will be broken into pieces in the same manner as this lotus flower.' He smashed a lotus bowl with his sword. He picked up a live cockerel and chopped off its head, and held the flapping body over a bowl containing wine and ashes of the burned yellow paper, and added its blood.

The New Horses knelt before the altar, and held out their left hands, then, one by one, the Vanguard deeply pricked the middle finger of each hand, and intoned:

'Do not reveal our secrets to others. If any secrets are disclosed, blood will be shed from the five holes of the body.'

The blood was added to the bowl. And each New Horse drank.

Now they were members of the Triad Society, sworn to a blood brotherhood from which only death could release them.

That ceremony held in San Francisco was the same as that held by the Hong Kong and London lodges of the 14K Triad Society, the same that had been held for hundreds of years, though somewhat shortened in accordance with the realities of the jet age. After all, the Manchu emperors had long since been overthrown, and the Triads no longer robbed the rich to pay the poor, so close attention to ritualistic detail was no longer so important: Now the Triads robbed everybody and paid themselves.

And another rule was no longer strictly enforced:

that which required recruits to undergo three years' faithful service before becoming eligible for promotion. Nowadays a man of wealth could buy high rank within the Triad Society immediately.

Choi Ho-man had become the 489, the Master, within two years of his initiation. Choi Ho-man was accustomed to buying what he wanted, but it was not his wealth alone that got him the rank of 489, it was sheer ability. He was a natural manipulator of people, and he had a genius for delegation of responsibility. He delegated so well that he did not even appear at the meetings of the officers of the Society. Most ordinary members had never even seen him. But he knew everything that was going on, both in the Hong Kong lodges and overseas, and his orders went out very effectively.

Choi Ho-man had joined the 14K Triad Society in order to acquire his own private army, world wide, with iron discipline and sworn by blood and fear to total secrecy and service. It gave him greater power than all the police forces of the world combined.

At the time that the Triad initiation ceremony was being performed in San Francisco, Choi Ho-man was in a limousine, entering the guarded gates of Buckingham Palace, in London.

Twenty minutes later he was in a large, gilded hall, at the end of which, on a dais, stood the throne of England. Seated on the throne, crowned and in ermine, was Her Majesty the Queen, Elizabeth the Second.

Choi Ho-man was kneeling before the throne, and Her Majesty rose and in her hand she held a sword. She raised the sword, and then ceremoniously tapped Choi Ho-man once on each shoulder. He almost expected her to say, 'Which is harder, the sword or your neck?' But Her Majesty said:

126

'I dub thee Sir Herman . . .'
Then she lowered the sword and said graciously:
'Arise, Sir Herman . . .'

FIFTEEN

It was like trying to eat soup with chopsticks.

She had vast sheaves of notes and transcriptions of tape recordings, she had facts running out of her ears, she probably knew more about Sir Herman Choi than anybody else alive, but she could not find a real chink in his Chinese armour. Plenty of scratches, even dents, which she could blow up into an embarrassing story about the bastard, but it would not topple him. Kid's stuff compared to the truth that somewhere in that pile of facts was a 489 official of the 14K Triad Society and one of the world's biggest dealers in narcotics.

What she needed was a Deep Throat, somebody close to the throne who would meet her at dead of night and give her inside information. Bernie Champion had been a mine of information generally, but on the subject of Choi he could only give her theory. McAdam the same. Harry Howard was the closest she'd got, and he had given her much useful information about the young Choi Ho-man, but when it came to Triads he could give her nothing solid.

The American Mess was empty but for her. The big dining-room table was covered in her notes and tapes. Now she paced the living room, holding her tape recorder in one hand and notes in the other. She had been dictating for over an hour.

'By the following year,' she said, 'the political crisis in China was over, Hong Kong booming again. With the help of the bank manager and an impressive donation, Choi Ho-man was appointed to the board of the

Society for the Blind and Physically Handicapped, and won respectability. Choi had been keen to join this charity because on the board sat several tai-pans and Legislative Councillors. These people would be useful in expanding his business interests, and he would also get inside information about the stock market. And, hopefully, they would yield a lot of information about new government fiscal policies, sales of Crown lands, introductions to many senior civil servants and to the corridors of power generally.

'Both hopes turned out to be correct, according to Harry. Through his fellow board members and a lot of intensive entertaining, Choi Ho-man doubled his personal fortune on the stock market with inside information. Friends of friends on the Trade Development Council could be persuaded, for a share of the business, to direct business to his import-export, shipping and insurance enterprises. Within a year Choi Ho-man was able to make several more impressive donations to charities and was awarded the OBE. He had let it be known amongst his Legislative Council friends that future donations would not be forthcoming unless thus acknowledged. And with his OBE he was offered a seat on the board of a local Chinese bank.

'There is enormous face in being a banker. Furthermore, as a director, he could surely arrange low-interest loans to his other companies – strictly illegal but, like so many other things in Hong Kong, done all the time. In his enthusiasm to accept, Choi did not consider this very point enough. At his first meeting of the Board he learned that the bank was in deep financial trouble – one of the directors was bankrupt, and the Official Receiver, suspecting illegal loans, had called in the Banking Commissioner, whose auditors had discovered that almost all the other directors were up to the same thing. Indeed herein lay the bank's special interest in having Choi Ho-man on its board: his OBE and his valuable contacts. He was outraged at these illegalities his co-directors had been perpetrating. He had been taken for a sucker for the first time in his life. But he recovered his disappointment by delivering a homily and agreeing to use his influence on two conditions: one, the chairmanship of the Board, and, two, all the bank's import-export, shipping and insurance business be channelled through his companies.

'Thereafter Mr Choi approached the leading partner of the firm of auditors who had discovered the irregularities. This firm was international, headquarters in London, with an impeccable reputation. However, good old Mr Choi was able to point a few things out to them. Firstly, they were auditors of the Society for the Blind and Physically Handicapped, and also of a number of banks, several of whom would be keen to take over this bank, if it were left with its honour intact; and secondly, that he, Choi Ho-man, his export business, his insurance company, his shipping company, the Lucky Man Development Company, the bank and all the business of his co-directors would consider changing to this English firm of accountants. The leading partners were impressed by these arguments. They consulted urgently with their London headquarters who, whilst maintaining their impeccable standards, reluctantly agreed to cover up the irregularities.'

Jesus Christ. What did this guy want to deal in narcotics for? Why did he want the might of the Triads behind him too? Why did he want to turn his multimillions into multi-billions with narcotics? The question had to answer itself: the man could not resist money. For more and more money he did not care whom he degraded, wrecked, impoverished, killed.

She took up the microphone again. 'Choi Ho-man's donations to charities got more spectacular. His selfless devotion to various youth organizations, trying to give the young in this pressure-cooker society an alternative to the Triad gangs, became renowned. In the normal course of events, a seat on the Legislative Council and later a knighthood were in the bag for our Mr Choi. And, make no mistake about it, he let it be known that his donations to charity would cease unless those two things came to pass, in that order.

'And sure enough, last week, Mister Choi Ho-man became Sir Herman Choi. At the tender age of forty-six.'

She threw down her microphone, stumped through to the bathroom and slammed on the cold tap. Today was water day in this neck of the woods.

She stepped into the cold bath, flinched despite her sweat, then lay down gingerly. Then she felt better, the cool water awash over her breasts. She picked up the microphone.

'But meanwhile, what about the Lucky Man Development Company?

'As a banker, Herman Choi was in a very strong position to raise capital. Hong Kong continued to boom, even during the recession years following the Oil Crisis. His Lucky Man Development Company quietly continued to buy choice undeveloped properties and slum tenements which, through their contacts in the Building office, they could have condemned as unsafe any time they chose. *Now* was the time to start developing.

'But not with his own money: with the public's. Lucky Man is to go on the stock exchange, with Sir

Herman Choi retaining fifty-one per cent. They are five-dollar shares being offered at ten dollars, and even at that price, Harry says, they are winners. They will open at fourteen or fifteen dollars. As soon as the slum tenements are demolished the shares will rise to twenty . . .'

The bathroom window was open. From where she lay she could see the steep jungled mountainside behind McAdam's apartment. Five hundred yards up she could see bulldozers gouging a huge terrace out of the mountain for a massive new apartment block.

She had always thought female pride was a load of old bananas. It had seemed perfectly in order for her to drive out to McAdam's boat-yard one fine day and say:

'Okay, Hogan, if the mountain won't come to Mohammed, Mohammed's quite prepared to go to the mountain. When am I going to cook you that dinner I owe you? A good American girl likes to repay her debts.'

But, all the same, she had had to rehearse it.

She opened the apartment door with one of the bunch of keys he had given her, and put down a large bag of groceries. Then she walked through the apartment, opening the windows. It was clean; his amah had obviously been every day, but the place had an air of neglect about it.

She paused in his bedroom. She had an urge to go through his wardrobe. For a moment she resisted the urge, then she thought, What the hell. Did he *have* any good gear? If she knew what the guy looked like naked, and had every intention of getting him likewise again tonight, she was surely at liberty to know what his clothes were like. She opened the big doors of his wardrobe.

As she had expected. Exactly two suits. A dark, conservative pin-stripe, well worn. And the other one was a black dinner jacket. She bet he hadn't worn that for a decade or two. And two police uniforms hanging there, one winter, one summer. Those truly went back almost a decade. The crowns of a senior superintendent on the shoulder tabs. There were his cap, gloves and swagger stick on a shelf. On the floor a briefcase, a jumble of shoes, his sword leaning in the corner. Jammed behind the sword were a number of scrolls. She pulled them out and unrolled one of them.

It was a university degree certificate. A Master of Arts, Political Philosophy, from Oxford University, England. She unrolled the next one. It had a big tea-cup stain on it. She read it. It was a citation awarding Assistant Inspector Jacob Hogan McAdam Her Majesty's Police Medal for Gallantry. Through the parchment, on the back of it, she could see a drawing. She turned the citation over. It was a child's crayon drawing of a princess with a big spiky crown on her head.

She smiled. She rolled up the scrolls and put them back. Olga had told her about the wife and child. She was about to close the wardrobe doors and go to the kitchen to start work. Then she saw something sticking out from under the police officer's hat.

She knew what it was before she lifted the cap. She stared at it. It was a pistol.

She did not pick it up. The first thing that went through her head was: Surely a thing like this should be locked away? Then the obvious answer: If you need a thing like that, you want it close to hand. Not locked away.

It was not a standard police revolver, such as she had seen Bernard Champion and constables wear. It had a silencer. This was no relic of McAdam's days in the police. It was the kind to carry in your shoulder holster, under a jacket. She had seen them before.

She could not resist it now. She knew she was prying, but she did not care. She had to know what was up there. She climbed the black iron spiral staircase up to the second floor and tried the door. It was locked. She searched through the small bunch of keys, selected the most likely-looking. It turned. She swung open the door.

It was an extraordinary sight, particularly because she knew what the apartment below it looked like. All the walls except those of one bathroom and two wardrobes had been removed, and the whole thing converted into one huge many-cornered room, with windows on all sides, flooding it with natural daylight. All the kitchen had been ripped out except the sinks, and shelves had been built all round them, holding masses of tins of paint. But the original bathtub, lavatory and bidet of the original master bedroom were still there, almost in the middle of the big studio, and over these he had built a wooden workbench: the washbasin and bidet were obviously used for cleaning painting equipment. Here and there still stood the whitewashed structural pillars supporting the apartments above, and fixed on them were batteries of adjustable spotlights. Hanging on every wall and stacked at floor level were scores of big canvases on frames. But they were all facing the walls.

She stared. It was like entering a ghost house. There was dust, no footprints. A rocking chair. The windows all closed. Everything so still. It smelled of old paint and canvas. Complete silence. Just the sound of her breathing.

She walked slowly around the silent room, looking at the faceless canvases, the equipment. It had an air of waiting. She approached the painting hanging on the wall nearest the front door. The first painting one would see as one walked in, if this were a gallery. For a moment she hesitated. Then she turned the painting round.

It was the Chinese girl. The same girl as in the big portrait downstairs. The girl called Ying. And she was beautiful.

She stared at it. Ying . . . She had a fine, handsome, squarish face. And big almond eyes, and thick eyelashes, and her pupils were large and black. And straight, jet-black hair. That was one of the differences from the portrait downstairs. The Ying downstairs had longer, softer hair, and she was smiling gently: this Ying was younger, and her hair was in two short tufty plaits that stuck out a little: her face was sterner, and the look in her eyes was almost haughty. She had a blue denim shirt on and she looked hot, as if she were walking in the mountains. Adding to this impression was the background. It was a valley, below, mauve in misty heat under a mercilessly blue sky.

She turned the next painting round.

It was Ying again. This time her eyes were bright with anger. It was a remarkable painting of a beautiful, indignant young woman. You felt the girl had just been pointing, accusing. There was a story behind that accusation, she could feel it: it was an important moment in time, and he had enshrined it here. And she wanted to know what it was.

She moved slowly to the next painting and turned it.

She knew it would be her. But she was unprepared for the difference. She wore big cat's-eye spectacles that had once been stylish, and her big eyes were fixed in concentration. And, poised in front of her, almost reaching out of the canvas, was an artist's paintbrush. And held up in her other hand, as if she had just taken it from her mouth, was a cigarette.

She stared at the beautiful, intense Chinese girl. In those concentrating eyes was a bright, almost serene, confidence; so different from the accusing Ying. Vanessa felt a twinge of unease.

God, the guy's good!

She went abruptly to the next painting. She almost did not want to turn it around.

Again she was surprised. And her journalist's mind said *Aha!* For here was the first bit of evidence. The girl *was* a Communist.

But oh, what a glorious one. In the background was a poster Vanessa had seen often around these parts, a marching column of joyous, robust Chinese peasants carrying big sheaves of wheat into a Red Star sunrise over China: and in front of it stood Ying, her square face resolute and her big eyes glinting; her mouth was open, and you knew it was in song. You knew she was leading others in the singing, and you knew it was the Chinese National Anthem, The East is Red.

She felt she did not want to look at any more paintings. But she could not stop now. She turned the next painting.

And oh, yes. A Ying so beautiful she almost did not like standing beside her. She was naked, though only her head and breasts were painted, and in her big eyes was the complete happiness of a woman in love, who had just made love, and her hair was longer and tousled, and she looked breathless and maybe she was even sweating.

Vanessa breathed tensely deep. She began to go through the rest more quickly. Ying on a rooftop garden, watering flowers with a big red watering can. Ying poised in the middle of a graceful Tai Chi Chuan exercise. Ying swimming in the sea, her hair plastered

136

wet to her laughing head, her big eyes sparkling. Ying underwater, diving like a seal, her black hair streaming behind her. Ying in glorious silhouette walking into the sunset with a dog at her side; Ying lying in a bathtub, reading a book. Ying . . . Ying . . . Ying . . . She had to find the end of the story. She was nearing the end of the hanging pictures now. Then she turned over the second last one, and stared.

Ying's face was gaunt, pale, her big brown eyes staring, exhausted, her full lips bloodless. And in those exhausted, staring eyes for the first time was irresolution. And grief. And yearning. And exhausted confusion. She wanted to say: 'Tell me – tell me what happened.' She could feel the grief in those eyes go straight to her heart.

She turned away from it. But she had to know now. She turned over the next picture and caught her breath.

Ying's eyes were full of tears, and through the tears shone a cringe of fear. Her head was partly averted as if she were expecting a blow: and splatting from her nose and over her open mouth was rich red blood. And on top of her head was a dunce's cap.

She stared, sickened. She could feel the fear of the next shocking blow.

A dunce's cap? Somehow that dunce's cap was more shocking and pathetic than the blood, than the cringe of her eyes.

And the painting was unfinished. As if he could suddenly bear to paint no more, had suddenly thrown down his brushes. And wept.

She locked the studio door behind her.

She walked slowly down the black spiral staircase. Her footsteps sounded loud in the empty apartment. She walked slowly to the kitchen, and began to unpack

137

the big grocery bag. Through the open kitchen window she could hear the distant roar of the bulldozer working at the site four hundred yards up the mountain.

SIXTEEN

Everything was prepared, the roast ready to go into the oven, the vegetables ready for boiling. All she had to do was go back to the American Mess and shower and change, come back and switch the oven on. As she rinsed her hands at the sink, she noticed the huge construction site up the mountain above her again. For the first time she looked at it. She could read the big signboard: *Lucky Man Development Company Limited.* So *this* was one of Choi Ho-man's projects.

She stared at it, her hands poised at the tap. And a very lucrative project it would be. That was a very big bite those bulldozers had taken out of the mountain; it was going to be one hell of a big apartment block in a desirable middle-class area, where rents were very high. Most apartment blocks in Midlevels were tall and slim, because land here was so expensive and hard to get; whereas this building was going to be tall and broad: a lot of apartments. Lucky Man was very lucky indeed: all the suitable land in Midlevels had been snapped up long ago and what was left was so steep it was unsafe for construction. That building up there was going to be worth a fortune.

She looked at the building site a moment longer, then looked at her watch. She had enough time.

She walked up the long, winding road. She had not realized how steep it was. So steep that the road had been cut in two big hairpin loops. Between McAdam's apartment block and the Lucky Man site there were only two private houses, cut into the mountainside; the rest was steep virgin jungle. She walked up the hairpin bends, sweating, and at last she came to cars parked along the road opposite the site.

She stood, panting. A high wooden hoarding had been built around the site. She wondered why. She walked up to it and peered through one of the joins in the planking. There were workmen everywhere. Concrete-mixers were roaring. One pile-driver was working already. The huge steel piston was hauled up mechanically to the top of the tall guillotine with a scream of steam, then it came crashing down on top of the big steel foundation pile, smashing it into the earth, like a huge hammer driving a huge nail, again and again.

She peered through other cracks. She was astonished at the size of the bulldozed area. It was about a hundred yards long, and at least forty yards deep into the mountain. She looked at the mountain – the slope was forty-five degrees here at least, maybe fifty. The back end of the wedge towered high, a huge cliff of earth. Dozens of workmen were busy plastering the cliff-face with cement, and building a retaining wall against it. That cliff was about one hundred feet high. And almost vertical. She could feel its menacing presence. She looked at the retaining wall of concrete bricks being built against it, and thought, Thank God they're doing that smartly.

Maybe it was the physical presence of that cliff, and the enormity of the wedge that had been cut out of the mountain; maybe it was the nerve-shattering scream and crash of the pile-driver making the earth shake, but she wanted to get away from this place. All the same she made herself look about her, trying to take in everything.

She turned around from the hoarding and looked at the view the apartments would have. Directly below, way down there, was Dragon Court, where McAdam lived, tall and slim. It was a magnificent view. And nothing would ever be built in front of it because of the two private houses below the road, and the steepness. This was probably the best site in the whole of Midlevels for an apartment block.

She walked along the edge of the construction site. Then she saw four Chinese men in suits emerge through a door in the hoarding, carrying briefcases, and she felt her pulse trip. One of the men was the dapper Sir Herman Choi.

She had seen him several times before in public, and she had seen many photographs of him. And every time it was hard to believe. Shortish, tubby but dapper, a pleasant face, a ready smile, twinkling eyes, a complete gentleman and a perfect Oxford accent. It was so hard to believe that once he had been a flunkey in a small shirt factory. It was just as hard to believe he was a dealer in living death.

She watched him go. He was followed by his two male secretaries. The same two had always been with him, every time she had seen him. Chunky, heavy-faced, in impeccable suits, hair smoothly combed. These were his heavies, his bodyguards. She watched them go, down into the road, towards the big Silver Cloud Rolls-Royce. She had an urge to run after them and get him to talk, try to squeeze something, anything out of him. But no. She would have her interview with Herman Choi one day. And she would be completely prepared. She watched him drive off.

She turned and looked at the advertising board. It had an artist's impression of the huge apartment block to be built, and the legend read:

140

For sale: Twelve floors of luxury bachelor, two-bedroom, and three-bedroom apartments. Children's playground and ample basement parking. Magnificent views.

She wondered why the bastards were going to sell them, instead of renting them. She looked at the views again.

Yes, they'd sell for a lot of money. And, yes, there was good *fung shui*, as far as she could tell. She had read a bit about the Chinese belief in the necessity of living in harmony with the elements. *Fung shui*, literally wind and water; according to the Chinese your house or office or grave had to be in harmony with nature, facing the right things, and if it did not it had bad *fung shui*, bad luck, and you should certainly engage a geomancer to tell you how to re-position your furniture and doors and windows and tombstone to mitigate the bad *fung shui*. One of the most important elements was water, and the other was dragons. Dragons slumbered in the bodies of mountains and they are benevolent unless rudely disturbed, in which case they're a veritable bull in a China shop. And from here she could see at least two dragon mountains, one on Lantay Island and one on Lama Island, with the magnificent tranquil sea between them. She guessed it was excellent *fung shui*, and the Chinese would pay enormous prices for these apartments. About the only thing that could spoil it was if a dragon had been slumbering right here where they had gouged out the mountain, and the bulldozer had rudely disturbed him. She turned back to the hoarding and peered through a crack at the cliff face: and then she stared, surprised.

The earth of that cliff-face was *reddish*! That was *bad*, man! Not only had this piece of mountain been the abode of a dragon, but the bulldozers had actually

141

wounded him! By the laws of *fung shui* that red colour of the earth was the dragon's blood! Oh brother, was this dragon going to be mad at Sir Herman Choi! The last time this happened, the Government had been cutting a road and the redness of the earth proved they had cut smack through some poor dragon's spine – and the dragon had kicked up a terrible plague of malaria in his outrage and half a British regiment had died and the Chinese population had made the Government put up a shrine to propitiate the dragon – Champion had shown it to her. And a Portuguese Governor of Macao had had his head chopped off by the outraged Chinese for doing the same thing!

Wouldn't that be fantastic? If a horde of outraged Chinese came and chopped Sir Herman's head off? She smiled bitterly. It was too much to hope, of course. But maybe she could make some capital out of it.

At first they felt strangely formal with each other, even nervous.

He had showered at the boat-yard, but tonight was his water-night and so when he got home he had showered and shaved again. He had even put on a tie. Maybe, he thought, it was the change in the apartment which made him nervous: it looked almost lived in. She had put flowers in the lounge and dining-room, and there were red mats, napkins, and candles on the table. And coming from the kitchen was the home-smell of cooking.

She had had her hair done and it shone soft and golden. She was wearing a full-length soft muslin skirt, flowing and gathered at her waist, and a white long-sleeved blouse of the same material, off her shoulders. He could glimpse the dark circles of her nipples through the fabric. She was beautifully, casually groomed, and

he knew she had taken a great deal of trouble over
herself. And he could tell she was nervous, too, through
her flippancy.

Now the candles were half-burned, they were drinking their second bottle of champagne, and they were
more relaxed: in the lounge his portable radio was
softly playing, and down there were the lights of the
magnificent harbour.

They did not talk about her work; she did not want
to question him about Hong Kong. The only questions
she wanted to ask were about himself, about that huge,
strange studio up there: she wanted to say 'Do you still
love her, Hogan? – tell me!' But she did not. They
talked about a lot of other things and they began to
laugh more. He did not want to talk about money, but
once he found himself thinking how good his apartment
was when it was lived in like this. He sighed and said:

'I really don't want to sell this apartment.'

'Do you really have to?'

'Not really. But it's academic anyway, because nobody wants to buy a monstrosity like this.'

She said: 'I think it's a lovely apartment.'

'It is tonight. Because you make it lovely.'

And the soft music playing; and the delicious knowledge of what they were going to do. He wanted to do it
so much that he was worried he would not be able to.
But first he wanted to dance with her: to turn slowly
with her in his arms, with the harbour lights down
below, not a soul to see them, to feel her golden skin
and the soft touch of her hair and her eyelashes, and
the brush of her lips and the sweet warmth of her
breath.

And later they did dance in the living room, by
candlelight, close together, and he could feel her soft,
strong body all the way down his, warm and tangible,

her belly against him, her thighs softly moving, her breasts against his chest, the beautiful feel of her body through the thin muslin, and the soft woman smell of her.

And they kissed, long soft kisses, and their hands slid, feeling each other, then he gently pulled her blouse down over her breasts; and she unbuttoned his shirt so they were against his chest, and they kissed more, and then he slowly peeled the blouse off over her head. The candlelight flickered on her, and his hand went to the back of her skirt, and he unclipped it. It fell in a flimsy heap to the floor, and there she stood in only her high heels, the candlelight flickering on her long legs; and she felt his hands tremble as he touched her.

Then he knelt slowly down in front of her and put his hands on her hips and kissed her flat belly, and then her thighs, and she felt his breath, then she put her hands down on his head and pulled his face gently against her. He kissed her soft intimate hair, and he felt the bliss well up inside him and buried his tongue into her warm softness. And she tilted back her head and held him tight against her and parted her long golden legs for him.

PART VI

Chiang Mei-ling lived with her parents in a Low-Cost Housing Estate and she worked on the beauty counter of a large department store. She was eighteen years old, and she was beautiful, and she was a virgin. She had a steady boyfriend, Mr Ignatius Ng, who was a clerk in a bank, and one day they were going to marry, when they had saved enough. Mei-ling had to stay a virgin until her bridal night, the day after which Mr Ng had to produce to his assembled family a bloodstained silk handkerchief to prove her virginity, whereafter she would have to kneel before her mother-in-law and serve her tea as a sign that she would always be a dutiful daughter. If she was not a virgin Mr Ng would furiously reject her and her own father would throw her out of his house and her whole family would shun her for ever.

That evening Chiang Mei-ling set off walking home through Mongkok to the bus terminus. Every evening she followed the same route. A lot of vice goes on in Mongkok, but Mei-ling felt safe; she knew many of the people by sight. She did not feel alarmed when a strange young man suddenly stepped out of an alley in front of her and offered to sell her a wristwatch. The next instant a hand pulled her into the alley and another slammed over her mouth. Mei-ling screamed into the hand and lashed out, but four men manhandled her down the dark alley and into a doorway.

Mei-ling was dragged, struggling, up two flights of stairs, then they pushed her into a dingy apartment. They threw her down on the bed and tied her struggling wrists together and rammed a gag in her mouth. She lay there heaving, wild-eyed, bound and gagged, her heart pounding with terror. The four men stood round her, grinning at her lecherously. The leader said:

'We are the 14K. You can choose which one of us is going to fuck you and he will be your protector afterwards. If you do not choose, we will all fuck you. Who do you choose?'

Mei-ling screamed and thrashed on the bed and beat her legs, and her screams were strangled in the gag. The five young men of the 14K Triad Society stood round and grinned and they knew they had made a good selection: once she was ruined she would not run away.

Mei-ling lay there rigid, sobbing into her gag, eyes screwed up; the young man wrenched her dress up over her stomach, and hooked his fingers under her panties and jerked them down. With a practised flash he pulled out his flick-knife; then he lowered it, and touched her breast with it. Then he swept it on high with a shout, and then he plunged it into the mattress between her legs.

He slashed the panties off her thighs. He grabbed her skirt and slashed it off in one wrench, then he slashed her blouse off her. And then he began to tear off his own clothes, shouting:

'So now we will all stab you!'

And he leaped between her writhing thighs and ground his penis into her and thrust with all his might into her body.

In all Chiang Mei-ling was raped nine times that night. Afterwards they made her wash the blood and semen off her thighs and private parts, while they all

146

watched. For three days they kept her in the room. Mei-ling did not resist them any more, she just lay down numbly on the bed when ordered and opened her legs. They brought her food, and they brought her clothes.

On the third day the 14K Triad member responsible for the protection of the Yellow Lotus Apartment House arrived to take her away. He was jolly, and he fussed over her, and she was so grateful she wept on his shoulder. They took her down into the street to a taxi. They guarded her carefully, but they knew she would not run away. She would never run home, for the unspeakable shame that had befallen her.

SEVENTEEN

Jake McAdam was forced to review the hard facts and make a decision. First he telephoned Harry Howard. Then he telephoned Superintendent Bernard Champion to borrow two hundred thousand American dollars.

It was a short meeting. They arranged to rendezvous in a girlie-bar in Kowloon. McAdam wanted a quieter place for such solemn business, but Champion insisted on the bar. But it was early, the girls were not yet noisy and the jukebox was still playing fairly quietly. Bernard Champion pulled out his cheque book as soon as he walked in, without talking any more about it, did a hurried calculation on the back converting American to Hong Kong dollars, and wrote out the cheque.

'Many thanks, Champ,' McAdam said sincerely.

Champion said gruffly: 'That's what friends are for.'

'What about a receipt?'

'You'll give it back to me. It won't be for long anyway. You can't lose on those shares.'

'Listen,' McAdam said, 'I'm not that far away from the bankruptcy court. You better have something to show.'

'You won't be bankrupt now. Fifty per cent profit, standing on your head. But if you want, I'll tell my solicitor to post you something. Just sign it and bang it back to him.'

'Okay.'

McAdam looked at him. He knew why Champion

was being so abrupt. Champion gulped his beer like a man who didn't know what to say and who wanted to get this over with. McAdam made himself say it.

'Champ? I'm sorry. About you and Vanessa.'

Champion shot him an embarrassed look then he looked away. 'It's not your doing.' He added gruffly: 'It's got nothing to do with the loan, a promise is a promise and I give it gladly. I knew it wouldn't work. She's too . . . good for me. I'm just a fool.'

'Champ? She's going soon, anyway.'

'Right.'

Champion glared at the bar, then took a swallow of his beer. Then he took a sharp breath.

'Are you in love with her?'

McAdam was taken aback. Then he shook his head.

'Champ, that question doesn't arise. She's going in a month anyway.'

'Well, it should arise.' He shot McAdam a hard look to cover his feeling. 'You've got to forget the past. Because Vanessa's not forgettable.'

Then he banged his glass down. 'All right. I've got to go now.' And he turned and walked hurriedly out of the bar.

They had a lovely time, that long hot month of July.

Sometimes he planned ahead and telephoned her or sent her a telegram from Tai-po village to make a date to take her out to dinner, and sometimes she rented a car and drove out to the boat-yard uninvited when she had finished her work or when she had easy dictating or transcriptions to do. She bought a big orange beach umbrella and a folding table ('You can have them when I go, Hogan'), and she set them up on the sand near the water. Sometimes she sunbathed while she worked, lying on the floating jetty. Every time they met they spent the night together, either at the boat-yard or at McAdam's apartment. But they did not get much sleep.

'Who the hell would want to sleep when they've got a stud like you in bed, Hogan?'

'Maybe you're an insomniac sex maniac.'

'Or maybe you just turn me on. You light me up like a pinball machine.'

'It takes two to work up a storm, Storm.'

'Why don't you ever ask me what I do on my free nights?'

'Because I want your orange beach umbrella when you go.'

She smiled. She stroked his eyebrows with her fingertip. 'Oh, Hogan.'

'What *do* you do on your free nights?'

'I don't have any free nights. When I do I come to you.'

'Ah, I get it. Silly me.'

She smiled. 'Hogan? I'm not screwing anybody else.'

He kissed her nose.

She said quietly: 'I don't want to.' Then more brightly: 'Funny, that. I better write to Xaviera Hollander about it.'

'And what'll she reply?'

' "Dear Miz Storm Williams, Evidently you're not a sex maniac after all. Pity. Watch it – you may be falling in love. Remember he really only wants your orange beach umbrella." '

Two week-ends they went hiking up in the mountains of the New Territories. She had hiked a lot of them by herself already, to get the feel of the place, to get to know this other side of Hong Kong. This was, as he had told her on their first lunch date, the old China of

150

before the battles long ago; these people had come from the age of feudal warlords to the age of the transistor radio without a revolution. After a hard week's labour building the boat-yard, McAdam did not want to go hiking; he wanted to spend the week-end in bed, with her, and those mountains held memories he did not want to evoke, but he did it to please her.

It was fiercely, humid hot, the sky blindingly blue: there was no rain in it for Hong Kong. He was surprised how strong she was. He considered she drank and smoked too much ('Jesus – the pot calling the kettle black, McAdam!') but she had no difficulty with those mountains and that heat. He looked at the glisten of sweat on her, on her flushed face, cheeks glowing through her suntan, tendrils of hair sticking to her forehead and neck; and he looked at her legs in those shortest of shorts and her sandshoes, and he loved that smell of woman on her too, and he wanted to tear off her sweaty clothes and fuck her on the hard mountain-side under the searing China sun. He leant towards her and kissed the sweet damp warmth of her neck and felt her heavy sweating breasts through her hot damp blouse and tasted the sweat on her wide soft mouth, and then did just that, high up in the mountains, naked and open under the wide blue sky.

They walked down through the jungled valleys, and through the terraced paddy fields with the water-buffaloes and the Hakka women smoking their pipes, and through the little duck farms and fish farms and cherry orchards. And hamlets where they hardly ever see a white man, or strangers of any sort. The farm-houses and hamlets had slate roofs with curly ends, and gods painted on the doorways to frighten off evil spirits. The alleys were narrow and cobbled, full of ducks and dogs and chickens and naked children, and old

151

temples with joss-sticks burning. The people were very shy, and stared at the foreign devils, but they were friendly. In the hamlets there was usually a place to eat, good Chinese food, sitting on small wooden stools, and there was usually cold beer and some kind of wine from China, which tasted like People's Republican Face Cream dissolved in vodka and had the kick of a People's steelworks.

And in the mountains and valleys there were streams, tumbling over grey rocks, and there were pools and soft grassy banks and shade. They slung down their knapsacks and tore off their dank sweaty clothes and jumped into the cool of the pools, the bliss of the cold water swirling over their hot bodies. He lay on his side on the soft bank, head propped on his elbow, smoking a cigarette, looking at her, and she smiled at him.

'What?' she said.

'Nothing. I'm going to miss you, that's all.'

She stopped combing her hair and smiled gently.

'I'm going to miss you too, Hogan. Miss you like hell. Don't let's even think about it.'

When they were lying side by side under the stars, the camp fire flickering, in the hour after love, she said:

'Why don't you build your crazy concrete boats in New York, Hogan?'

'Maybe I will one day.' He added: 'I'll just rent that bit of beach next to the World Trade Centre. Good spot.'

She sighed. 'Oh Hogan, Hogan, beautiful Hogan . . . I'm a New Yorker. Through and through. The big bright apple and all that jazz. And you build concrete junks on the China coast. To stop the natives chopping down trees.' She turned her head and looked at him. 'This isn't a very realistic discussion, is it?'

'No, it isn't.'

'Let's forget it took place,' she said.

They walked along the coast from Deep Bay in the west almost to Shataukok on Mirs Bay in the east, through the fishing villages with their oyster rafts that once upon a time had saved Wong, and up through the fish farms and duck farms built out into the tidal flats, and then up into the mountains at Lokmachau overlooking China. They walked through the jungle along the stout British diamond-mesh fence, built to keep the China refugees out, and just one hundred yards down there through the fence was Communist China, the paddy fields of the Shamchun River Valley with the peasants working under their big red banners, and the People's Liberation Army guards standing in their concrete pill-boxes. Once upon a time he had been the police inspector in charge of this border, and he told her something about those days, the Year of the Hungry Tiger, the year of the great fear of famine and the people swarming over this river and this fence. She said:

'Why did you quit the police force, Hogan?'

'That's a long story.'

'In a nutshell?'

He shook his head. 'It won't go in a nutshell.'

'Were you in trouble with the Communists?'

He smiled bitterly. 'In a manner of speaking.' Then he shook his head. 'They were also in trouble with me.' He thought a moment. 'I quit for many reasons. And they're all connected. In the big black rat-race of politics, human beings are expendable.'

They sat on the top of the highest part of Robin's Nest and looked down on to China, and far away over there was a town with smoke rising up off the People's factory

153

chimney, and a bus grinding down a dusty road, and the Kowloon–Canton railway stretching across the plain to the faraway, misty mountains, and the vast horizon of China beyond: and the sun was going down over one quarter of mankind, flaming red, and the mountains and the plain turned to mauve. He was staring at it silently and she said quietly:

'She's somewhere over there in that vastness, Hogan.'

He was brought back to reality. He did not say anything.

'Do you still love her?'

'It's a long time ago, now,' he said.

EIGHTEEN

A lot of other things happened those days, those weeks. Every day about one hundred illegal refugees from China got into Hong Kong, by swimming Mirs and Deep Bay, and packed down in the holds of the snake junks of Vacations in Happiness and Tranquillity from Macao. Every day an average of three point two people committed suicide. A total of twenty-nine tons of raw opium from the Golden Triangle was smuggled in by junks, ships and jets by the five Mister Bigs and was converted into three tons of heroin in a total of twelve laboratories, for export to America and Europe. Vanessa Storm Williams tried to get an appointment with Sir Herman Choi and was told that Sir Herman was very busy for the next fortnight. An unknown number of multi-millions was won and lost in a hundred and forty-seven illegal gambling casinos, restaurants, apartments, joints and alleys. Jack-the-Fire rescued a would-be suicide from a rooftop by tying a rope around his own waist and diving at him out of a helicopter. The four stock exchanges in the Colony hit an all-time high and the newspapers again warned of another crash. A Triad battle was fought in Shamshuipo between the 14K and the Wo Hop Wo, with axes, knives and bicycle chains, and six youths were killed. Over two hundred and seventy brothels did a roaring trade as usual. An average of two buyers a day expressed interest in Jake McAdam's apartments, then declared them either far too big or far too expensive to remodel.

The walls of the boat-yard's big shed were almost finished, but McAdam was beginning to run out of materials and he had not yet bought the roofing and windows. The pylon foundations on the Lucky Man apartment block were finished and the walls were growing up at a phenomenal rate with two shifts of builders working twenty-four hours a day. The Lucky Man Development Company published a two-page prospectus in the *South China Morning Post* of its assets and liabilities, giving legal notice that it was to turn itself into a public company, inviting the public to subscribe for shares.

Chiang Mei-ling was persuaded by a kind young man to run away from the Yellow Lotus Apartment House, which was a brothel protected by the 14K Triad Society, to the Oriental International Apartment House, which was a brothel protected by the Wo Hop Wo Triad Society.

In New York City, San Francisco, Los Angeles and Chicago eighteen Mafia hitmen walked into six Chinese restaurants and shot the owners at point-blank range. The next day the Prefect of Paris Police received an anonymous telephone call from a man speaking French with an Indo-Chinese accent, from a public call box, advising him that, contrary to official belief, heroin refineries in Marseilles were still functioning, and providing him with the address of a big one. The Chinese man promptly hung up and disappeared into the crowds of Pigalle, but within an hour the Marseilles police had had a shoot-out in a surburban villa with a number of Sicilians and seized a large quantity of heroin, worth four million dollars on the streets of New York. The next day a Beechcraft aeroplane, loaded with the morphine base of heroin, piloted by two Italians from America, mysteriously burst into flames when it was refuelling at an airstrip near Kuala Lumpur in Malaysia. The day after that the United States Coast Guard received anonymous information as a result of which a Mexican fishing vessel was boarded as it hove to off San Diego and one ton of raw opium was found cemented under the concrete ballast in its bilges.

These were record hauls and they made international headlines; the police were jubilant and claimed that they had broken the spine of the Mafia supply route. It shook the Mafia to their family foundations. Their traditional method of war had backfired on them. And how had the Chinese known? And who had given the orders? It indicated an organizational cohesion beyond their dreams. As a result there was going to be a shortage of heroin on the streets of New York and San Francisco. A gap the Chinese Triads aimed to fill.

That week a fishing trawler set sail from Bangkok in Thailand and in her holds were many bales of black raw opium, bound for the heroin refineries of Hong Kong. It was a massive consignment of twenty tons, which would become two tons of pure heroin, worth many million dollars on the streets of America. Choi Ho-man was going to hit the Mafia's distribution network like a typhoon, and make a killing.

*

That same day the subscription lists for the shares in the Lucky Man Development Company officially opened. The application forms, accompanied by cheques, were received by Sir Herman Choi's bank, and from early morning and right through the day there were queues of people right down the street, waiting to hand in their applications.

Sir Herman Choi threw a charity luncheon at the Hilton Hotel in aid of the Society for the Blind and Physically Handicapped, and Vanessa Storm Williams wangled a press invitation out of one of her friends at the Foreign Correspondents' Club. As she was introduced to Sir Herman she presented him with a gift-wrapped parcel, with her most dazzling smile, and by her pre-arrangement a press photographer's bulb flashed. Inside the gift-wrapping was a birdcage and inside the cage was a carrier-pigeon and a letter which read:

Dear Sir Herman, I have been trying for weeks to arrange an interview with you for my American readers but I can't get past your secretary. Please place a note in the pigeon's ring saying when you will see me, and release it out of the nearest window.

Everybody guffawed, including Sir Herman Choi, and then and there he scribbled a note granting Miss Williams an appointment for the following week, and he released the pigeon out of the Hilton's window, to more roars of applause, and the flash-bulbs went again.

That day a meeting was held in a Chinese restaurant between a heavily-guarded representative of the 14K Triad Society and a heavily-guarded representative of the Wo Hop Wo Triad Society, to discuss the matter of

Chiang Mei-ling. They were not very important members of their respective Triad Societies; all except the two negotiators were only muscle-men, and the business they were discussing, namely one Chinese prostitute who had fled from the protection of one society to that of the other, was of no great economic importance to either, for there were plenty more where she came from. Sir Herman Choi did not even know about the meeting and would not have been much interested in the outcome if he had. But what was important was the principle, and both negotiators had the full authority of their respective Red Rods: it was loss of face to that branch of the 14K who had provided protection to the Yellow Lotus Apartment House that the Wo Hop Wo had stolen Chiang Mei-ling from them, and they were demanding thirty-six thousand dollars in compensation, a sum which would have made the Wo Hop Wo lose face. The representative of the Wo Hop Wo refused to pay and the meeting broke up ominously, and both sides knew that meant war.

And a thousand miles away over the South China Sea, the typhoon called Rose was roaring round and about herself.

PART VII

First there was the vast mass of moist air over the warm Pacific Ocean. Because warm air is lighter it rose and formed an area of low pressure, and because of this more warm moist air moved over the sea to take its place. This air rose also, and thus the winds spiralled inwards and formed a rotating eye. As the warm moist air rose the water vapour condensed and heavy rain fell; and tremendous amounts of latent heat were released into the eye and heated the air, which rose faster and harder, and more warm wind rushed in to take its place. Now the bands of wind were a roaring wall around the eye, black with rain, and the whole mass was five hundred miles wide, moving across the Pacific, feeding off the sea, and the winds were over one hundred knots.

Mervin Katz passed Vanessa a photograph of it.

'The weather satellite sends us three photographs a day – that's the third.'

It was taken from space, and it showed a mass of black cloud, spiralling anti-clockwise, thickly inwards round the eye, like water circling into a drain. The black clouds were streaked with grey; the whole mass was beautiful and violent.

'It looks so magnificently ominous.'

'Ominous,' Katz said, 'and omnivorous. And omnipotent. *And* omnipresent,' he added. 'Any time of the year, the bastards form over the Pacific because it's warm. But *now*, July, August, September, they're the real bad months. And it's my job,' he added, 'to forecast the bastards.'

It seemed like the first time she had smiled in days. He went on with his guided tour:

'Every three hours we prepare weather maps, to determine movement and development. To do this we collect over six thousand weather observations every day from land stations dotted all over South East Asia – radioed to us; and observations from more than seven hundred ships and five hundred balloon-borne instruments in various South East Asian countries.'

She had her tape recorder playing.

'Plus the information we get from the weather satellites which are continuously orbiting the earth, taking photographs and measuring the radiative temperature of the cloudtops. We also get information from the US Navy reconnaissance planes that fly into the typhoons in our general area.' He added: 'That's a terrible job, even worse than mine. You know Kurt Marlowe, the American pilot, don't you? He does that. All the same, there're still huge blank spaces we receive no information on. And often the information is conflicting, particularly from shipping and aircraft. Nonetheless, we're expected to make accurate forecasts. Now I ask you, what kind of job is that for a nice Jewish boy?'

She smiled, but her nerves were tight. 'What's your degree of accuracy?'

'With ordinary weather forecasts, anything could happen. You calculate your accuracy by distance. The winds may change and the weather you forecast happens fifty, a hundred miles away.

'But typhoons march, like Genghis Khan's army.

160

They can stop, curve, loop, swoop. All without warning. Our average error in forecasting twenty-four hours ahead is between ninety and a hundred miles.'

'That doesn't sound too bad.'

He looked at her with disgust.

'It's *good*! Tell your readers it's *good*, for Chrissakes. You're dealing with a vast unpredictable machine of destruction out there! Roaring its way through millions of cubic miles of airspace! Generating enough energy in one day to keep Hong Kong in electricity for one hundred and fifty years if only we could harness it! And the whole terrible ensemble roars along twenty-four hours a day, for weeks and weeks, going anywhere it likes. And *I've* got to forecast where this massive sonofabitch is going to be twenty-four hours from now! And my average error is only ninety-odd miles!'

'It's good.' She smiled.

'It's bad.' He walked across the room. 'Do you realize what those ninety miles mean in a tiny place like Hong Kong? It means the difference between widespread destruction and death and millions of dollars worth of damage, or . . . no damage at all.' He looked at her reproachfully. 'What a responsibility that is! For these sagging, rounded shoulders!'

'But surely you give the appropriate warnings . . .'

'But do you realize the millions of dollars it costs to press the panic button and order the warning signal raised? All ships and cargo lighters must move to typhoon anchorage sand buoys. That means all movement of cargo ceases. Have you any idea what it costs to have a ship standing idle for a day? Let alone the stevedores. And all work must stop on building construction. And all the fishing junks come in and the ships that can't get typhoon anchorage must put out to sea to try to steam away from the danger. And planes are diverted and the tourists are stuck in their hotels. And all factories must shut down, all employees are sent home, and the school kids and Christ knows what else . . . The whole bloody place grinds to a halt.' He placed his hand on his chest. 'And all because Mrs Katz's little boy pressed the panic button.'

She smiled. 'What about radar?'

'Sure. But it can only reach two hundred and forty miles. We can see the typhoon beautifully on radar once it gets within two hundred and forty miles But by *that* time the damn thing's almost on top of us Come, I'll show you the thing.'

He led her out of his office, down the wide old colonial wooden staircase, into the first room.

Telex machines were clattering and radio operators sat with headphones and there were banks of telephones, and all the Chinese operators were intently concentrating. He led her into the next room. The walls were lined with racks and in the middle were big draughtsman's tables. A man with a beard and a pipe was poring over a map, sketching in lines through placid clouds of smoke. Mervin said:

'Preparing the latest map.' The man straightened and smiled at her around his pipe. The map showed the South China Coast, Vietnam, the Philippines, Taiwan. And drawn all over it were sweeping lines with little fletches on them. They all spiralled inwards to a central point.

'That's the eye. The wind bands spiralling in towards it. Building up speed all the way. Until here round the eye, they're a hundred and fifty knots. Roaring concentric walls of wind. Black as pitch. And blasting rain. From inside the eye the whole thing looks like the towering black walls of a vast well.'

She said: 'How far away is she now?'

'Nine hundred miles.' He picked up a smaller map. It showed a heavy dotted line studded at intervals with twirls. Next to each twirl was a date.

'That's her course to date. Look at it . . .' The dotted line veered and looped, swung from north to south and doubled back on itself. 'She's been looping around like that for over a month.'

'Is that unusual?'

'Typhoons can change direction without the slightest warning. But this bitch? I've never seen one do this much. Ever.'

She said: 'Do you think she's going to hit us?'

Mervin Katz breathed out through his hairy nostrils.

'As a meteorologist? Anything can happen. But if you want to know what I feel in my water?'

'Yes?'

He looked at her. 'She's coming,' he said. 'I got the feeling in my water. Suddenly, one day soon, she's going to veer north-west. And then keep coming.'

NINETEEN

McAdam had arranged to take her out to dinner that night, and he had uncharacteristically even reserved a table. But when he got to his apartment after dark to shower and dress he found a meal prepared in the kitchen and a flippant note telling him not to touch the oven, she had gone back to the Mess to perform her ablutions, and not to fetch her; she would get back under her own oomph.

Her bright mood was still to the fore when she came in, looking lovely, but he could see behind it. She kissed him and breezed into the kitchen. He followed her in and poured two beers but she busily examined her pots and the oven. He leant against the sink and said:

'What's wrong, Vanessa?'

'Nothing.' She shot him a smile over her shoulder and went back to work.

'Is anything wrong at work?'

'No.'

He looked at her back. She was so beautiful. All right, he thought. He had lived long enough to know that he would find out soon enough. She said without looking round:

'Everything's going swimmingly with work. Like swimming against the tide.' She added: 'Any advice from an old China hand about how I handle Sir Herman Choi at the interview next Thursday?'

He felt sorry for her. She had worked so hard on that bastard. And she had put together an excellent, polished

164

article; she had let him read it. It would embarrass Choi, it would make excellent scandal reading. But it wouldn't get her far. If all the Queen's horses and all the Queen's men and Interpol and the FBI couldn't crack Sir Herman Choi's armour, he didn't like her chances in one interview in his mansion surrounded by his unseen bodyguards. And he didn't like her chances of winning a libel action if he sued her, either. But there was no stopping her; she had the bit between her teeth and he admired that.

'What are you going to throw at him?'

She said: 'Play it cool. And charming. And then start in on him. Provoke him to anger. Finally accuse him directly. Then – ' she turned around and folded her arms grimly – 'I can at least publish his angry denials. "No, I am not a Triad member – No, I am not a heroin trafficker! No – all the rumours about me are vicious gossip!" A clever journalist like me can do it. And also publish the horse-laugh between the lines.'

He smiled.

'Yes. Good.' He added carefully, so as not to dampen her: 'But what about libel?'

'The Law of Libel is something we journalists are well schooled in, Hogan. Better than most lawyers. I'll squeeze it through the Law of Libel, all right. Just like he squeezes through the Criminal Law.'

He felt proud of her. And he regretted that he had not been of more practical and moral help to her, that he had been so preoccupied with his business problems. He said quietly:

'You're great, Vanessa.'

For the first time ever he saw embarrassment flicker across her face. 'Thanks, Hogan.' She turned back to the stove and stirred a pot unnecessarily.

He said carefully to her back:

'I just hope you find a publisher prepared to risk a libel action.'

'I will. When they see how cleverly I've written it.'

She kept her back to him. She hesitated, then said: 'Would you publish it? In the *Oriental Israelite*.'

McAdam was taken aback an instant. 'Yes,' he said. She did not turn round. He added: 'But you don't want a monthly magazine like the *Israelite*, with its tiny circulation. You want a big daily like the *South China Morning Post*. And in my financial position I want a libel action from a big gun like Choi with all his millions – even assuming I win – like I need a hole in my head. But . . .' He took a deep breath: 'Yes, if you can't get anybody better to stick their neck out, the *Israelite* will.'

She kept her back to him and said quietly:

'Thanks, Hogan.'

It was a restrained dinner, although she tried to be normal. She talked as if he was an old acquaintance whom she had not seen for some time. McAdam sat there, waiting for it. He wanted to put down his knife and fork and take her hand and say: 'All right, Vanessa. What is it?' But he waited.

She said, 'I've got something else up my sleeve, too, for Sir Herman Choi.'

'Oh? What's that?'

She played with her wineglass.

'It probably doesn't add up to much. On the other hand, it's a nice bit of local colour. It could be a good way to begin the story. *Or* end it. And with a bit of luck,' she said, 'it may adversely affect the value of his goddam Lucky Man shares. Particularly if the story appears on the first day they hit the stock exchange.'

McAdam's fork stopped in front of his mouth.

'What?' he said.

She smiled wanly. '*Fung shui*,' she said.

He stared at her, then felt relief flood over him. 'Oh? What about it?'

She said: 'My sub-headline will be "*Un*-Lucky, Man, *real* unlucky!" That may frighten off the Chinese share-buyers.' She pointed at the wall. 'That huge apartment block that he's building just up there? Bad *fung shui*, man.'

He smiled. 'I'd have thought it had excellent *fung shui*.'

She shook her head. 'Oh yes. It overlooks the water and two mountains with dragons. On the face of it, excellent. But,' she held up her finger, 'they had to bull-doze out the mountainside. And *that* cut slap bang through some poor dragon's spine!'

McAdam tilted back his head and laughed. 'Who told you that?'

She smiled. 'Don't laugh at me, Hogan. It makes a good little story. And it could help. And God knows I need help. Nobody told me. I went up to the site, and I saw it.'

'What did you see?'

'There's a huge cliff-face where they've cut a massive terrace in the mountainside. And that cliff-face, Hogan,' she said, 'is *red*. And as any Chinese will tell you, that's the poor dragon's *blood*.'

McAdam felt the smile freeze on his face. He stared at her. 'Red what?'

'Clay. And soil, of course.'

'Clay? And soil? Not rock?'

'No. A few bits, sure. A dragon can't be too choosy where it sleeps, you know. But mostly clay. And *red*, sir.'

Trying to wipe the consternation off his face, he

picked up the wine bottle and sloshed some more into both glasses. He smiled hastily at her joke, but his mind was racing. *That cliff-face was made up of clay and soil? Not solid rock?* Jesus. In a mountainside that steep? He knew enough about building to know that that should never be allowed, particularly in Midlevels with its bad record for landslides. A terrace that big would cut all the natural support out of that piece of mountainside and the whole building and all could collapse if it wasn't on solid rock. And he knew enough about building law to know that a cut that big into ordinary soil would not have been allowed officially – some silver must have changed hands. He tried to say it casually:

'How steep is that cliff-face?'

'Vertical. Or very nearly.'

Jesus. A cut like that just had to be into solid rock, anybody who knew anything about building knew that. She didn't know it yet, but she had found a big fat crack in Sir Herman Choi's armour. She had found a story that would really land the bastard in trouble, a prosecution for corruption, public fraud, God knows what. But Christ – he had just invested two hundred thousand borrowed dollars in Lucky Man, and he didn't want her beautiful little story breaking until he had sold his shares. On the very first day. Nine o'clock next Friday morning. He put his knife and fork together casually and said:

'Are you sure it was *red* clay, Vanessa? And soil?'

'Saw it with my own eyes.'

'Well. I'll go up tomorrow morning and have a look at it.'

'Too late, Hogan, the bastard's too smart for that. It's bricked over already. Why? Don't you believe this reporter?'

He smiled. Thank God for that brick wall. 'Of course. But I think you'll find he's employed a geomancer. To appease the dragon. Government often has to do that, to keep the Chinese happy, with all the mountains we bulldoze down for resettlement blocks.'

'And *does* that satisfy the Chinese?'

'Yes. Costs Government a fortune.'

'So you don't think I'll get anywhere with that story?'

'No,' he said. 'I don't.'

She twirled her wineglass.

'Well, I'm going to publish it anyway.'

He said: 'When?'

'Next Friday morning. The day after his shares hit the market.'

'Have you told the editor of the *South China Morning Post* about the *fung shui*?'

'No. I'm keeping that as a punch-line.'

'Is he definitely going to publish it?'

He lit a cigarette. He had to work on it to keep his hand from shaking.

'He hasn't seen the story yet. But he's interested. If it were a big enough story to blow earlier by itself, I would. To hurt his shares *before* they hit the stock exchange. But it's only any good as a punch-line to the bigger story.'

He inhaled his cigarette deeply.

'I'll publish it. As a bit story. In next month's issue of the *Israelite*.'

'I thought you said it wasn't of any value?'

He smiled. 'We'll blow it up into a big story. We can even put it in context of my editorials about Nature. *Fung shui*. Living in harmony with nature. The vanishing wilderness. The way man is ruining it. Overcrowding the planet. Hong Kong's the microcosm of what the world's going to be like in fifty years' time . . .

High-rises and everybody living on top of each other. No room for dragons any more.'

He was trying so hard that he believed himself. And then, by God, he knew he did believe it – he *would* do it. But, please God, only after next Friday.

She smiled at him.

'Thanks, Hogan. You're a lovely man.'

She had it rehearsed. She was just waiting for the right moment.

'Hogan?' He glanced up from the table. 'Please don't interrupt me. Let me say what I must.'

He looked at her. Then nodded.

'Hogan? This is the last night I'll see you. Because ... I'm going home one of these fine days, and I must control my feelings.' She took a big breath. 'I'm still in control of them: and I'm going to keep it that way. But if I saw any more of you it would become very difficult.'

She lit a cigarette and puffed out smoke hastily.

'Nothing can come of us, Hogan. You live in Hong Kong. And I live in New York. And neither of us wants to change. And in those circumstances I certainly don't want to be in love with you, ten thousand miles away.'

She paused.

'And I certainly do not want to get married.' She looked at him. 'Please believe me. This is not some kind of female ploy. I think one day I will get married. If I want to have children. But certainly not now.' She added: 'If I ever get married it will be somebody like you. In fact, I would want it to *be* you. You're a great guy, Hogan. With a big heart. But it won't ever be you, if only because we live on opposite sides of the world.'

She puffed hard on her cigarette, then blew out smoke.

'And please don't think that I imagine that you want

to marry me, either. I don't believe you do. Possibly for several reasons. But the most important is that you're still involved with the past. You're still in love with Ying.'

He didn't say anything.

'Please don't try to answer or analyse that. That's something you must do for yourself, and maybe you're doing it, but I think you're not out of the woods yet. And that's your business, Hogan. Because I'm not making any demands upon you, in fact the opposite – I'm leaving you. For my own reasons. But before I do so, I just want to say a few things. As your friend. As your admirer . . .'

She looked at him.

'First of all, she must be a very worthy person to have your love for so long. And she's a very lucky person: because she's got your love, wherever she may be or whatever she's doing, she's got that with her and that's a gift and a tribute beyond price.' She looked down at the table. 'But the most important thing I want to say is this: I think you must get out of those woods of the past, now, Jake. Because there's a whole beautiful world out there in the open, and you deserve the best of it. And you're not really like me in at least one respect – you *do* want a deep, permanent relationship with one woman.'

She glanced up at him. He was staring at the centre of the table.

'But . . . Few women could live with you with Ying still in your heart.'

They were silent for fully a minute. She stared at nothing, her cigarette burning away. McAdam stared at the centre of the table, thinking, unable to think. He had been expecting it, and hoping it wouldn't come. He

171

didn't know what he was going to say, what he wanted to say. She said:

'Please, Jake. If you love me the slightest, don't say anything. My mind is made up. Please don't even try to delay the evil hour – because that's the best we could do. And I'm going to get out of Hong Kong as heart-whole as I came in.'

She stood up and looked down at him.

'Good-bye, darling Hogan.'

He stared at her. Then she gave him her dazzling smile, but her eyes were moist. She turned on her heel and walked out of the apartment.

He sat where he was, staring at nothing, stunned. He listened to her footsteps ringing down the corridor to the front door.

For an hour he sat at the table. Then he slowly got up. He picked up his keys and walked slowly out of the apartment. He rode down in the elevator to the basement parking lot. Then he got into his car and drove through the night, back to the boat-yard.

TWENTY

He did not sleep that night. At three o'clock in the morning he got off his bed and lit a pressure-lamp, went out to the shed, mixed up concrete and began to work, the sweat running off him in the moonlight. And Sunday dawned.

That Sunday was bad. It was completely quiet, the sun beating down out of a mercilessly blue sky, and it beat back up off the hot hard China earth at him, hazy, shimmering, all the way to the horizon, and the sea was oily blue and flat. There was not a sound but the lonely noise of his trowel slapping mortar and bricks. He did not have a hangover, but his body was sick for sleep, and the whole world seemed bad, and heartbreakingly lonely. At four o'clock that Sunday afternoon he could take no more, and he threw down his trowel and flung himself on his bed. But he could not sleep. He did not fall asleep until midnight, and he was suddenly wide awake with the dawn of Monday, his nerves cringing for sleep. And there was nothing else to do but get up and start working again.

At five o'clock that Monday afternoon he knew what he had to do. He walked solemnly to the end of the jetty and dived in. Then he waded ashore and pulled on some clothes. He swallowed half a glass of whisky, got into his car and drove back to Hong Kong.

The amah answered the door. As he walked towards the living room he heard a man's voice, and then he heard her laugh. The living room was empty. Through the french windows, he saw Kurt Marlowe sprawled on a wicker chair on the big verandah. Then he saw her, half hidden by a potted palm. There was a bottle of whisky on the cane table between them. If it had been anybody other than Marlowe, he would have turned and gone away and waited until tomorrow. McAdam stood in the french window.

'Good evening.'

She looked around at him, surprised. Then he could see she was a little drunk. She was wearing a flowing Japanese kimono. 'Hullo,' she said.

Marlowe said nothing, just looked at him with one eyebrow cocked. McAdam looked back.

'Do you mind leaving us alone for a while?'

Marlowe stared at him indignantly.

'Yes,' he said. 'Yes, I do.'

McAdam looked at Vanessa. She blinked and slowly turned her head to Marlowe.

'Better take a powder, Kurt. I'm sorry.'

Marlowe sat poised. Then he put down his glass. He stood up theatrically, bent over her chair and kissed her forehead.

'See you soon.'

'*Hasta la vista*,' she said.

Marlowe turned and strode past McAdam into the living room. He closed the front door with a slight bang behind him.

'Well, Jake?'

'I'm sorry about that.'

'Like hell you are.' She sloshed whisky into a glass for him. 'Cheers.'

'Did you have a date with him?'

She laughed. 'It's happened! I never thought I'd see the day when Jake McAdam asks me what I'm up to. No. He just blew in with the typhoon. Just dropped by to see if he could get into my pants.'

McAdam sat down. He took a big sip of whisky.

'I said I didn't want to see you again, Jake. You're not being very fair.'

He said: 'Why don't you call me Hogan?'

'I don't want to call you Hogan any more. Quit stalling. Why did you come? Not for the same fluffy little thing as the beautiful Kurt Marlowe, I hope.'

McAdam took a firm breath. He said:

'I don't accept what you said last time.'

She looked at him.

'The hell, Hogan. What can we do about that? Because I'm going, Jake. As surely as the sun will rise in the east. And you live here. And ne'er the twain shall meet.'

'Don't go.'

174

She said with quiet exasperation:

'Hogan. Stay and do what? I'm a damn Yank, through and through. My career's there. My whole life.'

He said: 'And live with me.' He held out his finger. 'Last time I heard you out without interruption, now you give me a hearing, please.'

She sat back.

'Live with me, Vanessa. You can get more leave of absence from your job. You can send home good articles from here. You can become an expert on China. On the whole Far East. With your talent for work and getting to know people. And you can get a job on the *South China Morning Post*: they'd jump at you. You could string for *Newsweek* or *Time*. Get your name known outside of America. And,' he said, 'you can work on the *Israelite*. Christ, it would be marvellous to have you on the *Israelite*. The only reason I haven't suggested it before was that we couldn't afford you. But we can now. I'm all but out of the woods financially. And you could up-grade the circulation, with your ideas and know-how.'

She was staring at the table, listening.

'And *live* with me, Vanessa. We could give ourselves a chance. Three months. Six months. A year . . . We've got a great relationship, Vanessa. Don't throw that away lightly. Believe me, they're hard to find, if you find it once in your life you're very lucky. We're very compatible. We could have a great life. We can take off on the junk and sail the world. It's within our power. We can get out there and do things that other people only dream about. We're both the kind that *do* go down to the sea in ships.'

He stopped and looked at her. 'Don't go, Vanessa.'

She said quietly: 'And what happens after our trial

period?' She held up her hand to interrupt him. 'What happens if it's a failure?'

'I don't believe it will be.'

She said: 'I'll go back to the States and I've got to start all over again. With a broken heart.'

'For God's sake take the risk!'

'And if the trial period is a success? What do we do – apart from go down to the sea in ships?'

'We'll get married.'

She nodded slowly. 'And what about the lady upstairs?'

He didn't understand her for a moment. 'What lady?'

'Upstairs in your gallery,' she said quietly. 'Ying.'

He stared at her. 'Have you been up there?'

She nodded, slowly. 'Yes.'

For a moment he was angry. Then he controlled it. 'Then you'll have noticed that the paintings are all turned to the wall.'

'But they're still up there, Hogan. And in the living room she's not turned to the wall.' She added: 'I'm not telling you to take her down. I'm just telling you that it's significant. Of your emotional condition.'

'My emotional condition is well under my own control now, Vanessa.'

She smiled wryly. 'I don't doubt it. Controlled. I've seen plenty of evidence of that. But in your controlled way you still love her.'

'There's an important difference in practical life between always loving somebody from a long time ago, and being *in* love.'

'I understand that too. But what I don't understand is how do you feel about me?'

'I'm in love with you, Vanessa.'

*

She stared a long time at her drink, then said quietly: 'Thank you, Hogan. I mean that.'

Then her blue eyes flashed: 'And I mean this too! *Bullshit, Hogan!* It's all nonsense! Oh, I admire your honesty! That you admit that you still love her. That you come to me tonight with a solid proposition of a trial period. And all that jazz. Fair enough! It's what you want. But don't – ' she jabbed her finger between her breasts – 'expect me to go overboard about it! You finally manage to admit that you're *in* love with me. Great. I'm touched. But – oh, *dandy!* To get you to say it was like pulling a goddam tooth out of you! Which is also fair enough – because it's how you truly feel. And believe me I don't want you to say things you don't truly feel, I want the truth. And the truth is you *don't* love me! If you had you'd have burst straight out with it. You'd have said, "Listen – I love you! – I'm not letting you go!" But no, you come here with a well thought out proposition and the final thing you mention, under cross-examination, is that you're in love with me. I don't believe it's true. You're still in love with *her*.'

'It is true,' he said quietly.

'And that's not the only thing I don't believe, Hogan. Listen. I've given this whole thing a hell of a lot more thought than you have. Because *I'm* the one who's going to get hurt – and *I'm* the one who's got to give up her life back home. And I'm a bit drunk now and I've been a bit drunk for two days. And this is what I think: we're *not* compatible, Hogan! For a whole lot of reasons. And one of them is that I'm not half as big and bold as I act! Much as I hate to admit it. Everything I've made in life I've got the hard way by working twice as hard as others. And charm. And I want to keep what I've got. I've never done anything adventurous that wasn't under the protection of my employment. But

177

you don't give a damn about security. About money. I'm *envious* of you. How's that for compatibility? Sure, I'll go down to the sea in ships. But only if you make me. And I'll be shit-scared.'

She glowered at him, then looked away. 'I'm a fraud.'

'Bullshit.'

She snorted and ignored the comment.

'But that's not the half of it. The other half is far worse. And that is this.' She looked at him unsteadily. 'You're a straight guy, sexually, Jake. You're a great fuck, you're a wonderful lover. But you're straight, like the rest of you. And I'm as kinky as hell. I'd shock you rigid if I told you some of the things that go on in my head. I'm a fantasist, McAdam. Believe that. I have sexual fantasies galore. Gang-bangs and threesomes and foursomes and more-somes! And I want to share them with you, to tell them to you, to turn you on to the same thing – and I can't. It wouldn't turn you on, it would shock you to the marrow. And it would haunt you, and finally you'd want out.'

He said, 'Try me.'

'You couldn't handle such thoughts – you wouldn't tolerate it. Let alone do it.'

He said, 'I don't think you would either, when it came to the crunch.'

'But I *want* to be able to! Don't you see? When the honeymoon's over between me and you and we get down to day-to-day living, I'll revert to type. A leopard don't change its spots. And I'll want to be able at least to fantasize with you.'

'You can fantasize with me.'

'Could I hell! You'd be so hurt – because you're that kind of straight, loyal guy. And I'm not – not naturally. Not until you came along. By nature I'm a whore!'

'You're not!'

She cried: 'Not a paid one – just a willing one! Do it for free. For kicks. And I'm bisexual – '

'You are not.'

'I am! Do you think I don't know what I want? Christ – you don't even believe I'm telling you the truth; that's how far apart we really are, Hogan!'

He said, 'I'm getting tired of this, Vanessa.'

She slapped her forehead.

'My God! – "tired of this," the man says. The arrogance of it! The sheer *ignorance* of it! Don't you realize I'm very solemnly telling you my sexual hang-ups – and you say you're getting tired of it! Of all the male chauvinist arrogance! You're so goddam straight and ignorant of how women can feel – of how *I* feel – so unimaginative about sex, that you don't believe it! Well, I'll tell you what, McAdam – take me to a whorehouse right now and I'll prove it to you!'

Insulted, he rose to the challenge, 'All right, I will.'

'Right!' She slapped the table. 'Let's go!' She stood up and picked up her whisky and gulped it down. 'Then see if you believe me! And *then* see if you can live with it!'

She swept off the verandah. 'I'm going to tart myself up!'

McAdam sat there, angry, stunned. He poured himself a big shot of whisky. He did not believe she would go through with it.

TWENTY-ONE

They drove in grim silence. She stared straight ahead. So did he.

'You're really going to go through with this nonsense?'

'Yes.'

But he was sure that when they got there she would chicken out. He pulled into the basement car park of Nanking Mansions, in Causeway Bay.

Almost everything was sold in Nanking Mansions. The ground and first floor were vast shopping arcades, signboards scrambling on top of each other; above were offices and sewing shops and wholesalers and apartment-factories that made plastic flowers and dolls and transistor radios and suits and shirts and handbags, and above that were ten floors of apartment-hotels with names like the Cherry Blossom and the World of Suzie Wong and the USA, and they were all whore-houses. On the sixteenth floor was the Oriental International Apartment House.

The elevator opened straight into the whorehouse foyer. There was a big mahogany desk with a reception foki sitting behind it with an abacus, and the lamp-light was dim red, and there was a strong smell of incense. Beside the main door were two little godshelf altars, with offerings of mandarin oranges and joss-sticks burning: one was to the god of brothels, the other to the goddess of fornication. The foki stared at them an instant, then professional inscrutability returned.

McAdam said: 'Can we see the Mama-san, please?'

Vanessa said loudly: 'And a drink, please?' She

looked around the foyer and sniffed. 'Sex, McAdam – the joint reeks gloriously of sex.'

The Mama-san came into the room. She knew McAdam but her eyes gave away nothing. 'Good evening.'

'Mama,' McAdam said, 'this lady is my brand new wife and she wants to see how I spent my money before I met her.'

The Mama-san's face broke into a smile.

'Long time no see!' She turned to Vanessa: 'Mister Mac not very good customer, you know – ' and she burst out laughing nervously.

They followed her through the reception room. There was a long mahogany bar and cane bar stools. Around the room sat a dozen girls watching television. They came out of their boredom when they saw Vanessa. They stared as she crossed the room. She flashed them a smile. One of them was Chiang Mei-ling, in a red dress.

Vanessa sat down on a bar stool and crossed her legs seductively. McAdam leant against the bar. 'Two double whiskies, please. Well, here we are.' He jerked his thumb over his shoulder. 'Which one do you fancy?'

She retorted: 'All of them. Which do you fancy? – you're going to fuck her too.'

'Oh, am I? Good.'

She turned around to the Mama-san. 'How many rooms do you have?'

'Twelve,' the Mama-san said. 'Very good. You like see?'

'In a minute. And are these all the girls?'

'Two working now.'

'Is tonight a quiet night?'

'Not busy,' the Mama-san said. 'Monday.'

'And how much are the girls?'

The Mama-san looked at her. 'You want girl?'

Vanessa laughed. McAdam smiled grimly to himself. 'But how much are they?' she repeated.

'One hundred,' the Mama-san said. 'About twenty US.'

'That's cheap: a good hooker in New York costs fifty. And how long does she stay?'

'Until you're finished with her,' McAdam snapped.

She turned around to him conversationally. 'That tall girl in the red dress – she's beautiful, isn't she?'

'She is.'

'Shouldn't we buy them a drink?'

'*All* of them?'

'I'd like to get a story. I've got my tape recorder. How does a beautiful girl like that one end up on the game?'

'We didn't come here to get a story. You'll have to get the girl aside. And pay her.'

She replied sweetly: 'How about you on one side and me on the other?'

'Anything you say. This is your trip.'

'Yes, it is, isn't it?'

He turned to the Mama-san. 'Can we see the rooms now?'

They followed her out of the room, down the corridor. The lights were soft pink under ornate Chinese shades. The Mam-san stopped at the first mahogany door. 'Venice Room.' She opened the door.

And there was Venice on the wallpaper all about them, the Piazza San Marco, and in the middle of the room was a double bed built into a gondola.

'Fantastic!' She walked into the room. She sat down experimentally on the bed and the Mama-san flicked a switch. The lights went out and stars appeared in the ceiling. The gondola bed began to sway gently, and from somewhere came the voice of a gondolier singing in Italian, and all about them were the night lights of Venice.

He followed down the corridor. He didn't know whether she was stalling or not. The next was the Tokyo Room. The floor was tatami matting and in the middle was the futon, the mattress; the walls were sliding Japanese paper screens and there was the tiny dressing-table one had to kneel before, and in the other corner the sunken bath. The Mama-san slid back one of the paper screens. On the wall behind it was a life-size photograph of a Japanese garden full of cherry blossoms, and a bird began to sing.

'Oh, wow.'

The next was the Bangkok Room. 'Occupied,' the Mama-san said. Then followed the Taj Mahal Room and the Manhattan Room – 'Occupied' – and the London Room and the Paris Room. All the walls were papered with blown-up photographs of the cities they were named after. Then they came to the Heavenly Pacific Room.

It was circular. The ceiling was domed, and the big double mattress was set in a bulbous mass of inflated white vinyl that looked like a cloud. 'Get on bed,' the Mama-san beamed.

Vanessa piled over the cloud-mass on to the mattress and lay on her back, arm outflung. The Mama-san switched out the lights. And suddenly the domed ceiling was a starlit sky and in one corner there was a brilliant sunset going on, sinking below a horizon of silhouetted palm trees, the glow flaming up as the sun inched down, and on the opposite side a silver moon was riding; then the Mama-san flicked another switch and the cloud-bed began to rise. It rose up gently towards the ceiling on a hydraulic jack, and out of the silhouetted palm trees came the fluted strains of Hawaiian music. Vanessa lay there on the cloud-bed laughing as it came down.

She slid off the bed and stood up. She looked at him.

'This one.'

'Very well,' he said tersely.

Vanessa Storm Williams lay spreadeagled on the cloud-bed, naked, waiting. Her tape recorder was on the chair. The door opened and McAdam came back in. He knew by the wide movement of her eyes that she had gulped her whisky straight down.

'Two minutes,' he said. 'None of these girls will do it; they're getting an expert down from King Winky's upstairs.'

He sat down on the edge of the cloud-bed and folded his arms. She said: 'Get undressed, Hogan.'

'Like hell I am.'

'Get undressed. You defied me and brought me here. Now I'm going to prove I was telling the truth. And I want you in it too.'

He glared at her.

'Very well.'

He took a big mouthful of whisky to try to get some drunkenness back, then stood up and started to undress. His fingers were shaking. She was so damn beautiful. Lying there, her big white breasts lolling magnificently, her belly flat, long golden legs, her golden hair outspread: she was the incarnation of sensuality. But he still expected her to chicken out. What she proposed was in principle one of the most sensually exciting things he could imagine, every man's fantasy. But he felt sick in his guts. She was watching him undress, her eyes slow with liquor, her wide smile mocking.

'What're you uptight about, Hogan? You don't think I'll do it?'

He said nothing. He didn't want to provoke more bravado.

'Hogan – this is supposed to be fun, most men would think so.'

'It is. I can't stop laughing.'

She tossed her head and burst out laughing. Then she almost held out her arms to him. 'Oh, Hogan.'

The door opened and a woman came in.

'Hullo,' she said.

They stared at her. She was about twenty-eight and European. She was tall, poised, with groomed black hair swept up on top of her head, and she was good-looking and pale and aloof.

'Hullo,' Vanessa said languidly.

'Okay,' the girl said, and they caught the slight American accent. 'Just relax, I understand what's wanted. If there's anything special, tell me.'

She began to get undressed. She slid her dress off her shoulders and it fell to her feet. She had long legs, in black stockings with a red suspender belt and brief white frilly panties, and her breasts bulged out of her brassière. She bent her arms behind her back and unclipped it and her breasts were free. Vanessa was looking up at her appraisingly. McAdam tried not to stare. He could just make out faint stretch marks of childbirth on her belly. He wanted to ask her who she was. The girl bent her knee and unclipped one stocking, then the other. She sat down on the chair next to the tape recorder and languidly peeled the stocking off. Then her panties and the suspender. 'All right,' she said. She came to the cloud-bed and smiled down at Vanessa professionally.

'You're very beautiful,' she said.

'So are you.'

'Sorry about the tan, don't get much sun in this job.'

Vanessa said, 'How did you get into it?'

The girl smiled. 'Just lucky, I guess.'

McAdam did not even manage a smile. He could not believe what he was witnessing, the two beautiful naked women confronting each other, about to make love; it was like a dream, and it did nothing for him. The girl put one knee up on the bed and said,

'Who takes charge?'

McAdam muttered, 'I think you'd better.'

Vanessa shifted over on the bed. The girl lay down beside her. Then she got up on to her elbow and smiled at Vanessa.

'Your first time? With a lady?'

Vanessa shook her head.

The girl smiled disbelievingly. 'Don't be nervous.'

She bent and slowly kissed her on the mouth. Vanessa lay there rigid a moment, then her arm went uncertainly round the girl's neck. McAdam stared at them kissing. He could not believe it. The glorious woman he thought he was in love with making love to another woman. He was in a sort of half-angry daze. The girl uncoiled an arm and felt for his, then pulled him down. He resisted, then he came down on to his elbow beside them, looking at them. Then Vanessa moved her mouth away from the girl's, and looked at him defiantly.

'Well, Hogan?'

He said thickly, 'Well, what?'

She started to say something else, then said, 'How do you feel?'

'Fine.'

'Enjoying it?'

'Sure. What man wouldn't? Unless he were arrogant, ignorant and unimaginative.'

She looked at him. 'Kiss her then.' She added: 'But kiss me first.'

He shook his head. Then she leant out of the girl's embrace, her face intense. He watched her mouth, then let her kiss him without yielding. She kissed him ardently, then she bit his lip and whispered into his mouth:

'Goddammit, McAdam, this is meant to be fun!'

186

She gave him a fierce smile and then she suddenly slid down the girl's body to her breasts and began to suck her nipple hard. McAdam looked at her, his woman's mass of golden hair on the girl's breasts, and the girl lay there with her eyes closed and her lips apart and her jet-black hair on the pillow; then Vanessa writhed down, fiercely kissing her stomach and her hips and her loins, and her mass of golden hair dragged down the girl's belly, and the girl sighed and her legs slid apart; and now Vanessa was curled between them, her golden head was between the girl's thighs, and the girl's hips were writhing and her hand was buried in Vanessa's golden hair, gripping it; and then one hand snaked up the girl's body and found her nipple and began to twist and pinch it and her other hand slid over and found his loins, and suddenly McAdam's dazedness snapped. It snapped in a rush of lust and angry hurt, and nothing else mattered and he was going to fuck these two women, and his hand flicked the hydraulic switch.

The lights went out, the Pacific night flicked on, Hawaiian music flooded the room. The cloud-bed rose through the Pacific night with the whore writhing in the middle of it, McAdam on top of her and Vanessa watch-him from the back, and he thrust deep inside her and now Vanessa had her arms around his chest and she was fiercely kissing his back and it was the most wildly erotic feeling in the world, a woman beneath him and a woman on top of him and their wet writhing warmth; and he thrust and thrust and thrust – then suddenly agony shot through him as Vanessa sank her teeth deep into his hip and crunched. He yelled and Vanessa hung on fiercely, then let go and lunged at the switch, and the Pacific night disappeared.

Disappeared with a snap in mid Hawaiian love-song, and the overhead lights came on bright, and the cloud-bed slid back down towards the floor with a thump.

Vanessa leapt off it and ran into the bathroom and slammed the door.

McAdam stared at the slammed door, shocked, feeling the pain in his hip, then a grim smile broke over his face.

'Vanessa! Come back!'

She yelled from within: 'Go ahead and fuck her!'

Then he heard the bloodcurdling yells down the corridor and the crash of axes and the screams.

TWENTY-TWO

The gang of 14K Triad men burst out of the elevator into the Oriental International foyer to avenge the stealing of Chiang Mei-ling, yelling and swinging their axes and cleavers and bicycle chains on high. The clerk ran backwards, arms flung up, and they bounded after him, swiping and slashing; an axe smashed his shoulder. They crashed their axes into the big mahogany desk and the chairs and then the door leading into the corridor, bellowing above the girls' shrieking, and the door smashed open on its shattered hinges and the Triad men burst through.

The girls scrambled screaming down the corridor for the fire-escape, as the five Triad men erupted into the bar where the Mama-san was shouting into the telephone. One swiped her with a club and another sliced the telephone in half with an axe and the others were smashing up the bar. Swinging their axes, bellowing and yelling, they smashed the mirrors and barstools and the sofas and chairs and the television set. Down the corridor the axes were smashing up the Venice Room and the Taj Mahal Room and the Tokyo Room and the

Manhattan Room and the London Room, hacking the beds and the windows and the wallpaper and the lights and the bathrooms. McAdam had flung himself at the door of the Pacific Room to lock it, then he heard the first girl fling herself against it, sobbing and wrenching the handle. He looked wildly for something to arm himself with, grabbed a chair and pulled open the door, and the girl reeled in. Three more stumbled past the door towards the fire-escape, but it was locked, and the girls were frenziedly shaking it. McAdam wrenched the last girl into the room, then flung the chair up in front of him and lunged out into the corridor to cover the other girls, and the axeman crashed into him.

The axeman swung the axe at him and it crashed off the chair back into McAdam's forearm, and he rammed the chair with all his might into the man's chest and crushed him against the wall. The man tried to swing the axe up again and McAdam rammed the chair with all his fury into his face, and his shriek was chopped off and the axe dropped to the floor. McAdam swung his fist far behind and hit him with all his might in the guts, and the man doubled over and crashed to the floor. McAdam reeled, rasping, the blood running from his arm. He grabbed the axe and looked wildly once up the corridor, and then a man bellowed something and the Triad men were scrambling out of the rooms and rushing back towards the elevator. And there was a shattering of a window behind him, and then the scream.

It was a scream of absolute terror and it came from the girl called Chiang Mei-ling as she leapt from the sixteenth-storey window. Mei-ling fell through the air, arms and legs outflung, her hair streaming behind her and her eyes and mouth wide in terror, and the wind tearing the scream from her mouth: she hurtled through the night down towards the street lights and she screamed all the way till she hit the pavement.

McAdam lurched up the corridor, panting, his right hand clutching the wound on his left forearm: suddenly there was just the hysterical sobbing of women. He looked into the ruined bar. The Mama-san was sitting in the corner, crying, clutching herself; he looked at the foki lying in his blood in the shattered foyer, then knelt down and felt his pulse. He was alive. He walked shakily back down the corridor to the Pacific Room.

'Vanessa . . .!'

The door opened immediately. She was dressed, wild-eyed, shocked; she closed her eyes and clutched him tight.

Then the elevator doors opened again. The police had arrived, led by Superintendent Bernard Champion.

He heard Champion speaking loudly and fast in Cantonese, giving orders, asking questions. There were other male voices; he could hear policemen checking the other rooms. Plainclothes policemen began to arrive, and ambulance men. McAdam leant against the wall of the Pacific Room while Vanessa feverishly wrapped a towel round his arm; then he shouted:

'Champion! Bernie!'

He heard Champion striding down the corridor, then he stood in the doorway in his uniform and riot helmet, big and hairy and astonished. 'Jesus Christ! What're you doing here?'

'Just visiting. I think I'd recognize one of them.'

'And *you*?' Champion glared at Vanessa.

Vanessa glanced at him then continued binding up McAdam's arm. 'I asked Hogan to show me what a Hong Kong brothel was like.'

Champion looked at the naked European girl in amazement. 'With a naked prostitute! *Jesus Christ,*

190

what are you doing to this woman?'

McAdam said, 'Mind your own business, Bernard! I said I'd recognize one of them.'

'It is my goddam business! Jesus Christ . . .' He stood there, outraged. Then he turned on the prostitutes and jerked his thumb. 'Out!' he shouted in Cantonese. 'Go and wait in the foyer – and you.' He strode and picked up the dress and threw it at the European girl.

They hurried out of the Pacific Room, sobbing and sniffing. McAdam was pulling on his shirt impatiently. Champion closed the door with a slam, then turned back on them furiously. He held out his finger, and it shook: 'Jesus Christ, why do you have to do this for your kicks?'

'Dry your eyes, Champ,' McAdam muttered. He started tying his shoelaces, with difficulty.

'Of all the . . . *twisted* things to do!'

Vanessa said, 'Please just tell us what happens now. Hogan's got to get to a hospital – '

Champion stared at her, quivering.

'What do you think happens now, Vanessa? Do you realize what you've got yourself into? Do you realize that a murder has been committed and that a girl lies dead in the street out there and that you're slap-bang in the middle of it as witnesses? That you're going to have to stand up in court and tell them what the hell you were doing with a prostitute – in a whorehouse? What's your newspaper going to say about that? How're you going to look? Like a goddam whore yourself! – Which you are!'

'Shut up, Champion!' McAdam snapped.

'I don't mind giving evidence, Bernard – it's my duty to do so,' said Vanessa.

'Don't you, indeed? . . . But that's only half the god-awful story, I'm afraid, Vanessa Storm Williams. Do you realize that this is a Triad murder – a Triad Society gang war between the 14K and the Wo Hop Wo over a prostitute that one stole from the other – the two biggest sonsabitches Triad Societies in the world who think nothing of murdering each other, let alone witnesses!'

McAdam said, 'She saw nothing – and even if she had there'd be no reason for her to give evidence.'

Champion turned on him furiously: 'But do you realize what you're doing to me? I arrive on the scene of a murder and I find you here, and somehow I've got to keep your names out of the case because of the scandal and because you're my friends – or used to be!' There was a sharp rap on the door and he barked: 'Come in!'

McAdam finished tying his shoe-laces. He looked up and saw an angry middle-aged Chinese man in the doorway. Bernard Champion turned to him. The man said in Cantonese: 'Can anybody identify them?'

'I don't know yet.'

The man replied in Cantonese:

'Then find out! I pay you enough! I want every one of them hanged otherwise it's war!' And he turned on his heel and strode down the corridor.

McAdam froze over his shoe-laces. He had understood the Cantonese.

Champion snapped: 'Go on – get out of here! Do you want to be taken to hospital for that arm?'

'No. I can get there myself.'

'Then get out of here fast. I'll telephone you tomorrow.' And he turned and strode angrily down the corridor.

192

TWENTY-THREE

The dawn was just breaking. They walked slowly down the steps of Queen Mary Hospital. The harbour lights were still on, the whole world quiet. His arm was numb from the anaesthetic. They walked silently across the dark, deserted parking-lot towards his car. They were both wide-awake exhausted: the night seemed unreal. They reached the car; and she stopped and turned to him.

'Hogan? I want to say something.'

He looked at her in the dark and waited.

'Hogan, I'm sorry. For what I put you through. That . . . sexual ordeal. For what I put *us* through. It wasn't a very . . . mature thing to do.'

He said quietly: 'On the contrary. Adult to adult, you set out to prove by deeds what words could not prove.'

She said, 'I don't know what I proved, Hogan.' She started to go on then shook her head. 'Hogan, this is not a retraction of what I said about . . . going home to the States. And what I said about . . . Ying. You're not out of the woods yet, with her. But what I do want to say is . . .' She closed her eyes and shook her head: 'Oh, Hogan . . . I am in love with you. But it's a . . . love affair, Hogan. I'm not sure what all the differences are, but a love affair . . . is something that's going to end one day. As we must. For all the reasons I've given. Except this, Hogan.' She looked at him in the dark. 'I don't want to do it again, what we did tonight. I lied to you, Hogan. I was just trying to tease you before . . . to get your wavelength. To see if it turned you on. Because, to be honest, the idea *did* turn me on. But not' – she shook her head wearily – 'now my emotions are involved.'

She looked at him earnestly.

'Okay? Do you understand?'

'I understand.'

She stood there, holding the roof of the car in the dawn.

'Oh Christ, Hogan – *hold* me.'

He sat silently at the kitchen table in the apartment while she cooked them steak and eggs, feeling the throbbing come back into his arm. She was quiet. He did not want to think about it, he did not know what to think. And he kept turning something else over and over in his head. And did not want to think about that either, what he had heard in the whorehouse. He *must* have heard wrong. Not Champion. Not big lovely Bernardo Champion, his closest friend in the whole wide world. He must have mis-heard: maybe his Cantonese was not good enough. But his Cantonese *was* bloody good enough. She said, without looking round from the stove:

'I'm not going to let Bernard cook that case to protect me from giving evidence. I got myself into it, I'll take the consequences.'

He suddenly thought of something.

'Was your tape recorder running all the time?'

She suddenly remembered it. 'Yes.'

'Where is it?'

'In my bag.' She went to her bag on the table and pulled it out.

'What do you want to hear?'

'Just the end. Just from when that man knocked on the door and spoke to Champion.'

She pressed the re-wind switch, then listened. Suddenly Champion's angry voice was saying ' – *the two biggest sonsabitches Triad Societies in the world!'*

'Okay, give it to me . . .'

He bent his head over it and listened intently. He heard the rap on the door and Champion shouting 'Come in' quite clearly. Then he heard the Chinese male speak rapidly in Cantonese in the corridor. It was very indistinct. He switched the machine off.

'Can you turn off the frying pan?'

'They're nearly ready, they'll spoil.'

He heaved himself out of the chair and started for the door.

'What are you listening for?'

'Hang on.'

He sat down on the sofa in the lounge. His body ached. He held the machine close to his ear and played it again and listened. He indistinctly heard the Chinese man say in Cantonese:

'Can anybody identify them?'

Champion said, more distinctly: 'I don't know yet.'

The Chinese man replied: 'Then find out! *I pay you enough.*'

He re-wound the tape and listened again. That time he did not catch it. He snapped it back to re-wind, then listened again. And he heard it again: '*I pay you enough.*' Vanessa came into the room.

'What is it?'

'Nothing.'

'I'm not a fool, Hogan.'

He looked at her grimly. 'I think Champion's on the take.'

'You've got to be joking.'

'If he is, it's in the nicest possible way. Just part of the general rake-off his staff sergeant collects, on his own Chinese initiative – it's almost traditional. Or was until the Prevention of Bribery purges. Oh, Christ – ' he shook his head wearily – 'I shouldn't have said anything. Until I can confirm it.'

She waved her hand at the tape recorder. 'But haven't you just confirmed it? What's this about the Chinese man who came in right at the end?'

'He's the owner of the whorehouse. And he's obviously protected by the Wo Hop Wo Triad Society. I heard him say to Champion: "I pay you enough. Catch them or it's war." And it's on the tape. In Cantonese.'

She was staring at him aghast. 'My God!'

He held out his finger. 'Now listen . . . If you think you're going to use this in a story, you're mistaken! Because this is a very serious allegation.'

'You're damn right it is! And what do you mean, "In the nicest possible way – it's almost traditional"? It sounds as if you condone it!'

'Of course I don't condone it! I'm saying it's an easy trap for a young copper to fall into and he's stuck with it the rest of his life – '

'Is that why you quit the cops, Jake?'

'Oh Christ . . .' he said contemptuously.

'Okay, I'm sorry! But I'm not having you cover up for any crooked cop! I've heard enough excuses for corruption in this rotten town, from Herman Choi down! If it's on that tape I'm publishing it!'

'Like hell you are! *I* won't have it. It's got to be properly handled!'

She cried, '*You* won't have it?! – you mean you won't let it be known at all because Bernard Champion's your friend?'

'Certainly he's my friend! And he's got the right to explain himself first.'

'You mean give him time to cover his tracks! Are you going to go to the Anti-Corruption Bureau with this story? No! You're going to go to Champion. And he'll explain it away and your conscience will be salved and we'll never hear anything more about it!'

His nerves were gone and he wanted to shout, but he controlled himself and said softly: 'Do you want to take it to Anti-Corruption Bureau? – Hell no, because then it'll be sub judice and you can't print your bloody story! You want your sensational story published *then* turn him over to the courts – *after* you've already judged him guilty!'

She snapped: 'He's lent you money for your boat-yard!'

'So what?'

'It's ill-gotten money – and you don't want to admit it to yourself!'

'Oh, bullshit. Of course I don't want to borrow ill-gotten money – but I didn't know, did I? And anyway I'm repaying him on Thursday. The only point is the guy's got the right to clear himself before you blow the whistle on him!'

'I don't believe you. How can you repay him all that money on Thursday?'

'Because,' he said wearily, 'he didn't lend it to me for the boat-yard, he lent it to me to invest in the stock market.'

'And you're selling on Thursday?'

'Right.'

She stared at him. 'Why not tomorrow? Why not Wednesday? Have *you* bought Lucky Man shares, Jake? – they go on the market next Thursday.'

'Yes. So what, again? Half the town's trying to buy Lucky Man shares.'

'Good God, Hogan! Herman Choi's shares!'

He sighed. 'How's this got into it? Lucky Man published a perfectly accurate prospectus in the papers

197

as law requires, certified by perfectly good accountants, and they're legitimate shares. I'm quite sure he's also got shares in San Miguel Breweries, Hong Kong Telephone and the Hong Kong & Shanghai Bank – should I sell my shares in those because of him too?'

She cried: 'Christ! Russian and Japanese goods you boycott because they still hunt whales! But you borrow Champion's ill-gotten gains to buy shares in Herman Choi's company! And you're the guy who's promised to publish my exposé on him if nobody else will stick their necks out! Well, I tell you – you better sell those shares pretty damn quick because that story about Champion is being published if I've got to shout it around like a town-crier!'

She snatched up her tape recorder, stormed into the kitchen and grabbed her handbag. 'Good-bye!'

She slammed the front door behind her.

PART VIII

It was Tuesday afternoon. It was fiercely, humid hot, the haze hung over the sparkling harbour, the sea was flat and the Mountains of Nine Dragons were hazy mauve and brown. She knew she should sleep but she was wide-awake, her brain clear: she had been drinking ever since she had left McAdam early that morning, while she furiously typed her story, but she was not drunk. Now she stood at the counter of Cable and Wireless and listened to the clatter of the telex machine as the operator sent off her long story.

The operator finished and gave her a copy of the text. She slapped her Press Credit Card on the counter and speed-read the story while he processed the invoice. She signed.

'Thank you.'

She turned and walked out of the cable office, a tall, beautiful woman with a face gaunt with tiredness. Determined to get drunk enough to pass out. And when she woke up she was going to wrap up her business and get the hell out of this God-forsaken place.

TWENTY-FOUR

The desk of superintendent Bernard Champion, Queen's Police Medal, Colonial Police Medal for Gallantry, was always piled with the investigation files of his junior officers, for he insisted on knowing everything they were doing and ensuring they did it fast and perfectly. He was scrawling a caustic directive on the investigation diary of a file when he looked up to see Jake McAdam standing in his office door.

'For Christ's sake!' he said angrily. 'Couldn't you have got yourself announced?'

'No. Because you've been avoiding me. Why haven't you returned my calls?'

'What do you want?'

McAdam closed the door firmly behind him.

'Is this office safe to talk in?'

'What d'you think we are, the CIA? What the hell do you want to talk about? I'm very busy.'

'Unbusy yourself. I've come about a very serious matter that concerns you.'

Champion leant forward. 'I am furious with you. More than that – disgusted! That's the only word.'

'I didn't come here for any homilies – my private life is my affair.'

'Then keep your perversions to yourself! – don't corrupt others! Good God – ' he sat back furiously – 'isn't she enough for you? Isn't one beautiful body enough? But no – your taste-buds are so jaded, so corrupted by a lifetime of promiscuity – '

Hogan snapped, 'Who was the Chinese male who came to the bedroom door in the whorehouse?'

Champion was taken aback. 'I've no idea who you're talking about. Probably one of my plainclothes men.'

'Bullshit. No staff of yours would speak to you like that! He was the owner of the whorehouse, wasn't he?'

'Oh *him*.' He shrugged. 'Bill Lu. Everybody knows Bill Lu. He owns one of the best whorehouses in Hong Kong, doesn't he? What about him?'

Hogan said: 'That was a rival Triad raid – you told us so yourself. The raiders were 14K. That makes Bill Lu a Wo Hop Wo, or he pays protection to them.'

'Brilliant. You really shouldn't have left the cops. I don't know how we've muddled along without you all these years.'

'I heard him say to you in Cantonese: "I pay you enough".'

'What,' said Champion slowly, 'are you implying?'

'I'm implying that you are in his pay. That directly or indirectly you are receiving a rake-off from him and all the other brothel-owners in your district.'

Champion's face was pale.

'I beg your bloody pardon? . . .'

'You heard me.'

Champion slammed his big hand down on his desk. 'I should throw you out!'

'You'd better deal with me rather than somebody else. I heard it distinctly. My Cantonese is plenty good enough.'

'What do you think you heard him say?'

'He said to you: "Can anybody be identified?" You answered, "I don't know yet." He said, "Then find out! *I pay you enough.* I want them all hanged otherwise it's war!"'

'I've absolutely no recollection of it! Come on! –

repeat that in Cantonese!'

McAdam looked him in the eye. He repeated it in faultless Cantonese.

Champion said shakily: 'I do not remember any such thing being said. You are mistaken! In all that hullabaloo how could you have heard anything clearly?'

McAdam looked him in the eye. He wanted to believe him. 'Champion, I've got it on tape.'

Bernard Champion stared at him, heart pounding. 'On tape?'

'Vanessa happened to have her tape recorder running.' McAdam felt his heart sink. Jesus Christ, he wanted to hear him say the right thing.

'I want to hear that tape.'

'You'll have to get hold of Vanessa. We aren't seeing each other any more.'

Champion slumped back in his chair. 'If this happened – which I don't remember – but if it did, he probably said, "*We* pay you enough," meaning we, the public, pay you, plural, enough.'

McAdam dearly wanted that to be true.

'It was very clear. And he went on to say that if you didn't catch them it meant war. That was a Triad man throwing his weight around with a policeman he knows.'

Champion snapped: 'He's not a Triad man as far as we know. He just pays protection . . . For Chrissake, Jake. You know me. Do you believe I'm corrupt?'

'I don't want to, but on the evidence I see . . .'

Champion's eyes were hard and hurt.

'I've heard you out, McAdam, only because it's the right thing to do between friends. But can't you see what's happened? We all know that the brothel owners try to pay off the police staff sergeants. And some of them take it. We can't prove it, we all know it's wrong but we also all know it's the system, and it enables the staff sergeants to lean on the underworld. I'm not de-

202

bating the rights and wrongs of it – but it works. And Bill Lu assumes that because he pays off my staff sergeant that I'm in on the business. And I was so shocked and angry with you that it sails right over my head! I was *stunned*. Can't you appreciate that? You can take that or leave it, Jake. But it's the truth!'

'I'm sorry,' McAdam said.

Champion said stiffly, 'You were quite right to mention it.'

'And I'm sorry about her. About hurting you.'

Champion kept his mouth grimly closed.

McAdam waited. Then he stood up.

'Come on,' he said. 'I'll buy you a drink.'

Champion remained seated. 'No, thanks.'

McAdam looked at him with exasperation.

'All right. Just one more thing. Don't keep our names out of the case for our sakes. In fact, I insist on giving all the relevant evidence needed.'

'Don't tell me my job.'

McAdam gave him a last look.

'So long, Champ,' he said. 'See you around.' He added: 'You'll have your money back soon. I'm selling as soon as they open on the market on Thursday morning.'

He double-parked his car outside the first public telephone box. It was fiercely hot inside. He dialled the American Mess. It rang and rang and rang.

He got back in the car and drove to the nearest Cable and Wireless office, where he wrote out a cable to Vanessa which read:

> *I am absolutely satisfied the man is innocent stop please repeat please do not publish differently love Jake McAdam*

203

Then he crossed out the word 'absolutely'.

He drove back into the New Territories, and resolutely put the subject of Champion out of his mind. He had plenty else to think about.

He detoured to the Sha-tin Heights Hotel. He sat on the verandah and chain-smoked and drank three beers, staring out over the valley and the hazy sea.

Then, finally, he got up and went slowly to the public telephone.

It seemed unreal. His hand was shaking a little. He dialled the Commissioner of Police on his private line.

'Jake, my boy!' the Old Man said.

'I'd like to claim a favour, sir,' he said. 'I'd like a meeting with you. With the Director of Special Branch present.' He added shakily: 'A political favour, sir.'

TWENTY-FIVE

She received both McAdam's telegram and a telephone message from Bernard Champion at the same time when she got back to the American Mess late that afternoon. She screwed up the telegram and threw it away. Her pulse had tripped when she had seen the name at the end, then had come anger. He had done exactly as she had said he would. She was about to screw up Champion's telephone message too: McAdam had confronted him, Champion had convinced him and now he was going to try to convince her too in case she wrote a story that blew everything up in his face. Well, not bloody likely! She wasn't going to oblige. It was for this very reason that she had decided against confronting the charming roly-poly bastard herself – he would huff and puff and look at her with his big brown soulful eyes and give some cock-and-bull story that could be neither proved nor disproved, especially now Hogan had alerted him. No way. The only good that could come out of it would be her personal satisfaction of telling the bastard what she thought of him. She screwed up the note and was about to toss it into the basket too, when she stopped.

She stood there a full minute, thinking. She only had five days left. She needed more patience. Leave no stone unturned.

She smoothed out the note.

Jake McAdam's footsteps sounded loud to him as he was escorted down the long, familiar corridor of police headquarters by the Commissioner's fresh-faced aide-de-camp. It was almost nine years since he had been here, but the place smelt and felt and sounded the same. He was not remembering those far off days when he was the blue-eyed boy of this police force; what he was numbly remembering now were the bad, haunted, nerve-screaming days. The aide-de-camp led him through the outer offices, and then there was the Old Man, standing up from behind his desk, his grey devil's eyebrows up encouragingly: 'Jake! A long, long time no see.'

'Hullo, sir.' Through the unreality of it he was surprised that the Old Man looked so much older. From an armchair in the corner the Director of Special Branch rose lankily, his hand languidly ready.

'Hullo, Jake.'

'Hullo, Dermot.' He shook hands with him shortly, without warmth. Dermot Wilcox returned to his armchair.

'Sit down,' the Old Man said. 'Can I get you a drink?'

'No thanks.' He did not want to sit either. He would

much rather just stand there and tell them what he wanted and get out. But he sat.

'How've you been keeping, Jake?'

'Pretty well.'

'How're your concrete boats getting on? Most impressive, I thought, when I saw it on television.'

'Fine.' He shifted in his chair, then looked at the older man squarely.

'I want to see Chester Wu,' he said, and it sounded loud in his ears. 'Very urgently.'

Dermot Wilcox murmured: 'I thought so.'

'I take it he's still up there as head of the Public Security Bureau in Kwantung Province?'

Dermot nodded.

McAdam went on shakily: 'I'd also be grateful for certain information, if you can give it to me, but even if you can I still want to see Chester. But, please, gentlemen, no deals. I won't do anything for you in exchange. You owe me a favour.'

The Old Man started to speak and Dermot cut in quietly:

'It might be argued that you owe *us* a favour, Jake. After all, you're still alive. And after all, you only did your duty, as a policeman. And we had trained you in espionage – at considerable public expense, I might add.'

McAdam let it go. He said grimly:

'I could arrange a meeting with Chester myself by going to see the Bank of China. Or the New China News Agency: they'd get hold of him. But it's urgent, and I'm sure you could do it for me immediately through your network. As long as Chester does not know that *you're* arranging it. He must think I'm acting alone.'

Dermot said mildly: 'When do you hope to see him?'

'Tomorrow night. Or as soon thereafter as possible.'

'And where?'

'The same place. On my junk. Or anywhere in China waters. Mirs Bay is best.' He added: 'Same identification signals.'

'And what makes you think he'll come?'

'He'll come. If he thinks I've got something to tell him. In the same way as you gentlemen agreed to see me.'

Dermot drawled, 'We thought you just might want to rejoin the Club.'

'So might Chester.'

The Old Man shifted in his chair. '*Are* you interested, Jake?'

McAdam shook his head. 'No thanks, sir.'

Dermot said: 'We can give you a new cover. Put you in KGB section. One favour deserves another.'

McAdam shook his head. 'I can go to the New China News Agency if you won't help me. It'll just take longer.'

The Old Man said: 'Why the urgency? There's a typhoon coming.'

Dermot Wilcox drawled: 'Because his girl-friend's leaving soon. Oh yes, I know about her and you. Just routine information.'

The Old Man sighed. 'And what exactly do you want to ask Chester Wu, Jake?'

McAdam took a big breath. It seemed unreal.

'I want,' he said, 'to ask about Ying.' He took a deep breath. 'Where she is. What she's doing.'

The Old Man was staring at the centre of his desk. Then he looked enquiringly at the Director of Special Branch. Dermot Wilcox shook his head moodily.

'I wish we knew. The last we heard she was in the People's Liberation Army. Intelligence corps. On the

207

Russian border, I think,' he said.

The Old Man looked back at his hands on the desk. 'Is Dermot right, Jake? This is because your girl-friend's leaving? And you've got to make a decision?'

McAdam nodded. 'I *want* to make a decision,' he said.

Dermot laced his hands together on top of his head.

'We'll help you,' he said. 'We'll arrange it for Friday, tomorrow's too soon. But on one condition. We want to hear everything Chester says. About anything. Including Ying. Is it a deal?'

'Yes. But that's all I'll do.'

The Old Man murmured apologetically: 'I'd like to say again how sorry I am, Jake.'

McAdam said nothing.

Dermot said: 'We'll have to get this moving. There's this typhoon.'

'I can make it,' McAdam said. 'China's not far.'

'I'm glad for your sake you're doing this, Jake,' said the Old Man. 'Chester Wu will probably tell you nothing, *he* doesn't owe you any favours, particularly after all the disinformation you've fed him. But at least you may lay a ghost . . .' He looked at him. 'You must forget the past.'

Thursday dawned riotously red into a cloudless sky. That morning McAdam listened to the seven o'clock weather report on his portable radio at the boat-yard. It was predicted that it would probably be the hottest day in the history of the Colony of Hong Kong.

Typhoon Rose is centred approximately six hundred and fifty miles south-east of Hong Kong and is continuing on her north-west course at a forward speed of about ten knots. If she maintains this speed and course she is expected to come within the four-

hundred mile radius of the colony about this time tomorrow, Friday, whereupon the Number One Typhoon Signal will be raised. If she continues thereafter she may be expected to pass near the Colony sometime on Saturday. This is an advance precautionary warning only, as no typhoon signal has yet been raised, but boat-owners and building constructors are advised to prepare themselves for the task of securing their vessels and scaffolding, and farmers should prepare themselves to secure their standing crops and livestock . . .

He switched off the radio. Tomorrow night. It was cutting it fine, with the typhoon. But he would goddam make the meeting. Then he stripped off his shirt and went grimly to work, until he could go and telephone his stockbroker.

At nine o'clock the stock exchanges opened. They were all crowded and clamorous as usual, the telephones ringing and the jobbers scurrying and signalling and the ticker-tapes clattering and share prices changing on the boards. Almost everything was up on yesterday's prices. But the most important share to be listed was Lucky Man Development Company.

At half past nine McAdam stood sweating in the public call-box of Tai-po village. He had a crumpled copy of the *South China Morning Post* in his hand. He had scanned it feverishly from cover to cover. Then he telephoned his broker.

'Okay, Mac,' the broker barked. 'I've sold them. At fourteen dollars a throw.'

McAdam heaved a sigh of relief. 'Thanks,' he said.

'I still think you're a fool. They'll be up to fifteen by tomorrow. Okay, I got to go now, it's like a mad-house.'

McAdam hung up. He stood there, mouth dry, the

sweat running off him. Examining how he felt.

Forty per cent profit. On two hundred thousand dollars – that was eighty thousand American dollars he had just made. He was rich again. His money worries were all but over. With eighty thousand dollars he could put the boat-yard in business.

And how did he feel?

Not a thing. Not a jot of elation. He had not earned it. He had been lucky. With his friends. And with Herman Choi's reputation as a brilliant business man.

He felt a fraud.

Then he went to the telegraph office. He sent a cable to Vanessa at the American Mess. He did not want to telephone, and hear her voice. It read:

In your own interests do not publish your Lucky Man story until you've seen me at Foreign Correspondents Club on Saturday love Hogan.

TWENTY-SIX

Captain Kurt Marlowe, United States Navy Meteorological Department, was a very handsome man, and he knew it. He was tall and grey-haired, with just the right number of lines around his blue-grey eyes, square-jawed and deeply tanned, and his teeth were white, even and perfect. Kurt Marlowe had had almost every woman he had fancied, except Vanessa Storm Williams. She thought him beautiful. She also thought he was a conceited pain in the ass, and anyway until recently he had been screwing her friend Olga, and Olga had been potty about the man. But she had to admit that on the closer acquaintance afforded by a lunch date at the

Mandarin Hotel, he could be absolutely charming.

Kurt Marlowe was playing it very cool with her today, and not – unless she was badly mistaken – out of any contrition for his past brashness: Kurt Marlowe, with a wealth of experience, was working on the principle that the conquistadorial instinct of beautiful women is best aroused by a display of male indifference. Furthermore, he knew full well that she wanted a favour from him, after having been pretty damn off-hand with him in the past. Kurt Marlowe was playing it charmingly cool. And she just wished that, with the miserable way she was feeling, she did not have to go through this bullshit. She said:

'Do you develop a sixth sense about these phenomena?'

He played with his wineglass.

'Yes, one does. And she's a bad one. I've never seen a typhoon that has hung about so much. Going round and round. She's like a recurring bad dream. Winds of over two hundred knots. Black as ink. And rain like I've never seen. I can't say where she's going, except she's going to hit the South China coast nearby and affect Hong Kong significantly.'

'How do you fly into something like that?'

He loved answering that question. Casually.

'Fly in low. About a hundred feet above sea level. *With* the wind, not against it. The winds are always going in an anti-clockwise direction, in towards the eye. So you edge into them,' he swept his hand in a slow circle, 'keeping the winds on your port tail,' he tapped the heel of his thumb. 'And in you go – and crash bang!' His hand dived and jumped and rolled. 'You're thrown all over the aeroplane, black and blue. And the wings are trying to tear off and the plane's trying to hurl itself into the sea.' He shook his head and gave her his charming grin. 'Hell of a way to earn a living.'

'And then?'

'Have to keep going like that. Trying to force your plane towards the eye. Can't see a thing, of course, you're flying by instruments.'

'How long does that last?'

'Depends on the typhoon. Gets worse all the time because the strongest winds are round the wall of the eye. When you get to the hard wall of the eye all Hell's breaking loose. The wings are really tearing off and the plane's flooded with water. Then suddenly –' he burst both his hands open – 'you are sort of *hurled* out of the wall into the eye . . . And it's dead calm.'

She was fascinated, despite herself. 'And what's it like in the eye?'

'Superb.' He held his hand above his head. 'Great wall of whirling clouds, miles high. Like being in a huge spinning well. A huge stadium of clouds, spinning round and round you. And you're in dead calm. And it's hot. And you can see the sea down there now, because it's usually clear sunshine in the eye. Though it's a sort of hellish glow. And the sea is like a boiling pot. Big waves crashing together and sucked upwards.'

'How close down to the sea do you go?'

'Right down. Twenty feet. Zoom across the top of the waves. To test the air pressure and the temperature down there. And the wind speeds.'

'And then?'

'When we get to the opposite wall –' he tilted his hand upwards – 'climb up. Circling up and up. Testing wind speeds and temperatures and air pressures and density. Up, up, up towards the sun. It's magnificent.'

She was considering the best way of saying it. The best was doubtless to use her charms, but she hated to with this conceited man.

'Could you take me with you on one of these flights?'
Then she gave him a forced seductive smile.

He had been expecting it.

'I could swing it.'

'I'd be terribly grateful. What does it depend on?'

He said: 'No trouble getting you aboard here – I'm
the senior officer. The difficulty would be if we have to
land in the Philippines.'

'Why would we have to do that?'

'If the typhoon keeps heading towards Hong Kong
I have to put down in Manila tomorrow night. Standing
orders. And she *is* heading this way. We'd have to
smuggle you off the plane. And,' he added casually, 'we
would be stranded in a hotel for a couple of nights.'

She noted the 'we'.

'That would be all right.' What the hell, she thought.
If that was the only way she was going to get to fly into
a typhoon. If it hadn't been for Olga, and then McAdam,
and if he hadn't been so conceited she would probably
have screwed him long ago anyway. 'I'd hate you to get
into trouble.'

He looked at her and his grey-blue eyes twinkled.

'Oh, I'm prepared to risk it, if you're game.'

She felt her anger flare but she controlled it. 'Game
for what?' she said sweetly.

'That depends.'

'On what?'

'On you.'

You brash prick, she thought. 'I don't understand . . .'

Kurt Marlowe was also no fool. 'On whether you're
game for a very rough flight,' he smiled evenly.

213

TWENTY-SEVEN

Staff-Sergeant Pang Man-kit was big and fat, and tough and he was a first-rate policeman. He knew Hong Kong in general and his own district in particular like the back of his hand. He knew every crook and their spheres of operations and influence, and those whom he could not get convicted under British law he could more or less control by other means. He was hard on those who crossed him, generous to those who helped him, and he kept his bargains. Staff-Sergeant Pang understood very well that working under the disadvantage of British law, plus the complications of dealing with the devious Chinese mind, the only way to maintain law and order was to live and let live as far as possible while packing a bigger punch, and a crook who owed you a favour was more useful than one who owed you nothing. Throughout his district he was respected, feared and even liked. No major reported crime had ever gone unsolved in his district during his tenure of office.

Staff-Sergeant Pang was furious about the raid on the Oriental International whorehouse. He was not so angry that the 14K Triad Society had abducted a woman into prostitution, nor about their subsequent raid itself, for both events were to be expected from time to time: he had been angry that his information network had failed to tip him off so that he could forestall the raid by leaning on the right people, and now he was more furious that though he had cracked the whip his network had still not come up with any information. He and his men had interrogated hundreds of people, scoured for clues, leant on the underworld for help, but nothing had been forthcoming. It was loss of face. Staff-Sergeant Pang was slipping, losing control of his district. It was a sign of the times. Police authority had been undermined, their prestige sapped by the purges under the Prevention of Bribery Ordinance, and the Triads were stepping into the power vacuum left behind them.

'I must increase the reward, sir,' Staff-Sergeant Pang said angrily.

Superintendent Bernard Champion glared at the file. In the old days Staff-Sergeant Pang would have set the reward without consulting him. The official scale of rewards to be offered by the police for information in this type of offence was set at one thousand Hong Kong dollars, about two hundred American dollars: but in the old days, and not so long ago, Staff-Sergeant Pang would have offered one hundred thousand dollars from his own pocket without batting an eye to make sure his network supplied the information. The trouble with nowadays was that such a reward would indicate that Staff-Sergeant Pang had assets beyond his policeman's salary, which in itself was an offence under the Prevention of Bribery Ordinance.

'How much?' Champion said grimly.

'Two hundred thousand, sir,' Staff-Sergeant Pang said. 'This is a murder.'

'Jesus Christ! You'll have Anti-Corruption Bureau round here in five minutes.'

'They are testing me, sir. If I don't show the Triads that I still have the power, things will get worse.'

'We haven't used any muscle yet. We could knock over some whorehouses to prove our power.'

But Champion knew that was stupid as soon as he said it.

'Too soon,' Staff-Sergeant Pang said. 'We use our power wrong time.'

He knew he was right. It was also a hell of a lot of work. He would get convictions, sure, after tying himself and his men up in court for weeks – and he would make a lot of enemies. And damage the network further – brothel operators were an excellent source of information. A blitzkrieg on the whorehouses to prove who was boss should be kept as a last resort. He snapped:

'You can raise the reward to fifty thousand. That's over ten thousand US dollars, for Chrissake.'

Staff-Sergeant Pang stood there solidly. 'Not enough, sir. I lose face.'

'If Anti-Corruption hears about it you'll lose your job! And your freedom. Fifty thousand is a great deal of money! And,' he held out his finger at him, 'not a trace, do you hear! If this ever comes out I'll deny this conversation ever took place!'

That same Thursday night, at a dinner party in a back room off a seafood restaurant in Tsimshatsui, Staff-Sergeant Pang, surrounded by bodyguards of constables in plain clothes, made his offer to a ranking representative of the 14K Triad Society: he would see to it that the charge would be reduced from murder to manslaughter; he offered two hundred thousand Hong Kong dollars' reward out of his own pocket for information leading to the arrest and conviction, for manslaughter, of four members of the gang who raided the Oriental International Apartment House. Terms of payment: one hundred thousand dollars on arrest of the four hoodlums: fifty thousand on completion of the police investigation file; twenty thousand on committal for trial by the examining magistrate; and fifteen thousand dollars for each plea of guilty to manslaughter in the Supreme Court. Staff-Sergeant Pang also made it very clear what would happen if the first part of the reward were not claimed within twelve hours: no 14K brothel and no 14K gambling operation would do any business for a long, long time.

It was an offer the representative of the 14K Triad Society could not refuse. It was a weighty offer, giving both Staff-Sergeant Pang and the 14K face; only four arrests out of twelve was still a victory for the 14K over the Wo Hop Wo, and manslaughter charges instead of murder were very good terms. The representative of the 14K Triad Society, in accepting, made it clear that Staff-Sergeant Pang had only barely recovered face.

That Thursday night Vanessa looked across Bernard Champion's living room and said quietly:

'I am not going to argue with you, Bernard. If I were sitting on a jury I think I might just, *just* give you the benefit of the doubt. But I am not on a jury. And so? . . . No, I do not believe you.'

Bernard Champion sat slumped in the armchair. His face was grey. He did not know what to say. He had had secret hopes that more would come out of this meeting than convincing her of his innocence. He had known from the moment he saw her again he was still hopelessly in love.

'And will you also write how you came to be in the whorehouse in the first place?'

'Oh yes, Bernard. The best way to get through this life is to have nothing to hide! I will not usurp the function of the court and say you're guilty. I shall simply write what happened. The truth – warts and all. Sue me, Bernard. I refuse to compromise with principle like everybody else here does! It'll be perfectly fair that if I stick my nose into politics I must expect to get it bloodied.'

217

'Politics?'

'That's a figure of speech, but of course it's politics! Money is politics and politics is money! How to get more wealth! And this godawful place is an example par excellence. Corruption is against the law but the law is disregarded because by so doing the whole place runs smoothly and Law and Order is maintained.' She banged her hand on the armrest. 'What a lousy paradox! And that's what everybody's doing in this godforsaken place! Even Hogan – even McAdam, who's so honest he won't turn his company public until he's proved its worth! But what does he do instead to raise his money? – he buys shares in Herman Choi's company. One of the biggest traffickers in human misery in the world, one of the biggest blackguards unhung! And whose money does he borrow? – yours!'

Champion opened his mouth, but she cut in:

'And Government's the same! For years Government knew its civil service was corrupt. But did it crack down? No! Because that *system* worked! So everybody turned a blind eye – and they find it politic to award Herman Choi a knighthood! Because he donates a fraction of his ill-gotten gains to charity. Oh Jesus! – '

She looked at him witheringly. 'I thought you were a man of integrity when I first met you. But by your own admission you permit your staff to abuse the very law that you've sworn by Almighty God to uphold. And where does this graft come from? It's almost *clean* graft, you say, because the law banning prostitution and gambling is stupid. Well *bull*shit, Bernard! Because that graft comes from narcotics too! – '

Champion whispered, 'It does not!'

'Crap, Champion!' she cried angrily. 'Those rackets are controlled by the Triad Societies and the same Triad Societies control narcotics!'

Champion rasped: 'The Triads have branches just like any other organization – entirely separate operations – '

'Big deal! They're still controlled by the same organization. Be a man and face facts, for God's sake. Here – ' She grabbed her bag, snatched out some newspaper pages and thrust them at him. 'Read these! The London *Times*. The heroin traffic. "The Hong Kong Connection," it's called. Triad gangland murders and addicts multiplying by the thousand! Your own countrymen! Amsterdam. Addicts everywhere! Paris – the whole of Europe being rapidly riddled with the stuff! And where does it come from? Not Turkey and Marseilles any more – not the French Connection any more. No, the Hong Kong Connection!' She jabbed a finger at him: '*Your* connection! Your district! Your beat, Bernard! And that's what you – you the policeman, the Christian – the human *being* for Christ's sake – that's what you're permitting your staff to share in. And you're *worse* because you have the authority to stop them.'

Champion was staring at her, white-faced. He said huskily: 'But not the practical power. Because if I did, the information network would break down – our whole leverage over the underworld – '

'Then destroy the underworld, Bernard! Come down with a crack of thunder and knock the living shit out of them. And start a new information system! Be a damn *policeman*!' Suddenly her eyes were brimming with tears.

TWENTY-EIGHT

She got McAdam's telegram when she got back to the American Mess late that night. She read it then screwed it up.

She hardly slept that night. Before dawn on Friday she got up, sponged herself down, and threw a few clothes into a small handgrip. She did not have anything to eat because Kurt Marlowe had warned her not to. Then she left in the sweating sunrise and set off for the Government Information Service offices. She sat in their library, fiercely trying to concentrate on refreshing her memory with their files on Sir Herman Choi and her own copious notes before the interview.

At eleven o'clock, she could stand the tension no longer. She went to the Hilton Coffee Shop and had a bottle of beer and a hot roast beef on rye to steady her nerves. Then she went to the Ladies' Room, tucked her mini-tape recorder into her panties, led the microphone wire up against her skin and fixed the tip of it into a buttonhole on her blouse. She covered the buttonhole with a brooch. Then she set off into the blazing midday to the mansion of Sir Herman Choi.

It was hard to believe. 'Miss Williams – how nice to see you! But where're your pigeons? Aha-ha-ha!' She had laughed too. He was so charming, his English so English (he *must* have taken elocution lessons), his house so elegantly, tastefully Victorian, his manners so gentlemanly it was hard to believe that she was in the presence of a ruthless trafficker in human misery and degradation. At least with the Mafia gents, those she had met, you *felt* their ruthlessness like you feel the catness of a cat, and even their clothes seemed to give them away: but with Sir Herman Choi? Even the electronically-operated iron front gate had been casually ajar. No guard dogs, no heavies, just a cat sitting in the sun on the path grooming itself. A beaming amah who had answered her knock on the front door. And the young men she had seen with him at the building site and every other time had turned out to be so quietly, almost self-effacingly courteous, so immaculately groomed in dark suits, that it had been almost impossible to believe they were bullet-proof-vested bodyguards. And here she was now sitting in the registered offices of the Society for the Blind and Physically Handicapped (there had been a big brass plaque on the front gate), while the two bodyguards in the general office studiously typed and worked away at the society's philanthropic business. She had to work on it to keep her mind mean. He was saying:

'We're trying to extend our activities from the physically handicapped to the youth as well. We'd like to be involved in things like Forward Bound, because it seems to us that in this cut-throat society the youth are in as much need of vocational guidance as the physically handicapped – probably more so, because of our peculiar social problems of congestion and the limited future of the colony. And there's a big difference between what these youngsters want and what they're likely to get. We Chinese *all* aspire to being white-collar workers, Miss Williams – whereas the colony's raison d'être is industry. They *need* our help.'

Beautiful, she thought. She said earnestly:

'Is it true, Sir Herman, that dope peddlers are actually selling drugs to school children outside the very school gates?'

Sir Herman Choi crossed his elegant legs and sighed.

'Unfortunately it is. I think you may have an exaggerated view of the *size* of the problem, but it is certainly true that that is happening in no small measure. Which – ' he spread his hands – 'is another reason for the youth needing our help. The devil finds work for idle hands, the saying goes. And what have these youngsters got once the school-bell rings? Where are their playing fields? I feel it's up to privileged people, and organizations like mine, to help them.'

Good. She knew exactly how she was going to write her story now. She was longing to slip the knife into him. But she had to provoke him, goad him into saying something indiscreet.

'Can't your organization help protect the youth from the predations of the Triad Societies?'

He spread his hands again.

'Alas, Miss Williams, even the police seem unable to protect them from the Triads. All my organization can do is offer youth some kind of alternative to Triad membership.'

'Moral leadership?' she said sweetly.

'Exactly.' He looked at her, then glanced regretfully at his watch. She said quickly:

'Just a couple more questions, Sir Herman, please . . .' She gave him her dazzling smile, and he smiled charmingly.

'First, are you a religious person, Sir Herman?'

He looked mildly amused.

'I am a baptized Christian. We Chinese are not generally renowned for our Christian piety. We are really a rather pragmatic race, who believe traditionally in many gods. And our code of conduct is still very Confucian. Should we say I am a Christo-Confucian?'

'Combining the best of both worlds?'

'I try to,' Sir Herman Choi said modestly.

Good quote. She said:

'Can you tell me a bit about your chairmanship of the board of directors of Lucky Man Development Company, which has just gone public . . . ?'

Sir Herman Choi looked mildly surprised. 'It is only one of many companies in which I am involved, Miss Williams.'

She said, 'Yes, but it's your latest baby, isn't it? The one you've been slowly building up for years, ever since you were a young man starting with nothing. It's such a success story in itself, it sums up your whole successful life – it's almost the American Dream. My readers will be fascinated.' She looked at him brightly. 'Oh I know all about you, Sir Herman, I've done my homework!'

He looked amused and flattered. 'Ask away, Miss Williams.'

'First of all, do you believe in *fung shui*, Sir Herman? The necessity to live in harmony with wind and water, to bring luck?'

He looked surprised, then laughed.

'Show me the Chinese who doesn't, Miss Williams! In his heart of hearts, no matter how cynically modern he is. Once a Chinese, always a Chinese; you can't expect too much of us. I'll even bet old Mao Tse-tung believed in *fung shui*. Why?'

'Well,' she said earnestly, 'I've read up a bit about *fung shui*, and it seems to me that where your company is building that massive new apartment block in Midlevels, it has excellent *fung shui*.'

Sir Herman Choi smiled. 'Oh yes, so they say. It should be a good spot to live.' He added: 'We bought that site years ago, before Midlevels was so congested.'

'You've got the magnificent view of the water, bounded by those two islands with mountains containing sleeping dragons. And equally important, the road up to the site is hairpin bends, which is excellent because Evil can only travel in straight lines?'

He smiled. 'So they say, true.'

She smiled, then said: 'Isn't it rather a shame that with all that excellent *fung shui*, you had to go and ruin it all by breaking a dragon's back when your bulldozers gouged out that huge terrace?'

He put an amused puzzlement on his face.

'I don't follow you, Miss Williams.'

She was surprised but delighted with his reaction. 'You see I notice that you've built that high wooden hoarding around the site so nobody can see in, except with difficulty. But I peeped in one fine day, and saw that the cliff-face which your bulldozers had cut was *red* clay. And anybody who knows anything about *fung shui* will tell you that when you cut a mountain and find red clay or soil, it means that you have cut a dragon's back. And that is terrible *fung shui*. Awful bad luck. And I wondered if you had built that wooden hoarding around the site to conceal the red soil of the cliff from prospective purchasers who would be frightened by the bad *fung shui*.'

'Miss Williams, you're not thinking of publishing such a ridiculous story, are you?'

It *did* sound rather ridiculous. 'Why not, Sir Herman, if it's true?'

He said quietly: 'Because it's *not* true, Miss Williams.' He waved his hand. 'Not just the *fung shui* – the whole story's ridiculous. Because that terrace is cut into solid rock.'

She opened her mouth to protest, then she stared at him. As the truth dawned on her.

'I see . . .'

And she wanted to slap herself on the forehead and jump for joy. *She had found it!* The chink in Sir Herman Choi's armour had been staring her in the face!

224

'I see. Solid rock. Of course, it would have to be, wouldn't it? Silly me.'

Sir Herman Choi smiled frostily. 'I'm afraid so.' He watched her.

She put on a straight earnest face. 'Because it's common knowledge that Midlevels is an area that has a lot of landslides.' She added hastily, 'I'm only quoting what I've read in newspapers, of course. But apparently the mountain slope is made up of jumbled soil and granite, and when the heavy rains come the weight of the buildings is sometimes too much for the mountain slope and the landslides occur.'

Sir Herman Choi nodded warily. 'Correct.'

'Now . . . I take it you've investigated this?'

He looked at her hard. 'Miss Williams – I am not an architect, I'm only a humble businessman. But I can assure you that this danger *has* been investigated, goodness gracious me!'

'But as Chairman of the Board, have you *personally* satisfied yourself there is no such danger?'

'Of course I have! Miss Williams, I sincerely hope that you aren't thinking of publishing any alarmist theories like that, which would be highly libellous and enormously injurious to the company.'

She pretended to be embarrassed by the rebuke, then went on:

'Have you inspected the site, Sir Herman – and seen the solid rock?'

Sir Herman Choi knew now that she was definitely a wolf in sheep's clothing: but he kept his cool.

'Miss Williams,' he smiled frostily, with dignity, 'I accept the certificates of my professional advisers in such matters. I have seen the site. Seen it, yes – inspected it, no.'

'And how much solid rock did you see, Sir Herman?'

He looked theatrically at his watch.

'Miss Williams. I resent your manner. But to answer your question: I don't recall, for the simple reason that the cliff-face was already concreted over. And now, Miss Williams – ' he stood up – 'I'm afraid I must ask you to leave.'

She said icily:

'Sir Herman, you visited the site three Tuesdays ago – and the cliff-face had only been partly concreted over. And the cliff was clearly not solid rock – it was red soil! I know because I saw it and I also saw *you* there!'

He said slowly, furiously: 'Miss Williams, I repeat, I am not a construction engineer. I believe the word of my architects and not the wild allegations of an insolent young foreign journalist! Now will you kindly leave?'

She sat on. 'In short, that is why Lucky Man is going to *sell* those apartments instead of *renting* them – to pass the risks on to the poor innocent purchasers! And that is why you put that big wooden hoarding round the site – and concreted the cliff-face so hastily!'

He clenched his fists at his side and his voice shook. 'If you print one word of these spurious allegations – '

She cut in calmly, 'I know very well what you are, Herman Choi, I've thoroughly checked you out! You're one of the world's biggest traffickers in narcotics – you're one of the world's biggest dealers in human misery and death! You're also one of the leaders of the 14K Triad Society! – '

'*Get out of my house!*'

' – which specializes in international narcotics traffic and prostitution and gambling! London, Amsterdam, Los Angeles, New York – *you* are the Hong Kong Connection! – '

'*Get out!*' he shouted.

She smiled brightly. 'I hope for an answer first, Sir Herman.'

'*I deny it!*'

'Knight of the Realm. All his charitable works – the Christo-Confucian who wants to help the youth – '

'*If you don't get out I'll throw you out!*'

'I'll print that too,' she said sweetly. 'And your denial of course.' She picked up her bag and stood up.

Sir Herman Choi got himself back under control. He hissed: 'You print one word of those libellous allegations and you'll regret it!'

'What'll you do, Sir Herman? Sue my newspaper? The news media of the world are very interested in the Hong Kong narcotics connection and we will have a lovely time proving my allegations are *true*. And proving beyond all doubt that that Lucky Man apartment block of yours is *not* built on solid rock! Because that wall would be very easy to chip away!'

She saw the fear flash across his Oriental face and she felt a thrill.

'Good day, Sir Herman!' She turned on her heel theatrically.

He did not move.

'There are other kinds of regret than losing a libel action, Miss Williams.'

She felt her pulse trip in fear for the first time. She stopped. But she could not show she was afraid, she had to goad him – goad him into saying something incriminating. She turned slowly.

'I beg your pardon?'

'There are more ways of killing a cat than stuffing its throat with libel writs.'

'Please be more specific. I always believed the pen was mightier than the sword, you see.'

Sir Herman Choi suddenly strode to the wall and jabbed a button. Instantly the door opened. One of the Chinese men stepped into the room. He looked at her with hooded eyes.

'Ah, the heavies. I was wondering where they were.'

'Drive Miss Williams back to her apartment.'

'Not bloody likely! If you think I'm getting into a car with one of your thugs you've got another think coming!'

She walked past the Chinese man. She was shaking; she had to control herself. She heard Sir Herman Choi snap something in Cantonese, then the footsteps coming behind her, and she broke into a run. She ran, panic-stricken, high heels clattering, through the general office and down the wide marble corridor for the front door. She looked wildly over her shoulder, and the man was striding after her with Sir Herman Choi behind him. She flung herself at the door, grabbed at the lock, wrenched the bolt back and pulled at the door, and it jerked on the chain. She cried out and grabbed at the chain, and the man and Sir Herman Choi were standing right there, smiling at her.

She stared at them, wild-eyed, panting. Sir Herman Choi smiled:

'The pen is mightier than the sword, Miss Williams? I have never seen a pen in such disarray.'

Her fingers shakily pulled the chain off its latch. She swung the door against her hip – outside was the short flight of steps to the big ornate iron gate. Sir Herman Choi stared at her a moment, then he said quietly in Cantonese to the man:

'Later.'

Then he said in English:

'This conversation never took place, Miss Williams.'

The man stood there with his arms hanging loosely at his sides, looking at her through narrowed eyes. She fumbled the door open and stepped through the doorway and down the steps out into the sunshine. Down the path to the open gate. Then she turned to Sir Herman Choi.

'The conversation, Sir Herman, is recorded verbatim on my tape recorder!'

And she flung herself through the gate and Sir Herman snapped in Cantonese:

'Get it!'

She ran away from the gate, and the man bounded down the steps after her. He charged through the gate as she was running down the street in her high heels. She swung around wildly and swiped her handgrip at him, lashing it across the side of his head, and he grabbed as it hit him and wrenched it off her wrist. She reeled round and ran on wildly down the residential street, gasping.

She ran flat out, hair flying, just carrying her handbag, then she saw a taxi at the intersection at the bottom of the street. She ran, waving her hand, yelling, and it stopped.

She clattered to a halt against it, and looked back over her shoulder. The man was gone. She swept her hair off her face and flung open the door. She sprawled across the seat and panted:

'Airport . . .!'

She lay there, sprawled, gasping. Then her hand went down to her stomach and she felt the little tape recorder.

She heaved herself up and looked through the rear window. She could not tell if any of the vehicles were following her.

The taxi pulled up at Kai Tak International Airport. She piled out and paid. Then she hurried into the big building. It was crowded, tourists flooding to get out before the typhoon, the tannoys rasping. She hurried, dishevelled, sweating, through the crowds, towards the Information Counter. She saw Kurt Marlowe waiting there, from some distance. His face lit up in relief when he spotted her and he came striding towards her in his uniform. 'Hi there! Where's your bag?'

'Lost it,' she panted. 'Listen, I've got to make an urgent phone call, where's a box?'

'Over there.'

She hurried to the booth, snatched up the receiver and dialled the Foreign Correspondents' Club.

'Mr Ball please.'

A voice came on. 'Yes?' it barked.

'Whacker? Vanessa. Have you got your tape recorder?'

' 'Course I got my tape recorder.'

'Hook it up to the telephone. It's urgent. It's a big story.'

'It better be . . . Okay.'

'Whacker, you got to do me a favour, I'm leaving in a few minutes to fly into this typhoon, then the Philippines. I'm going to dictate a story. For Christ's sake transcribe it for me and edit it – it's worth a case of whisky to you. Okay?'

'Must be some story,' Whacker Ball growled. 'If it's that good I'll publish it myself. Who's it for?'

'The *South China Morning Post*. The editor's agreed to publish something as soon as he can. Probably Monday. Or as soon thereafter as he's got space. Okay?'

'Okay. I suppose.'

'But, Whacker? – have you got any shares in Lucky Man?'

'Some. I was lucky, lady, real lucky. Aha – ha – ha.'

'Well, if you're smart you'll get rid of them. You'll hear why now.'

PART IX

It was blinding, hazy, sunshine hot; but way over there beyond the horizon the sky was black for hundreds of miles, and the black winds were roaring at two hundred knots, and the sea was howling, great waves crashing and flying in galloping canyons. And beneath the great spiralling eye of the typhoon, the sea was sucked upwards into a seething dome, a hundred and fifty miles wide, billions of tons of crashing waves. And from way, way up, high above the earth in the brilliant sunshine where the weather satellite was orbiting, taking photographs, the typhoon called Rose was a silent, gigantic, slowly-moving, writhing whirlpool, making its way across the curvature of the earth.

For over thirty days that picture had been coming through on the recording equipment of observatories round the world – Manila, Saigon, Hong Kong, Peking, Taipei, Tokyo, Guam. For thirty days they watched her at the Royal Hong Kong Observatory, digesting and collating data about her from satellites, ships, aircraft, and from the American reconnaissance aircraft which flew into the middle of her almost every day. For twenty-seven of those days she had moved erratically, twisting, turning, looping, north-west, south-west, south-east, doubling back, massively, slowly; but for the last five days she had been turned towards Hong Kong.

TWENTY-NINE

From five thousand feet up and a hundred miles away she did not look like the satellite photographs. Vanessa sat behind Kurt Marlowe in the cockpit of the United States Navy aircraft, and said into her tape recorder above the roar of the engines:

'Just a vast blackness that blots out the whole sky ahead, the whole horizon. You cannot see where it begins and ends . . . awe-inspiring. And ominous.'

She was not sure how much the tape recorder was picking up. She was wearing a flying helmet, with earphones and mouthpiece that enabled everybody to speak to and hear each other, but she had switched hers off to make the note. She saw Kurt Marlowe's mouth moving, and she switched in and heard him saying:

' – fifteen hundred thirty-five hours, our speed two hundred and fifty knots, we're encountering the first real winds now on port tail, approximately forty knots.'

She was wearing a flying suit, with a lifejacket on top. She was strapped tight into her seat around her waist, with another set of straps across her shoulders and breast. Next to Kurt Marlowe sat the co-pilot, who had the unlikely name of Fairweather. Next to her, across the flight-deck aisle, sat the radio operator, and behind him the navigator. Aft, seated at portholes just behind each wing, sat the two observers, watching the engines. They had taken her aback – God, if you need a guy to tell you your engines are knocked out . . .

The crew looked young and all-American-boy naïve, with the exception of Big-wheel Kurt Marlowe. She had to admit that he did look exceedingly dashing. At this moment he was the most important man in her life, because he was the one who was going to get her out of this machine alive, and that gave him an importance that was almost sexual.

She stared through the perspex at the vast black violence ahead, and at the sea down there, blue-black in the afternoon sun, white caps flying off the swells; she tried to notice everything and to live every moment of it. She had to concentrate hard to bring her mind back from her encounter with Sir Herman Choi – and from a small bay in Tolo Sound. The radio operator spoke over the intercom:

'Latest report from Hong Kong. She's slowed right down again.'

Kurt Marlowe said over the intercom:

'Descending to five hundred feet.'

The nose began to turn downwards, and she felt herself straining against it. She forced herself to relax and leaned forward to look. The sea was looming up at them, nearer and nearer. The sun was left behind, the light was turning grey. The aircraft nosed down, lower and lower, and now she could see the spray flying in thick, white, hurtling sheets across the grey-black sea, and she could make out the height of the swells. And now the lashing sea was coming up, up, up to meet them, then the nose levelled out, and Kurt Marlowe's casual drawl came over:

'Five hundred feet. Our speed one hundred and fifty knots, wind speed eighty-odd knots on our port tail. Height of the swells fifty-odd feet at present.'

Ahead was only dense black through the grey light. He half turned his head and said to Vanessa over the intercom:

'We'll be cutting back our speed soon. We'll keep the winds on our portside tail and we'll be curving in towards the eye with them. Anti-clockwise.'

She said, leaning forward:

'How long before we get into that black stuff ahead?'

'Not long. These winds here are just the outside edge; they're getting stronger every minute. She's a bad one. Are you scared?'

'Are you?'

He grinned: 'Not yet.'

She looked around at the rest of the crew. They were all grinning at her. But they looked pale and nervous behind their smiles. 'What do you mean, "Not yet"?'

'I'm shit-scared every time. I really should have joined the infantry.'

She did not like hearing him talk like that, but for the first time she almost liked him.

Fifteen minutes later she felt the winds really hit them hard. Outside the perspex it was dark grey and the sea down there was flying black and white. The winds hit the aircraft on her portside tail and the machine lurched sideways and down towards the black sea, and Kurt Marlowe pulled on the controls and the whole cabin strained about Vanessa and the straps wrenched at her guts and her head was flung sideways. The aircraft lurched and dived, and then roared up again, and the blackness out there plunged in front of her eyes, and through the shock of it she heard Kurt Marlowe say:

'Getting into it now.'

The aircraft roared into the blackness. The howling walls of winds and hammering rain hurtled the aircraft along with its engines screaming, the big wings leaping and bucking. It staggered and shook and fell, and she was wrenched about in her seat; her head jolted and jerked, her stomach heaved. The aircraft staggered and fell again and screamed upwards again, and the whole crew were thrown against their safety straps, clutching at their instruments. The rain smashed against the perspex and came spurting into the cabin at the joints, the instrument panel was leaping in front of her eyes, her stomach was heaving against her ribs and Kurt Marlowe was rasping into his mouthpiece:

'Windspeeds one hundred and ninety knots – thick driving rain – visibility nil – estimated radial distance from the eye forty-five miles –'

She grabbed for the plastic bag and tried to get it up to her mouth and her hand shot one way and her head flew the other, and she threw her head towards the bag and out it came, her corned beef on rye and San Miguel beer in a big choking eruption.

THIRTY

In Hong Kong it was bright, blue, blazing hot, and the air was motionless. From high places in the Colony the Number One signal showed, the big black letter T and the three bright lights, the standby alert. It was broadcast across the Colony by government and commercial radio and television in English and Cantonese:

Attention! Attention! The Number One Typhoon Signal has been raised by the Royal Hong Kong Observatory. Typhoon Rose is situated approximately three hundred and ninety miles south-east of Hong Kong. She is following a due north-westerly track at a forward speed of ten knots. If she maintains her present course and speed she will enter the

Colony's waters at about noon tomorrow, Saturday. However, strong winds can be expected from the south and south-east within the next twelve hours.

The last reports from shipping and reconnaissance aircraft indicate wind speeds near the eye in excess of two hundred knots. Rainbands within one hundred miles of the eye are strongly formed and heavy rainfall can be expected, which may cause severe flooding, landslides and rockfalls. Tide heights can be expected to rise from ten to thirty feet above the normal high tide levels with substantial flooding in low-lying areas.

All reports and observations indicate a continued intensification of this typhoon, and there is no reason to suppose that she will not continue on her present course.

But out in the harbour, packed with ships and junks and ferries and cargo-lighters and sampans, and down in those narrow teeming streets of shops and banks and godowns and money-changers and bars and tenements and resettlement blocks and squatter shacks cut into the steep jungled mountainsides – down there that Friday afternoon it was business as usual.

In Number Three Court of Causeway Bay Magistracy the magistrate was conducting the committal proceedings in the case of Regina versus Ong Man-kit and three others, charged in respect of the raid on the Oriental International Apartment House. Superintendent Bernard Champion sat next to the police inspector who was the prosecutor. At the back of the court sat Staff-Sergeant Pang. On other seats sat the other witnesses: the Mama-san, some of the prostitutes, and Bill Lu, the owner. They had all given their evidence. Beside them sat various members of the 14K Triad Society, listening.

Committal proceedings are only a preparatory examination of the evidence of the witnesses, at the end of which the charge is put to the accused, whereupon the magistrate decides whether or not to send them to the Supreme Court for trial.

The prosecuting inspector said:

'I close the case for the Crown, your worship. May charges of manslaughter be put to the accused.'

He handed the prepared typed charges to the orderly, who handed one up to the magistrate and one copy to each accused. The interpreter began to translate the charge aloud to each of them. Then he turned to the magistrate and said:

'Each defendant understands the charge, your worship.'

The magistrate sat forward. 'Well, there's something *I* don't understand, Mr Prosecutor,' he said.

'Yes, your worship?' The prosecutor stood up.

'I don't understand why on earth you are only charging the accused with manslaughter,' the magistrate said. 'My view of the facts and the law is that the charge should be murder.'

Superintendent Bernard Champion, sitting beside the prosecutor, felt his stomach contract. The prosecuting police inspector stood there, looking helpless.

'I am only following instructions, your worship,' he said. Then he added: 'None of the accused struck the deceased. None of them pushed her out of the window, she jumped by herself.'

The magistrate snapped: 'She did not jump by herself – of her own volition! She was forced to do so to escape the accused gang who were brandishing murderous weapons and who looked like murdering her! For the purposes of the law she was forced to jump – *by the accused.*'

The prosecutor mumbled: 'As your worship

pleases . . .' Bernard Champion sat white-faced. Staff-Sergeant Pang glanced across the gallery at the 14K man. The man glared at him, then narrowed his eyes. The four accused in the dock had not understood the English.

The magistrate was writing on the charge. Then he looked up and said:

'Mr interpreter, tell the accused that I am amending the charge to murder. It now reads as follows: " . . . that they did, upon the same date, and at or near the Oriental International Apartment House in Hong Kong, wrongfully and unlawfully and maliciously kill and murder Chiang Mei-ling, contrary to Common Law." Then formally read that charge to each one of them again.'

The interpreter said 'As your worship pleases.'

He started to read the new charges to the accused. Bernard Champion sat waiting for the reaction. As the interpreter read, incredulity came into the faces of the four accused. Then the first one's face contorted in outrage.

'Protest!' he shouted.

The magistrate looked up.

'Behave yourself, young man!'

The accused pointed at Staff-Sergeant Pang and shouted desperately at the magistrate:

'He made a deal with the 14K! He paid two hundred thousand dollars for us to be arrested if we pleaded guilty to manslaughter only! He promised not murder! Now he breaks his deal!'

The magistrate stared at the accused, astonished, then he picked up his pen and said quietly:

'Say all that again slowly . . .'

Fifteen miles away, the other side of the Mountains of Nine Dragons, Jake McAdam and Wong Ting-tak were feverishly securing the last sheets of asbestos on to the roof of the new boat shed. If they did not get it on in time the winds would rip the rest of the roof off and two hundred sacks of cement would be swamped with the lashing rain. They still had to finish emplacing the sliding doors in the entrance. The concrete junk lay moored at the end of the jetty, ready.

It was mid-afternoon when the roof was finished, and the big sliding doors were in position. They stood, panting, sweating, looking at it. But he did not feel elation.

He took a bottle of whisky and the portable radio. There was beer and water and hard rations on the junk. He said to Wong:

'I'll be back early tomorrow morning, at sunrise; be sure to be here. Then you will have to take the boat to the typhoon shelter.'

He turned and walked down to the jetty and climbed aboard the junk. He ground the engine over, released the decompressor, and the big diesel took sweetly and loudly. He nodded, and Wong cast off the two shore-lines from the jetty. Then McAdam shoved the gear lever into forward, opened the throttle, and the junk pulled away from the jetty. He turned the wheel and the bows surged round, to the mouth of the little bay.

The junk went chugging up Tolo Sound towards the open sea. He had quite a long way to go before night through the many islands, before he came to Kat O Chau island, and the China waters of Mirs Bay beyond.

The vast horizon was hazy blue and the wind blowing on his sweating chest was warm. On the horizon he could see many junks, coming in towards Hong Kong already, running from the typhoon.

Ten miles away, over the Mountains of Nine Dragons, the Red Rod of the 14K Triad Society received certain instructions through a messenger of Sir Herman Choi.

239

The instructions needed no discussion. The only question was how the orders should be carried out, and that was his decision alone, for the Red Rod was the expert in matters of murder.

But certain aspects of the job were immediately apparent: there was a typhoon coming, and if the killing could be made to look like the typhoon's work, so much the better. Drowning was the obvious possibility. Being hit on the head by a heavy flying object was another. Being buried alive was another. Or falling from a big height, as from a verandah, or down a stair-well. Strangling, knifing, or shooting should not be used for such a death could not be attributed to a typhoon.

But it was urgent. His instructions were that the woman would most likely be found either at an apartment known as the American Mess in Hillside Road of Midlevels district, or at the apartment of one McAdam, an ex-policeman, in Dragon Court, also in Hillside Road.

The murder would have to be carried out by stealth, and not by hit-and-run. The killer would have to be expert at picking locks, as well as an expert in accidental deaths.

The other part of the instructions which the Red Rod of the 14K Triad Society received was much more simple to execute. It was that nothing was to be published in the English language press about Sir Herman Choi or the Lucky Man Development Company until further notice.

That was easy to arrange. The 14K had Triad members amongst the typesetters of both the *South China Morning Post* and the *China Mail*, and men who could exercise control over the printers' union and call a strike on some pretext or other.

THIRTY-ONE

For another hour the aircraft flew around the outside of the eye, fighting further and further inwards; for another hour the plane roared and screamed and bucked and plunged, with the winds getting fiercer and fiercer; for one more hour Vanessa clutched her seat and did not hear the things the crew were shouting to each other, and she did not care, all she wanted was to die: then suddenly, when the black winds were at their maniacal fiercest, the aircraft burst brokenly through the roaring wall of wind, and suddenly the blackness was gone and the cockpit was flooded with eerie sunshine and the aircraft subsided into smoothness.

'We're there,' she heard Kurt Marlowe rasp.

The eye.

She sat slumped in her seat, held up by the straps, the sweat running off her in a sheen, her lipstick smudged, and the taste of vomit in her mouth. She stared at the splendour in front of her – the magnificence, the great walled arena of black clouds, fifty miles in diameter, bathed in sunshine. The black cloud-banks spiralled up, up, like vast tiers of seats, and they looked stationary in the sudden deafening tranquillity. The light was golden-grey and silver. The engines were a lilting celestial drone. Then Kurt Marlowe was rasping over the intercom:

'Report wind speeds round the eye of over two hundred knots. Barometric pressure in the eye still falling . . .'

She looked dazedly around at the rest of the crew. The radio officer's eyes were red from vomiting and he had a big bruise over his eye. His right hand was strapped to his instrument desk. The navigator grinned at her ruefully. Kurt Marlowe said:

'You all right, darlin'?'

She was so relieved she could have kissed him.

'Fine.' She breathed deep and quivered. 'What's the significance of the barometric pressure still falling?'

'The typhoon is still intensifying.'

Then he nosed the aircraft downwards, and she saw the sea again, just five hundred feet down below. It was a vast cauldron, grey spray and froth flying off the crests, and the troughs were seething from all directions and clashing together. Marlowe took the aircraft low over the leaping pinnacles of sea, taking the meteorological readings, while the radio officer was sending the information back to Hong Kong. They droned across the vast arena, flying low over the sea round the edge of the eye, the winds like a black wall on the portside wingtip. Right the way round the walls the aircraft flew, then began to climb.

Round and round and upwards and upwards, a tiny battered flying machine against the roaring walls of wind: way up to the very top it flew, and now the eye of the typhoon was a vast black well below them. The sun shone eerily down the great black well-shaft; and the barometric pressure was still falling, the forward speed had increased and the whole roaring mass was still heading north-west, straight towards Hong Kong. For two hours the aircraft flew round the well of the typhoon, and all the time Vanessa was muttering into her tape recorder and taking photographs, and dreading when it was time to fly out again.

Kurt Marlowe said over the intercom:

'Give me a bearing for Manila.'

Vanessa sat, strapped in her seat, sweating, her hair sticking to her temples and neck, her empty stomach squirming, staring with dread at the black wall ahead across the leaping sea, and she did not care that she had to spend the night in the bed of Kurt Marlowe in Manila; all she cared about in the whole world was that she lived through the next two hours.

The black wall was looming closer and closer, stretching way up to the top of sky, and now the edge of it was only five hundred yards ahead, now four hundred, three hundred, and the aircraft turned. It turned its starboard wing to the black wall, and now she could see it like hurtling smoke, and she sat braced in her seat, every muscle tense and her knuckles white: the aircraft roared at the blackness, fifty, forty, thirty, twenty yards off, then the starboard wingtip disappeared into it. In an instant the whole wing had disappeared, the whole machine jolted, her head flew forward and then blackness roared over the perspex.

And the vast arena of the eye was empty again.

The sun was going down over Hong Kong, riotously red.

All across the horizon there were the navigation lights of junks coming in, to get to the typhoon shelters ahead of the rush. In the harbour big ships were getting ready to move to typhoon buoys, and those that could not get them were getting ready to put out to deep sea ahead of the typhoon to ride out the storm. They would be loading and unloading cargo all night, the lighters clustered around them. Shopkeepers were beginning to board up their windows. But in the bars and restaurants and clubs and brothels it was still business as usual.

A hundred miles away, south-east over the South China Sea, the Thai fishing trawler from Bangkok was ploughing full throttle towards Hong Kong with its cargo of bales of black raw opium. It was doing twelve knots, about the same forward speed as the typhoon which was only one hundred and fifty miles behind it.

A professional assassin always sticks to his preferred method of killing. The strangler will not use a knife, the knife-artist will not shoot, the gunman will not bludgeon to death. But the trick-killer is the most versatile of all. He studies his victim's circumstances in as much time as he is allowed, and then uses any effective tactic permitted by his instructions. The Triad man who was sent to murder Vanessa Storm Williams was a very good trick-killer, one who specialized in making the death look like misadventure.

As the sun was going down that Friday evening, the killer entered a public telephone box at the bottom of Hillside Road. He was short and lean and very strong, and his face was wide and yet also lean, his eyes flat and cold. But he was wearing a business suit and at a glance he looked like any Chinese white-collar worker returning home. He put some coins in the slot and dialled the number of the American Mess. It rang a few moments, then the amah answered.

'*Wei?*'

'Is Miss Williams there, please?'

'Nobody here.'

'What time are you expecting her home?'

'Hah?'

'What time she come back?'

'All missies come back different time.'

'Do you know where she is?'

'Tonight Friday, always party, you phone FCC.'

'Where?'

'I give you number.'

The amah consulted a list on the wall and then slowly read him the telephone number of the Foreign

Correspondents Club.

'Thank you,' the man said.

Then he dialled McAdam's apartment in Dragon Court.

The telephone rang and rang in the empty apartment.

Then he telephoned a third number. It was answered promptly. This time he spoke in Cantonese.

'My face is pale, but my hands will be red.'

Then he hung up.

He walked up Hillside Road towards Dragon Court in the early darkness. Another man came up a ladder street, and nodded to him casually.

The second man went on into the gathering darkness. He made his way to the old-fashioned apartment block in which was the American Mess. He climbed the stairs to the third floor, inspected the lock on the front door, then the back door. Both were simple. Then he investigated the steps leading up to the rooftop. From the corner of the steps he had an excellent, concealed view of both the front and back doors. He walked over the dark rooftop and looked down on to the big open verandah below. A long drop, but easy enough to climb back up. He marked down the corner of the rooftop steps as the place where he would settle down and wait, once he had searched the apartment for the tape.

The first man walked casually into the foyer of Dragon Court and summoned the elevator. He got out at the sixth floor.

The sixth-floor foyer was empty. He tried the door. It was locked. Then he dropped to one knee and took an instrument out of his pocket, inserted it into the keyhole and delicately turned it, listening carefully. The lock slid open. He stood up, wiped the door handle with a handkerchief, pulled on gloves, entered the apartment

245

and closed the door behind him.

He went quickly, silently through the dark apartment, checking it out and looking for the best place to hide. Then he saw the spiral staircase.

He climbed cautiously up it. He tried the door. He listened intently. Then he picked the lock.

The door swung open. He stared inside. A thin smile crossed his face. It was an absolutely ideal place to wait. It even had its own front door, opening on to the seventh-floor foyer.

As the last of the sun went down, Jake McAdam's junk chugged into the tranquillity of Double Haven. It was a beautiful stretch of deserted water, surrounded by steep green islands. About two miles ahead, around the point, was the village of Shataukok. Down the middle of Shataukok ran a road called Chung-Ying Street, which means China-England Street, and on one side stood the Union Jack and on the other the red flag of China with the five gold stars. It was the official border between the British Crown Colony of Hong Kong and the People's Republic of China, and this was the only place where no fence separated the two countries.

About a mile ahead was the steep ridged island of Kat O Chau. McAdam's face was gaunt as he steamed towards it across Double Haven. It was the first time he had been to this beautiful, deserted place in eight long years, and the last time it had been to meet Chester Wu, whom he was going to meet now.

He looked at the island in the sunset. Once upon a time, a long time ago, he had come here with her, and they had planted their two pine trees up on top of that ridge.

He looked at his watch, then cut his engines, and just drifted. It was suddenly very quiet, magnificently still in

246

the hot sunset. He had an hour and a half to wait before he had to sail round that island and out into China waters.

It was unreal, being here again. And hauntingly real. But now he was here he did not want to think about it, to remember and feel and find out, which was the very thing he had come here for. And he did not want to look for those two pine trees against the sunset.

He uncorked the bottle of whisky, and took a big swallow. The liquor burned down inside him.

All right, he thought.

And he picked up his binoculars. He swung them up to the ridge of the island in the sunset, and he looked for them, and his eyes were burning. Then he found them.

There they stood, side by side in silhouette against the sunset. As if they were on fire, black against the vast glowing red. Side by side, and their outstretched branches were just touching.

THIRTY-TWO

Six hundred miles away, Vanessa walked unsteadily through Manila International Airport towards the ladies' toilets. She could still hear the roaring of the engines in her ears and the marble floor was heaving up and down. She was pale, and she knew she looked like death, and apart from the fact that she knew she felt terrible, she felt marvellous. She did not care what she looked like, nor even that she had peed in her pants and that it showed loud and clear – she didn't care about a goddam thing except that she was out of that typhoon. She tottered into the toilet. It was empty, but she did not expect that to last too long, and she did not care about that either. She went to the corner and ran taps in two basins. Then she started to undress. There was only one way to handle the mess she had got herself into.

She kicked off her shoes, stripped off her blouse, undid her skirt, then peeled off her panties. She shoved everything into one basin of water. She squeezed two handfuls of liquid soap out of the dispenser and then swished it vigorously into the soaking garments. She sank the top of her head into the other basin, and sighed as the cool hit her scalp; then she tossed her wet hair over her neck and splashed her face with cold water. Then, stark naked, she lifted one long leg up on to the basin and proceeded to sponge off her body, vigorously and entirely.

Ten minutes later it was all over. A dozen people had interrupted her and she had ignored each one cheerfully. She had dried herself off, wrung out her clothes and pulled them on wet, combed her wet hair and put on her face. She took one last look at herself in the mirror.

Then she picked up her handbag jauntily and walked out. She crossed the big marble concourse with her wet clothes sticking to her and headed for the bar to meet Kurt Marlowe.

She gulped her first brandy down in one go, slapped ten dollars on the bar and said, flushed, 'Another round.'

Kurt Marlowe grinned at her and put his hand in his pocket.

'No,' Vanessa said, 'let me buy you a drink for that ride.' She held up her new brandy at him. 'You flew that machine magnificently.'

'Thanks.' He smiled modestly. He glanced appreciatively at her nipples, showing through her wet blouse.

She took a gulp of brandy.

'It'll all be in my story next month: "Those magnificent men in their flying machines".' She added: 'Let me buy you lunch when you get back to Hong Kong.'

He looked at her, quizzically. 'When *I* get back? You'll be flying back with me.'

'No more typhoons for Mrs Williams's little girl, darling! I'm flying back by good old scheduled airline and that's only if there isn't a train.' She finished off her brandy in a gulp and then smiled at him dazzlingly and put her hand on his shoulder: 'Thanks awfully for taking me into that holocaust – and even more for getting me out! It was really very kind of you. And now I really do have to rush . . .'

He stared at her. 'Where the hell to?'

'There's a Philippine Airlines for Hong Kong in forty minutes – probably their last flight until the typhoon's over.'

Kurt stared at her indignantly. 'Hey, we've got a deal!'

'A deal? I don't understand . . .'

'Don't come the coy and girlish bit with me, baby! – You know very well that we made a deal at lunch – a tacit one – but clearly understood!'

'What, *me*?'

He said softly: 'You bitch . . .'

She gave him a coy smile and wagged a finger at him: 'Now now, Kurt, don't spoil your image!' She bent forward and gave him a big kiss on his cheek. 'I really must dash. Fly carefully!'

She twiddled her fingers at him and turned on her heel and hurried away. She looked back once and blew him a bright kiss and twiddled her fingers again. His lips mouthed, '*Bitch!*' She did feel a bit of a shit, but her heart was singing.

Jake McAdam's junk ploughed slowly past the point of the island of Kat O Chau. The engines were going *doem – doem – doem* in the silence of the black sea. On his port side, the lights of Shataukok twinkled slowly past. Ahead was Mirs Bay, and China waters.

There were no lights of other vessels within miles. Far away, up there across the black sea, twinkled the lights of a commune. He looked back at Shataukok's lights. Up in the mountains behind, on Hong Kong's side, the police searchlights swept slowly along the fence down at the bottom. And far away behind him, beyond the black silhouettes of the mountains of the New Territories, the lights of Hong Kong glowed dimly up into the starry night sky. Behind him, too, on this side of Kat O Chau, was a small fishing village. It belonged to Hong Kong, but the villagers were Communist and China's fishing junks and motor gunboats often put in there to show the flag. He swung his binoculars slowly across the black horizon. Far away he could just make out a string of navigation lights. That would be a fishing junk fleet putting back to China ahead of the typhoon.

He rubbed his fingers across his brow, and he felt them tremble. He did not want to remember. He did not want to remember the heartbreak, the dread of those many times he had been here long ago, the dread of what they might tell him, and the hopes. Oh God. The hope, every minute of every day, that at the next meeting Chester would say, 'Okay, Jake, old man, it's all worked very well and we're moving on to phase two now – we're letting Ying go back to Hong Kong and you two can get nice and respectably married and go to the top of the Hong Kong police force – and keep spying for us, of course.'

He did not want to remember. And the raw solid fear that any time Chester might have said, 'Jake, old chap, you've been feeding us disinformation all this time, haven't you? Her Majesty's been using you as a double agent all this time, hasn't she? And here you are in China waters! I'm sorry, old man, but I've got to arrest you as a spy. There'll be a trial of course, but I'm afraid we're going to shoot you. *And* her of course . . .' One day, any day it could have happened, it was bound to happen. And the only hope was to keep stringing them along, feeding them play material and disinformation until they let her come back. And, oh God, the dread, every minute of every day, of what they would do to her if they found out. But she had saved him from that, although she did not know it. She had thought she was only saving his honour. That was the last time, and Chester had brought her with him, the hostage, and she had blurted out defiantly at both of them:

'I do not love you any more, Jake! I despise you! I will have nothing more to do with this disgraceful business! I love China but I despise you for spying on your own country and I refuse to be used any more! If I ever come here again it will only be if they drag me in handcuffs! And I shall stand mute!' And she had turned her back to them, shaking, and she had stood silent from that moment on. And there had been no way he could tell her what he was really doing.

He looked behind him at the silhouette of Kat O Chau; then at the lights of Shataukok, trying to calculate his position in the dark. Then he cut his engines. He was about inside China waters. He left the wheel and made his way up to the bows. He threw the anchor over.

Then he went back to the wheel. He sat in the silent dark, waiting, and trying not to think.

THIRTY-THREE

It was after ten o'clock. The typhoon was still more than twelve hours away. Hong Kong's Kai Tak Airport was still in business, but not as usual.

A jet-airliner can land, discharge passengers, refuel, take on passengers, turn around and take off again in forty-five minutes if it has to. Aircraft were still arriving and leaving, but only those whose schedules provided for a quick turn-around: planes that normally had a long stopover in Hong Kong were being diverted to airports in Taiwan and the Philippines with their passengers. All the hotels were jampacked, with tourists arriving and tourists trying to leave ahead of the typhoon, luggage everywhere, people crowding in the foyers, the lounges, the passageways, the bars, round the reception desks, people asleep on the lobby chairs, children grizzling, the reception clerks hustling, bustling, answering the same questions over and over, the telephones shrilling.

Vanessa was the first off the Philippine Airlines jet, the first through Immigration. She did not have any luggage to wait for, so she dashed through Customs. She hurried across the huge clamorous marble concourse, dodging people, making for the public telephones. She grabbed the only empty one, deposited fifty cents, dialled.

Across the harbour the telephone suddenly rang in McAdam's dark, silent apartment. Upstairs in the gallery the killer stiffened, his eyes alert. The telephone

252

rang and rang.

She waited, excited, nervous. She could imagine the apartment, empty, dark, the sound of the telephone.

Then she hung up impatiently.

She got her coins back, redeposited them, fingers shaking. She dialled the American Mess. Maybe there was a typhoon party on there, maybe somebody there would know where he was.

It rang shrilly in the big, old-fashioned apartment.

Outside on the dark stairs that led up to the rooftop, the second Chinese man heard it ringing. In the servant's quarters, beyond the kitchen, the old amah, Ah Li, stirred in her sleep. She lay there, hoping the ringing would stop, then she got creakily out of bed. She shuffled through the kitchen and down the long wooden corridor, her long pigtail hanging down behind her. All the missies' bedroom doors were open, which meant that none of them had come home yet, and she knew very well that maybe none of them would come home on a Friday night, especially with a typhoon coming. On the other hand they *all* might come home, with *all* their boy-friends. As she shuffled up to the telephone it stopped ringing. The old woman swore in Cantonese, turned round and shuffled back down the corridor, mumbling.

Vanessa banged down the telephone and recovered her coins. Then she redeposited them and dialled the Foreign Correspondents' Club.

'Hel*loo* . . .' a cheerful voice said. In the background she could hear laughter and singing.

'Is Jake McAdam there, please?'

'Haven't seen him. Hang on . . . Nope.'

She sighed, impatiently. 'Is Mr Ball there?'

'Of course Whacker's here. Hang on . . .'

'Who is this?' Whacker barked.

'Vanessa. Do you know where Jake is, Whacker?'

'I thought you were in the goddam typhoon!'

'I was, but I've just flown back from Manila, I'm at the airport. Is Jake there?'

'No. Haven't seen him for days, thank God. Probably messing about with his boats in the dark. How he expects to run businesses. Listen, I've got to talk to you! That's a hell of a story.'

'I still owe you a case of whisky, Whacker. Have you given it to the editor of the newspaper yet?'

'No. Listen, lady, a story that big you don't dictate over a telephone and chuck at an editor. It's a *scoop*, woman! You've got to write it properly and you've got to check out the facts with the Building Ordinance Office, look at architects' plans and see the certificates of solid rock. Jesus, don't go off at half-cock! You'll spoil the impact. This will put the bastard in jail –'

'I know – I didn't have time before I left and I wanted to be sure the story didn't get lost if I plunged to my death in that fucking aeroplane. I'll check out the Building Ordinance Office tomorrow – '

'Typhoon's coming tomorrow and everything'll be closed, and anyway it's Saturday. You'll have to wait till next week. You got to take your *time* and cover every angle before you blow a story this big, girlie! And it's going to bring his Lucky Man Development Company crashing down on top of him. And send him to jail for a long, long time. You don't want him to slip through the net.'

She felt the thrill all over again. 'I know – it's just that it was an emergency, Whacker – your lips are sealed, aren't they? I wouldn't have told anybody but you.'

'Yeah, they're sealed,' Whacker grunted. 'I'm too old to be ambitious any more. Why else would I work on the *Israelite*? But you still owe me a case of whisky.'

'Sure.'

'But needless to say I sold my shares. I might be mad to work for McAdam, but I'm not stupid.'

'Whacker?' she sighed. 'If you see him tell him I'm looking for him, please.'

'Okay,' Whacker Ball grunted. 'There's a typhoon party starting here; it'll be going all night and tomorrow, he may blow in, I'll tell him. But tomorrow I'm on duty at the Typhoon Emergency Centre.'

She sighed happily. She said:

'I'm going to rent a car and go check out the boat-yard now, Whacker. If he's not there I'll go and wait in his apartment.'

'Okay,' Whacker said, 'I'll tell him.'

She couldn't resist saying it, she was so happy. 'And Whacker? – I love you too!'

She drove as fast as she could over the rough tracks, her headlights bouncing ahead of her, the rented car jolting, her eyes far away, her heart singing. She slammed to a stop at the top of the hill and looked down into the boat-yard's cove.

His car was down there! But there was not a light shining, even a crack. She slammed her hand on the horn and gave a long blast. Then waited, her heart hammering. Then she shoved the car into gear and ground down the hill.

She wrenched on the handbrake, slung open the door.

'Ho – *gan!*'

She went round the side of the cottage, to the front. No light. 'Hogan!' She tried the door. Locked. She rattled the door hard, and shouted his name again. He *must* be in there, his car was here.

Then she noticed the junk was not at the jetty.

Of course! He had taken the junk to the typhoon

shelter at Tai-po.

She gave a frustrated sigh.

Damn. He was just a few miles away down Tolo Sound in that typhoon shelter. But she would never find his boat in the dark amongst all those hundreds of junks that were crowding in there. And ten to one he was asleep already down below, he would never hear her shout.

Oh Hogan, Hogan, beautiful Hogan. Don't tell me you're going to spend the typhoon on that junk when we could be spending it in bed making beautiful love!

But, no, he wouldn't stay on the junk – Wong would be there to look after it, and anyway he had sent her a telegram to meet him at the Foreign Correspondents' Club tomorrow. He would leave the junk to Wong as soon as it got light and come back here for his car. Maybe any time now, maybe even now he was walking across the hills in the dark.

Well, she would wait for him right here. Here where his car was. She didn't want to go anywhere else. She just wished she could get into that cottage and lie in his bed and wait for him and smell his body on the sheets.

She went to his car, opened it and slowly got in. She ran her fingers over the steering wheel, to feel close to him. It was completely quiet.

Maybe she should go home and bath and have something to eat, and sleep until daybreak.

Or go to his apartment; she still had a front-door key, though she'd given the key-ring back to him. And have a lovely long bath with a long glass of beer. And then get into his bed.

THIRTY-FOUR

He saw the navigation lights of the junk long before he could hear it, just the small red and green pinpricks. He stared at the lights. They were a long way off yet. He had about fifteen minutes to get himself under control. He lit a cigarette and inhaled it deeply.

The lights blinked off once and then came on again. He got up, went to his control panel, flicked a switch and blinked his navigation lights off, then on again.

The silhouette approached in the dark, the engine quietly thudding in the silence. Then a flashlight swept the junk and blinded him. He shielded his eyes.

'All right,' he snapped, 'switch that damn thing off.'

'Are you alone, old man?' Chester's voice said, in his perfect Oxford accent.

'No, I'm bristling with marines. And I've got a submarine shadowing you. Pretty wild, huh?'

'Mind if we check, old chap?'

'Go ahead.'

The junk hove to against his and half a dozen men came aboard with submachine-guns. They went clattering below. A tubby silhouette stepped over. McAdam stayed seated.

'Jake,' Chester Wu said. 'How nice to see you again.'

'Hullo, Chester. Sit down.'

'I'd rather you came aboard my old tub. New boat, huh? Concrete, I hear. That's pretty wild. Stand up, old man. Hands above your head.'

McAdam stood up with a sigh, and raised his hands. Chester Wu frisked him.

'Okay, you're clean.'

'Of course I'm clean, I don't want trouble.'

'Come on, then. Up to the bows? It's cooler.'

McAdam picked up the whisky bottle and his cigarettes. He stepped off his junk on to Chester's and followed him up to the bows. They sat down on the bows. Chester smiled at him in the dark.

'What makes you think I won't arrest you, old man? As a spy. For all that horrid disinformation you fed me.'

McAdam took a small swig of whisky, then passed Chester the bottle. 'Got any glasses?'

'The bottle's all right. Well?'

'Because if you were going to liquidate me you could have done so easily enough in the last eight years. Because I'm more useful to you alive than dead. Or rotting in a People's Prison.'

'And how can you be useful to me now?'

He steeled himself to keep his voice level.

'I can be useful, all right. But first you've got to be useful to me.' He added: 'Please.'

'Oh? How?'

He took a deep breath. His voice sounded loud.

'How's Ying?' he said.

Chester said carefully:

'Why should I tell you how she is?'

McAdam's voice almost trembled.

'For two reasons. First, as a man. For compassion's sake . . . You're a decent human being at heart, Chester!'

Chester smiled. 'That's true. But what favours do I owe you? As I recall, *you* were the one who arrested *me* that night many years ago and had me deported.'

'Of course I arrested you! You were a superintendent

in the Hong Kong police and you were a spy and I caught you red bloody handed! I'd arrest you again!' He glared in the dark. 'But you won't arrest me now, Chester. Because I can be useful to you. Which is my second reason why you should tell me about Ying.'

'How useful?'

'I'm rejoining the club.'

Chester stared at him in the dark.

'You don't say!'

'All right – don't believe me.'

'Which end of it?'

'Not the China end, obviously. Not directly.'

'Okay. We'll check your story out.'

'*If* you can.'

'But what's your price?'

There was a short silence.

'How's Ying?' he said again.

Chester Wu looked at him.

'She's fine . . .' he said.

'And?'

'And what?'

'Where is she?'

'She's in Canton. Just up there,' he added.

'Doing what?'

'Teaching. School.'

You fucking liar, McAdam thought. *You want to keep the carrot on the old string.*

'Well? – what's happened to her? Has she married? Has she got a baby? A boy-friend?'

Chester said hastily: 'No . . .' Then his tone changed. 'I'm not impressed by all this drama, Jake. I know very well that you've got a new girl now. An American blonde bombshell called Vanessa Storm Williams. Quite taken Hong Kong by storm I hear, aha – ha – ha.

259

I know all about it.' He added casually: 'Just routine tabs we keep on you.'

McAdam made himself smile.

'You don't say?' He breathed. 'And what about Ying's private life? If she's allowed one in the People's Paradise.'

Chester said airily:

'I don't know about any boy-friend.'

'And how does she feel about me?' It wasn't as hard to say as he had thought it would be. He added: 'Surely your Thought Police know.'

Chester smiled indulgently at the little joke.

'That's for you to find out, Jake . . . through me. In due course. In return for information. I don't pay in advance.'

McAdam felt his anger flare. And suddenly he knew what he was going to do, what the real outcome of this meeting was. And what the truth about her was. And what he had to do, because – *no way* was he going to be put through that agony again. *No way* was he going to put *her* through that again! He stood up and picked up the whisky bottle.

'Okay. It's no deal.'

He turned towards his junk.

'Just a moment, old man!'

He knew he should not say it:

'It's no deal, Chester! Because you're lying about her! And you're lying because she still won't co-operate with you. You've known about this meeting for forty-eight hours, don't tell me you haven't asked her. And if she were co-operative you'd have her here right now to show me. But it's no good dragging her here in handcuffs and her standing mute again, is it?'

Chester said: 'She still loves you, Jake.'

'Then why haven't you brought her here?'

'She still feels the same – '

McAdam jabbed a finger at him: 'You see – you admit she's still a handcuff case! You've shown your cards, Chester! And that's not all you've lied about. Because she's not just up there in Canton, she's up there in Manchuria! And she's not teaching school – she's in the People's Liberation Army Intelligence. You can't order the Army to do a damn thing, can you? They'd tell you to stick your handcuffs up your arse if they wanted to. And that's not all of it! She's probably married since she's been Rehabilitated and Thought-Reformed. To some nice colonel. She's probably got a family. She's got her own life now. She's *gone*, Chester! From you *and* me!'

He turned and stepped across on to his junk angrily.

'You're wrong, Jake.'

'Okay, I'm wrong! Tell your guys to get off, I'd hate to do them the favour of taking them to Hong Kong.'

'You presume too much.'

'Yeah, okay, anything you say!'

Chester Wu stood on the gunwale of the junk. 'What makes you presume I'll let you go, just like that, after all the trouble you've caused me?'

McAdam pushed in the decompressor and turned the ignition. The engine ground over, then took, *doem – doem – doem*. He was so sickened that it was easy to lie.

'Because I'm rejoining the club, Chester. I'm much more useful to you alive and back in the business than dead. And any information you could squeeze out of me now is eight years old. And I don't even know what the truth is of the information I gave you eight years ago. I was just *told* what to say.'

He left the wheel angrily and went up to the bows and hauled in his anchor. Then he untied the rope holding

261

the two boats together. Chester watched him.

'You'll be back, Jake.'

McAdam was back at the wheel. He looked at him squarely.

'Yes,' he lied. He added: 'Don't call me, I'll call you.'

Chester looked at him.

'Any messages for Ying?'

He felt his bitterness flare, that the bastard was still trying to use her.

'Yes! The message she didn't send me. Give her my love.'

He rammed the gear lever into forward and opened the throttle.

As the junk swung round back towards Kat O Chau he looked up at the ridge. He could just make out the two pine trees against the night sky.

'Good-bye,' he whispered. 'Good-bye, Ying.'

And he rammed the throttle up to full.

PART X

At three o'clock that Sunday morning the first winds came. The typhoon was still many hours away: these were just the peripheral winds. They came out of the dark sky, gusting over the black sea, a short erratic burst, then still again, then another, jerking the trees and bushes, ruffling the sea, then gone again. Then another one, harder, so the windows slammed and curtains billowed and the sea slapped, then gone again into the darkness.

Most of Hong Kong was battened down. And out there, the black sea was studded with the red and green lights of junks coming in from deep sea at full throttle, making for the typhoon shelters.

THIRTY-FIVE

The first gusts of wind whipped through the banana trees at McAdam's cove and beat against his car, and she woke up. She sat up, startled. She looked at her watch. Almost three. She was muzzy with tiredness. She squeezed her eyes with her fingertips and then looked at herself in the rear-view mirror.

She was hot, her wrung-out clothes creased and sweaty. *I look awful.* She sucked her lips as she ferreted in her bag for lipstick. Then she pouted in front of the little mirror, put the stuff on. She looked at herself in the mirror. Bared her teeth. Not even a toothbrush.

There was only one thing for a smart lady to do. Leave a note on the steering wheel, go and have a proper sleep, tart herself up. And *then* come back.

In many places in Hong Kong the typhoon parties were in swing, the parties that kept everybody captive for twenty-four hours at least and where everybody ended up sharing beds and carpets and sofas. At the Foreign Correspondents' Club it would go on all week-end, and from there typhoon parties would develop all over the colony. Vanessa had never been to one in her short time in Hong Kong but she had heard about them. As she pulled up in her rented car outside her apartment block at four o'clock that Saturday morning she knew by the unusual number of cars parked close together up on the sidewalk, some of which she recognized, that there was a party going on upstairs at the American Mess.

She sighed behind the wheel. She wanted to be alone with her thoughts, she could not bear the noise and the laughter and the bullshit. And probably somebody was screwing in her bed. And she wouldn't get a bath with everybody in and out of the john. She put the car into gear, and drove the extra fifty yards to McAdam's apartment block. She swung the car down the concrete drive, down into the basement car-park.

It was dark. She drove the car into McAdam's parking space, cut the engine and switched off the lights. The slam of her car door sounded cavernously loud. Then she started walking for the elevator, her footsteps ringing on the concrete. She pressed the elevator button, and waited. Just then another gust of wind came whipping in off the sea and up the mountainside and between the apartment blocks and she heard the creak of the trees outside. Suddenly the elevator doors opened with a rasp. She got in.

She was not feeling sleepy any more. She just wanted a bath and wanted daylight to come. So she could get back out there looking beautiful and find Hogan before the typhoon cut them off from each other. And she needed something in her stomach.

The elevator doors slid open on the sixth floor. She stepped out.

Her footsteps sounded loud in the silent foyer. She stood at the door, rummaging in her bag for McAdam's key. She found it, and unlocked the door.

She shut it behind her. It was dark, but some light came in from the stars. She walked slowly into the living room and sighed happily.

She felt she had come home. And she wanted to *smell* the place. She walked slowly to the big french windows and looked out at the harbour.

Ah, yes – what a view.

The sea was studded with lights of the junks coming in, running from the typhoon. There was a big freighter putting out to sea. All the buoys had big ships tied up to them, all lit up, all facing the same way, swung with the tide. She looked down and sideways at the American Mess. Without opening the windows she could see the verandah, people on it.

Thank God she was here.

She turned and walked briskly down the corridor to the main bedroom, unbuttoning her blouse as she went. She snapped on the light and went into the bathroom. She spun the taps and water gushed into the tub.

At the top of the spiral staircase the door silently opened a crack. The killer listened to the sound of running water, then smiled faintly.

In the bathroom she peeled off her blouse and slung it on the floor. Then the telephone rang.

She turned off the taps, and dashed out of the bathroom, across the bedroom, down the corridor. She flung herself into McAdam's study and snatched up the telephone in the dark.

'Hullo!'

There was a moment's surprised silence. Then:

'Is Jake there?'

She recognized the voice. Disappointment swept over her.

'For God's sake, Bernard, it's four o'clock in the morning!'

She heard him breathe deeply.

'I'm sorry, but I've got to talk to him.' He added: 'I've been awake all night.'

'He's not here, Bernie. I think he's at Tai-po typhoon shelter. I'm going there at daybreak to look for him. What message can I give him?'

She heard him sigh again. He sounded a little drunk.

'Can I come with you?'

She closed her eyes. *No no no . . .*

'Look, I'll tell him to phone you.' She added: 'I haven't seen him myself for some time, you see.'

Silence.

'Yes, I see . . .'

'What is it, Bernie?'

'Vanessa? . . . Are you up?'

'Right this red-hot moment I'm up at the telephone.'

'Can I come and see you?' He added: 'Please . . . I've had a sleepless night. I've got to talk to somebody.'

She closed her eyes in the dark and suppressed a sigh.

'Okay. But I must leave here before daybreak. And I must get a bath in. How long will it take you to get here?'

'Five minutes.'

'Five minutes,' she said. 'Okay, Bernie.'

Through the crack of the door at the top of the spiral staircase the killer was listening.

He silently closed the door.

He needed more than five minutes.

She put down the telephone. She went through to the kitchen and switched on the electric kettle.

He had big dark rings under his eyes. He stood at the window, staring at the harbour, while she read the letter he had thrust at her.

Dear Sir,

In terms of the Prevention of Bribery Ordinance, I hereby require you to account within seven clear days of today's date, for all your assets, of whatever kind in all parts of the world, and the means whereby you acquired them. Failure to comply with this requirement constitutes a criminal offence.

*You are further advised that failure to account sat-
isfactorily for all your assets raises a legal presump-
tion against you in a court of law that you acquired
the assets by corrupt methods.*

The wind buffeted the window.

'But . . . have you *got* a lot of assets?'

'More than are good for me.'

'But,' she waved her hand, 'you're a bachelor.
You're a senior policeman on a good salary. You play
the stock market. Can't you account satisfactorily?'

Champion snorted, turned to the bottle and poured
another large whisky.

'No.'

She stared at him. Her reporter's mind was working.
'How did this arise?'

He said bitterly: 'That bloody whorehouse raid that
you were involved in. My staff-sergeant paid a massive
reward for information. We made a deal with the
accused. Manslaughter instead of murder. The bloody
magistrate changed it back to murder. The accused
squealed and blew the whole story. This was yesterday
morning. By last night that letter was served on me. I've
been with my lawyer most of the night.'

He sounded near to breaking.

'What did your lawyer say?' she demanded.

'That I'm in trouble . . .' He added: 'He also told me
how to get out of it.'

'How?'

He turned and walked across the room, his face grey.

'Run away. To England. Or America.'

'*England?* I would have thought that was the worst
place. Hong Kong's a British colony.'

He sighed. 'The safest place. Because our extradition
treaty only applies to Hong Kong crimes which are *also*

crimes in England.' He turned wearily without looking at her. 'There is no such crime in England as failing to account for your assets. Or in America.'

'I see. Have you still got your passport?'

He snorted softly. 'Yes. That's a loophole in the law. I'm not on any kind of bail, either. I haven't committed any crime yet, until I fail to provide the explanation. They could physically stop me leaving if they caught me trying, but that's all. That's all I've got to do. Just get through that airport without them spotting me.'

She said sharply: 'What do you want me to do? And Hogan?'

He turned and his eyes were suddenly full of tears.

'Nothing! Just sit there! Just be my friend!'

He looked out of the window.

'Do what? Go where?' He turned slowly, haggard. 'Run away?' He shook his head. 'You can't run away from yourself, Vanessa.'

She knew that too, now.

'You've got to live with yourself, Vanessa . . . You've got to be able to look yourself in the eye. And say . . .' Then he whispered: 'Oh dear God . . .' He half turned and looked at her. 'What's important in life, Vanessa? Honour?' he appealed.

He waited. Then he cried:

'Help me! I'm asking you! What good is honour going to do in prison? What good is it going to do to say I owned up?'

'What do you want to hear?'

He smashed his fist down on the back of the chair.

'What you think! You're a woman of the world! You know how this town works!'

She took a big breath. 'Bernard, listen to me. No, I do not want to see you in prison! But Jesus Christ, I cannot and will not make up your mind for you – '

'*I'm not asking you to make up my mind! I'm asking you to tell me about honour! In this dishonourable town!*'

He stopped, glaring at her.

'Yes, Bernard. Honour is absolute.'

There was a long silence.

Then she said quietly:

'What are you going to do?'

'I don't know,' he said.

Outside the windows the winds came in gusts. The very first light was coming into the sky. She said softly:

'I must go now.'

He said dully: 'You haven't had your bath.'

'Yes, I must have it. And go.'

He sat there, staring at nothing. Then he said, thickly:

'Can I stay here till you go?'

Her heart went out to him.

'Yes,' she said.

At the top of the spiral staircase, the Chinese man had listened to everything.

He turned and silently crossed the gallery. He opened the front door, and stepped outside.

He would have to wait until later in the day.

THIRTY-SIX

All over the sea, from all directions, the junks were converging on Hong Kong for shelter, even junks of Communist China. By dawn all the typhoon shelters were almost full: junks, fishing trawlers, sampans, pleasure craft, lashed to each other, forests of masts,

270

sails tightly furled and lashed down.

With the first light McAdam was throttling down Tolo Sound. He was wide awake – exhausted. He did not think he had ever seen so many junks. Every few minutes the short gusts of wind lashed down the Sound. His portable radio was tuned in to the Government's Cantonese broadcasts, which gave hourly reports on the situation at the various typhoon shelters. And it sounded as if Tai-po was one of the worst.

> *Your attention. The Royal Hong Kong Observatory has raised the Number Eight Typhoon Signal.*
>
> *This is a warning that a gale is approaching from the south-east of Hong Kong and winds of at least seventy knots must be expected, and may exceed one hundred and fifty knots.*
>
> *Typhoon Rose is centred within three hundred miles south-east of Hong Kong, and is heading north-west at an average speed of thirteen knots. However, gale force winds must be expected within the next ten hours.*
>
> *The following precautions should be taken by everybody . . .*

Twenty minutes later McAdam rounded the point of his boat-yard bay, and there was Wong waiting on the jetty.

He edged up against the jetty and Wong swung aboard; McAdam shoved the gear lever astern, and put back out into the Sound.

He did not even think about his car.

He gave the wheel to Wong. He went to the main-mast with the binoculars, climbed up the foot rungs and looked at Tai-po with the binoculars in the sunrise.

The mouth of the typhoon shelter was dense with junks, forests of masts, all sizes, crowded tight as an armada; blue clouds of diesel fumes were rising and hanging. He could smell the urgency of *tai-fung*, the typhoon, in the air.

Twenty minutes later he steamed up to the edge of the crowded boats. There was the roar of engines manoeuvring, the stink of diesel fumes, the junk-masters waving, blowing on their whistles to their crews, the sea churning at the propellers. It was light now. He gave the wheel back to Wong and scrambled up the mainmast again. He looked over the junks into the typhoon shelter.

The mouth was jammed for three hundred yards ahead of him with acres of masts. Somewhere in that mass was a channel with junks manoeuvring down it to find a place to tie up to another junk. He heard Wong shout to the junkmaster on the next junk:

'What is going to happen, Elder Brother?'

The junkmaster looked at McAdam's boat.

'Is not this the boat that is made of stone?'

'It is made of concrete.'

The junkmaster shrugged, inspecting the junk. 'We shall soon see how well stone floats.' His daughters, who were manning the tiller, giggled. 'It is madness,' the junkmaster said. 'How can a boat be made of stone? Nobody will want to be tied up next to your boat, Elder Brother. Because when it sinks like a stone it will drag the other boats with it.'

McAdam smiled grimly at the conversation. He swung down the mast and went back to the wheel. He was dog-tired now.

'Did you sleep last night, Elder Brother?'

'Yes, First Born.'

McAdam dragged his hands down his face.

272

'We will wait two hours,' he said. 'Then if it does not look as if we will get in, we will go elsewhere.'

'Where?'

'Down there.' He pointed down the foot of the L-shaped sound towards the village of Shatin. 'It is quite well protected by the mountains there.'

He took off his wristwatch and gave it to Wong.

'Wake me in two hours.'

He turned and walked slowly down the hatch into the cabin. He threw himself on his back on the bunk and pressed his fingers to his eyes.

The sun was up by the time Vanessa was jolting along the hill-top track towards the boat-yard. The gusts of wind were harder up here in exposed places: they buffeted the car, and flattened the grass and bushes. She came to the hill-top overlooking the boat-yard and stopped.

His car was there! She rammed hers into low gear and ground down the steep track. As she got near the bottom she stuck her head out of the window and bellowed:

'*Ho-oh-gan.*'

She slammed to a stop beside his car and climbed out. A gust of wind whipped through the banana trees, whipping up her dress, and she clutched at it.

'Ho-gan!'

Then she saw her note, still on his steering wheel. She snatched the note and turned it over to see if he had written anything on the reverse. *Nothing.*

She hurried round to the front of the cottage. She shook the door for confirmation. Then she walked disconsolately back to the cars. She got into his with a sigh and sat there, staring at the Sound. Junks were thudding past out there.

Well, she would just have to wait.

Another burst of wind came and the banana trees bent. She peered up through the windscreen. The whole sky was hazy now. And over there towards the south it was grey. The sweat was running off her again. And she still had not had anything to eat.

She would wait a couple of hours. If he wasn't back by then it would mean he was stuck on his goddam junk.

In the typhoon . . . She closed her eyes. For the first time in her life she was afraid for somebody else.

By eleven o'clock that morning the sky was getting dark. The gusts of wind were coming harder and more often now, and out there the South China Sea was swelling and breaking higher. Tolo Sound was protected from the winds and the open sea by the Mountains of Nine Dragons, but swells were seething under the gusts and the waves were breaking along the rocky shoreline.

At eleven o'clock McAdam's junk was steaming down the foot of the L of Tolo Sound. He had given up trying to get into the shelter. A lot of other junks were doing the same, and some of the bigger ones were putting back out to deep sea, to try to ride out the typhoon far away from rocks.

The sun was almost gone behind the haze, and the sea ahead was nearly black. Way ahead was Shatin village. All the way down the long jagged Sound, on both sides, were other junks, anchored far apart. All the anchored junks had their bows pointed south.

He had to give himself plenty of space. When he was approaching the end of the Sound, he swung the junk around and went steaming back up the channel again. He chose his place and swung the wheel to starboard. He put the engines astern, then into neutral. Wong scrambled up to the bows. He grunted as he picked up the big anchor. He slung it overboard with all his might.

McAdam heard its splash. He waited, sweating, for the junk to drift and take up the slack in the anchor rope. Then he went up to the bows himself to look.

The anchor rope was tight, stretched out. He paid out a bit more, until he estimated that he had the correct drag, maximum resistance to the weight of the boat. Then he untied the smaller Sanforth anchor. He stood up, heaved the anchor above his head, and hurled it with all his might.

He pulled in the slack. Then he tested the main anchor, pulling on the rope firmly. It held. He pulled it once more a little harder, and it came loose out of the sandy mud.

He cursed and then hauled the anchor in with all his might, hand over hand. He heaved it up out of the black water, on to the deck, then stood there, heart thudding. The smaller anchor still held the big junk.

'Bring the dinghy.'

Wong lowered the rubber dinghy into the chopping sea. He rowed it round to the bows, then stood up and hung on to the gunwale. McAdam heaved the big fifty-pound anchor over the edge and lowered it down into the little boat.

'Out there.' He pointed.

Wong rowed the dinghy through the slapping water. 'There.'

Wong left the oars and scrambled up, and heaved the anchor over the side with a big splash.

McAdam waited, then pulled in the slack.

'Hold fast, you bitch!'

He tested it. It held. He looked around at the shore-line, at the nearest junks. At the sky. A gust of wind swept over the Mountains of Nine Dragons and funnelled down the Sound.

There was nothing more they could do. Except wait.

At noon that Saturday morning Vanessa was driving her rented car down the tarmac road back to Hong Kong. She had left another note for McAdam, on his steering wheel.

She had stopped at Tai-po and tried to see his junk amongst the masses, but it had been impossible. Now, as she drove through the gusts of wind down the edge of Tolo Sound, she was not looking for his boat, but she was glancing at the profusion of junks at anchor. Then suddenly she thought she saw it, and slammed on her brakes.

It was the yellow rubber dinghy that she spotted, half a mile away across the Sound. She peered across the water at it. Yes – she was sure!

She gave a long blast on her horn, then a burst of short ones, then scrambled out of the car. The wind flapped at her as she ran stumbling round the car to the edge of the road, where the stone embankment dropped straight into the slapping sea.

'*Ho-oh-gan!*' she bellowed, waving frantically.

She shouted and shouted, dashed back to the car and blasted the horn some more. The wind snatched her shouts away to nothing, and the spray hit her. For ten minutes she tried.

For another ten minutes she sat in the car, watching the junk, the wind buffeting. A few times she could just make out a figure moving about.

Then she sighed, started her car again, and drove slowly back to Hong Kong.

Her note said that she would wait for him at his apartment. That was where she wanted to be. But she could not bear to go there yet, with nothing to do but wait.

276

PART XI

The radar screen of the Royal Observatory was a little bigger than a television set. Mervin Katz stood beside it, with an air of morbid proprietorship. Vanessa stared at the machine. The rotating radar beam showed up in the screen as a thin white line going slowly round. And in that rotating beam showed Typhoon Rose.

With each sweep the typhoon glowed, a big curling mass, spiralling blackly and brightly inwards to the eye.

Her nerves were going. She had only had three hours' sleep last night in the car, and she was sick with worry for McAdam on that junk. That terrifying mass on that radar screen, that same holocaust she had flown into yesterday – it was going to hit him, on the sea, on a junk. She tried to force herself to concentrate.

Katz pointed to the black eye.

'The eye's still two hundred and fifty miles due south of us. But the nearest big winds are only about fifty miles away at this moment.'

'How long before they hit us?'

'About four, five hours. But the first big gusts will hit us in half that time. You should get home soon.'

'Could she still turn? Or stop?'

'See here.' He turned on the overhead light. On the table was the latest weather chart. The lines of wind were drawn on it, curving inwards. 'She's going this way. In front of her, towards Hong Kong, lies this trough of low pressure, here, moving in front of her. A typhoon will keep moving into that trough of low pressure, because it helps her suck moisture up from the sea. She'll hit us.' He looked at her. 'That was a pretty impressive business, flying into her yesterday.'

She nodded bleakly. 'I'd rather watch her from here.'

Mervin Katz shook his head. 'You should have stayed in Manila.'

She pressed her fingertips to her eyes.

'I wish to God McAdam had got into a typhoon shelter.'

'Don't worry. McAdam's the luckiest guy I know.' Then he went on tactlessly: 'Can't rely on typhoon shelters anyway. If Typhoon Rose arrives on schedule she'll coincide with normal high tide.'

'Oh my God, Katz . . . What happens?'

'Okay, forget it.'

'Tell me!'

'Well, in 1932 a typhoon coincided with high tide and caused a bejezus big wave that knocked out all the typhoon shelters. Eleven thousand people died.' He said apologetically: 'You know about the dome of sea a typhoon causes?'

'No.'

'Well, a typhoon causes a dome of sea to rise up. By a kind of suction. And that moves with the typhoon. And if that dome of sea arrives at the same time as normal high tide it can be very bad.' He added apologetically: 'Look – don't worry – '

'Don't worry! Look – do you think I could get a boat to go out to him and get him off? Or a Marine Police launch . . . ?'

He smiled and put his big hand on her shoulder.

'Listen. There are thousands of junk people going to be on their boats. And Jake's on his precious boat for one reason – he refuses to leave it. Wild horses wouldn't get him off. And he also wouldn't leave that boat-boy of his to his fate.'

She stared at him, then turned away and paced across the floor.

THIRTY-SEVEN

The China sun beat down through the haze that hung over the sea and the islands. It was muggy hot between the hard gusts of wind. The streets were almost deserted, all the shop windows boarded up.

There were still a few taxis running, a few trams. There was one Star Ferry shuttling back and forth across the harbour but it was almost empty. Some junks were still coming in. The big typhoon buoys were all full of big ships, the 'B' buoys all empty because they were not heavy enough to hold a ship during a typhoon.

The radio repeated at half-hourly intervals in English and Cantonese and Chiu Chau and Tanka:

Here is a special announcement. The Royal Hong Kong Observatory has raised the Number Nine Signal . . . All precautions should already have been completed . . .

All precautions were being taken; in the Police, the Fire Department, the Public Works Department, Marine Department, the Army, Navy, Air Force, the Volunteer Services, Government Information Centre. All policemen were on emergency standby. The Special Operations Room next to the 999 Room was opened up, with the big maps hanging on the walls, the flags and lights marking positions, the hot-line telephones connected up to all other stations, to Special Mobile Units, the Public Works Department, the Government

Information Centre, HQ. In the Public Works Departments the emergency officers and their equipment were ready, from bulldozers to drainage maps.

In the Fire Department daily routine had been done in full kit, from hitting the pole to fire drill, climbing drill, rescue drill; hoses, ladders, pumps and engines had been tested, fire engines were revving and roaring. Now in all the fire stations round the colony the firemen were lying on their dormitory beds, boots on, ready to hit the pole within sixty seconds of the alarm bell ringing for fires, floods, jammed elevators, landslides, house-collapse. The Army was on standby for manpower duties and engineering jobs, the Air Force for helicopter rescue operations, the Navy for sea rescue operations. Government Information Staff and certain trained volunteer servicemen were on duty all the time: camp beds, coffee percolators, sandwich boxes were everywhere, telephones and teleprinters were tingling with anticipation.

'And we still can't get it right,' Whacker Ball said, disgusted.

'What?' Vanessa said. Her nerves were stretched tight. But it was better to be here, at the Government Information Centre, trying to learn something, than going out of her tiny mind alone in his apartment.

'Information. Christ, with all this sophisticated apparatus you'd expect it to go like clockwork. But no. Wrong information is our greatest problem. Imagine,' he said irritably. 'All hell's breaking loose and this idiot looks out of his stormy window and sees something and he telephones in hysterically and tells you there's an electrical fire. But really it's a landslide, the fire's the least of it. And it's smashed down two streets. What happens here? We press the panic button for a fire and all the relevant equipment goes screaming out. And what do we find?'

'A landslide.'

'Not only a bloody landslide! It's a landslide that's smashed down two roads, so the area is inaccessible. And it's burst all the big drains and there's tons of water gushing and the surrounding streets are like Niagaras. And not only that! – the landslide's flooded the ground floors of two apartment blocks with mud, and it's drowning everybody from their ankles up! And meanwhile, of course, what has happened?'

'What?'

'What about the equipment these poor rescue bastards are lugging along to the disaster area through this howling typhoon? They're setting out for an electrical fire! What do they find they need when they eventually get there?'

'A bulldozer?'

Whacker Ball winced.

'Of course they need a bulldozer! They need ten bulldozers! But how the hell are they going to get a bloody great bulldozer along all those narrow streets which have been smashed away by the landslide? Bulldozers! – they're the *last* things to get to the scene! *Hours later!* No – they need a sludge pump! Half a dozen sludge pumps! And they've got to have a bloody great generator to drive them.' He sighed, disgusted. 'Happens all the bloody time.'

Suddenly, simultaneously, on all four television sets, came the next typhoon warning:

We interrupt this programme to issue the following urgent typhoon warning. The Number Nine Signal has been hoisted. Typhoon Rose is centred approximately one hundred and eighty miles from Hong Kong and is proceeding towards us at a speed of approximately ten knots. If she maintains her present speed and direction she will pass directly over the Colony in approximately eighteen hours, or at noon tomorrow. However, winds will definitely reach sixty knots within two hours. The following precautions should already have been taken . . .

The *Fat Hong* had sailed the China coast for forty years as a passenger ship, a cargo ship, a gunboat, a floating casino, a night club, and, for a few spectacular weeks, as a pirate ship. In those forty years she had been sunk four times.

Now she was a ghost ship. Now she mostly lay on her moorings, pockmarks of machine-gun bullets across her bridge and patches on her hull, waiting for somebody to charter her. She was an unlucky ship.

Neil O'Bryan, Captain of the *Fat Hong*, considered himself a lucky man, however. He was seventy years old and lucky to have a job at all. He lived aboard the old ship in solitary splendour. Every morning when the sun was over the yardarm, Captain O'Bryan stepped down the accommodation ladder into his little old motor boat and went chugging across the harbour, and then went to the Foreign Correspondents' Club and drank gin until the sun went down. Then he rode back across the harbour to his ship, went into the silent empty galley, opened a can of pork and beans, carried it through to the old empty dining-room, and laid it on the captain's table, with linen and silver, and even a butter-knife. He went to the bandstand, selected a gramophone record, placed it on his old record player. Later he climbed up to the bridge and made his nightly entry in the log. Then Captain O'Bryan retired to his stateroom with the London *Times*.

But this Saturday was different. Captain O'Bryan

woke up not so brightly because he had been drinking into the early morning with his old friend Commander Horace J. Mooney II of the USS *Dreadnought*. The USS *Dreadnought* had sailed into Hong Kong, given a nineteen or so gun salute, tied up to a 'B' buoy, and turned all hands loose for seven days' rest and recreation. Captain Mooney had been holed up in the Hong Kong Hilton resting and recreating only three days when the Number Five Typhoon Signal had been raised. Standing Orders required United States Navy ships to put to sea and execute a square around a typhoon, but Captain Mooney was not going to, for several reasons. One, because he did not care much for Standing Orders, two, because it is highly unpleasant, not to say unsafe, to leave the security of a harbour during a typhoon, and three, because he had been resting and recreating in his favourite port for only three days.

Both Captain O'Bryan and Commander Mooney woke up at about noon, neither feeling very clever. Commander Mooney opened a can of beer and Captain O'Bryan hurried shakily out on to his bridge in his underwear. The *Fat Hong*'s skeleton crew of ten men were preparing for emergency sailing. Captain O'Bryan picked up his binoculars. There were junks everywhere, pouring into the harbour, full sail and throttle. He tottered to the communication tube. Wang bellowed up the tube from the clanking of the engine rooms: '*Wei!*'

Captain O'Bryan winced, then croaked angrily in Cantonese: 'How much steam have we got?'

'*Two more hours!*' Wang slammed the tube closed.

Captain O'Bryan stared furiously at the tube then jabbed the buzzer hard and long. '*Wei?*'

'*Wei?!*' Captain O'Bryan bellowed. 'You say *Yes Captain* to me, do you understand!?'

'*Wei?!*' Wang bellowed. '*Wei! wei! wei!*'

'*Do you want to keep your job?*'

'*No! You come down if you so smart make steam!*'

Captain O'Bryan stared at the tube, wanting to rant and rave and beat his fist against the bulkhead. '*We sail in two hours, then you swim ashore if you like better!*' he bellowed.

He swung his binoculars, angrily looking for the USS *Dreadnought*. He found her, still tied motionless to her 'B' buoy.

'Stupid bastard!' he croaked.

At five o'clock the Thai fishing trawler, carrying twenty tons of raw opium, was only ten miles from Hong Kong waters. It was in China's national waters, ploughing in the big swells which rose up high above the wheelhouse, engines thudding flat out. The gusts of wind were thrashing spray across the rolling decks, hammering on the glass of the wheelhouse. Scattered over the heaving sea there were still junks, heading for Hong Kong, rolling and pitching. And through his binoculars the skipper had seen several China motor gunboats today, patrolling.

The China gunboats were what the skipper was terrified of. If one of them stopped him and searched the trawler, it would be the end. A very quick trial before a People's Court, then he would be publicly shot. But today was an excellent day for delivering a cargo of opium because there were so many junks about making for shelter from the typhoon, and the China gunboats were more concerned with looking for vessels in distress than with stop-and-search.

The risk was almost over now. A few miles ahead was the International Shipping Lane leading into Hong Kong. That was where he had to rendezvous with the

Hong Kong junk. He was almost there. He shouted to his deckhands:

'Throw the goods over!'

The deckhands struggled their way to the hatch of the main fish hold, just forward of the mast. The spray thrashed them. They wrestled up the big hatch-cover. And there, in the hold below, were the big plastic bales of black opium, in four fishing nets.

The deckhands unlashed the derrick on the main-mast, and winched up the fishing nets containing the opium on to the heaving deck. Then, one by one, they swung them out over the gunwale on the derrick, then lowered them down into the sea with a splash. They lowered the four nets twenty feet below the keel of the trawler, two on each side, then made the nets' lines fast to the big iron deck-bollards.

The trawler ploughed on through the swells, dragging its cargo of death unseen beneath the sea. It slowed the trawler down, but she was built for dragging tons of fish in her nets. She was nearly at the rendezvous area, in the international shipping lane. It would be a quick job, simply to transfer the four lines holding the nets from his deck to the junk's. And if a China gunboat did head towards him, all he had to do was chop through those net-lines with an axe.

It was almost foolproof.

The skipper of the Thai fishing trawler was a Chinese, although he lived in Thailand, and he was a member of the 14K Triad Society, and so were all his crew. But he did not know for whom his cargo of opium was ultimately destined. He did not even know the identity of the person to whom he would hand it over at the rendezvous area, not even what he looked like. All he knew was that a junk would appear, with a piece of green rag tied to its rigging as a windsock, and that certain passwords would then be used. If he were caught, he could never divulge who the purchaser of the opium was, not even under the worst torture, because he simply did not know.

Normally the transfer of the cargo was foolproof. A fishing trawler trawls round and round for fish in international waters. And that is all he had to do, until the junk hove to, correctly claimed the cargo, and paid him. In American dollars.

But this time it was a little more tricky. Because of the typhoon.

The trawler was doing about two knots. The sea was running in big troughs in the gathering dusk, the trawler rearing up and then crashing down so the water flew in sheets and the swells seethed over the deck. The skipper was searching the surging sea through his binoculars for the junk that was to meet him. He was on the edge of the international shipping lane: ahead, all about him, were the outlying Communist islands that fringed Hong Kong; dead ahead, five miles away, was the group of Communist islands called the Lemas, with their gunboats and cannon, guarding the international lane, and the skipper watched them feverishly. That was the direction from which the gunboats would come, if they came. He scanned the sea again: there were still junks, but they were all heading towards Hong Kong, none were heading towards him. Then, out of the hazy dusk, the first wind hit him.

In a roar that made the spray fly like grapeshot, the swells broke and crashed against his hull. The trawler heeled and the swells broke over the bows. The skipper clung tight in the wheelhouse, trying to scan the heaving horizon through the dusk and the spray. In half an hour it would be pitch black. In two hours at the most he would have to run for the shelter of Hong Kong. Dragging his nets laden with twenty tons of opium in this sea would be suicidal. With each of these bigger swells, as his trawler tried to ride up them, the weighted nets wrenched her back and the water crashed over his decks. And he dare not run for Hong Kong carrying opium. But if he cut loose the nets he would not be paid, and the entire expense of this journey would have to be paid by him. And if he did not deliver he would never be hired again for this lucrative work. Indeed he might be quietly killed, as an example to others, if the 14K suspected bad faith.

Another burst of wind came, harder than the last, and the swell crashed over his gunwales and over the deck and the spray flew in sheets hammering against the wheelhouse. The skipper knew what he had to do: if the junk did not show in thirty minutes, he had to cut the net lines and plough for Hong Kong, or go down.

For twenty-eight more minutes the trawler crashed and wallowed and staggered in the swells and troughs, the winds coming harder and harder all the time. Now the sunset was invisible against the black of the west, and the skipper could hardly see the lights of the Lemas Islands ahead through the spray. Then, as he was about to cut the net lines, some navigation lights could be seen through the blackness, then more behind those.

They came from astern, from deep sea, not from Hong Kong's direction. And suddenly there was a spotlight blinding him. A voice bellowed over a megaphone:

'Do you need help with your catch?'

The skipper clung desperately to the door of the wheelhouse and bellowed into the blinding light:

'No!'

The voice shouted:

'Do you have womenfolk aboard?'

'*We have no womenfolk!*'
'*From whence comes the wind, brother?*'
'*The wind comes from the south!*'

And the spotlight swung off the skipper. In its beam he saw the green rag tied to the rigging.

THIRTY-EIGHT

As the first high wind came, Vanessa swung her rented car down into McAdam's basement car park. The wind howled through the dark cavern. She clutched her dress about her and bent her head and ran back up the drive-in, into dark Hillside Road. She battled her way down to her own apartment block and dashed into the entrance.

She took the back service staircase because she did not want to walk into the American Mess typhoon party – she was going to sneak in by the back door. She climbed up the steps, her skirt billowing up above her hips, her hair flying. She let herself quietly in at the kitchen door, and she was hit by the party.

Music, laughter, loud talking. The kitchen was a mess of bottles, glasses, food, wrappings. She tiptoed hurriedly down the corridor to her bedroom. She opened the door quietly and was confronted by a large pair of spread female buttocks on top of male thighs.

'Oops – sorry.'

The girl slid off the man hastily and clutched the bedspread up to her breasts. The man lay there, drunkenly unsurprised, his erection unabated. She didn't know either of them. 'Come and join us!'

'Do you mind if I take a rain-check?'

She hurried to the wardrobe and grabbed a few things.

Then to the dressing-table, and snatched up a few cosmetics.

'Bye – have fun.'

She didn't mind. If her bed had been empty she would have collapsed on to it, and then regretted it when she was woken by a drunken revelry. And she would have been trapped. Oh no, all she wanted was his apartment, his things about her. And some peace to keep praying in. She hurried to the bathroom and got her toothbrush, hair conditioner – and her bath salts. Yes – it was still bath-day, lucky old her. And two sleeping pills.

If she wasn't beautiful when he came out of this goddam typhoon it wouldn't be for want of trying.

Then she tiptoed back to the kitchen, and sneaked out of the door. The wind coming up the stairs billowed her skirt up again.

Upstairs in the gallery, the Chinese killer heard the front door open in McAdam's apartment below. He sat dead still in the rocking chair behind the closed door at the top of the spiral staircase, and listened.

She came in panting because she had climbed the six flights of stairs. She knew better than to trust an elevator during a typhoon. She locked the front door behind her. Then she flung herself on to the sofa.

She lay there a full minute in the near darkness, eyes closed, getting her breath back. Then the wind beat against the windows and she opened her eyes in a sudden realization: the windows had not been fortified with tape to hold flying glass.

She sighed. She was dead tired. Then she heaved herself up off the sofa.

It was almost like night outside, now, though she knew that somewhere behind that blackness the sunset was still going on. It was an unearthly darkness, full of foreboding. She could hardly see the sea, but the lights of the apartments and ships were burning. She walked to the french windows that led on to the verandah, and opened them. There was no wind at that moment. She stepped out into the hot darkness.

Then another burst of wind came.

Hard and sudden, and the trees below bent in the darkness. She clutched on to the verandah rail, and her hair blew and her skirt flapped and the curtains billowed into the living room. She clung there, feeling its strength; and she wanted to stand out here and feel the winds that would blow McAdam, and share them with him.

At the top of the spiral staircase the door opened a crack. The killer stood there a moment, looking down. Then he opened the door.

He stared down the iron steps, silently. Carefully. Below him, in the dark, were the open french windows. Outside on the verandah, she stood holding the rail, eyes closed, waiting for the next burst of wind, concentrating on McAdam, trying to communicate with him by thought. And behind her in the dark living room the man came silently down the spiral staircase to kill her.

One smart blow on the back of her shoulders and one grab at her knees to tilt her up, and over she would go. A wild scream, clutching at the air, arms and legs outflung as she plunged six floors to a sudden sharp death on the dark concrete below. Nobody would see her go in the dark, and nobody would hear her, with all windows closed.

Then the big gust of wind struck. She jerked and opened her eyes. Behind her the french door banged against itself, and she turned. She strode through the french window, into the dark living room, and slammed the window closed behind her. Six feet from her the killer froze on the spiral stairs.

He stood absolutely still in the dark as she bolted the french windows. Then she turned her back on the spiral staircase, snapped on the air-conditioner, switched on a reading-lamp, and walked out of the room to look for insulation tape to secure the windows.

The killer retreated silently up the staircase.

She found a big roll of adhesive tape in his office, and a pair of scissors. She spread the tape across the glass, from corner to corner and side to side, like a spider's web. She went methodically from window to window, room to room. She was very tired. But it was better to be working, doing something.

It was night by the time she finished with the windows in the bedroom. And outside the wind was coming harder now, beating against the glass almost all the time. She threw the roll of tape on to the chair, walked into the bathroom and spun the taps. She threw in a big dash of bubble suds. She sat down on the edge of the bath, eyes closed, waiting for it to fill.

Then she suddenly remembered the gallery upstairs. She had to tape those windows as well.

Well, she'd better do it now, before she zonked out.

She heaved herself up, went to the bedroom, picked up the tape and scissors, and walked down the corridor into the living room. She crossed to the spiral staircase and began to mount it.

She plodded slowly up it, round and round. She got half way.

Then she remembered. She didn't have the bloody key . . . It was on McAdam's key-ring. She stood there, wearily, considering what to do. It was serious. If those windows went . . .

There was nothing she could do. But she'd better try

the door anyway. Maybe by some chance he had left it unlocked.

She sighed and pulled herself forward on the handrail and started on up the stairs again. She came to the second last turn.

Then she remembered the bath. The taps were still running. She could hear them.

Damn!

She hesitated, then turned and clattered back down the spiral staircase.

She hurried across the living room, down the corridor, into the bathroom. The bath was full, the bubbles frothing up to the rim, the room full of steam. She spun the taps closed. Then she bent and felt the water.

It was good and hot. She hesitated again.

Well, even if that door to the gallery was open, it would take her an hour to tape all those windows. And by then this lovely bath would be cold. She wasn't going to waste that.

She would check the gallery afterwards, before she went to bed.

She began to unbutton her blouse.

At the top of the spiral staircase the door quietly opened. The killer listened, then he began to come down the stairs.

Outside in the blackness the wind beat the windows and howled up the stairs, but it was quiet in the apartment. She sat naked on the lavatory, eyes closed.

The killer heard the tinkling, the most defenceless sound in the world. He stopped at the beginning of the corridor. Absolutely still. He wanted her *in* the bath. He did not want to leave bruises or splashes or other signs of struggle. He stepped silently backwards into the living room, and waited.

Then he heard the sound of the lavatory flushing.

She piled her hair up on top of her head, pinned it; then she climbed carefully into the bubble bath. It was very hot. She stood a moment, adjusting to the heat; then she slowly lowered herself into it, and eased herself down the bath, so the suds slid up over her breasts. Just her head and neck were exposed.

She sighed and lay there, eyes closed.

Bliss.

Down the corridor, in the living room, the killer did not hear her getting into the bath because she had done it so slowly. He waited, absolutely alert, listening.

She lay silently in the bath for a full minute, just feeling the heat soak into her tired limbs. Then she felt the beads of sweat forming on her face. She slowly opened her eyes.

What she wanted was a long cold beer and a cigarette to relax with in this lovely bath. She lay there half a minute considering it. Then she heaved herself up out of the water.

The killer heard the splash of the water, and he thought she was now bathing. He came on tiptoe down the corridor.

Vanessa came naked, soapy, through the bedroom door, heading for the kitchen, then she saw him. All she saw was the terrifying dark shape of a man coming at her down the corridor, and she screamed.

She stumbled backwards into the bedroom, and the killer lunged down the corridor. She grabbed wildly at the door to slam it as he threw himself at it. She flung herself against the door with all her might, her wet feet skidding on the floor, and she shoved and shoved, screaming and heaving, and the door flew open.

She reeled back wild-eyed down the side of the bed and the killer burst into the room. She threw herself at the open wardrobe and grabbed wildly for McAdam's gun. She snatched it out, and as he lunged at her she jerked the trigger. There was a sharp popping noise, and the silenced gun leapt in her hand. The bullet smashed into the wall and the killer threw himself sideways against the wardrobe.

She scrambled up on to the bed, holding the gun in front of her with both hands, her breath coming in juddering gasps. The killer shoved himself off the wardrobe and lunged at her. She screamed in terror and pulled the trigger again and again, and the gun jerked in her hands and the bullets smashed into the wall. She leapt off the bed and fired again with both hands, and the bullet hit his chest just below his shoulder.

He crashed on to the floor, blood welling out of the side of his chest; she stood shuddering, her face contorted in horror, mouth open, the gun shaking in her hands. For a long instant the killer lay sprawled on the floor, his face creased up in agony; then he looked up at her, and began to get up. She gave a strangled cry of terror, levelled the gun at him blindly and fired again.

The last bullet in the gun smashed through the other side of the killer's chest and knocked him back to the floor. The blood was now spreading out from under him.

She crouched by the wardrobe, whimpering, the gun still pointed at him in both trembling hands; she pulled the trigger again, and the gun went click.

His chest covered in blood, his hands and face smeared in blood, his face screwed up in murderous fury, he got to his knees. He stretched out both his bloody hands towards her, and staggered up to his feet. She threw down the gun, and lunged into the wardrobe to grab McAdam's sword.

She wrenched off the scabbard and thrust the sword

desperately in front of her with both hands. The killer's eyes glinted. For a long terrible moment he stood there, the blood pumping out of him, then he bared his teeth in a horrible grin, and lurched towards her. She swung the sword wildly up over her shoulder like a club in both hands and ran towards the bathroom door, swinging the sword on high, and the killer came at her and she screamed and swiped at him. The sword slashed the air in front of him, and she threw herself hysterically through the bathroom door, reeled round and slammed it. The killer lurched against the door and she screamed and heaved against it with her naked shoulder.

Suddenly the door burst open and she lurched backwards. Her legs hit the edge of the bath and buckled, and the killer grasped for her.

She crashed backwards into the water, legs upflung, the sword in one hand, and the killer grabbed her foot. She screamed and wrenched and kicked and swung the sword, and he grabbed her wrist. She twisted and thrashed, and then thrust with all her might. The point of the sword stabbed into his breast, and he staggered back against the wall.

She scrambled up out of the bath, gasping. The man slumped against the wall, the blood spurting out of his chest, then he lurched towards her again. With the sword in front of her in both hands like a bayonet, eyes screwed up in horror, she rammed it with all her terrified strength into his stomach.

The killer doubled over, clutching the sword in both bloody hands, and hung on to it. She wrenched it out of his bloody grasp, then rammed it again with all her might into his guts. The point hit the wall behind him. The blood was pouring out of him, and her screams of horror were just hysterical gasps.

The blood welled up and out of his mouth, and he looked at her once, then slumped, and slid down the wall. She looked in horrified disbelief at the bloody man, then staggered across the bathroom and flung herself through the door clutching the bloody sword, naked, sobbing.

She wrenched open the front door. The wind howled up the stairs about her as she almost fell down them. Face contorted in terror, she escaped into Hillside Road and the howling night, and the wind got her, and she fell on hands and knees. She scrambled up, and lurched into a staggering run towards the American Mess.

PART XII

At about ten o'clock that night the first big wind came from the north, rushing in a black curve across the South China Sea, roaring like an express train. The wind lashed the waves up before it to send them crashing up on to the waterfronts and across the streets, and leaping up high over the rocks and the big concrete breakwaters of the typhoon shelters, and the packed junks rolled, timbers grinding, gunwale to gunwale. The ships in the harbour suddenly heaved against their buoys. And with the end of the first big wind came the first rain.

The rain swept across the islands in great black furls like curtains, and through the streets and up the steep mountains, lashing the jungle and the squatter shacks. And the water came rushing down the mountainsides, cascading down on to the roads and ladder streets between the apartment blocks and tenements, frothing, rushing down on to the foreshore.

But Typhoon Rose was still a hundred miles away and her winds were very much stronger than this.

THIRTY-NINE

The two deep-sea fishing junks had taken delivery of the four fishing-nets loaded with opium well before the first big winds struck. They too were dragging the nets behind them under the sea, although the likelihood of being challenged by a Hong Kong Marine Police launch at this stage of a typhoon, and at night, was remote. The junks were ploughing with the sea towards the land, and they made good time despite the weight of the nets. It was almost plain sailing.

The crews of both junks were also members of the 14K Triad Society, but they did not know for whom the opium was destined. All they knew was that near a certain deserted beach in Tolo Sound, they would see a single paraffin lamp blink. The place, the beach, the passwords, the people, were different every time.

The junk's skippers saw the paraffin lamp blink on the deserted beach and they hove to, the passwords were exchanged, and all lights were extinguished. The fishing-nets were hauled up, the bales of opium were hastily emptied into the holds of the sampans, and the junk crews were paid. Then the sampans were sculled ashore to the beach.

Waiting in dark near the beach were five vegetable trucks with canvas-covered backs. One of these trucks was completely loaded with vegetables. The sampan crews hastily loaded the bales of opium into the backs of the four empty trucks. Then they covered the bales with the vegetables from the fifth truck. The sampans were cast adrift to be smashed up by the typhoon, and the trucks ground away over the rough mountain track.

Even these truck drivers did not know where the opium was bound, nor who had purchased it. All they knew was that they were to drive through the wild typhoon night by different assigned routes to the general farming area called Sekong. And in that area, at assigned places, they would stop in the darkness to examine their right front wheel, whereupon a man would step out of the bushes, passwords would be exchanged, the newcomer would pay and take over the vehicle, and the first driver would walk away into the blackness.

The new drivers drove the vehicles to a certain remote farm and delivered the cargo to heavily armed guards, who paid and then handed the cargo of opium over to the chemists within the farmhouse. And the chemists set about converting the black raw opium into 999 heroin, signifying ninety-nine-point-nine per cent purity.

Even the chemists and their armed guards did not know who the owner of this heroin was, although they were all good 14K Triad men. All they knew was that when they were finished they would be handsomely paid and then new armed guards and new vehicles would take the stuff away.

The only persons who could assist the police in their enquiries, the only persons who knew the identity of the master-mind and financier of the whole operation, were the Red Rod of the First Lodge of the 14K Triad Society, and the Vanguard. And the Red Rod was surrounded by many brave and iron-disciplined men; he was the headmaster of a well-known Chinese school, and the Vanguard was a Chinese priest in the Church of England.

As soon as the typhoon was over, the heroin would

be aboard a number of 747 jumbo jets, heading for America and Europe. Not in pickle jars and tooth-paste tubes aboard steamships, nor built into motor cars – that was old-fashioned. The modern need in the Hong Kong Connection was speed. And *jumbo* jets, because of the large number of lavatories. On the lava-tory bulkheads are panels which can easily be un-screwed. The couriers boarded the aircraft, carrying the heroin in their hand luggage, and during the flight they placed it behind the panels in the lavatories. When the aircraft reached San Francisco, the couriers got off, empty-handed, and their job was done. If they were searched by Customs officers there was nothing to find. In San Francisco new American couriers boarded the aircraft, bound for Chicago or some other destination. They went to the lavatories, unscrewed the panels, retrieved the heroin, put it in their hand luggage. When they got to Chicago, they were not searched thoroughly by Customs officers because theirs had been only a domestic flight.

And the heroin bound for England and Europe went via America too, for those couriers had not been near the Far East either.

Herman Choi's other favourite system required the collaboration of aircraft maintenance staff at the air-ports concerned. The electrical engineer passed through the airport security gates unchallenged, with the heroin in his toolbag. He hid the narcotic in the 'Fl section' of the aircraft, that area under the cockpit deck which is full of highly complicated electrical gear and wiring, a place where only an expert would venture. On arrival the narcotics would be removed by another engineer, who would also pass through Customs unchallenged.

Both systems were ninety-nine-point-nine per cent foolproof.

FORTY

The firemen were spreadeagled on their bunks, exhausted, dirty, grazed. They were in full firefighting gear, dripping water and ashes and blood, the sweat pouring off them, smoking their first cigarettes for hours, their feet up for the first time in seven hours, but with their fireproof boots still on, because when the alarm next went they had to hit the pole within sixty seconds.

Always with our fucking boots right on, Jack-the-Fire thought. He sprawled on his back on his office floor, eyes closed, face streaked with black, hair matted. He had been wearing his boots for a hundred years. He was clearly going to die with his boots on, because he was going to die any fucking moment. The mere sound of the next alarm bell would kill him by itself.

The two-way radio was rasping all the time next door; he was trying not to listen to it. Fires, landslides, collapsed houses, collapsed roads, floods – firemen and fire-engines and fireboats being ordered here, there and everywhere at once. There was a big fire in the Chaiwan squatter area, the winds spreading it faster than the lashing rain and the fire-engines could put it out. Two other squatter areas had been hit by landslides, firemen and soldiers were digging, dragging out the bodies in the lashing rain. There was an electrical fire raging in the power station, half of Kowloon was plunged in blackness, half of Kowloon's firemen were fighting it, trying to save the transformers so that Kowloon's factories would not be out of work for weeks. There were twenty-one fires on both sides of the harbour and in two typhoon shelters.

'Fire alarm at Nanking Mansions – '

'Jesus,' Jack-the-Fire muttered, eyes closed.

Then the alarm was shrilling and they were leaping off their bunks and running for the pole and hurtling down it to the red fire-engines below, and Jack-the-Fire was yelling:

'Come on!'

In exactly fifty seconds the last man was clinging to the fire-engine and the big red machines roared out of the doors into the typhoon. The fire-engines lurched in the wind and the men clung fiercely on, heads down. The engines raced down the street, bells clanging, lights flashing, swerving round rocks and branches and debris. At the corner a big drain was burst and water gushed out like an oil well and the winds lashed it away. A car was overturned. Ahead was a wide road rushing like a river in the headlights. The fire-engine roared across the rushing street, wheels spinning, and then a big neon sign came hurtling down the concrete canyon, and it would have gone flying over the fire-engine, but at that moment Fireman Chan lifted his head, and it hit him on the back of his helmet at a hundred miles an hour. The mass of flying steel sliced off the top of Fireman Chan's skull as if it was a boiled egg, and took his body with it, hurtling into blackness. Nobody saw him go.

The fire-engines stood axle-deep in rushing water, arc-lights beaming up, fire hoses jetting. The fourth to the tenth floors of Nanking Mansions were ablaze, the winds driving the fire upwards. The fire had started in an illegal plastic-goods factory on the fourth floor. The people below the fourth floor had fled downwards, and huddled in the rabbit warren of shopping arcades, the black water crashed down the stairs around them. But many people above the fourth floor had fled upwards, scrambling, trampling each other, whores, pimps, sailors, screaming, shoving, coughing. And firemen were fighting up the flooding stairways.

Big Cheri was lying on the bed in King Winky's penthouse brothel, admiring her magnificent breasts in the mirror and humming untunefully, and Harry Howard was pacing about fully dressed, wringing his hands, dying to get the hell out of this terrible sinful place and back to his ever-loving wife, when suddenly the bedroom shook and there was a roar of wind in the corridor, and then black smoke gushed under the door. Harry stared at it uncomprehendingly, then Big Cheri sat up so her big tits bounced. 'Gosh,' she squeaked, 'Fire!'

'Fire?' Harry Howard croaked. 'How can there be fire with all this rain?'

'Don't just stand there, Harry,' Big Cheri squeaked. 'Go put it out!'

'Oh my God,' Harry gargled. 'Oh my God – water – water – '

He went scrambling into the bathroom looking for something to pour water into, and there was nothing except the two toothbrush glasses, and he bellowed at Big Cheri who was still clutching her breasts: 'Call Room Service for a bucket! – ' and turned the taps on full blast, and all he could think of was what he would tell his wife when she heard that the fire-brigade had rescued him from King Winky's whorehouse.

'Oh Room Service, where are you, Room Service, call the fire brigade,' she squeaked into the telephone.

At that moment the front doors of King Winky's whorehouse exploded open under the force of the black wind roaring up the stairwells, and with the wind came the screams of the people struggling up the stairs. The wind roared through King Winky's whorehouse and smashed the windows at the end of the corridor and the long carpet went sucking out, and the wind hit Harry

Howard's door and blasted it open.

The door sent him flying backwards on top of Big Cheri. He scrambled up, clutching his bloody nose, and screamed '*Get out!*' He grabbed Big Cheri's arm and heaved her up and lunged, choking, into the teeth of the blast, dragging her after him, and the first of the fleeing mob came stampeding up the corridor. Harry and Big Cheri were crushed up the stairs that led to the rooftop, choking, up against the iron door. Harry beat on the door, feeling wildly for the bolts, and rammed them back, and the iron door suddenly disappeared, whipped into the howling blackness by Typhoon Rose, and it took him and Big Cheri with it. They were flung out on the rooftop and over the concrete, on their faces in the lashing wind and rain, and the mob came fighting after them.

Thirty minutes later there were still a hundred people trying to fight their way along King Winky's corridors and up on to the rooftop, but the ones at the end would not make it. There were over three hundred and fifty people packed on to the rooftop between the water tanks and the elevator housings, on top of each other, and there was no more room to scramble to. The rooftop heaved and surged with bodies trampling each other in the blackness, trying to get away from the terror of the fire that was now leaping red and yellow through the black smoke of the doorway. Fifty people lay roasting in King Winky's corridors. The rooftop was getting hotter from the flames below. For the moment the lashing rain cooled the concrete and the winds tore away the smoke and the intense heat. But when the eye of Typhoon Rose passed over, the winds and the rain would stop, and it would be deathly still.

It was nearly daybreak. Then the rain stopped, and there was only the roaring of the winds.

FORTY-ONE

Captain Neil O'Bryan in the *Fat Hong* knew from the screeching radio that there were thirty-one ships dragging anchor at this moment but he could only glimpse flashes of lights through the lashing spray. He could not see how close to the rocks of Lantau Island he was. He could not even see the waves, he could only judge them by their massive pounding on his hull, and great sprays flying over the bridge. The bows crashed down into the troughs so the whole ship shook and the waves resounded like cannon.

Captain Neil O'Bryan clung to the bridge-wing, lashed, sodden, eyes screwed up, his skinny legs braced. The *Fat Hong* was dragging both her anchors, but he had his engines grinding ahead to diminish the drag. '*Hail Mary, Full of Grace,*' he croaked fiercely over and over into the lashing rain, '*Hallowed be Thy Name . . .*' And he could not even hear himself.

Suddenly he saw bridge-lights through the lashing rain. He lurched frantically towards the wheelhouse.

'*Do you see them – lights?*'

The helmsman could see nothing through the rain-lashed glass. '*Up anchors!*' Neil O'Bryan bellowed at the bridgeman, and he reeled at the telegraph and rammed it up to half ahead. '*Starboard forty-five degrees!*' Then he shouted into the radio transmitter:

'*Ahoy there! Fat Hong calling unknown ship bearing down on her off Lantau. Heave over for the love of God! Fat Hong turning east on her starboard. Do you read me for the love of Jesus!*'

The Chinese seaman was fighting his way over the

foredeck. He threw himself at the port anchor winch and began to heave in the anchor. Then through the rain the blurred bridge lights of the USS *Dreadnought* could suddenly be seen, heaving upwards, fifty yards ahead, then they were gone again. The next wave smashed him away from the starboard anchor winch before he could turn the handle, sucked him over the rail, and he was gone.

The *Fat Hong* was heaving to starboard, her old engines pounding, but one dragging anchor was still holding her. She was broadside on to the big galloping troughs now, and she heaved over under each impact in a massive roll, then rolled back again in the bottom of the trough, then the next wave hit her and she rolled again, and Captain O'Bryan was hurled into the corner of the bridge-wing. He lay stunned, then he started to scramble up, and then he saw the lights again.

'*For the love of Jesus and Mary!*'

Twenty yards off his port side bridge-wing, looming blurred and terrible way up above him as his ship rolled. The *Dreadnought* was broadside on to him, crashing and rolling with the waves; for a long instant he saw her, then she rolled to port as the *Fat Hong* rolled to starboard, and she was gone in the spray and rain. Captain O'Bryan bellowed into the gale: '*Starboard hard!*' and flung himself into the wheelhouse and rammed the telegraph to full ahead. He grabbed the megaphone and clawed his way out on to the port bridge-wing. The *Fat Hong* rolled to port as the *Dreadnought* rolled to starboard. The bridge-wing came rolling towards him, and he yelled into the megaphone:

'*Get out of the way for the love of Christ!*'

The wave broke over him and *Dreadnought*'s bridge missed him by two yards. He clung to the bridge-wing, gasping as it swooped upwards and away from the

Dreadnought like a ferris wheel with her starboard roll, then she began to roll back. *Fat Hong* crashed into her portside roll and Captain O'Bryan saw the *Dreadnought* bridge-wing coming swooping down towards him, the big wing of steel looming huge, and he screamed into the wind and reeled backwards to get out of the way of the mass of steel, and the *Dreadnought*'s bridge-wing crashed down on to his.

The *Fat Hong*'s port bridge-wing was torn off the wheelhouse with a terrible cracking under the crashing spray, and O'Bryan went with it, headlong into the sea below. He fell between the two mangled ships as they tore apart and rolled in opposite directions again, but he did not fight the sea because he could not any more. The two ships started rolling back towards each other, and O'Bryan was crushed between the two steel sides as they cannoned against each other.

Again and again the two ships rolled and crashed against each other in the blackness, and already they had made gaping holes in each other, and the *Fat Hong* was taking water fast when she capsized and sank.

It was almost daybreak.

The rain had stopped, and with the daybreak McAdam could see the lights of junks ploughing up Tolo Sound like he was, taking the troughs head-on.

He clung to the main-mast, lashed to it by his waist with a lifeline, one hand trying to shield his eyes from the seas and wind. The bows reared up again into the running swell, then swooped down the other side, and the sea hit him full blast, and the lifeline wrenched at his guts. The winds were fiercer than ever. But he hardly felt them – all he felt was the sudden exhausted elation that the horror of being blind was almost over. He could just see the shore-lines on both sides now, and he could see something on the sea, and it was marvellous to know that there was nothing ahead. He clung tight on to the mast as he feverishly untied the bowline around his waist, then he staggered back to the wheelhouse.

'Daybreak, Elder Brother! And the rain has stopped!'

Wong clung to the wheel, sodden and exhausted. 'But the typhoon is not over.'

'But it will not be like last night again! By tonight it will be gone!'

The junk shook as it crashed down into the trough, and the spray lashed the wheelhouse in a sheet. He could not even hear the pounding of the diesel engine just beneath his feet.

'Just hold her there! There is nothing ahead.'

McAdam lurched across the wheelhouse and down the hatch into the cabin. He pulled open the drawer and his hand found the whisky bottle. He staggered back into the wheelhouse and braced himself. He felt marvellous. His concrete boat had performed perfectly. He passed the bottle unsteadily to Wong.

'Drink! It will be good for you!'

Wong took a swallow, choked and suppressed a retch. 'Again!'

Wong clung to the wheel, head down, shuddering. McAdam clapped him on the shoulder.

'Be joyful, Elder Brother! It is nearly daylight! And our ship of stone has survived!'

FORTY-TWO

Suddenly, when they were at their blackest and fiercest, the winds vanished.

Suddenly the sky could be seen again, a circle of blue, with the great amphitheatre of black walls rising up to it, and the light was eerie. It was humid sweating hot. Suddenly the jungle stopped threshing and hung there, sodden, broken. Suddenly there was no more roaring, only the noise of the water cascading down off the mountains and rushing down the streets. It was like a silent battlefield, just the water swirling, the broken cars and the neon signs scattered up the streets. And the waves were no longer battering the waterfronts, just big swells seething, confused. Out on the rocky coastlines of the islands eleven big ships lay wrecked, but ships which had been dragging anchors suddenly held; Hong Kong was inside the eye of the typhoon.

The broadcast went out again and again:

We repeat, this is only a temporary lull. The eye of the typhoon is passing over Hong Kong. We are on the inside edge of the eye. It will pass in approximately sixty minutes, whereupon the winds will return at the same velocity, but from the opposite direction. All people should remain indoors. All vessels should prepare to receive the wind from the opposite quadrant. Shipping is warned that the return of the winds will coincide with high tide and bigger waves can be expected . . .

At the Royal Air Force strip the helicopter was being

rolled out of the hangar.

'In,' Jack-the-Fire shouted to his firemen. 'In!'

The helicopter flew flat out, roaring low over the rooftops. They could see the smoke from Nanking Mansions. Jack looked through binoculars at the Chaiwan squatter area and he could see that a big rockfall had cut a broad swathe through the huts. He looked at his Chinese firemen. They were wet, dirty, tired, like him. But the shine on Jack's face was not water, it was sweat. Good cold fear. Even in big airliners Jack never flew quite sober: he was terrified in a helicopter. 'How long?' he said to the pilot.

'Half a minute less than the last time you asked. About one minute more.'

'How much time have you got to get this flying machine back before the shit hits the fan again?'

'Forty minutes.'

'What'll you do if the typhoon comes back before you've made it back to base?'

'File a complaint.'

The helicopter went chopping into a big circle, approaching the rooftop of Nanking Mansions. The smoke belched up in a dense black cloud. The flames leapt through the windows, orange and yellow and red and black. They could not see the people on the rooftop through the smoke. On the next rooftop, across the yawning chasm of the street and fifty feet lower, there were firemen waiting. 'What do you want me to do?' the pilot shouted.

Jack was leaning out of the door, clinging on tight, trying to see the rooftop through the smoke, some point to drop on to without falling seventeen floors down to the street. The helicopter lurched in the rising heat, the smoke whirling away from the propeller blast. And down there on the rooftop the piled bodies were writhing, clawing, gasping, suffocating, dying; people were hanging over the wall, trying to scramble away from the roasting concrete. Jack spoke into the intercom:

'Hover over the centre. About twenty feet. We'll bale out by ladder. Then keep hovering there to blow the smoke clear while we rig the slide.'

The helicopter came chopping back over the concrete canyons. Way down there were the fire-engines and ambulances. Jack did not look. The propellers were blasting the smoke off the rooftop and he could see the gesticulating people clearly now. 'Hover!' Jack rasped. 'Away the ladders!'

The rope ladders unrolled, and the first man was already scrambling down, the helicopter rocking under the shift of weight. Jack swung down the ladder in the propeller blast. The first two firemen were dragging the dead and injured clear.

Jack dropped down on to the concrete and began to shove his way towards the steel door, pushing people aside, shouting into his gasmask, 'Make way!' He saw a naked woman with magnificent breasts and a mass of blonde hair, and she was cradling the bloody head of a man saying, 'There, there, Harry, there there . . .' The last firemen in the helicopter were throwing the equipment down. Jack lowered his helmet and disappeared through the black smoke of the doorway.

He could see the flames leaping, and feel the heat beating on his asbestos suit, roaring up the corridor towards the open steel door like a chimney. And below this floor there were half a dozen more ablaze, roasting that rooftop, without the wind and rain to cool it. He scrambled back up to the rooftop. Seven firemen were shoving through the people towards him lugging fire extinguishers. They scrambled through the door, gasmasks on under their visors, and disappeared into the smoke.

Jack-the-Fire struggled across the rooftop to the water reservoirs. A nylon rope had been fired across the chasm from the rooftop to the next apartment block, and the cable had been dragged across.

Jack's men were rigging their end of the slide, lashed around a water reservoir; now they were pulling across the chair on the running tackle. Jack pulled off his visor and gasmask, grabbed the nearest woman by the arm and bellowed:

'Women first! – into the chair!'

The firemen swung the chair underneath her buttocks. 'Hold tight!' Then she saw the yawning chasm beneath her feet and screamed. 'Away!' Jack bellowed, and away she went, screaming out into thin air, eyes screwed-up, hair flying, through space down towards the firemen on the rooftop below. Now the people were heaving and clutching to be the next to go. Jack was back underneath the roaring helicopter at the rope ladders.

'Come on!' he roared. 'Up! – Up!'

He grabbed a woman and she started scrambling wildly. Now they were mobbing around the rope ladders. '*One at a time!*' he bellowed. '*No grabbing!*'

Three minutes later the helicopter was full. It went rocking up, into the sky, then it banked away, chopping over the concrete jungle towards the Police Sports Club where the ambulances were waiting.

A second helicopter was coming towards the rooftop. Jack was shouting into his radio: 'We need another helicopter! Heat intense, these people can't take much more. Also oxygen-starvation. The only chance is to blow the water reservoirs and then follow it with men – so get another fucking helicopter and stuff it full

of firemen and get its ass up here because I'm going to
blow them reservoirs before these people roast alive!'

The circle of blue sky was almost gone over the Mountains of Nine Dragons. The black wall was coming back
over the sea. There were thirty people left on the rooftop. The smoke was billowing out of the door again,
black and choking; people were hanging over the wall,
coughing, gasping. Jack knelt at the base of the water
reservoir, placing a plastic explosive charge. He slid the
detonator in, then scrambled backwards, trailing the
electric wire. Another man in the chair went hurtling
off over the canyon. Then the third helicopter came
overhead and the propeller began to blast the smoke
away.

Jack waved it down, it hovered and the two rope
ladders unfurled. 'Up!' Jack roared. They started clawing frantically up, people surging, shoving to be the
next to go. 'Last one!' He grabbed Big Cheri by the arm.
'Up, lady!'

Big Cheri squeaked at him: 'Excuse me, Mr Fireman,
but I think my friend should go and I'll go on the slidy
thing – '

All Jack saw was the big smudged mouth moving
through the mass of flying hair, and the magnificent
breasts. He shoved her regretfully:

'Get up there, lady!'

'But Mr Fireman, Sir!'

A man shouldered her aside and swung on to the
ladder, and Big Cheri staggered backwards, and then
another man grabbed the ladder and started clawing up
it. Jack yelled at the pilot: *'Get out of here before they
pull you down!'*

The helicopter rose, lurching, straining, with the two
ladders full of wildly clinging people; it rose two feet,

three, four, six, and the ladder laden with people was swinging across the rooftop. Harry Howard lunged blindly as it swung past him in the roaring blast of the propellers, and grabbed it with two hands and clung on for dear life, and he was swept kicking off his feet in the roaring blast, and the helicopter keeled under its swinging weight as it roared across the rooftop. The wall was sweeping towards him with the terrible nothingness yawning below, and everybody was shouting at him to let go.

'*Come back, Harry, you'll fall!*' Big Cheri screamed, and she lumbered after him as he was swept across the rooftop, and her clawing fingers just got him by the pants and she clung on as she was dragged on her knees screaming, '*Let go, Harry!*' Jack-the-Fire was bounding after her bellowing, '*Leggo for Chrissakes!* – ' and Big Cheri hit the wall and let go. As she was about to crash over the wall, Jack-the-Fire hit her from behind in a sort of wild rugby tackle, both arms flung around her waist and his face squashed against the side of her ample buttocks, and the helicopter keeled out over the chasm. It roared down with the two ladders swinging wildly, the pilot wrestling to get her back under control. The helicopter fell twenty feet, sideways, then she came back under control, lurching and staggering. The pilot gave her full throttle to drive her up out of the chasm, and she began to lift. She lifted slowly, shuddering, and she was going to make it; she was gaining altitude slowly but surely, juddering, and now her screaming propellers were almost level with the rooftop again, and Jack bellowed:

'*Mind the wire!*' and as he yelled, the propellers hit the cable stretched across the concrete canyon and the blade smashed and went spinning off into the air. For a moment the helicopter seemed to stagger at the top of the concrete canyon, then it lurched sideways and fell.

A roar went up from the street below and inside the helicopter there were screams of terror; it went down fifty feet, then it hit the side of the blazing building at the tenth floor and went skidding straight down the blazing wall, then it burst into flames – great orange flames that billowed into a ball around it. Then it bounced off the wall and went tumbling down through the air for the last sixty feet, and crashed in a splat of flying flames on to the street below.

FORTY-THREE

McAdam sat slumped over the wheel, sodden, his head in one hand, his other holding the whisky bottle. Wong lay stretched out on the wheelhouse deck, fast asleep. McAdam yearned to lie down but he knew that if he did he would pass out. His whole body felt bruised from the sea hitting him.

It was steamy hot. Directly overhead the sky was blue, but just beyond the mountain it was black again, the walls of winds silently coming closer and closer. He sat, waiting for them. They had taken a new anchorage, in good water, the bows pointing south-east now, whence the backlash of the winds would come. The sea seethed in the eye of the typhoon, heaving and slapping against the hull, as if it did not know where to go.

He got up stiffly.

'Wong!'

Wong did not stir.

'Wong, Elder Brother!' He crouched down wearily

and shook him.

Wong's eyes opened and he sat bolt upright, staring.

'The winds are coming back. And it is nearly high tide. The waves will be even bigger.'

Wong creaked to his feet. McAdam hefted his life-jacket on.

'I go to the mast?'

'No. We should be able to see enough with the daylight.'

He put the whisky bottle away and lit a cigarette.

Then the howling winds came back with a dragon's roar.

The tidal wave that got McAdam and Wong came from way out in the South China Sea. It came rolling towards the South China Coast and it hit the outlying islands and went crashing and leaping far up them and round them; and it went rolling through Hong Kong harbour, thundering against the big ships and over the junks, leaping over the waterfront and sweeping cars down the streets and piling them up on top of each other; it was more than twice the height of a man, and it smashed down shopfronts and swirled into the doorways of the tenements and up the stairs. The great wave heaved up the freighter *Gonzalez* and carried it over the waterfront and down on to the street.

When the wave was about five hundred yards away McAdam saw it, through the rain and the flying spray lashing his face and eyeballs. The junk had dragged its anchors again and they were in the middle of the sound, Wong at the wheel, McAdam lashed to the mast. It was the biggest wave he had ever seen, a great wall of water coming galloping down towards him. '*Watch out!*' he roared to Wong, and it was a roar of terror and fury and hate and the knowledge that he was going to die.

318

Through the fury he knew also that he somehow had to make his beloved concrete junk take this terrible wave head-on, try to plunge it up and over it and down the other side. McAdam bellowed to Wong into the wind and he untied himself from the mast and clawed his way forward to heave in the dragging anchor.

Wong could not see the wave through the rain-lashed glass, but he could see McAdam heaving in the anchor and trying to bellow something to him above the bedlam of the wind and sea. It was not until the wave was one hundred yards off that Wong saw the wall of water looming; for a moment he stared at it, not comprehending, clinging to the wheel, then suddenly he understood what McAdam was bellowing at him – *Head straight into it!* and he gave a strangled shout of terror and exhaustion, and rammed the throttle full ahead, clutching the wheel tight. McAdam fought his way back to the mainmast, and started desperately to undo the knot of his lifeline so he could get back to the wheelhouse. He bellowed '*Hold her into the wave! –*' and wrenched at the knot with one hand. He wrenched and wrenched and he could not do it with one hand and he bellowed a terrified curse and let go of the mast and wrenched with both hands and he fell. A wave crashed over him and he toppled on to his knees and grabbed for his knife and he could not find it. He bellowed again in fury and looked wildly into the lashing spray, and he knew he was not going to make it. The wave was fifty yards off now, rearing up and coming as fast as a man can run, and McAdam knew the only thing he could do. He flung his arms around the mast fiercely and yelled over his shoulder to Wong:

'*Hold fast!*'

Wong held the junk fast head-on. He could see almost nothing through the rain-lashed glass except

McAdam at the mast: Wong clung to the wheel, legs apart, braced for the terrible wave he knew was coming and that was surely going to kill him.

When it was thirty yards away he saw it again through the sudden clarity of the glass, the approaching wall of brown sea, the spray lashing off it and the waves driven before it, and Wong knew that the junk could never get up and over that wall of sea, it would smash right over him and drag the boat to the bottom. He gave one long howl of terror, and swung the helm hard to starboard.

The bows came round and McAdam saw the wave suddenly swinging crazily aside and he bellowed: '*No! No! – Back!*'

Wong held the wheel hard over and the bows came right round. McAdam looked back and saw the terrifying crest coming curling over behind him, then he felt the stern of his boat riding up up up the slope of the killer wave.

Then it hit the stern like thunder and crashed over the wheelhouse, and the wave picked the boat up and carried it. Like a giant surfboard, the boat was hurtled down the sound towards Shatin Village. The wave carried the boat down the sound for six hundred yards, then it hit the beach with a crack like cannon and exploded over it, and the junk rolled over on to her side and went with the wave over the beach and over the road and into the paddy-fields beyond.

McAdam was flung with it by the rope round his waist, upside down and head over heels, trying to thrash his way to the air; then the mast broke and his life line was gone. He fought wildly to get back to the air, then his head broke surface and he too was carried over the road into the paddy-field.

Five hundred yards down the beach, the wave ex-

320

ploded over Shatin Village sea wall, and went marauding right through the village carrying all before it, junks and sampans and carts and people, across the road and into the paddy-fields and over the railway-line; the wave went a thousand yards up the Shatin Valley, before it began to draw back towards the sea.

For thirteen hours Typhoon Rose raged across the Colony, and the winds reached one hundred and ninety miles an hour. Ten walls collapsed at a Low Cost Housing Estate. Three aircraft were destroyed when their hangar blew down. Five hundred Army, Navy and Air Force catering staff worked round the clock feeding sixty-two thousand homeless people. Thousands of tourists were trapped in their hotels. Over one thousand junks were wrecked and over two hundred boat-people drowned. A groom at the Shatin Riding Stables saw the tidal wave coming and managed to turn ten of the horses loose to fend for themselves, and they swam wildly against the waves, but the rest were drowned, kicking and whinnying in their stables. One hundred tons of boats were lying in the middle of Kai Tak Airport runway. A rock as big as a tram crashed down the mountain, buried eleven squatter shacks, and cut a swathe through the Chinese Cemetery below, leaving tombstones and coffins and bones everywhere. Four men were swept off rooftops trying to save their cocklofts. Big Cheri Fontaine flew naked through the typhoon on the slide to safety, clutching her magnificent bosom. Twenty-seven typhoon parties were a roaring success. The anchor of an American freighter dragged up the cross-harbour telephone cable and Hong Kong and Kowloon could not contact each other except by radio. Twenty-seven thousand other telephones were knocked out. The Fire Department rescued over five thousand people from being burned, suffocated, drowned and crushed. Over four thousand motor cars were destroyed, flooded, overturned. Altogether thirty-seven big ships were wrecked on the rocks.

Typhoon Rose was heading northwards into China. Gradually, the winds began to get slower. And slowly it was getting lighter now, the sky no longer so black; there were moving banks of grey, and you could see the harbour again through the rain, the water rushing down off the mountains, great yellow muddy torrents pouring down the streets, and the new piles of landslides, and the cracks in the roads and the crumpled cars, and the rocks and the debris.

Then the typhoon was gone, and the great rains came.

PART XIII

The rain came down out of the vast dark mass of clouds moving like molasses across the China Sea in the wake of Typoohn Rose. It came down first in furls and curtains with the last of the winds, sweeping across the rooftops and hammering down the streets, on the wreckage and devastation and the stretchers and the ambulances. Then the wind was completely gone, and down it came, straight. Grey and hard and thick as fingers, and the harbour was invisible again. More water came rushing down off sodden mountains, cascading down over the embankments and swirling down the steep winding roads, carrying rocks and branches and debris. The rain came hammering down as it had never done before.

FORTY-FOUR

The rain drummed on the hood of Vanessa's rented car as she came out of Lion Rock tunnel above the Shatin Valley. In the car with her were two policemen. The valley was misty grey in the rain, but she could see the junks lying wrecked in the paddies, the sheen of water over the whole valley. She hunched close to the windscreen as she drove fast, her tyres roaring on the wet tarmac, the windscreen wipers sloshing. But she could not see the sea through the rain. She took the final bend down in the valley.

Ahead the road disappeared under a sheet of water.

The Chinese inspector beside her said:

'I think it is too deep, madam, better we go back through Sekong.'

'No dammit! That'll take hours.'

She rolled her front wheels into the water, then declutched down to low gear and accelerated. The sea water curved up off her wheels. She could not see the road. It was like driving into a lake. But she was not going to give up. She drove through the water, hunched over the wheel. The inspector sat beside her peering anxiously.

'Is the road straight here?'

'I don't remember, madam.'

She did not care a damn about the car – Mr Hertz's problem – the only desperately important thing was that she didn't plunge into a paddy-field and have to proceed on foot. She saw a dead horse on the left. She glimpsed some junks, lying on their sides, up there in the valley.

She drove another two hundred yards, then she could just make out the first buildings of Shatin Village ahead through the rain: she was sure the road was straight the rest of the way. She roared her engine and slammed up to second gear, and suddenly the car ploughed nose first off the road and jolted into a ditch.

'Oh, *shit!*'

She sat behind the wheel, furious with herself. She slammed the car into reverse and roared the engine. The rear wheels screamed in the water and the car did not move.

'Oh, *fuck!*'

She flung open her door without hesitating and grabbed her umbrella. 'Sorry, gentlemen. Come on!' She sank up to her shins in water, slammed the car door. The water was only just below the top of her gumboots. The policemen came plodding stoically after her in their regulation boots. The inspector was speaking into his two-way radio in Cantonese, telling Headquarters what had happened.

She came splashing up the sunken road into the outskirts of the village, the policemen splashing beside her. There were dead chickens and dogs and cats everywhere, and some dead water-buffaloes and more horses. The rain teemed down. Ahead she could see the red fire-engines and the big blue police trucks and the ambulances, and the people milling. She saw the collapsed walls, the roofs smashed off. There was a junk crashed on its side right on top of a building. People were loading the dead into sampans and rafts. She looked desperately around. There were firemen and policemen everywhere but they were all working. She saw a fire officer standing by a Land-Rover, talking into a radio transmitter. She hurried over to him. He was saying:

325

'. . . Dead, one hundred and seventeen so far. Over and out.' He looked at her wearily, the rain splashing off his helmet.

'I'm sorry to trouble you, but I'm trying get to Tai-po; are there any vehicles going through?'

'No, madam. Road's washed away. So is the railway line. Only way is via Sekong, the long way.'

She waved her hand behind her. 'My car's gone off the road down there.'

'Sorry, can't spare any vehicles to tow you out yet.'

'No, of course. I'm looking for a man called Jake McAdam, do you know him?'

'I know *of* Mr McAdam. Was he in Shatin at the time of the wave?'

'He was on his boat around here.'

The officer looked at her. 'If he was on a boat . . .' He took a weary breath. 'Come with me, please.'

He led her between the vehicles and people, up towards high ground. Her policemen hurried after her. They both had their hands on their gun holsters now, eyes darting everywhere. They came upon a big mass of people. The officer parted them. Then she blanched. There was a long row of dead people laid out, over a hundred yards long. Chinese were crowding past and bending over them, weeping and sobbing.

'There're a few Europeans. Would you care to look?'

She stared at the row of dead, muddy faces. 'Oh my God, Hogan . . .' She walked down the rows of bodies, heart pounding. They were all lying on their backs, face up. There were many children. She felt sick, stunned. She could not feel proper compassion, only dread. That she was going to see his dead face lying there. She could not look at the faces of the children.

She walked slowly, dazedly, down the long, dreadful line, glancing at each battered face. A woman was bending over a baby, examining its head; she looked up, stricken, and then laughed hysterically. She came to the first dead European, she did not look twice, and her heart thudded faster. It was an elderly priest. Then the next. Out of the corner of her eye she saw two ambulance men stagger up with another body. Somebody in front of her shouted:

'Here's one alive!'

The ambulance men thumped the stretcher down in the mud and came running. They splashed down on their knees beside the body and one grabbed its wrist and the other rammed his mouth over the body's and began to give it mouth-to-mouth resuscitation. She hurried on. She could see one more European body ahead, and it was young and with brown sodden hair.

She stood in the teeming rain, aghast, staring at the body and shaking her head, then she plunged her hands into her face and gasped:

'*It's not him!*'

And she reeled around, sobbing and laughing hysterically into her hands: 'It's not Hogan!'

She looked about joyfully for the fire officer to tell him so he could rejoice with her. He was coming towards her through the rain.

'Is Mr McAdam the man with the concrete junk?'

'Yes!'

He pointed back at the valley.

'I've made some enquiries – they tell me the concrete junk's down there.'

She ran through the rain, splashing down the flooded road, half sobbing, the policemen running beside her. She fell on to her hands and knees, scrambled up and ran splashing on. Then she saw the first junk lying on its side in the grey paddy and she yelled:

'*Hogan!*'

She ran on, panting, her hair plastered to her head. The junk was too small for McAdam's. She could dimly make out more junks further ahead.

'*Ho-gan!*'

The rain deadened the shout. She ran on, stumbling, splashing, gasping, until she was opposite the junks. They were two hundred yards off; she tried to shield her eyes from the rain. And her heart lurched. She was sure the furthest junk was Hogan's. It was the right size.

She jumped off the edge of the road and landed with a splash on the edge of the paddy, on her hands and knees. She picked herself up, and her boots sank up to her shins in mud, the water up to her thighs. She pulled herself forward, plodding fiercely. The policemen followed her. She waded, her feet sucking in the mud. When she had gone fifty yards she had to stop. Her breath was coming in painful gasps, her legs trembling. She stood, shielding her eyes, trying to see through the rain. The inspector panted:

'You stay here . . . I will go . . . to look . . .'

'No. Thank you.' The junks had disappeared again in a heavier curtain of rain.

When she was a hundred yards off she saw the junk more clearly in a gap in the rain. *It was Hogan's junk!* She saw six water-buffaloes up to their bellies in front of the junk. Four men were heaving on the junk and the water-buffaloes were straining.

'*Ho-o-gannn!*'

She ran, splashing, sobbing, clawing the water.

'*Please God . . .*'

She staggered on, blindly, splashing, and she could not see the junk any more, and she was crying now. When she was fifty yards from the junk she saw it again through the rain and she cried out: 'Ho-gann!' – and she fell again. She picked herself up, muddy, crying, and then she saw him.

He was splashing through the water towards her, his hair plastered to his head. She cried out and staggered, and she fell into his arms. And he clutched her tight against him and she kissed him fiercely, crying and laughing.

FORTY-FIVE

The rest of that day was confused. And exhausting and shocking. And happy.

All the bloodstains had been outlined in chalk, the photographs taken, the exhibits taken into custody, the statements recorded: then the apartment had been cleaned up. The bullet marks on the walls and the splintered wardrobe were the only evidence that remained. The superintendent of the Criminal Investigation Department was showing McAdam a pile of glossy photographs. The officer said:

'He crawled down the stairs to the second floor before he died.'

'Good God.' He could not believe it. He looked at the photograph of the dreadful body sprawled, head downwards on the stairs, the blood smeared all the way down behind him, blood trickling down the stairs ahead of him out of his mouth. Then he looked at the photograph of the body in the morgue. The killer eyes still staring. Vanessa sat beside him on the sofa, but she could not look at the photographs.

'You took his fingerprints?'

'Yes, sir. And traced him through Records. He's a suspected 14K Triad member, but we can't prove it.

He's got a few convictions for wounding and affray, and he's suspected of being one of the 14K hit-men, but there's absolutely no way we can prove his connection with Herman Choi, I'm afraid.'

'Jesus . . .' He heaved himself up off the sofa and paced, exhausted. 'And what did Choi have to say about Vanessa's story?'

'His lawyer said it for him. Flat denial. Seething with righteous indignation. Miss Williams rudely made these scurrilous allegations and he told her to leave. She forgot her overnight bag and he promptly sent it to the nearest police station.'

'And what are you going to do about her story? That that cutting up there is not into solid rock.'

She said grimly: 'Whacker Ball's going to examine the architectural plans in the Building Ordinance office when they reopen tomorrow.'

He said to the superintendent: 'But are you going to open up that retaining wall he's built against the cliff-face, to see if there *is* solid rock?'

'Yes, sir. But we'll have to get a court order for that. And it would have to be supervised by experts. We can't just go and do it off our own bat. We've only got Miss Williams's word for it, and with all due respect to her, she's not a trained observer in these matters.'

McAdam cursed. 'A court order will take weeks!'

'Well, a week, anyway.'

She said angrily, 'Well, I'm going to go ahead and publish my story. As soon as it's finished.'

'Certainly,' the superintendent said. He added bleakly: 'Just give me a chance to sell my Lucky Man shares tomorrow. If the stock market isn't under water.'

She smiled wearily.

McAdam said, 'I think we'd better get out of this

apartment, in the circumstances. Go to a hotel.'

The superintendent sighed. 'I can't stop you going anywhere, sir. But it will be much harder providing police protection at a hotel. And I must emphasize that Miss Williams needs the best protection we can provide.'

Vanessa shook her head. 'I don't want to go to a hotel, Hogan. Shut up in a room, a cop at the door. Here we're at home, everything we need . . . I'm not scared of this apartment, with you here.'

The superintendent said, 'Here it's easy, sir. We'll just billet a couple of men upstairs in your gallery. And one guarding the front and back doors; you won't even know they're there.'

'How long's this going to go on for?'

'At least until Miss Williams has given evidence at the inquest.' He added: 'And if your theory's right, Miss Williams may need even more protection after she's published her story. And Lucky Man goes bang. And Herman Choi up for public fraud. She would be a vital witness.'

McAdam dragged his hands down his face.

'We must go away,' he said. 'A holiday. And come back for the inquest and the trial.'

'If the theory's right, that the Triads are after Miss Williams – especially if she's going to be a witness at any trial of Choi – '

'There'll be a trial all right,' McAdam promised.

'– then going away where we can't protect you isn't very wise, sir. The Triads are everywhere these days.'

McAdam stared out of the grey window at the rain. Then he sighed and said: 'Fly, fly away . . . somewhere where it's clean, and sunny. And safe. To Africa . . .'

Later, when he was to try to do so, he could not remember the details of what happened the rest of that day, and the next. All he remembered were feelings, and the rain coming down. Feeling exhausted, feeling outrage, feeling happy, feeling stronger; feeling drunk, feeling sensuous, feeling lust, feeling love. Even feeling safe. But the strongest of these was the love. Only these feelings would he remember, no matter how hard he tried to break them down and say: Now when did that happen? How did that come about? But this he would know loud and clear, and forever: that he was glad with all his heart about these feelings. In his dreams he would remember and relive them, be happy again, wonderfully happy and alive, and she too, tall and strong and smiling and laughing and in love: oh God, alive. What he remembered he would be glad with.

They hardly slept that night. They made wild, exhausted love on the big double bed, drank champagne, and then made love again. Her long legs wrapped around him, her arms lashed around him and her hips and breasts grinding up at him and her mouth locked on his, sucking and biting. '*Oh fuck me fuck me fuck me,*' she cried. And the joyous bliss of her body in his arms again, strong, soft, smooth, locked writhing into him and around him and under him, and her hair outflung on the pillow, and the glorious smell and taste of her, and the slipperiness of their sweat and the warm wet depth of her.

And they lay beside each other, panting, sweating, happy, exhausted. Neither of them wanted to sleep. He would remember she said softly:

'For weeks I've been talking to you in my head, Hogan. Why should I sleep now?'

And he leant over and looked down into her eyes, and said:

'I love you.'

And she looked at him and then kissed him.

332

'I love you too, Hogan,' she said.

He said: 'Then why didn't you come back?'

'Why didn't you? Why didn't you send me flowers and all that stuff?'

'Because you wouldn't have come back if I had.'

'No, I probably wouldn't have. But what're the other reasons?'

'Because I was in love with you. And who wants to be in love with somebody who has every intention of taking off to the wide blue yonder?'

'That's why I wouldn't have come back if you'd sent flowers. Why does a girl like me have to fall in love with somebody who doesn't want me taking off for the wide blue yonder?'

And she lay there, on her side, her golden head propped on her hand, and she looked at him, smiled softly and said:

'I'm back . . .' And she kissed him. And kissed him and kissed him again. 'I'm back,' she whispered.

And the rain came down.

She said quietly: 'Every time I saw anything beautiful I thought, I must tell this to Hogan. Every time I read something interesting I thought, I must discuss this with Hogan. Every time I got steamed up about something I wanted you to get steamed up with me. Every time I got excited about something. Every time I got angry. Every time I heard a joke I wanted to tell it to you to laugh with me . . . I didn't want to fall in love, Hogan. I wanted to be free.' She spread her arms. 'I didn't want to have to gear my life around anybody else. I wanted to come and go as I liked. The power of that kind of freedom. Nobody can hurt you, nobody can tell you what to do.'

'Except it doesn't work for ever.'

'It works fine, until your emotions become involved. Then other laws take over. And you're just like everyone else who's ever been in love.'

She lay back on the pillow, then flung her arms wide.

'Except, of course, nobody has ever, ever been as in love as I am.'

They had a bath together, then. There was plenty of water again in Hong Kong's reservoirs. She stood in front of the steamy mirror piling her hair on top of her head, the steam rising up, her breasts moving as she pinned her hair.

They lay deep in the hot bath drinking cold wine, and they were completely happy. She said:

'What are we going to do about your junk?'

'I'm going to leave her right where she is in the middle of the paddy-field for a month. And I'll rig a spotlight on her. She's a wonderful advertisement like that. The concrete junk that crashed five hundred yards inland and did not spring a single leak. Not a *crack*! And I'll get the television people out there when I tow her out. With a team of water-buffaloes and thirty men. And we'll push her straight back into the sea. And she'll float like a bloody cork!'

She threw back her head and laughed in the steamy bubble bath.

'McAdam – the only guy who can make a gimmick of his disaster. You better come to America, they'll pay a fortune for you on Madison Avenue.'

They lay in the bath, feeling the hot balm of it on their exhausted bodies, and they talked about some of the wonderful things they were going to do, and see, and feel.

And the rain came down.

FORTY-SIX

It rained without ceasing.

It beat down on the steep jungled mountains, came cascading into the basements of the apartment blocks, and the big drains choked and burst; and it soaked down through the sodden slippery clay of the mountains and down through the jumbled soil and granite, and the landslides came. That night there were over twenty, and over fifty people were caught in them. The Army and the police and the firemen were everywhere digging for bodies and dragging out the survivors, and all the time the rain hammered down.

He woke up late that Monday morning. She was standing at the window, looking at the rain. She was wearing his silk kimono and the grey light from the window made it transparent.

'Hullo,' he said. 'Come back to bed.'

'Come and look at the rain.'

They stood at the window side by side. They could only dimly see the harbour down there: the tugs and the ships had their lights on. Somehow it felt good and earthy and exciting: they were together, and they were rested, and they were safe, and there was nothing in the world they could do about the rain except stand there and wonder at it.

They had a lovely morning. She had been up since early and she had finished her story on his typewriter and she was going to deliver it today to the editor of the *South China Morning Post*. And then McAdam was going to take her out to lunch, the best damn lunch in town, bodyguards and all. They had plenty to celebrate. They went through to the kitchen together to make breakfast. They had to put the lights on. She opened the refrigerator, and there was nothing in it but beer and three bottles of champagne and some cheese and olives.

'There's nothing to eat – not even milk for coffee.'

'Then we'll just have to have champagne.'

But they did not get dressed yet. They took a cold bottle of champagne into the living room and sat cross-legged on the carpet, drinking it. He would re-member the first cold sips, going down good and clean and sparkling. The police had delivered a newspaper but neither of them wanted to read it. It was full of photographs and headlines of the typhoon damage, and now more about the rain damage. When the first bottle of champagne was nearly finished, she got up to get cheese and biscuits and olives and she brought back another bottle of champagne with her. After this bottle they were definitely, but *definitely* going to get dressed to go out for lunch. He opened the bottle and the cork hit the ceiling with a pop and champagne spewed up frothing and they grabbed for the glasses. They were both laughing.

It seemed an excellent idea, more champagne.

And the rain soaked down through the clay and jumbled granite of the mountain and the massive weight of the sodden jungle pressed down. The water rushed down over the vertical man-made cliff behind the Lucky Man apartment building; it poured down on to the foundations and soaked down to the deep concrete piles: and gradually, slowly, sucking, widening, the man-made cliff that was not solid rock began to part from its mother mountain, under the massive weight of the apartment block. Then suddenly it gave way in a great wrenching chunk, three hundred yards wide and fifty feet deep, with a great roar above the hammering of the rain, and it began to slide.

It slid uncertainly at first, a chunk of mountain slowly tearing itself out, and the apartment block heaved and teetered, tottering on its foundations, still erect; then it slid. It came sliding, massively, invincibly, for maybe thirty terrible yards, still erect, then the moving chunk of mountain hit the road below, and the apartment block keeled slowly over. It hit the steep mountainside below with a crash like an explosion and the mountain shook and then the whole mass of building and mountainside came crashing down the steep slope.

'What's that?' She frowned.

He listened, then got up and went to the back window.

'Good God . . .'

She was already beside him. Together they saw it.

At first they did not understand. They saw the great scar of earth three hundred yards wide way up there through the teeming rain where the Lucky Man apartment block had stood. 'What's that up there?' Then they saw the whole of the mountain moving, and they still did not understand. Mountains should not move. Then they heard it above the hammering of the rain, the distant rushing roaring, like a faraway train. And then they saw it come.

They saw the great mass of jungle and mud and concrete coming sliding down the mountain, and behind it the great mass of mountainside lumbering down itself towards them, tearing itself up and getting bigger and bigger, like a wave; and then they could see whole floors and walls and pillars tumbling in the terrible

337

mass, and they understood; then they saw it hit the first hairpin bend of Mountain Road.

The huge mass smashed down on to the road and the road disappeared, swallowed up; and the great avalanche did not falter, it just kept on coming, huge chunks of road tumbling with it, ploughing up the jungle in front of it. They stood there, staring. This was a phenomenon, something happening far away. Not yet fear, just astonishment, at the mass of mountain carrying all before it. But of course it would stop. For ten long astonished seconds they stared at it, seeing it come crashing down through the rain towards them; now it was fifty yards away, now forty, now thirty, and now they could hear the roar of it, like the roar of an express train. And it was not going to stop.

'God, Hogan!'

He grabbed at her and shouted, '*Jesus!*'

And it hit Hillside Road behind Dragon Court. The avalanche hit Dragon Court at the second floor; one hundred thousand tons of landslide hit the wall at thirty miles an hour, and the whole building shook under the tremendous impact, then the concrete caved inwards and the building broke. She screamed as the floor staggered beneath them, and he shouted '*Vanessa!*' and clutched at her wildly, to drag her away from the terrible thing that was happening. He reached for her as the room caved sideways and she was wildly trying to scramble up, her face shocked and terrified, one arm desperately outstretched to him; for a long terrible moment the building seemed to waver, trying to recover its balance, then it began to fall over, and Vanessa slid. She slid screaming on her hip across the floor with her hand outstretched, and he lunged after her, the floor giving beneath him, to throw himself on top of her to protect her from the terrible weight that was going to

338

crash down on her.

The tall apartment building went over slowly, smashed in two, fourteen floors of apartments leaning over like a giant felled tree, slowly at first, then more quickly. McAdam flung himself at her across the floor, bellowing above the crashing of furniture, desperately trying to get to her; then the whole world exploded in smashing blackness. Fourteen floors of apartment building crashed down on top of itself; and he heard only the deafening explosion and her screaming in his ears.

PART XIV

It was completely black.

He came to, with the instant realization of what had happened, the horror of where they were. He jerked his head up and bellowed:

'*Vanessa!*'

And his forehead hit concrete. He tried to pull his legs up, and they were held crushed under concrete. He tried to fight himself free and he smashed his face again on concrete six inches above and fell back, stunned. Warm blood in his eyes and mouth.

'Vanessa! – answer me! – '

He tried to lunge sideways, but his right hand was held, crushed. But his left arm was free. He swept it sideways and his knuckles scraped concrete. 'Vanessa!' he roared. He lunged his hand again and swept it in an arc as far as it would go, and he wrenched and wrenched at his right hand to get it out from under the concrete, and shouted:

'*Vanessa! – Vanessa!*'

In his frenzy he did not feel the blood and the agony of the wrenching, all he knew was the desperate fear for her, Vanessa lying here somewhere in the blackness under tons of concrete. He would fight through all the concrete in the world to get to her – he lunged and wrenched and kicked and roared her name a long time.

Then he heard her whisper:

'Hogan – '

'*Yes! – Vanessa! – where are you? –* '

And he wrenched again, then fell back, gasping, to listen, and all he could hear was his heart and his own rasping, and all he knew was that she was lying somewhere near in the blackness, under tons of concrete but *alive alive alive*, and he felt strong enough to tear the stuff off her hunk by hunk and drag her out of there by sheer force.

He shouted again:

'Vanessa! – Where are you? – Keep calling!' He tried to wrench his right hand free again.

'Vanessa! – Is my voice coming from your right or your left?'

And she answered in a whisper: 'My right . . .'

'Then stretch out your right hand!'

And he flung out his left hand as far as it would go. It seemed the most desperately important thing in the whole world that they could just touch hands. '*Stretch, Vanessa!*' he cried, and he felt the flesh tear on his right hand, but all he cared about was throwing his left arm as far out as possible, and suddenly skin and nails tore off his right hand and it came free from under the concrete and he could lunge sideways further, and then his fingers touched hers in the blackness.

Just her stiff, quivering fingers, and he cried, 'Oh Vanessa – I'm sorry . . .'

Oh God, when you love somebody, and she lies dying: her flesh lying there in the terrible blackness, her life being slowly crushed out of her. McAdam swelled his chest and roared and heaved to throw the concrete off him to get to her and drag her out before she died. But he could not shift the terrible weight, he only beat and smashed himself against the concrete six inches above his bloody face. He wrenched and heaved, but all he could do was touch his love's fingertips.

FORTY-SEVEN

After a short time he got himself back under control.

He lay there, shuddering, his eyes screwed up, trying desperately to think.

The living-room carpet was underneath him. But not under her hand. She was a little higher than him, on his left. His head was higher than his feet. To his right, the broken floor rose, then dipped away. This was the living-room ceiling, just six inches above him. How exactly was he held? By his thighs. He could feel nothing pressing on his knees. His feet – he could just move them. He felt with his fingers, and he could feel the beam across his thighs. He stretched his feet as far as he could, and he thought he could feel the carpet bunched up. Somewhere over there on his left would be the remnants of the iron spiral staircase. He reached his left hand up behind him, groping for the ceiling, and he felt it slope away upwards sharply. There would be space to crawl there.

He clenched his teeth and tried to push with his heels and ease his body upwards, out from under the concrete beam. He felt the flesh of his thighs pull, unbearably hard. He slumped again, then took a breath and tried again. Then he tried sideways, trying to shift his body and legs leftwards under the beam. No . . . To the right? He tried, holding his breath: the beam held him firm, his flesh pulled unbearably. He slumped back: He was feeling the searing pain in his raw right hand now.

Then he remembered the policemen in the gallery. They would be just a few feet above him.

'*Police!*' he bellowed.

He waited, listening. No reply.

'Police!'

Nothing. Only the distant roar of the rain.

He lay still, trying to think: it was no good shouting for help above that roar. Save your strength until help is near . . . He tried to hold her hand, and all he could do was press her fingertips.

'Vanessa? Are you in pain . . . ?'

He waited for her answer, heart pounding, heart breaking.

'*Vanessa! Are you in pain?*'

'No . . .'

Then he heard her sob out loud once.

'*I can't feel my legs, Hogan . . .*'

Oh God . . .

'Your legs are all right – It's only because your nerves are pinched.'

She didn't say anything.

'Vanessa, do you hear me?'

'Yes . . .'

He took a big shuddering breath and he was so desperate for her he wanted to shout. 'Your legs are all right! Believe me! . . .'

'Vanessa, how are you lying?'

She whispered: 'On my back.'

Thank God. 'Is your head higher than your feet?'

'Yes.'

'Where is the concrete pressing?'

'On my stomach . . .'

'*Can you breathe all right?*'

'Yes . . .'

*

345

'Vanessa . . . ? Don't talk, just listen. Save your breath. If you want to say yes, press my fingers once . . . If you want to say no, press them twice. All right?'

She pressed his fingers once.

'Vanessa . . . Don't struggle. Save your strength until they come. Just try to rest. Do you hear me?'

She pressed his fingers once.

'The fire department will come soon, Vanessa. They *will*.'

She just lay there.

'They must be here already. It doesn't take them long to get on to a disaster like this.' She did not do anything. 'They're here already, Vanessa, working to get us out.'

She pressed his fingertips. He took a juddering breath. Desperately trying to think what was happening. What to say to her, to help her. Trapped, impotent under tons of concrete and not knowing what was happening to her body. Where the Fire Brigade was. How long it will take. And oh God, how many tons of concrete were lying on top of them and how do they move it without crushing her!

He screwed his eyes tight in the blackness.

'They're experts at this. They know how to do it. We can *breathe*. We can last a long time like this. For days. For *weeks*. They'll get us out, I promise you!'

She whispered: 'Are you cold, Hogan . . . ?'

He was not cold. He had not yet thought about cold. But now he knew she was cold! Tons of concrete crushing down on her guts and she was cold! All he could do was press her fingertips.

'No. Are you?'

'No,' she lied. 'I'm just exhausted, I guess.'

He tried to think whether she should sleep or whether she should fight to stay awake. Maybe she

346

would choke in her sleep. Maybe her body would not fight the cold if she was asleep. 'Don't fall asleep. They'll be here soon. Vanessa, save your strength but don't fall asleep, can you do that?'

She pressed his fingertips.

He tried to listen for the sound of rescuers, and all he could hear was the rain.

And the rain came down. Running down through the mass of concrete in thousands of little waterfalls, gurgling, rushing. He tried to listen above it for sounds of people. Eyes closed, trying to hold the panic down. *How long have we been here?*

Suddenly he remembered his watch. He worked his left hand over his chest. He got it up to his chin and peered through the blackness. No luminous dial. He jabbed his wrist against his shin to feel for it. Nothing. *Wasn't he wearing his watch at the time?* He twisted his head and peered at his right arm in the blackness. Nothing.

He twisted to look to his side, for the glow of the dial, he crashed his forehead against the concrete above him, he twisted his head furiously again, and he saw it – the tiny glow of the dial. And he gasped out *Thank God* and lunged his raw right hand out towards it. He could not reach. He worked his head and shoulders sideways, then stretched again. He still could not reach. He breathed furiously and stretched again, his raw bleeding fingers quivering, his forehead pressed up against the concrete, and the tip of his middle finger just touched it. And he gasped out, fiercely, and tried to stretch one inch more, feeling the new desperate fear of not knowing the time, of infinite blackness going on and on, not knowing what day it was, how long pain, how long thirst, how long hunger, how long help, how long life, the terrible blackness stretching on and on for ever! He ground his forehead against the concrete, stretching and he wanted to bellow, *For Christ's sake help me, just one inch* – and then he collapsed.

He lay still, breathing long and slow, trying to get his strength and control back, trying to think.

How long have we been here? One hour? Two? *They must be here now!* Firemen, policemen, ambulances, digging.

Why can't I hear then? *Why can't I hear them?*

All he could hear was the water. No bangs, no shouts, no machinery. And no light. Just blackness.

'Vanessa, can you hear me?'

She pressed his fingertips once.

He took a long slow breath.

'We're in pretty good shape. They're working on getting us out right now . . .'

She said, more loudly: 'How will they get the concrete off?'

'They're the most expert people in the world at this sort of thing, Vanessa. They have the most experience. Piece by piece. Just listen to me . . . There's plenty of air getting through. There's no water getting to us, we won't drown. No broken bones. We're not even really in pain. All we've got to do is wait, Vanessa. It will only be hours. Just rest . . . Have you heard me?'

She said, louder: 'Won't the concrete crash? . . . when they try to move it . . .'

'No! They're absolute experts! Just for Christ's sake don't think about it!'

He did not say any more about it. To stop her thinking about it.

Try your body again, he told himself.

He tried his feet. They moved. Stiff, cold, constricted, but they moved. He tried to tighten his leg muscles; he could just feel them move, numbly, under the weight.

He slid his hands down the side of his hip, and he felt the tip of something metal, and he knew it was his transistor radio.

He pulled it up his side, heart thudding in anticipation. He dragged it up to his chest. The switch clicked and he waited. Nothing happened. Then he remembered the volume. His fingers found it, and suddenly the blackness was filled with song:

'Will you still need me
When I'm sixty-four?'

He snapped the radio off.

'Vanessa! You hear that?'

She did not answer. He felt his stomach lurch in panic.

'Vanessa! Answer me – !'

'Yes?'

Relief flooded over him.

'Were you asleep?'

'There's a radio playing . . .'

'Yes – listen to it, try to stay awake. Do you hear me . . .?'

'Yes.'

'Vanessa – tell me what's happening to you. Are you in pain?'

He waited, heart thudding.

'I can't feel anything . . . Just let me rest . . . I've had a busy week-end . . .'

Oh God, yes, just let her rest and feel nothing!

'Save your strength for when they come . . .'

She whispered: 'I thought you were going to take me out to lunch, Hogan?'

His eyes burnt. 'Oh, I will. The best bloody lunch in town . . .'

She whispered: 'So he got me after all, Hogan – that bastard.'

'He hasn't got us, Vanessa! We're getting out!'

Then she whispered softly: 'There goes my story, Hogan. Everybody will know it now, no Woodward and Bernstein scoop for me . . .'

'Oh, Vanessa, what a thing to worry about now!'

She snorted. 'Once a journalist, always a journalist, you can't expect too much of us, Hogan . . .'

And he thought his heart would burst for wanting to fight and save her.

He switched the radio on again. Suddenly he was shivering. At first he thought it was the shock. Then, suddenly, he was deep-down-to-the-bones cold. And with the cold came the numbness, his back and shoulders numb where they pressed to the floor. And the terrifying unfeeling in his legs.

FORTY-EIGHT

High above the black masses of clouds the airliners circled, banked up, waiting for Air Traffic Control's permission to land. It was brilliant sunset up there. Then, one by one, they came down into it, the black suddenly hurtling past the windows, the rain beating against them. They came screaming in over the rooftops, flying entirely on instruments, and only at the last moment could the pilot see the blurred lights, then the runway lights through the rain.

Kai Tak Airport was mobbed with people. Tourists held back by the typhoon were trying to get out, airlines had laid on extra flights, incoming traffic which had been delayed by the typhoon was arriving as fast as Air Traffic Control could let them in. The marble floors were messy with trampled rainwater, the vast concourse smelt of damp clothes and umbrellas.

Bernard Champion stood tensely in the queue for the Pan American flight to Los Angeles and Mexico City. He was wearing his police uniform under his civilian raincoat. On the pocket of his tunic, concealed now by the raincoat, was his Airport Police Security identification pass. His face was haggard. But he did not look about him. The security pass was what he relied on. With that he would not have to go through Immigration Control, he could simply walk through, as a policeman. Immigration Control was where they would be watching for him.

But maybe the airlines had been told to watch out for him too. The check-in counter in front of him was his first hurdle. He was sweating. If only he had thought ahead he could have bought a forged passport in another name in Macao and bought his airline ticket in that name. But it was too late to regret that. The man in front of him was at the counter now. The airline girl looked tired. Thank God for that. The man moved on. Champion picked up his suitcase and put it on the scale. 'Good evening.'

He passed her his ticket. His hand was shaking.

'Mr Champion?'

She had her head down, scanning her list.

He waited, heart pounding.

'Passport, please.'

He handed it across the counter, his hand trembling.

She opened it to the photograph. She looked up at him. He felt his stomach lurch. Then she lowered her head.

'Champion . . .'

Out of the corner of his eye he saw two figures in khaki approaching. He glanced sideways furtively. Two Chinese constables were walking towards him. He looked hastily away, heart thudding. But they were strolling. He fumbled for his cigarettes, to light one to shield his face. The airline girl was talking to her supervisor now. He felt himself go white. 'Mr Champion?'

'Yes?'

The supervisor looked at him.

'When did you book?'

'Yesterday. Through a travel agent.'

'We don't have you on our list.'

'But I was in the office when the agent telephoned, I heard it confirmed!' He had to get on this plane. 'Is the plane fully booked?'

'Completely. Except first-class.'

He closed his eyes.

'I'll go first-class.'

He wrote out the travellers' cheques, hand shaking.

He had closed himself up in his apartment for three days. He could not bear to see anybody, nor to be seen. He had wanted to hide, to turn his face away from the world. He had hardly eaten. He had sat through the typhoon, slumped in his armchair, drinking, and unable to get drunk, listening to the typhoon without caring. Then the rain. He had not listened to the radio. He had not looked at the newspapers that had been pushed under his door. He had not wanted to know. To know, feel, even see, in any way to be involved in the place that was no longer his home.

He walked through the airport crowds, sweating, dry-mouthed. This was finally it, the end of a life. The end of twenty-two years' service as a policeman. This time tomorrow policemen would be looking for *him*.

He was in a state of emotional daze. Even his nervousness at the weigh-in counter seemed a long time ago. Ahead was the Immigration barrier. As he walked he unbuckled his raincoat. He pulled it off, slung it over his arm. There were long lines of people waiting. He walked past them, towards the nearest Immigration officer sitting in the glass kiosk.

He walked to the top of the queue, stepped around the woman being processed. The Chinese Immigration Officer looked up at him, Champion pointed to his Security Pass on his tunic. The officer nodded. And Champion walked through. It was as easy as that.

Bernard Champion walked numbly into the departure lounge. It was full of passengers. He headed for the lavatories.

He locked himself into a cubicle, and opened his hand grip. He pulled out a shirt, sports coat and slacks and hung them on the peg. Then he took off his tunic and shorts, and put on the shirt and slacks. He stuffed his uniform into the grip. Then he left the cubicle and went to the wash-basin. He stared at himself in the mirror.

This was what his life had come to. Shedding his police uniform, his career, in a public lavatory. Everything he knew, all the law, all the tricks, all the expertise, all the people; he would never use them or know them again.

He was a criminal. On the run.

He stared at his white, gaunt face.

He did not care who saw him. He walked through the crowded departure lounge. He was not going to the bar, he was not looking for a seat; he was just walking. He had intended to stay hidden in the lavatory until his flight was called but he had to get out, to move. To try to contain his welling grief. If one person, any person, had given him sympathy he would have broken down.

He heard the television say soberly:

'. . . at the Dragon Court disaster in Midlevels. So far the death toll is seventeen . . .'

He stopped. The television was mounted on the pillar right in front of him. He stared at it.

It took him a long confused moment to register what he was seeing. A huge black and white pile of rubble in glaring arc-lights. Misty in the continuous rain. Firemen and policemen and soldiers toiling. Then the picture vanished and the newscaster reappeared, talking about something else.

Bernard Champion turned abruptly. He strode dazedly back towards the lavatories. He locked himself into a cubicle, unzipped his grip and pulled out his tunic. His fingers were shaking almost uncontrollably. Then he ripped off his shirt.

FORTY-NINE

Requests. 'Lemon Tree.' 'Yellow Submarine.' There was a little red light on the radio's dial; he lay shivering, staring at it, singing under his breath. There was a time-check and all he caught was 'twenty-three', and he lurched up and hit his forehead on the concrete. It was after that that he passed out the first time.

He heard the American accent saying cheerfully:

'Now for some more bad news! Latest reports from our frantic friends at the Royal Observatory are that it will continue to rain cats and doggies tomorrow! – bringing the rainfall up to its highest since the founding of the Colony. But every cloud has a silver lining, and it's for you lucky people who thought you had to go to school tomorrow. Yes, you've guessed it! Our lovely friend the Director of Education has announced . . . Wait for it! *No* school tomorrow! How about *that* for a silver lining! So just stay tuned to your favourite Far East Rayyy-di-oh! And here we go with that mind-blowing, deee-eep brown voice of Lee-ee Marvin, singing that all-time smash hit – yes, you've got it . . .!'

Lee Marvin's voice filled the blackness.

'*I . . . was born . . . under a wa-a-a-andering star . . .*'

He lay still in the blackness, eyes tight closed, trying to concentrate on the music and not feel the cold and the numbness. The announcer's voice was saying:

' – another report on the Hillside Road disaster, and we have our man Kevin Gray reporting from the area! Come in, Kevin.'

'Thank you, Mike! And a real disastrous-looking scene it is in the glaring arc-lights and pouring rain. Dragon Court lies in a huge pile of rubble and jungle and mud and broken furniture. Firemen and police and army are here in force. The whole area has been cordoned off, to hold back the crowds of friends and relatives of the poor people trapped in the debris. Hundreds of willing people are helping. Over three hundred people, men, women and children, are lying dead and alive in that horrific mess. It is a desperate race against time. Already twenty-five people have been unearthed but nineteen of them were dead.

'I am told by the fire officer in charge, Jack Evans, that one of the major dangers is of further landslides. And that the weight of the men working to move the debris will cause the mass of concrete to shift and crush the people still alive. Wooden barricades are being built to try to stop further slides. What more can they do except work and pray?'

The tears were running down his face and he wanted to shout and laugh and cry.

'*Vanessa! – They're here! – They're digging for us!*'

He flung out his hand to hers to wake her to rejoice:

'*Vanessa! Wake up! – They're digging! Everything is all right –* '

She was asleep. He lay back, panting, the happiness and relief choking up his throat. He had to restrain himself from bellowing to them. And he wanted to clutch her tight in his arms and laugh and hug her.

Ten minutes later he felt the water. Suddenly water was trickling through the crack in the ceiling above him, on to his chest. Then he felt the water on the back of his head and under his shoulders and he put his hand up to feel, and he felt the mud.

Then he smelt the gas.

The rain poured down, silver in the glaring arc-lights. Jack-the-Fire rasped into the two-way radio in his command tent:

'Priority, priority. Strong smell of gas coming out of upper levels of disaster site. Instruct Gas Company to cut off at source, repeat Gas Company to cut off gas supplies for this whole area immediately – do you read, over.'

The voice came crackling back from Headquarters: 'Affirmative, over.'

'And send Gas Company technicians to scene immediately. Use of oxy-acetylene cutters has been stopped until gas is cleared – and we desperately need to use them. Also send K 12 cutting equipment urgently. Also an extra lighting unit and generator. Over.'

'Two numbers K 12 already en route to yours. Two army mechanical shovels also en route, over.'

'I don't think we can use mechanical shovels yet, due to tenderness. Or we could bring the whole lot down on top of us and victims. We have to go by hand at this stage, using great care to avoid dislodging debris. We're still attempting to extricate the four people reported in my last message. Can now confirm that they are a family all from one apartment, the man confirms that he lived on the twelfth floor and he thinks the thirteenth floor was empty. We'll have them out in about ten minutes and can then probe down to eleventh floor better. A good access into the tenth has been found, two men are in there now searching as far as light permits. Calling into the debris is producing some response from victims but we badly need those additional lighting units. We've only got one petrol generator going near the lower level at the moment – we've moved it well away from the gas and I don't think it's any danger at the moment but we can't rely on it. Message ends. Over.'

'Roger, can confirm that additional lighting units are en route. Can also now confirm that Gas Company will have cut off gas at source within a few minutes, but they say that it will take some time for gas in pipes to dissipate. Also the Electricity Company is leading an extra power line in, the engineer will report to you for your disposition when connected. Over.'

'Roger. Since this message began can now report arrival of fifty troops of Welch Regiment with additional porto-power and lighting. We should be all right for lighting and manpower for the time being. Over and out.'

Jack-the-Fire rammed his helmet back on his head. He turned to Bernard Champion and the Building Ordinance officer. 'Figured out anything?'

Champion looked at him, plastered wet. 'He thinks

the sixth floor – McAdam's – he thinks it's taken the brunt of it. The building probably broke about the seventh floor. Floors seven to fourteen probably came down like a concertina, all on top of six.' Then he turned furiously on the Building Ordinance officer: 'Why the hell did the goddam Lucky Man block come down? Which idiot in your office approved the plans?'

'He's retired now.'

'Well he's bloody well coming out of retirement! Where is he now?'

The Building officer pulled a wry face.

'Not far. He now works for Lucky Man Development.'

'Oh yes! Lovely!' said Jack Evans. 'All right, Bernie. Just do as you're told. No heroics. He may be your friend but this is *my* disaster.'

He turned and plunged out of the tent into the rain. Champion stared at the Building Ordinance officer. Then he grabbed him by the shoulder and pulled him out of the tent. He pointed furiously at the disaster site in the dazzling arc-lights.

'Whereabouts is the sixth floor?'

FIFTY

First there was just a faint whiff of it.

McAdam lay still, eyes staring wide in the blackness. *Gas.* His instinct was to scramble away from the killer smell, to writhe and shout out to her. He lay rigid, holding his breath: then he had to breathe out. He held his lungs empty as long as he could. Then he began to breathe in lightly. Immediately he smelt it again. He cut the breath off.

Stronger.

He lay there, mind trying to race. She was out, asleep! He breathed in slowly, and it stank all the way.

His hands were at his shirt. He clenched his teeth against the agony in his raw right-hand fingers, then sank both hands into bunches in the fabric, and ripped. He felt the cloth tear.

His broken finger nails caught in the fabric. The pain screamed through his hand. He ripped again, the nail tore off his finger. He lay there rigid, gasping, his fists bunched at the agony.

Then he thrust the strip of shirt out into the blackness, feeling for the water coming through the ceiling. He soaked the cloth, then he groped fiercely for her.

'Vanessa! Wake up!' He found her hand. 'Vanessa! Put this over your face!'

'Hogan – ?'

'Put it over your face!'

And then he was coughing and choking and his hand groped for his face, trying to filter the terrible gas through his clawing fingers. He sucked in a big lungful and tried frantically to spit it out and grab some clean black air; then his head was swimming and he fell back.

Where Bernard Champion was working, the rubble was forty feet high, the highest part of the disaster. Somewhere in there was the sixth floor. The upper floors, as the Building officer had said, had crashed down like a concertina on to the sixth. Champion was working with a gang of soldiers under the leadership of a Chinese fireman. They stood in a phalanx, the front row heaving the chunks off, hefting them over to the row behind.

Champion worked like an ox, mud up to his knees, the rain beating down on his back. His heart was pounding from the exertion. There was a strong smell of gas still, although the Gas Company had cut it off. He seized a chunk of concrete.

'Here's one . . .!'

Just an arm was sticking out. They grabbed the next slab of concrete and slung it to the side. Underneath it was another slab. They heaved it up, grunting, slipping underfoot. And there lay a Chinese girl of about twelve.

'She's alive!'

Her eyes were closed and her face was pulpy with blood but her chest was moving. '*Stretcher!*' the soldier bellowed. Champion and the fireman were throwing the concrete off her legs. 'Broken leg . . .'

The fireman pulled out his walkie-talkie radio. 'Stretcher needed at position F. One Chinese girl, broken leg.' Champion knelt beside her and said in Cantonese:

'You're all right now. What was your apartment number?'

The girl mouthed: 'Nine . . . B . . .'

'Who else was with you when it happened? Just shake or nod your head. Your mother and father?'

The girl stared at him dazedly, then nodded.

'Brothers and sisters? Two? One?' The girl nodded. He rasped to the fireman in charge: 'Family of four.'

The ambulance men came sloshing through the mud. Champion got out of the way, his mind racing. If that was 9B, where the hell was 6A? The rubble was thirty feet high above the girl. Then sloped off down the hill, past G, H and I sections, down to where Jack was working. Further uphill towards Hillside Road, past positions, E, D, C, B, the rubble was not as high but it was smothered in mud. Was 6A further uphill or deeper into that pile in front of him – or at the very bottom of it? The ambulance men started lugging the girl away.

She was crying hysterically now. What the hell should he do? The soldiers were back into the rubble. 'Another one!' somebody shouted. Then the fireman bellowed:

'*Watch out – !*'

There was a loud grating above the hammering of the rain, and everybody looked up and saw it move, a big slab of concrete beginning to slide off the top of the pile: it slid slowly six feet, sending tons of small rubble before it, and everybody was scrambling backwards in the mud, then it came in a rush. The soldiers scattered backwards, and as the fireman scrambled backwards he fell. He flung one arm up over his head and tried to get to his feet, and the concrete slab hit him across his right thigh and he fell back with a shout and the whole slab crashed down on top of him. He lay half buried in the mud. Champion went over to him.

'My leg – !'

Champion unclipped the fireman's walkie-talkie:

'Position F calling Command Post – we need a cutter or a pneumatic drill – we'll need a stretcher too – over.'

The fireman gasped: '*Saw a foot sticking out – over there – *'

The smell of gas was much stronger, flooding out through the dislodged debris. And the rain drummed down.

FIFTY-ONE

The arc-lights glared up the steep mountainside above Hillside Road, on to the huge swathe of collapsed earth, three hundred yards wide four hundred yards long. The army engineers were erecting barricades across the vast raw wounds in the earth, to try to hold further landslides.

At Hillside Road the army engineers had laid steel plates to replace the collapsed road and the barricade there was nearly finished, big walls of timber and steel struts. Water came rushing down the great raw swathe of the collapsed mountain in tumbling streams, carrying mud and rocks and branches. It hit the barricade and leapt up over it, gushing down on to the collapsed apartment block below. Scores of soldiers were feverishly digging ditches to try to lead the water away. The Director of Fire Services said into his radio:

'Colonel Tompkins of the Engineers considers there's a fifty-fifty chance of another landslide and his barricades will only hold a small one. We need more lights and barricades higher up. I want a geologist's survey of the area – try the Building Ordinance office, they should have one, if not try the University. I have ordered look-outs to be posted on the tops of surrounding buildings to watch for further slides.'

Just below collapsed Hillside Road, the army engineers were erecting the steel and concrete base of the heavy-duty lift-crane that would be able to swing over the mass of debris and lift the concrete slabs off. At B and C sections, three good tunnels had been found through the piles of jumbled concrete. Firemen were crawling, squirming through like chimney sweeps. They had found seven people, but five of them were already dead. The two survivors were heavily trapped by concrete. The fire officer in charge said into his walkie-talkie:

'The smell of gas has almost gone up here and I consider it safe to use the K 12 cutters. But now we've got water problems. It was draining away well but now something must have blocked the exits. We're rigging a pump to go down with the cutters, over.'

Down at the bottom of the disaster site, Jack replied:

'Are you sending down an air-line as well? Are the victims in danger of drowning? Over.'

'We're getting the air-compressor set up now. One victim is in distinct danger of drowning, the water is already up to his chin, but Mr Johnson is down there with him and he's got a piece of tubing to breathe through if it goes over his nose. Over.'

'Well, get those cutters going and report as soon as possible, I daren't use the mechanical shovels down here until your guys are out of those tunnels. Out. Command Post: send this message back to HQ Control: Strong smell of gas persists down in lower and middle sections, so we still can't use the cutters. Nor can we use the Army's mechanical shovels because of tunnel work on upper sections. However, we are doing very well by hand down here and with the Army engineers' heavy duty winches, which are doing a great job. We have uncovered another six persons, four alive but in bad condition. We have found two access tunnels and are penetrating them now, we believe we've reached the tenth floor. However, until the gas clears and we can use the cutters, it's getting slow. My boys are exhausted, we need some temporary relief. Haven't they got any more CAS personnel on standby? Also get six more crowbars. Christ knows what's happened to them all. Also get another pneumatic drill from somewhere. Over.'

The voice came back from the Command Post tent:

'Roger, can confirm another twenty-odd Civil Aid Services have reported for duty and are being sent already. Also Queen's Gurkha Rifles en route from border area, don't know how many yet, over.'

'Roger, and tell HQ we need something to eat and drink, water, water everywhere and not a drop to fucking drink. Over and out.'

Down there in the blackness the gas was still percolating through the honeycombs, locked in pockets between the slabs of concrete. And the water ran through the debris, damming up here and leaking away there. And the rain came down.

Dreams ended and mind-wandering began.

He knew they were trying to kill him and he roared and thrashed and fought, and they ran away. But he knew they would come back and he lay there hiding, cunningly quiet, waiting for them.

And he was by a stream and the water ran sparkling clean over the smooth stones and little rapids and he walked along the banks casting into the pools and eddies so the trout would not see him and he knew this stream from a long time ago, every pool and rapid, and he went down it fishing every place expertly, fleetingly; then he came round a bend and there was the lemon tree, and she climbed up out of the stream and her legs were golden, smooth and strong and he kissed her lovely thighs as she stood on the bank and they were cool and soft against his face and she looked down at him smiling and she touched him with just her fingertips and they were icy and she whispered, smiling:

'Will you still love me when they cut my legs off? Tomorrow they're going to cut my legs off you know – '

And he shouted: '*Over my dead body – !*' and he was fighting up the bank and it was made of black concrete and he was crashing his head against it roaring *Over my dead body – !*

And the blood was thick in his eyes and he could taste the salt of it and his head was pounding. 'Vanessa!' he roared, 'Vanessa – !'

And he lashed out into the blackness for her hand, and he found it. He collapsed back, crying for joy because it was only a dream. And the gas was gone.

When he woke up again the thirst had set in. And he could not open his eyes.

His fingers scrabbled frantically on his blood-caked eyelids and he forced them open, blinking and shaking his head, and the scabs got in his eyes, rough and sandy, and he lurched and rubbed his eyes frantically, and the scabs scratched across his eyeballs and he wanted to roar and shake his head. Then he forced himself to lie back, to control himself.

And the dry, raging thirst. *Water.* His left hand felt out blindly in the blackness for water. Nothing. The leaking through the roof had stopped. And he could hear water everywhere, water gurgling, the rain roaring down.

'Vanessa . . . ?' His tongue was caked, stiff.

'*Vanessa!*' he rasped, and his hand groped desperately for hers. And he found it, feeling for his.

'Are you . . . thirsty . . . ?'

He waited. Then she pressed his fingers weakly once. 'Feel for water. Both hands . . .'

Her hand moved away. *Oh God, let her find water.* He lay there, eyes screwed up against the agonizing scratching. He felt her hand come back, feeling for his.

She pressed his fingers twice.

He clenched his teeth to control the fury.

'Were you asleep?'

A long pause. The rain. She pressed his fingers once.

'Go to sleep,' he whispered.

He lay, eyes screwed up, trying to breathe through his nose. He gripped one eyelid and pulled it down to make it weep and wash the scabs out of his eye. Then he took his other eyelid, too, with his raw right-hand fingertips. And slowly, slowly, the blood-scabs began to melt away across his sticky eyeballs. He blinked, and tried to open his eyes, and there was grating pain again and he could not tell in the blackness if he was seeing anything.

Saliva. He clamped his mouth shut and tried to breathe through his nose. But he could not. *Saliva.* He held his breath and tried to suck the saliva up out of the roots of his jaws. His tongue stuck dry to the roof of his mouth.

Then he felt the cold again. The bone-chilling cold. But many times worse was the horror of the numbness from the crushing concrete he could only half feel; and a thousand times worse was the knowledge of her flesh crushed and torn and bruised, bloody, senseless also. He groped in the blackness for her hand.

PART XV

The rain glinted on the oilskins and bare skins and the khaki.

Men toiling everywhere, clambering, lugging, digging, manhandling the big chunks of concrete aside, chunk by chunk; the pneumatic drills were roaring, the electric cutters screaming, breaking up the beams and the big slabs of concrete, winches and ropes and steel cables, and the stretcher-bearers plodding up steep muddy slopes to the ambulances. Kevin Gray's voice came over McAdam's radio in the blackness:

'You can hardly hear yourself above the rain, and it's hard to see. And with the water coming down the mountain, it has turned the whole disaster area into a treacherous bog, further hampering the efforts of the rescuers.

'There have been several other minor landslides in the night which threatened to crash down on the rescuers. But makeshift barricades have held most of it back. Soldiers are digging channels frantically to divert the water but a lot is getting through and it is feared that it may either drown trapped survivors or cause the massive pile of wreckage to shift and crush them.

'It is difficult, tragic work indeed. Nonetheless a great deal of progress has been made through the night, with reserves replacing men who wear out. It is a scene of heroic activity against tremendous odds to save the victims trapped underneath the wreckage.

'But why did the disaster happen in the first place? Why in this modern age of building construction was the disaster not foreseen and prevented? To try to get some answers to these questions we approached Leo Ball, Editor of the well-known *Oriental Israelite* . . .'

Whacker Ball's gravelly voice barked:

'Greed! And corruption. That's the answer!'

'Whose greed, in particular, Mr Ball?'

'Government's, and the greed of the private individuals who built the apartments. The Hong Kong Government is greedy for lucrative sales of Crown Land. Real-estate developers are willing to pay fortunes for land in this area to pack in even more apartment blocks. But this area is unsafe for such heavy high-rise buildings and Government knows it! It's steep and unstable. We had a similar disaster near here in Kotewall Road in 1972.'

Kevin Gray said: 'You also said corruption was responsible . . .?'

McAdam wanted to shout, *Don't blow her story, Whacker!*

'Yes! The Building Ordinance Office is responsible for approving building plans and safety measures. It is clear that the landslide started at the Lucky Man Company's apartment block, where because of the steepness a great cliff had to be cut out of the mountain. That cliff was almost vertical. A vertical cliff is forbidden unless it is cut out of solid rock, and the architect said that the cut *was* being made into solid rock. But this was a lie. You can go up there now and *see* there's no solid rock. And this, together with the fracturing caused by the building's foundations, plus the weight of the building and then the rains, caused the landslide. Now – how come the Building Office didn't spot these irregularities? We know that the Building officer who approved the plans now *works* for Lucky Man! But the whole credit for unmasking this monstrous public fraud must go to a young American lady journalist called Vanessa Storm Williams, who herself lies trapped in that wreckage – '

And Kevin Gray's voice cut him off with, 'Thank you, Leo Ball.' He went on: 'So far forty-seven people have been rescued alive, and the bodies of forty-nine other people have been recovered. Most of the living are suffering from serious injuries, and all are suffering from shock . . .'

The disc-jockey's voice came back brightly. 'And we say au revoir for a moment to our man Kevin Gray for a few words from our *sponsor* . . .!' and the strident jingle of the advertisement for Dab After-shave Lotion came over:

'Dab! Dab!
'Dee! – Ay! – Bee!
'If you like girls
'Use Dee – Ay – Bee!
'(And even if you don't like 'em, be sweet to your-
self . . .)'

Somewhere in the blackness something shifted and through the cracks and crevices it came, the mud.

First he felt it on the back of his shoulders, and he reached his hand back and felt the cold stickiness. He put his fingers into his mouth and felt the grit. He spat it out. *Mud.*

He lay still. If mud was coming through now, so must water. He rasped:

'Vanessa – wake up! Feel for water . . .'

He waited.

'Mud . . .? Or water . . .?'

She whispered: 'Mud.'

'Water will come soon . . .'

The mud came slowly at first, then faster. It was down the side of his legs now, oozing across the carpet in a thick sheet. Now it was round his feet, banking up where the carpet was bunched.

The mud banked up slowly round his legs, blocked by the carpet at his feet. Then it was up to his knees. Then up to his hips, and he felt panic. He clenched his teeth, trying to control it, the desperate fear of death by mud. Mud slowly rising up to her chin, to her mouth, to her nostrils. He scooped with his good hand, trying to sweep the mud away, trying to make waves to shift the blockage below. He moved his feet, trying to push against the bunched carpet.

The mud lay like a black swamp around him. He groped for her hand. There was no mud touching her yet: she was higher than him.

He did not want to frighten her. The only hope was to scoop the mud over the low crest in the broken floor to his right, away from her. With his bad hand. Sweep the back of his right hand through the mud and scoop it into the blackness beyond.

He felt his right hand. The flesh raw down to the knuckles, the fingernails half ripped off. He clenched his teeth tight and sank his hand into the mud. He screwed up his face and swept his hand furiously through the mud, over the broken sloping floor.

FIFTY-TWO

It was Tuesday noon, dark misty grey in the rain. The arc-lights were blazing. Jack-the-Fire Evans had had six hours' sleep, but his body ached for more. He stood in his command post tent and snapped into the radio transmitter:

'CFO Evans reporting, taking over from Mr Wang. Army and Civil Aid Services personnel changing shifts also in the next few minutes. We need the following items immediately:

'At least another one heavy-duty rock drill. Ask Public Works Department.

'Ten numbers minuteman cylinders.

'Ten numbers three thousand pound BA cylinders.

'Ten or twelve numbers oxygen cylinders.

'And a dozen or so kerosene pressure lamps. And more blankets. And we've got to have better supplies of hot food than last night! Half of us were hungry and a hungry man can't work properly. Are you reading me, over.'

'Roger, items requisitioned will be on their way. About the food, private caterers have been contracted for and have been delivering well this morning. Over.'

'And send a large jar of instant coffee. Hold there! ...'
His walkie-talkie radio was rasping to him. He listened, then said to Headquarters:

'Mr Wang says we're going to need a coffin van soon. They've just made contact with a whole bunch of bodies on the ninth, must've been a typhoon party, and they're all very dead. They'll be decomposing soon, no sense burdening the ambulances, they've got enough to do. Out.'

He picked up his walkie-talkie and said:

'Evans to Director Fire Services, good morning. What's the position with the army heavy-lift crane? I see it still isn't working, over.'

From somewhere up-mountain the voice came back:

'Good morning, Jack. They've been having trouble building a strong working base because of shifting mud. But Colonel Tompkins expects to have it functional in a few hours. Over.'

'Well – hope must be fading fast for the rest of the survivors, they've been down there nearly twenty-four hours. How're the barricades, any more slips?'

'Barricades have been considerably strengthened. Only one minor slip from high up, but the barricades stopped it. Look-outs still being maintained. But a lot of water and mud is still getting through the wreckage. Over.'

'Yes, so Mr Wang complained. All right, sir, out.'

He plodded out into the rain, eyes crinkled up, aching for more rest. The relief crews were getting to their positions, the old shifts coming out, sodden, covered in mud, exhausted. He saw Champion.

Bernard Champion was up to his shins in mud, head down, hands on his knees, just letting the rain hammer down on him. Jack walked up to him, dropped his hand on his shoulder. 'Have you been here all the time?'

Champion turned his head up. Muddy, haggard, greasy. 'No, had some rest, came back early . . .'

'You're finished, Bernie. Go home, you can't work like that.'

Champion rasped: 'I'm staying . . .'

'Bernie? There's not much hope, mate. It'll be a long time before we get into those middle-floor sections. There's simply no access.'

'Then I'll make an access!' He shook his muddy gloved hands in Jack's face. 'With these hands!'

'You'll do as you're told. Or I'll have you sent home. *No unauthorized person goes into any tunnels!*' Then he turned and strode away downhill.

Champion glared furiously after him, chest heaving. Then he turned and plodded towards the wreckage.

Inside his sodden gloves his fingers were almost raw.

Twenty minutes later he found it, behind a great slab of flooring: a big jagged opening in the wreckage. He crouched down and looked. The opening disappeared into blackness over broken rubble. He pulled out his torch.

The yellow light shone in ten feet, then hit fallen concrete. But the tunnel curved there.

He looked around. The fire officer in charge had his back to him.

He dropped to his hands and knees, then to his stomach. He crawled and wriggled into the hole.

His elbows scraped painfully. He had only short sleeves on his police tunic. His knees tore. He shoved himself forward, cursing himself for not thinking about long sleeves and trousers, trying to take the rubble on the flats of his forearms. He filled his lungs and bellowed again:

'Jake . . .! Vanessa!'

His shout hit the concrete, deadened. He lay listening for an answer. The roar of rain and the rushing of water. His torch shone ahead, yellow, making black shadows. The concrete was two inches above his back. The broken ceiling sloped down on one side. On the other side was crushed bedroom furniture. Water was dripping everywhere, glinting in the torchlight. There was no answer.

He worked his way forward on his stomach, the torchlight jerking ahead of him. The ceiling sloped upwards, giving him more room. He could crawl. Ahead was a red carpet. A child's doll. He was out of the bedroom now. If he could find the front door he would know what floor he was in. He thought it was the seventh. He looked to his right, downhill.

There was no floor, only crashed ceiling. A hand stuck out. Female. He shone his torch on it, panting. He pulled off his glove and touched it. Cold. He lifted a finger. It was rigid.

'McAdam . . .! Vaness-a . . .!'

Nothing. Just the rushing of water.

Now he was crawling on fallen wall. A corridor? The collapsed ceiling was just above his back again. On to his stomach again. He saw a porcelain ornament, of the type stuck on doors. It read, *Wendy's Room*. He stopped.

'Wendy . . .!'

Nothing.

'*Anybody here . . .? Wendy!*'

He looked for an opening to Wendy's room. He carefully shoved the rubble on his right. He pulled a piece; it came away. Another. Then another. Then here was a small opening, a space beyond. He shone his torch in.

Yes, this used to be Wendy's room. Under the rubble he could see the golden hair of a big doll, a drawing of a donkey, some crayons, a corner of a patchwork quilt, the smashed legs of a bed.

He pulled away some more rubble. Put his head into the hole.

The room was squashed down to a height of eighteen

inches, except in one corner. There the floor had fallen away, and there was a jagged black hole. Above the hole was another, into the ceiling. Water cascaded through the upper hole, disappeared into the lower. In the other corner the bed and dressing table had been crushed. More dolls, a slipper, broken glass.

'Wendy!'

Then he saw her. The golden hair was not a doll's, it was Wendy's. 'Oh Christ . . .' He stared at her, panting. He pulled away another chunk of rubble. He shoved his whole shoulder in; his hand touched her face.

He lay, trying to interpret what he was feeling. The eye. Cold. He felt down her little nose. He waited, trying to feel breath on his fingertips.

'Oh, little girl . . . I'm sorry.'

He pulled himself out of the hole feverishly. He wriggled forward on his guts. Ahead was a big block of concrete, blocking his way, but he could see the shadow of a hole on one side. He shone his torch in.

It used to be the living room. He could see crushed furniture, a smashed television. The front door must be somewhere in there. And beyond that the elevator foyer. Then the west wing, McAdam's. He began to tear rubble out of the hole.

He pushed through on his stomach. The ceiling was six inches above him. Rubble and glass on the floor. A carpet. The sofa and armchairs were crushed on the far side. He wriggled towards where the front door should have been. A dining-room table was smashed in front of him. He shone his torch around it.

Beyond, the ceiling was crushed right down to the floor.

No way through there.

Then he saw the corner of the front door.

It was under the table. And the cross-beams of the

table would just let him get his hand in. He wriggled into position, grunting, and stretched in, feeling for the number on the door. He swept away rubble, groped. Then he found it.

He pressed his cheek against the table, his arm stretched in. Carefully his fingertip traced the metal number.

Five . . .

5B.

He pulled out his hand, his heart hammering. So the sixth floor was one up. 6A was just a few yards above and on the other side of that collapsed wall and elevator foyer. Oh Jesus . . .

He scrambled on his belly across the rubble towards the crushed sofa. He peered all around, flicking the torch. Absolutely no way out.

The only way was up through Wendy's room.

He turned around and scrambled back towards the hole he had come in by. He cracked his head on the ceiling but he did not feel it through his riot helmet. His elbows and knees were raw but he did not care. *Thank God for Wendy's room.*

He reached the hole. He got both hands to a chunk of rubble and jerked it. It came away in a cloud of dust. He stared at the crushed ceiling above him. It stayed still. He got another chunk in both hands, tugged. It came away.

He tugged out four more pieces and the low jagged hole was just big enough for him to crawl through.

He wrestled through the hole into Wendy's room. The ceiling scraped the top of his helmet. He pulled himself through the rubble, shoving with the sides of his boots. The ceiling scraped across his back, but he could just make it. Then he was at the hole in the corner.

He could not turn himself around and lower himself

into the hole feet first, then climb upwards. There was only one way in, and that was head first. He clenched his teeth and shoved his head and shoulders into the cascading water, down into the hole. Now he was looking upside down into the room below.

He gasped as he looked straight into the staring eyes of a dead man.

The head was six inches from his inverted eyes, face up, eyes open, bloody, streaked with the spray from the water.

Champion shoved himself further into the hole. His helmet touched the floor. He shoved with his feet. Now his waist was over the edge of the hole; he bent his neck. Now he was bent in the shape of a U. He shoved again. He could not move.

Could not move.

His buttocks were jammed against the edge of the upper hole. His spine and neck could bend no more. The blood was rushing to his head. He tried to scrabble his feet to find some purchase and they just slipped. Panic swept through him. He groped upside down into the squashed room below for something to grab, to pull on. All he could grab was the corpse. He grabbed it by the shirt and pulled. He could not budge. The jagged edge of the hole was digging into his stomach. He heaved again with all his desperate strength and the shirt tore.

'Jesus Christ!'

He was gasping, whimpering now. The blood pounded in his head, water ran into his mouth and eyes and nostrils. He coughed and spluttered and kicked and wrenched wildly. And he tried to push himself back upwards, shoving with his hands, and the jagged edge of the hole gouged into his flesh. All he knew was the horror of being stuck like this, unable to move one way or the other, and the water choking into his nose and mouth, the horror of dying like this upside down. He grabbed desperately at the corpse and got him by the chin and one armpit and he sank his fingers into the dead flesh and heaved with all his might over the jagged hole.

The corpse's head and arms moved stiffly under his frantic pulling, but its legs were jammed under concrete. Champion wrenched and wrenched again, his face about to burst with blood, spluttering, and he jerked another two inches with all his might.

Bernard Champion crashed into the hole, half on top of the corpse.

FIFTY-THREE

The message came through the rain from Headquarters to the Command Post and from there to Jack's walkie-talkie.

'Urgent informative – reliable report received that Queen's Tower apartment block above Hillside Road on the edge of the landslide area appears to be leaning over – '

Jack jerked round and glared uphill through the rain.

'Oh shit!' Then he shouted furiously into his walkie-talkie: 'Sound the alarm!'

The low-pitched siren began to wail. Jack was running uphill, ploughing through the mud, rasping into his radio.

'Call PWD building inspectors . . . tell Colonel Tompkins meet me at Hillside Road – '

Rescue workers were scrambling through the mud away from the wreckage. Jack ploughed through them, boots sucking in the mud, up to Hillside Road. His legs were trembling. He peered through the rain up at Queen's Tower.

'Jesus . . .'

The tall apartment block on the very edge of the landslide was definitely leaning over at a slight angle. He shouted into his radio:

'Evans to Command. Evacuate Queen's Tower. Send two men to each floor ordering people out – no use of elevators, stairs only. Cordon off the area. Also evacuate the apartment block immediately below it, and the one next to that.'

Colonel Tompkins of the Engineers came hurrying through the rain.

'She's leaning all right.'

'I want sentries, please. I'm cordoning off the whole area. What do you think of her chances of falling?'

'With this soil? Anything can happen. Elsewhere, on hard ground, I'd say she's fairly safe.'

'Oh shit!' He glared at the colonel as if it were all his fault. 'If she falls, she won't come down on top of us. She'll hit those apartment blocks there.'

'Depends on how she falls, Mr Evans. If she falls on her side – '

'She won't fall on her side, for Chrissake! She's leaning more downhill than sideways.'

'It also depends on how she breaks up. Part of her could certainly fall on your men on this side. And on the wreckage.'

'Oh *Christ*!' He shouted into his radio: 'Where're those goddam building inspectors?'

Then he snapped at the colonel: 'Well, *my* men are going back to work! Are yours?'

Bernard Champion half straightened himself in the hole.

The water cascaded on to his shoulder. He shone his torch into the room above Wendy's. The sixth floor.

It was squashed flat.

Almost absolutely flat. Only rubble and smashed furniture held ceiling and floor apart. He cursed. His chest and stomach were red with blood. Then he reached up to the next floor. He put one foot on Wendy's floor and heaved himself up.

The seventh floor.

And *yes* . . .!

The ceiling had collapsed in the middle: but on one side it was held up by a heavy desk and a filing cabinet. They were half crushed but they held the ceiling twenty inches off the floor. He shone his torch down the side of the desk. Then he worked his head and shoulders into the gap. He reached into the room grunting, looking for something to grab. The edge of the hole cut into his chest again.

The only thing he could reach was the filing cabinet.

He hooked his fingers round it. He gave it a tug. It held. Then he kicked his feet up from Wendy's ceiling, grunting, and heaved his stomach over the edge into the room. Now the cabinet was taking almost all his weight. He swung his knee up over the edge; it crashed against a spike of concrete. He cried out, then swung it up again.

He just got it over. He clung there, half in, half out, gasping at the pain in his knee and his raw stomach. He heaved his other knee into the room, then the filing cabinet gave way.

It went in a screech of steel on concrete and the ceiling crashed down another inch, then stuck. Champion lay on his guts, terrified, in a shower of dust. Then it was still.

He lay gasping, eyes wild. The dust still falling.

Then it came again. It began as a long, creaking, tearing sound and Champion screwed up his eyes in terror and tried to make himself flat. The noise screeched deafeningly, and the ceiling crashed another inch; and then stopped. Dust everywhere.

He opened his eyes, and he saw the desk crunching further.

Then it stopped.

He lay there, heart hammering. He looked at the desk in the torchlight. He did not know whether to scramble on or scramble backwards. If the ceiling didn't come down now and kill him it could come down in two minutes or two hours. And he could never get back.

Then he clenched his teeth and scrambled wildly forward.

He pulled aside the rubble in the kitchen and peered through the hole. *Stairs!* He could see them plainly. That meant McAdam's gallery, 7A, was just over there on his left. He pulled out another piece of rubble feverishly.

'Excuse me, sir . . .'

He whirled around on his side. His torch shone into the ghostly face of a small, wide-eyed boy. Champion stared, heart pounding.

'Who're you, son?'

'Mike Stevens, sir. Are you a fireman?' The little face was gaunt and stained with dried tears.

Champion closed his eyes.

'No, I'm a policeman. Are you all right, Mike?'

'Yes-sir. Are they coming to get us out?'

'Yes. It won't be long now. Where do you live?'

'8B,' Mike Stevens said.

'This isn't 8B, is it?'

'No-sir. I came down a hole when I heard you. 8B is upstairs.'

'Where're your parents, Mike?'

'They were at work. There wasn't any school because of the rain.'

'All alone?'

'Yes. It was the amah's day off.'

'Have you found anybody else?'

'No. I heard some people talking, but they stopped.'

'Are you hungry? Thirsty?'

'Not thirsty,' Mike Stevens said. 'There's plenty of water even though it's dirty. I'm hungry, all right.'

'Here.' He pulled off his glove and wrestled his hand into his pocket. 'Boiled sweets. Good for energy.'

'Thank you, sir. You can come up to my room if you like, sir, there's lots of room, I can almost stand up in one place.'

Champion smiled, exhausted.

'Are you scared, Mike?'

'I was, sir, not so much any more, they must be here soon. I've got my dog, you see. And my torch.'

'Where is he?'

'Up in my room, sir, I couldn't bring him down the hole. I called, didn't you hear?'

'No, I'm sorry. Listen, son, you've got to get out of here.'

'Yes, sir,' Mike Stevens said earnestly.

'Now, listen. I know a way. But there's somebody I want to look for first. You come with me.'

'Yes sir, thank you. Can I fetch Billy?'

'Yes, of course.'

'If I lower him down the hole, you just take him.'

Mike Stevens crawled upwards across the kitchen with his flashlight. In the corner was a hole, as in Wendy's room. He disappeared up it like a monkey. Champion wriggled after him on his belly, grunting.

'You there, sir?'

'Yes.'

'Here he comes.'

The hindquarters of a young fox terrier appeared. Champion took it by the chest. He could feel its heart beating. 'Good dog, Billy.' He brought the dog down. It tried to lick his face. 'Come on, Mike.'

Mike appeared, feet first.

Champion said: 'I'm looking for Mr McAdam's flat, 6A. He also owns 7A. Do you know a way to get there?'

'No, sir.'

'All right. Follow me.'

The number on the smashed piece of door was 7A. Champion pulled feverishly at the rubble again and bellowed into the hole:

'*Jake . . .! Vanessa!*'

He lay, trying to listen above the muffled roar of the rain. All he could hear was water.

He grabbed more rubble with both hands and heaved. Then more.

'*McAdam!*'

Nothing. The hole was not yet big enough for his head.

'Mike? Can you stick your head in there, and your torch? And tell me what you see?'

Champion did not even feel the rubble on his raw flesh. Mike Stevens wriggled his head into the hole.

'A spiral staircase, sir. And mud.'

'*Mud . . .?* All right – come out!'

He gripped another chunk of rubble with both hands. He wrenched it out. Then another, then another. Then it was big enough.

Mud. The crashed floor of 7A was about two feet above the floor of 6A, here partially supported by the iron spiral staircase. There was a big hole there, down into McAdam's tomb. But the slanting floor of 6A was deep under mud.

'*McAdam!*'

Nothing. Champion scrambled down the hole around the spiral staircase, into the mud below. On to his hands and knees. The ceiling of 6A was above him, the lounge floor caved upwards in the middle.

'Jake! Vanessa!'

Nothing. Just the wild hammering of his heart. He got down on to his stomach in the mud and scrambled upwards towards where the dining area used to be. He could just get under the ceiling. He shone his torch desperately at where the kitchen used to be. He shone the torch the other way. Then he saw her golden hair in the mud.

'*Vanessa!*'

He started frantically towards her, clawing across the sloping floor.

FIFTY-FOUR

She was completely still. The back of her head in mud, up to her ears, mud up to her chest. Her right arm was buried in mud. '*Vanessa!*'

He shook her shoulder, then he ripped his sodden glove off, felt her forehead. But his cold fingers could not register temperature. He looked desperately downwards, trying to see how she was pinned – her hips disappeared into mud. Then a hand rose out of the mud right in front of him.

He jerked back. A man's big hand, dripping mud and blood, groping at him. He swung his torch sideways. 'Jake!'

The mud was right over McAdam's ears, mud lapping at the corners of his mouth. His head was twisted desperately upwards, encrusted with blood, his mouth open, trying to speak.

'Jake!' He grabbed his hand. McAdam's eyes were desperate, his mouth tried to say 'Vanessa . . .?' Champion looked wildly around the hell hole, then he grabbed a flat chunk of concrete.

'Putting this under your head – get it out of the mud . . .'

He burrowed his fingers under McAdam's head, lifted it. Then slid the chunk of concrete under.

'I'm going to try to drain the mud.'

McAdam mouthed, 'Can't hear . . .'

'What?'

His hand rose up out of the mud again, running red with blood, and he brought his muddy fingers to his left ear and began to try to poke mud out.

Champion writhed round on his stomach. 'Vanessa . . .?' He groped his muddy hand on to her face, then wrestled the torch on to her. He tried to lift her eyelid, then cursed. The mud on his fingers. He buried them into his mouth and sucked them clean. Spat. Then he groped back at her face, and lifted her eyelid.

Her eye stared blankly. But he could not see properly. He scrambled his fingertips to her nostrils. He held them there, holding his breath, trying to feel her breathing. He could feel nothing. He slid his hand frantically down to her left breast.

He lay there, his hand over her heart, holding his breath. Then he cried out:

'She's alive!'

He grabbed McAdam's shoulder and shook it joyously and yelled:

'She's alive!'

McAdam closed his eyes and his blood-caked mouth

broke into an incredulous grin.

'Mike!' he shouted.

'Yes, sir?'

'Come in! We've got to get this mud drained!'

Champion writhed down the sloping floor into the mud on the other side of McAdam. At the bottom he could get to his hands and knees. He felt feverishly for what was blocking the mud. The bunched carpet. 'Hold the torch, Mike!' He got a grip on the carpet and tried to heave it up. The weight of mud held it down. He heaved again fiercely. It sucked slowly away from the smashed corner of the floor. He held it with all his might with one trembling hand, and with the other he groped under, feeling for a hole.

None.

He whimpered and heaved the carpet back further with all his strength. Then stretched in and seized another two handfuls under the mud and heaved. And there was a big sucking noise and the mud began to pour out of a hole.

'Shine the torch down more . . .'

Arms trembling with the strain, watching the mud drain out in the torchlight, the carpet tearing at his bunched hands. Then his fingers could take no more, the carpet tore from his hands. He crouched there, arms aching.

Then he manoeuvred his hand into his pocket for his knife.

He got down on to his stomach in the mud. It swamped over his back. He shoved himself forward. Then he groped in under the crashed ceiling, as far as he could reach. But he could not reach far enough. There was only one thing to do.

He took a big breath, screwed up his eyes and plunged

his head under the mud. He groped furiously under the carpet, heaved it up off the hole with one hand, and with the other sank the knife into the fabric, and sawed.

He ripped the knife towards him, then he twisted his head sideways and got his mouth out of the mud and gasped in air, spat, then plunged his head back under and sawed again.

He sawed a gash sixty inches out of the carpet, then sawed off the long strip. Then he writhed backwards, black with the muck.

He crouched on his hands and knees, gasping, letting the mud run off his face.

'Jake! It's all right. It's going.'

He wriggled into the crushed wreckage of the kitchen. He found what he was looking for straight away: a large empty beer bottle. Two. And there, lying under rubble, was a bottle of whisky. But no water!

'Mike – you know where there's water . . . ?'

'Yes, sir. Up in my apartment, lots. If you keep Billy.'

'For Christ's sake be careful.'

Champion writhed back across the floor.

'Jake? We're getting you water.' He shone his torch on Vanessa. Her eyes were open. '*Vanessa! Are you in pain?*'

She turned her face to him, the mud on her neck and hair. Her lips were cracked and dry. She closed her eyes and shook her head and tried to smile.

She whispered: 'Come to . . . pull us out of . . . the shit again?'

'It's all right, Vanessa! I've drained the mud. Water's coming. Then I'm going to fetch them to get you out. Everything's going to be all right!'

'Hogan . . . ?' she whispered.

'He's fine – look at him.' He writhed backwards out of the way and shone the torch on Hogan. He had his bloody head turned to her; he tried to smile.

'Do you want some whisky?' Champion panted.

She shook her head and whispered, 'Water.'

'It's coming . . .' He shone his torch down her body. Her legs were still under mud. So were McAdam's. The concrete ceiling was pressed down on her stomach. Why wasn't she in pain? The cold? Numb?

'Sir?' Michael Stevens said behind him.

'Good boy, Mike . . .! Help Mr McAdam . . .'

He grabbed the first bottle and wriggled closer to Vanessa, panting. 'Vanessa? Open . . .' He brought the bottle shakily to her mouth. She opened her cracked lips, they groped for the bottle rim. He pushed it in gently and she sucked.

The water ran out the corner of her mouth, she spluttered, swallowed. Her muddy hand came up and took the bottle from Champion's. She sucked and sucked.

'Hold it in your mouth and swirl it round . . .'

She swirled it round her mouth, eyes closed, trying to get it to soak through the dry membrane, then she swallowed blissfully. McAdam held his bottle and drank, and swallowed and drank. Champion and Michael Stevens lay there on their stomachs, watching them.

'There's more bottles in the kitchen. Can you fill two more, Mike?'

'Yes, sir.'

'And do you have a big ball of string?'

'Fishing line, sir. If I can find it.'

'Good boy . . .' He grabbed the lad's skinny shoulder and shook it. 'You're a good man, Mike!'

Michael Stevens blushed under his muddy pallor,

then wriggled away manfully into the blackness.

McAdam finished his bottle. He lowered it, then smiled brokenly at the ceiling.

'Marvellous . . .'

'Do you want some whisky?'

'Yes . . .'

'Just take one mouthful. It'll go straight to your head . . .'

'Vanessa first.'

Champion turned to her. She was just finishing the water. 'Vanessa – take some whisky.'

She smiled through cracked lips. She whispered, 'Think of everything . . . or are you . . . trying to get me drunk?'

She took the bottle shakily. She closed her eyes and took a sucking mouthful. She rolled it round her mouth, then tried to swallow and gagged, and the liquor snorted out of her nostrils, and she coughed. She wiped her muddy hand across her mouth. Then she lay still, eyes closed, getting back her breath.

'Hey . . .' she whispered, mud on her mouth, 'that's good.'

'Some more.'

She squinted in the torchlight at the bottle, brought it shakily to her muddy mouth. She took a big mouthful, eyes closed. She whispered:

'Now Hogan . . .'

He gave the bottle to McAdam. He took a mouthful, while Vanessa watched him.

'Hey, Hogan . . .?' she whispered. 'Where're we dancing tonight?'

'Here, sir,' Mike Stevens piped out of the blackness. He had two more bottles of water and also a reel of nylon fishing line.

'Beautiful, Mike!'

Champion put a bottle next to each of them. The mud was almost all drained out now. Now if he got his head down low he should be able to see what was holding them. He writhed forward down the muddy floor, until he was stopped by the beam that held them. He put his cheek flat and wrestled the torch into position. He peered under the beam in the yellow torchlight.

At first he did not grasp what he was seeing. He saw the ceiling crushing her legs. Her legs were covered in mud. He could make out her knees. But there was another bend in her muddy flesh that should not be there. Another beam was lower than the rest of the ceiling, across her thigh. And her thigh was bent. And sticking out of her muddy flesh was a spike. He stared at it, not comprehending. He thought it must be a piece of wood sticking to her. Then, he saw the red, realized it was blood; he saw the red-black raw flesh of her thigh; the thing sticking out was bone.

He stared, horrified. His mind fumbling: *But she feels no pain.* Then the terrible fact dawned on him:

She feels no pain because she's paralysed!

He stared, shocked; then he felt the anguish sweep over him. Then he screwed up his eyes and scrambled backwards.

'I'm going now! To fetch them – We'll be back in no time!'

He grabbed Mike Stevens's fishing reel, peeled off a length of line and tied it round a piece of rubble feverishly.

'I'll leave you Mike's torch. The whisky's here.'

'Sir, shall I stay to look after them?'

'No,' McAdam rasped. 'You go, Mike. Thanks.'

Champion slithered round and scrambled away. The fishing reel spun in his hand, peeling off line. The tears

390

were welling in his eyes. He did not hear her try to call, 'Thanks, Bernie . . .'

Then she said: 'Hogan . . .? When we get out of here . . . I've got to stop my story about Champion being published . . .'

FIFTY-FIVE

Queen's Tower and the apartment blocks below had all been evacuated. The whole area had been cordoned off.

The men were back at work in the rain and arc-lights. The army engineers had finished erecting the heavy-duty crane. It swung out over the middle of the wreckage and two soldiers were standing on top of the rubble, ready to hook up the first load. Then one of the look-outs posted on top of the apartment blocks saw the new landslide starting, and he shouted into his radio, and the siren moaned.

Bernard Champion and Michael Stevens heard the siren. They were just scrambling out of Wendy's room, the dog called Billy trotting quickly behind them.

'Quickly!'

He scrambled forward flat out on his stomach, his forearms bloody. The fishing reel peeled off line. He came to the end of the crushed corridor. He stopped, desperately trying to remember which way he had come. Then he scrambled right. And there was the hole into the first room he had entered.

'Come on . . .!'

He scrambled into it, hitting his head. He looked behind him for Mike, then went on, the torch jerking in front of him. Then there was a hole to the outside world

391

ahead of him. The siren was still wailing, the hammering of the drills had stopped.

'Through!'

He squeezed aside and grabbed Mike by the scruff of the neck and dragged him towards the hole. Then Champion writhed through after him. And the rain hit him, and the siren roared in his ears.

The grey light was blinding bright. He clambered up, staggering, and looked through the rain for the danger and he could not see the landslide coming. He grabbed Mike Stevens by the wrist and ran him five paces across the steep muddy slope, slipping, sliding, and through the siren he heard the shouts, and then he dropped the fishing reel. He let go of Mike Stevens and shouted:

'*Run!*'

And he doubled back for the reel, and as he picked it up he saw the new mudslide coming.

It was seventy yards above him when he saw it. Coming big and terrible in the arc-lights, a great mass of orange mud seething down the steep raw mountain, dragging its long tail behind. He saw it hit the second-last army barricade. And the stout wall of wood and steel buckled and the great head of mud flowed over it, and then the barricade burst. And the mud came head-long on down the mountain towards Hillside Road, and Bernard Champion did not hear the people shouting at him, all he knew was that it was going to hit the wreckage of Dragon Court and kill Vanessa and McAdam and he stood there rooted, outraged, and then he waved his arms and bellowed into the rain,

'*No – No! They're in there! No – !*'

And the mudslide hit Hillside Road in a great roaring swoosh, and leapt over it just thirty yards up there, and Bernard Champion recovered his senses, and turned and ran.

He ran furiously across the muddy slope, downhill at an angle, and all the time he was yelling at the sky:

'*No, you bastard! No – !*'

And the mudslide hit the wreckage of Dragon Court so the earth shook, and mud flew in sheets and crashed on down the steep slope after Champion. When he was two-thirds across, he fell flat on his face and for a moment he did not care – he would die bellowing his outrage to the sky – then Jack-the-Fire got him. Jack charged through the mud, screaming:

'*Get out – !*'

He grabbed him by the collar and dragged him blindly, stumbling, slipping, out of the way.

Jake McAdam and Vanessa did not hear the siren. They only felt the tremble as the mudslide hit Hillside Road; then there was a long slow grinding sound in the blackness, and he felt the concrete creak underneath him and he clutched for the torch and shouted:

'Vanessa – !'

He heard her cry out in the blackness, and then the whole black terrible world cracked.

Cracked and shifted, and the blackness gave way underneath them. He heard her scream and he crashed his forehead against concrete and his feet were going down and his head was coming up; then it came to a grinding, jolting stop.

For a long moment there was nothing but stunned silence.

Then the sound of her gasping.

'*Vanessa!* Vanessa – !' He groped desperately for her, and his hand touched her knee.

'*Vanessa – ?*'

And he slid his hand up her leg, groping for her hand. And his fingers groped the sharp hump of flesh in her thigh, then the sharp point of her thighbone sticking out and the next instant his hand touched hers.

She screamed into the blackness and he was shouting, *'Vanessa! – Vanessa!'* and he wanted to lunge out and grab her in his arms and clutch her close and bellow his anguish and absorb all the shock and terrible injury into himself. *Oh God let it be my body!* His hand scrabbled desperately for the torch and he was gasping:

'Oh my darling, I'm sorry – I'm sorry.'

And her scream suddenly cut off in a swoon, and she was silent.

He cried out again *'Vanessa – !'* and his hand found the torch and he flicked it on and saw her leg within arm's reach, and it was bent in the middle of her thigh, the sharp spike of bone was sticking out, muddy, glinting in the torchlight. And he filled his lungs so his neck swelled and he bellowed to God:

'Why don't you come down and help us?'

But God did not.

She whispered in the blackness:

'Hogan? I'm all right now . . .'

He lay there, eyes tightly closed, squeezing her hand tight. He did not know whether she knew about the bone. And, oh God, he did not want her to know.

'Hogan . . .? It was just the . . . shock that made me scream. Not the pain . . .'

He started to speak and she whispered:

'There's no pain, Hogan . . . There really isn't.'

She breathed deep. She did not know whether he knew about the bone sticking out of her leg, and she desperately hoped he didn't. And there *was* no pain. And that was really why she screamed. Because she had realized that she was paralysed. Because her back was broken.

She breathed deeply and her voice caught:

'I only screamed . . . in delayed shock . . . About the concrete crashing . . . But I'm fine now, darling . . .'

He lay rigid, holding her hand tight, and the tears were running down his face.

'Sure,' he whispered. 'We'll be fine, Vanessa. They'll have us out soon . . .'

FIFTY-SIX

She whispered softly:

'Hogan . . .? Now shut up, you lovely bastard, and listen to me . . . I feel like talking . . . Where's that goddam whisky? Don't use the torch, save it.'

He groped for the bottle in the dark, found it. He did not want to use the torch either, he did not want her to see her leg. He unscrewed the top, fingers shaking, the tears running down his face. 'Here . . .'

Her hand took it. She manoeuvred it to her mouth. She took a big trembling mouthful.

'Have some, Hogan. Let's go out in style . . .'

He hissed fiercely: 'We're getting out of this, Vanessa! Not "*going* out".'

She whispered, 'Sure, Hogan . . . I meant that. We're going to have a great life, darling. So let's drink to that . . .'

Through his shock and his anguish he did not think she should drink – *people in shock with gaping wounds should not drink:* but he would have given her the world. He just wet his lips with the whisky, to save it all for her. He held the bottle out into the blackness. 'Take it . . .'

He felt her hand grope for it. Then she said hoarsely:

'God, that's good stuff, Hogan . . . What every girl in a landslide shouldn't be without . . .' Then she said:

'Hogan . . . ? This stuff is going straight to my head.'

Oh, my lover. 'That's all right, Vanessa . . .'

'Hogan? Isn't it a pig . . . ? Just when I had that bastard Choi over a barrel . . . and we were going out to lunch . . .'

He lay there in the blackness, teeth clenched.

'Don't talk about it, Vanessa.'

She cried softly, 'I *want* to talk, Hogan . . . ! This is my story which I worked so hard on! And I alone cracked it, found the chink in his armour . . . It should have been a landslide victory for me . . . and instead he nails us. With *his* fucking landslide.'

'Oh, my darling, I'm sorry! – *Talk* about it!' And he cried out inside for her to be in a soft white hospital bed, to scoop her tight in his arms and hold her and take her anguish from her and love her and tell her that it didn't matter, that he would still love her. 'It's still your story . . . Whacker was on the radio, and he gave all the credit to you.'

She breathed deeply, then took another swallow of whisky.

'Sure. The only thing that matters . . . is that we got him . . . But . . . it's a pity it isn't my scoop any more . . .'

'It *is* your scoop, Vanessa! We'll see to that! And that bastard Choi's going to jail for the rest of his life . . . ! If the cops stop me shooting him first . . .'

He held her hand tight, the tears choking his throat. 'Vanessa! We're getting out of here. We're alive . . . we've survived . . . and as soon as we're out of here we're going to fly away, darling! To Africa. To anywhere you like. And see the animals . . . and we're going to drink lots of wine in the sun . . . and stay in the best damn hotels . . . and we're going to sail that junk around the world.'

She lay in the darkness, her teeth clenched to stop

herself sobbing out loud, and her fingernails dug into his arm and she whispered:

'Yes, darling . . .'

But her heart cried out, *Oh, listen to me, you darling Hogan, it's not going to happen because there's no way in the whole wide world I'm going to live with you in a wheelchair!*

'And we'll make those beautiful nature movies, Vanessa . . . And you'll write wonderful stories . . .'

And she wanted to cry out, *They're going to cut this leg off, darling Hogan! We've got to face it! What I'm going to have here is a goddam stump!*

And she held his arm fiercely, clenched her teeth and her voice shook:

'Oh yes, darling . . .'

She lay in the blackness, her chest heaving, holding his hand tight, the tears running down her cheeks and into her ears. Then she took a juddering breath and said:

'Let's have some light on the subject, Hogan. And I don't mean my luscious legs. I want to see your beautiful eyes . . .'

He groped for the torch. He pointed it up the slope so that when he switched it on she would not see her leg, and as he was about to switch it on she said:

'Hang on, Hogan . . . a girl likes to look her best.'

She tried to rub the mud off her tearful face. She passed her hand over her matted hair, and sucked her lips. 'God, I bet I look a wreck . . . Okay, Hogan. But first a beat-up girl needs a drink in adverse circumstances . . .'

She groped for the bottle.

'Wow . . . that's good stuff.' Then after a moment: 'Okay, Hogan . . . Lights. Action.'

He switched on the torch.

She was looking at him, her lovely eyes anguished, dried tears on her dirty cheeks, and her heart was breaking. She put her fingertips on his arm and trailed them gently, then her eyes filled with the most wonderful smile he had ever seen, loving, pitying, and she held out her arm to hold him tight, to pull him to her, and all she could do was hold out her arm to him; and he held her arm, and nothing in the whole terrible world mattered except that she was alive.

She whispered:

'I love you, Hogan. Just remember that ... always ...'

The tears were running down his face.

'I love you, Vanessa.'

FIFTY-SEVEN

He did not know how long she was unconscious, from the whisky, and the weakness, the exhaustion. He remembered the torchlight getting dimmer; her body faintly glowing, swollen, crushed, and the blood running out of the dreadful hole in her thigh; 'Vanessa ... Vanessa ...!' he whispered, but she could not hear. *Oh, God, just let her lie there, unconscious, just let her know nothing until they get us out of here.*

He tried to feel her pulse. But each time his stiff trembling fingers could feel nothing; not even any warmth, just cold flesh. And he panicked, staring at her ashen face, trying to see if she was breathing, and he could see nothing in the dying light, and he cried out, 'Vanessa!' and he lurched at her, shining the torch, and he saw her breathing. And then shuddering, watching her breathing, shallow, so shallow; and the great slab of concrete so close to her breast. *But, oh, God, God, why didn't you hold it off her legs . . .!*

He roared:

'Champion! – Come back and help us – !'

He shouted many times, but he did not know how long it was since the last time. And he prayed, his eyes tight closed, trying to concentrate, trying to pray constructively to the God he did not believe in. *Please God, protect her . . . Please God, her leg is going to be all right . . . Please God she is not paralysed. Please God give her strength – Please God give me strength to shout.*

Later in that long, terrible blackness the gangrene set in. And the delirium.

Her moans and her shouting and her laughing and her sobbing and her talking. He did not know how long it lasted between silences: all he knew was the sick shine of her sweat in the dying torchlight, glinting silvery yellow on her contorted face.

Sometimes she passed right out; her arm outflung, her matted hair wet with sweat, mouth open, quivering, the infection spreadeagling down her leg: and he lay there, praying, *Please God, make her stay asleep, please, God, keep her still –*

But God did not keep her still. At some time the flashlight began to fade right out, and he tried desperately to save it for her – for what? For some last awful emergency when she screamed out for him? In the last dying light he saw the gangrene spreading out round the big hole in her leg as she lay there. He hoarsely cried:

'God, come down and help us!'

But God did not come down. Neither that long black night, nor the next long, terrible, black day. That next afternoon he could hear the drills, and he tried to shout, but he could only whisper. That afternoon her delirium got very bad. Sometimes he managed to get her hand,

and sometimes she did know who it was, and she tried to speak, but she could not murmur more than a few words, then she pulled her clenched hand away. The drills and bangs got louder in the blackness, and he wept tears of despair and joy, but his shouts were only dry, thirst-scabbed croaks. He did not remember the last few hours.

He only knew the sudden shaft of black night sky in the wonderful hammering and crashing, and then a Cockney voice shouting *'Here they are – !'* and then Champion's voice shouting from above:

'Jake – it's all right now!'

And he was laughing-crying:

'My wife has a broken leg – '

And the blackness was flashing with blinding torch-light, and a Chinese face was shouting for a concrete-cutter saw, and somewhere behind the Cockney voice was shouting 'Morphine!' And then her moaning went wonderfully silent, and he was crying tears of desperate happiness. Then a spout was being held to his lips and he was sucking, spluttering, choking, but he could not taste the water through the dry scabs in his mouth.

'Do you need morphine?'

And he remembered trying to say, 'Only if you cut me.'

Jack-the-Fire's voice was saying: 'Get another saw, we can't winch this lot up in one go – '

Champion's voice said, 'Where's that bloody doctor?'

He tried to shout:

'Don't let them cut her leg off, Champion – !'

And he felt the needle slide into his arm.

The rest was very confused. He had the feeling of not caring any more, of complete trust in the skill and good-will of their rescuers, the joy that she was safe. *She was safe*, and they were digging them out of this place and taking them to hospital where doctors would put the bone back into her leg and heal her up and she was lying deep in clean soft white sheets. The noise of power drills and saws was all around him in the flashing torch-lights, and he just wanted to laugh and make jokes, except that it was all a great effort. He said:

'How is she – ?'

'She's fast asleep, sir; we've got her out.'

And he wanted to take his hand and tell him he was a wonderful fellow. 'Are you a soldier?'

'That's right, sir, Medical Corps. Just you relax, we're starting on that beam now from the other side – '

'I'll buy you a drink afterwards, you and me.'

'That's right, sir.'

'My wife and I want to invite you all to dinner. And Jack-the-Fire. And Champion. The whole fucking lot of you!'

'Very good, sir.'

'*Jack-the-fucking-Fire*, you lovely fellow you, I'm taking you to dinner tonight – '

She was the first to go, but all he saw through the flashing shadows was a kind of metal stretcher and he shouted, 'Good luck, Vanessa . . .!' But she did not answer. Then somebody saying:

'Your legs are free now, see if you can move them.'

And somebody was getting a rope under his armpits, and he had a wonderful feeling of security and trust; everything was going to be all right, and she was running into the sparkling blue sea and she dived so her whole body was golden, taut and perfect, flashing in the sunshine, and he swam underneath her and she was gloriously satiny, shimmering, slippery, against him, and they broke surface laughing, gasping, kissing.

PART XVI

At three twenty-one a.m. that Thursday, Vanessa Storm Williams died in Queen Elizabeth Hospital, without having regained consciousness.

First there is just shocked disbelief; it does not register as something that has really happened. Then slowly, through the disbelief, while they are explaining it, and you are staring at them, and demanding answers, and they are answering, kindly, firmly, slowly through this awful disbelief there begins to seep the terrible realization. And a kind of sick, white ringing begins to well up in your ears, and though you do not believe it yet you also believe it, but you are trying desperately not to. *No, no, no, it hasn't happened* . . . And suddenly, like a long, stretched-out piece of elastic being released, there is a snap, and you believe it. It really is true, the whole awful truth – this has really happened, to her. *To her*.

And it came suddenly welling up his throat, from his heart and guts, the outcry, and the despair, and the outrage, and the pity, pity, pity, and the grief, grief, grief.

FIFTY-EIGHT

The rain came down. Many of the telephone lines were washed out, but he could hear the attorney in New York very clearly. The man said:

'The Italian Embassy has been very helpful and thorough. I'll write you a full explanatory letter of course, but briefly, the facts are these:

'Her mother was a Miss Stormo, an immigrant from Italy, and her father is indeed Senator Williams. However, her parents never married.

'I have spoken to Senator Williams and he admitted his paternity, privately, but he would put nothing on paper. He says he's never had anything to do with his daughter, for everybody's sake, and he doesn't intend starting now. You can understand that it wouldn't do his political life any good. He makes no claim on the estate either.

'Miss Stormo, her mother, was in the theatre. Vaudeville stuff. Music hall. Her stage name was The Tempest. She died when Vanessa was an infant, of drugs. She was a heroin addict.

'At the time Miss Stormo was living with a Mr Pacino, a man well known here as an important member of the Mafia. Mr Pacino was murdered last year, in a raid on his restaurant. But I have spoken at some length with his brother and he was co-operative enough, although once again he refused to make an affidavit: he said that Mr Pacino had been very fond of both the mother and the child.

'However, after her mother's death, the child was brought up by her aunt, the mother's sister, a Mrs Mazziotti, in Brooklyn. Now also deceased.

'Mrs Mazziotti died when the child was nine and she was brought up thereafter in boarding schools paid for by Mr Pacino. However, he would not foster the child because he thought his gangster life would be bad for her, and she was farmed out to friends for holidays. Apparently, as she grew up, Vanessa became very antagonistic towards her gangster background and refused to have anything to do with Pacino. However, Mr Pacino secretly set up a trust fund of a quarter of a million dollars for the girl, to be received on her twenty-fifth birthday.

'There are no other known relatives.

'The estate is substantial. There's the quarter of a million dollars, plus, according to the newspaper and magazine syndicate she wrote for, substantial royalty payments yet to come in, and salary. She was highly thought of by them.

'None of those people I've mentioned makes any claim to the . . . er . . . body.'

McAdam sat in the hospital matron's office, numb, the telephone at his ear.

'Well, I do!'

'I understand. Well, in that event, you only need some kind of burial order from the Hong Kong authorities to . . . er . . . go ahead.'

Outside the Matron's window the rain came down.

'What about the other matter?'

'Yes. I have approached the magazine syndicate and asked them to withdraw her story about Mr Champion. It seems it will be impossible. Nearly a hundred thousand copies of the magazine have already been printed and it will cost a hundred thousand dollars to withdraw them.'

He said huskily:

'I'll pay it! But that story is not to be printed!'

There was a moment's hesitation.

'A hundred thousand dollars, Mr McAdam . . .?'

'Yes! That's what she wanted. And that's what she's going to get!'

He walked slowly back down the corridor towards the reception room. The Chinese nurse walked beside him, but he did not need her.

Bernard Champion was waiting in the reception room. He was alone, standing staring out of the window at the rain. He turned as he heard McAdam. He was holding a big bunch of roses. Standing there, two yards apart, they looked at each other; then Champion's big blue chin trembled and his face crumpled, and he sobbed out loud and blundered into McAdam's arms, and they clutched each other.

They walked slowly down the corridor. Then outside on to a covered concrete area. The rain drummed on the iron roof. The nurse stopped ahead at the double doors and smiled nervously:

'Mortuary.'

Champion looked at McAdam and said hoarsely:

'You sure . . .?'

McAdam whispered angrily: 'Who else should do it? She's mine, isn't she?'

'You go first door on left, please,' the nurse said.

McAdam walked into the chill building, then turned into the room on the left.

She was lying on a slab, covered in a white sheet. A Chinese attendant was standing at the sinks. The nurse went to the slab and put her hand on the sheet, then looked at McAdam nervously.

He nodded.

The nurse peeled back the sheet.

'Do you formally identify this body as Vanessa Storm Williams?'

'Yes.'

The nurse replaced the sheet. 'Will you sign now?'

'Later . . .' Then he said angrily: 'Only the identification document. No post mortem permission. I'm not having anybody cutting her up!'

'Yes,' the nurse said nervously. 'Do you want the attendant to help you?'

'No. Alone. You go too, please. And you, Champ.'

They turned to go. He said without turning round, hoarsely:

'And I want the undertaker to fetch her as soon as I've finished cleaning her. She's not going back into any more damn refrigerators. And no more plastic bags!'

'Yes,' the nurse said. 'Do you want me to cut off the plastic bag?'

'No. *I'll* do it.'

The door closed behind him.

He stared a long trembling moment, staring at the sheet. His eyes were full of tears. Then he slowly peeled back the sheet.

He looked down at her.

'Hullo,' he whispered. 'Hullo, Beauty . . . I've come to tidy you up . . .'

He took a big quivering breath and the tears were running down his cheeks.

'And to tell you what I'm going to do . . . but most of all to make you beautiful, my Beauty . . .'

Afterwards, he walked back up the concrete path under the drumming iron roof.

Champion was waiting in the reception room, at the window. Beside him was the suitcase with the change of clothes he had bought for McAdam. He turned.

McAdam said, thickly: 'Well . . .?'

'He refused to make a statement. His lawyer spoke for him. That he is not an architect or builder, he simply accepted the advice of his surveyors, he didn't know it was not solid rock.' He shook his head at him, his eyes still full of tears: 'We've got nothing to pin on him.'

McAdam stared at him, then said thickly:

'I want to borrow a gun.'

Champion's red-rimmed eyes were astonished.

'What for?'

He said, 'To kill a man.'

And the rain came down.

FIFTY-NINE

The rain hammered on the taxi roof. The windscreen wipers went slosh – slosh.

He told the driver to stop at the corner. He paid him, got out painfully into the rain. He opened his umbrella. Then he walked grimly, carefully up the street. He tested his legs, bent the knees. They were all right. He stopped outside the gates of the big house. He pressed the bell.

He stood at the communication panel, waiting. The rain drummed on his umbrella, splashed his trouser legs. Then a Chinese male voice said:

'*Wei?*'

'Good afternoon. I would like to see Sir Herman Choi, please. In connection with the Foundation for the Blind and Physically Handicapped.'

The voice hesitated, then replied in English:

'The office for the Blind is closed now, it is the lunch time. Can you please telephone this afternoon?'

'No, I leave this afternoon. I wish to make a donation, you see.'

Hesitation. 'One moment please, sir.'

He waited. The rain drumming on his umbrella.

Then the voice came back.

'Come in, please, sir.'

A buzzer sounded and the iron gate opened.

He walked up the path in the rain. The big front door opened. There stood a Chinese man in a dark suit, smiling.

'Sir Herman will see you now.'

'Thank you.' He furled his umbrella carefully.

He followed the Chinese down the marble corridor. The man opened a door. On it was written: *Foundation for the Blind and Physically Handicapped.* Inside was a reception room. They walked through it. Through double doors, into a general office. Desks and typewriters. Empty. Through more doors. Into a big room full of equipment for the physically handicapped. Empty. Charts on the wall. Then a big door. The man knocked, then entered.

Sir Herman Choi stood up from behind a desk, smiling, his right hand extended. McAdam held out his left hand.

'Excuse my appearance, I had an accident.'

'Oh, I am sorry . . .'

'I'm sorry to disturb you, sir, but I wish to make a donation and I'm leaving town.'

The Chinese man withdrew and closed the door. Sir Herman Choi beamed.

'The Foundation is never too busy to receive money. Do sit down . . .'

Sir Herman Choi began to sit down in an armchair.

McAdam put his left hand inside his jacket pocket. He pulled out the gun.

'Put your hands on your head,' he said.

Sir Herman Choi sat and stared, astonished, the smile half fixed on his face.

'This gun has a good silencer; it won't be heard. Hands on your head.'

Sir Herman Choi put his hands slowly on top of his head. 'Who are you?' he whispered.

McAdam kept the gun on him and walked backwards to the door. He dropped the lock. He walked back into the centre of the room.

Sir Herman Choi stared at him.

McAdam lowered the gun muzzle and fired. There was a flashing pop and the bullet smashed into Sir Herman Choi's right thigh. He gasped, and his hands clutched his leg. He stared, shocked, at the hole in his suit trousers, the blood welling out.

'That is for her broken body you caused . . .'

Sir Herman Choi looked up at him, his face creased in shock and pain.

'What do you want?'

The gun popped again and the bullet smashed his other thigh. He cried, and his hands clutched at the wound. The blood welled out between his fingers.

'That is for her broken flesh.' McAdam stepped up to him, grabbed the man's hair and yanked back his cringing head, and his bandaged hand rammed a handkerchief in the man's mouth.

'Spit it out and I'll put the gun in your mouth.'

He stepped back. Sir Herman Choi looked up at him, eyes bulging, terrified, his mouth stuffed with handkerchief. His hands clutched his left thigh. McAdam pointed the gun at him. He whispered, shaking:

'You are a dealer in death. In slow, degrading death . . .'

He spat the gag out and gasped:

'*I'll give you . . . one million dollars . . . American dollars . . . Two million –*'

He grabbed the man's hair and yanked back his head, and rammed the hot muzzle into the back of his mouth.

'Where's your heroin refinery?' He twisted the gun hard.

Sir Herman Choi's cheek bulged round the gun muzzle, his eyes wild, his lips distorted. His tongue worked and his lips closed, distorted round the steel.

'New . . . Territories . . .'

'Where in the New Territories?' He twisted the gun. The lips and tongue worked.

'Sekong . . . Yung Kee . . . Duck farm . . .'

'How far from Sekong?'

'Two . . . mile peg . . .'

'Who's your supplier in Bangkok?'

The bulging mouth twisted round the steel.

'Major . . . Pattikorn . . .'

'Of . . . ?'

The lips worked. 'Police . . .'

McAdam twisted the gun hard.

'Who do you supply in San Francisco?'

The eyes bulged, the lips mouthed, distorted, saliva dribbling.

'Ernest . . . Chang . . .'

'Address?' He twisted the gun hard.

'China . . . Youth . . . Club . . .'

He jabbed the gun. 'In London?'

'Tran . . . Tranquillity . . . Funeral . . . Home . . .'

McAdam pulled the gun out of the man's mouth and rammed the handkerchief back in deep with the gun muzzle. He stepped backwards.

He levelled the gun at Sir Herman Choi's head. The man stared at him, horrified.

'And this is for killing her.'

He took trembling aim, then squeezed the trigger fiercely and the bullet smashed through the middle of Sir Herman Choi's head.

He did not hesitate. He yanked out the magazine clip in the pistol's handle, and rammed in a new one. He swung the gun on the door, then walked backwards towards the telephone. He picked it up, trembling, and dialled. It was answered immediately. He kept his eyes and gun on the door. He said hoarsely:

'Narcotics Bureau.'

There was a click. He said:

'Whoever you are . . . get this on tape . . . Herman Choi's heroin refinery is at Yung Kee duck farm, two-mile peg, Sekong road . . .'

It took him less than thirty seconds to dictate it all. When he finished the officer said:

'*Who is this?*'

He said: 'Jake McAdam. Ex-Hong Kong police. I am also reporting the murder of Sir Herman Choi. By me. I'll be reporting to Headquarters in about twenty minutes.'

The astonished voice said: 'Where are you? We'll send a car – '

'No,' McAdam said. 'I'd rather walk, thank you.' He hung up.

He went shakily for the door. He turned back the lock; then stepped to one side. Then opened the door. The exhibition room was still empty. He walked through it towards the general office. He stood to one side. Then opened the door. He walked through it. To the reception room. He held the gun behind his left thigh. He opened the door. Also empty. He walked through the reception room, opened the door to the marble corridor.

The Chinese man was coming down the passage. McAdam said:

'Sir Herman wants you, please.'

The man came, smiling. McAdam stepped aside to let him come through. He closed the reception room door behind him. Then he walked out of the Foundation for the Blind and Physically Handicapped.

Down the marble corridor. He carried the gun, dangling, just behind his left thigh. He saw his umbrella at the front door.

He picked it up. He opened the front door. Stepped out into the rain.

Then he remembered the buzzer on the gate. He looked back inside, saw the panel. He pressed the switch. The gate buzzed and opened.

He closed the front door. He walked down the path.

At the gate he slid the gun back inside his jacket.

He walked through the gate. Pulled it closed behind him.

He walked down the street in the hammering rain. He forgot to put up his umbrella. The rain drummed on his head, and the tears ran down his face, and his heart was breaking.

THE END

THE YEARS OF THE HUNGRY TIGER
by JOHN GORDON DAVIS

Hong Kong . . . crossroads of East and West, city of teeming streets and crowded harbours, of rickshaws and coolies and markets and girlie-bars.

Hong Kong . . . where Jake McAdams, a successful young British policeman met Ying-ling, a Communist schoolmistress – a union as dangerous as it was unlikely and as beautiful as a sunrise over the Mountains of the Nine Dragons . . .

THE YEARS OF THE HUNGRY TIGER is a poignant love story and an exotic journey through the last decade of Hong Kong's history. Against a background of savage typhoons, killer rains, espionage, riots, unlawful sex and the shock waves of Mao's Cultural Revolution, McAdams and Ying-ling fight for their love and Hong Kong comes alive in this unforgettable novel of a city in torment.

0 552 10437 X   £1.50

CAPE OF STORMS by JOHN GORDON DAVIS

This epic novel of whales and whalermen in the Antarctic seas centres round James McQuade, a young marine biologist from South Africa. Every summer he went south with the whalers to the Ice, and this season the crew was a particularly flamboyant mixture of personalities. On board was a beautiful nurse, Victoria Rhodes, who rapidly became the target for frustrated male lust . . . Despite the mystery about her origins, McQuade fell violently in love with Victoria, and when the whalers returned to port, he could not bring their affair to an end . . .

0 552 10447 7   85p

HOLD MY HAND I'M DYING by JOHN GORDON DAVIS

'This is the best novel coming out of Africa that I have read for a number of years. It is Africa today. It has the inevitability of a Greek tragedy. The characters develop in the skies and spaces of the continent. Love, battle, boredom, drink, all woven into the tapestry of Rhodesia. It is seldom that one gets a book of this kind that is both moving emotionally and full of adventure.' *Stuart Cloete*

0 552 11241 0   £1.25

THE ODESSA FILE by FREDERICK FORSYTH, author of THE DAY OF THE JACKAL

The life-and-death hunt for a notorious Nazi criminal unfolds against a background of international espionage and clandestine arms deals, involving rockets designed in Germany, built in Egypt, and equipped with warheads of nuclear waste and bubonic plague. Who is behind it all? Odessa. Who or what is Odessa? You'll find out in *The Odessa File* . . .

'In the hands of Frederick Forsyth the documentary thriller achieves its most sophisticated form – Mr Forsyth has produced both a brilliant entertainment and a disquieting book.' *The Guardian*

0 552 09436 6   £1.25

A SELECTED LIST OF
FINE NOVELS
THAT APPEAR IN CORGI